DOUBLE TAKE

DOUBLE TAKE

Ellen Violett

DOUBLEDAY & COMPANY, INC., GARDEN CITY, NEW YORK, 1977

All of the characters in this book are fictitious, and any resemblance to actual persons, living or dead, is purely coincidental.

Library of Congress Cataloging in Publication Data

Violett, Ellen.
Double take.

I. Title.
PZ4.V792Do [PS3572.I587]   813'.5'4
ISBN: 0-385-07440-9
Library of Congress Catalog Card Number 73–83679

To my mother. In memory of my father.

With special thanks for the help of my friends: Mary P. R. Thomas, Damien Martin, EDD, my special editor Betty Prashker, special artist Alex Gotfryd, special agent Gloria Safier.

And remembering LeBaron Barker.

DOUBLE TAKE

Under the Credits

The liveliest tenant on the thirteenth floor moved in as if there were no tomorrow. She was trailing a horde of hippie helpers to wire the place for sound and light and make it more truly her own. As if her first lease signed alone was the last on Manhattan's East Side, and she planned to live happily ever after in a glorified one room, misadvertised as a STUDIO 3! On a HI FL, tactfully misnumbered for those with a need not to know. Which was practically everybody who bought those MOD LUX BLDG myths about FULL SECURITY, ALL CONVEN's, to put up with a sterile confinement behind paper walls.

She was different. She saw sterility as a challenge, the perfect empty space on which to impose her personal, relevant statement. Otherwise, all rents being equally ridiculous, she might have managed a separate bedroom along with the usual built-in charm of an UNUSUAL ATTR. BROWNSTONE FLR THRU! But atmosphere, capital A, she said, was back there somewhere with parquet floors and teak end tables. There was no teak in her statement.

The message got through loud and clear to her neighbors the first time she rang the bell, sweetly seeking help, apologetic, startling. "I'm sorry—I know it's early (or late) but I'm Maude Lee Evans in 14B," she would begin breathlessly, "and I have to blow up my sofa." And so on from one apartment to the next. There were only eight on each floor, two with bedrooms in the back on either side of her, overlooking the garden, allegedly. Though, in fact, at least half the picture windows—even she had two—were eyeball to eyeball with the kind of hotel that features beer cans on the sills, where air conditioners should be. Whereas on the street, where it was noisy, and cheaper, the five smaller studios across the hall looked north for blocks over tidy rooftops—through one window each, naturally. She checked out all seven views to find the stand-up vacuum which, unlike hers, could inflate furniture. Or whatever else she was looking for.

And got. With that unbelievable smile. The whole opening shot was effective, but it was the smile which made people say she was beautiful. And her body, almost a shock the first time out on the sun roof, after her blue jean period for demolition. Though she never dressed to stress it—cool in hot pink or slim in slacks, for office or party—an unexpected reticence in a blond bombshell who came on with a three-barreled name to borrow a hammer. Unless being a girl had been a different kind of bomb once, when wary pride was learned, before puberty came as it must to all children and taught nature's darling what she could get away with. Whatever she thought was fair.

It turned out that her name had been Mud in her school days, an exasperating period, too easily recalled while trying to fit white tile next to black in a tight corner. Like poor Mud-Maude cornered in preadolescence, trying to fit by becoming

Lee, which converted so hideously to Leesy she went back to the original after high school. But differently this time, entering college on the wings of new-found butterfly confidence, insisting on the *whole thing* for her professional life. At least until her present job in the monkey-see, monkey-do world of television where everybody called her Evans because her boss did. A big man with a lousy memory, adamantly unable to retain more than one label per lesser body.

Certainly television was a consistent choice for someone who took sterility as a challenge. In fact, to hear her tell it, mass communication was the *only* relevant game in town for statement making, the last meaningful frontier where it really mattered to hold the individual line against corporate pressure for conformity. Though exactly how a go-for held the line while going for the master broadcaster's coffee was the stuff sitcoms were made on. And the dingaling picture she conjured up as she tripped along, getting by with the help of her friends. The light-fingered, moonlighting set designers. The contacts with contacts who made commercials, which got her those breaks, which got her by. More or less. No one could figure *all* the angles, against the future shock of shortage—that much seemed breathlessly obvious. Otherwise, all salaries being equally withheld and laughable, she might have done better on unemployment, while collecting under the table from underground filmmakers to support her generation's mania for motion pictures. But the stuff that got shot in lofts, she said, was somebody else's mania—old smokers from yesterday, freaking out on mañana. As irrelevant as teak and the sterner stuff Establishment dreams were made on. Stern dreams seemed to go with the territory only for other residents, never getting a nod from her, or so much as a mention in passing, as she rose to Fun City's challenge. For the fun of the challenge, only—always. Never the status or power. Or money.

Until one mañana a new statement appeared in the country's largest newspaper, about the second-largest television network. Announcing that someone called Maudley Evans was now to be something called East Coast Executive Consultant on Dramatic Specials. Replacing the big man with the lousy memory, newly promoted to Executive Creative Co-ordinator. (*Titles*, she sighed, just labels to them. Never who you were. It was always the same.)

She was different? Exactly how began to blur along with that famous name, as the upward mobility of her progress became self-evident. She was breathless from climbing, there were some who might say. Like the boys at the office—(who won that rat race, fellas?). Not to mention the girls in Consciousness Raising, holding the line for Woman—(who had told her before *that* was the relevant statement). From object to symbol to person, we're coming the long way, baby. Challenge-with-a-smile, but watch out for the smile that's a turn-on, an old number, out of sync with the dance of the peer group. And dangerous.

And yet, somehow, from the outsider's view, it all seemed a little unlikely. That so light a step would go the distance, in the crunch, make that heavy scene, to do or die for a piece of the rock. Anywhere. Not that rose, flower child or phony, living so fully in the moment. The truth lay somewhere in between. You only had to know her for a day. But that was the problem. Which day? Perhaps it's the problem with anyone, even after a lifetime.

Until the last day, when suddenly only memory serves. And the zaniest prop becomes dull evidence bereft of the animating presence, like a dress that's nothing in the hand. While personal essence, unique and intangible, survives as it can the perception of friends—raconteurs, with fancy ways, or literal loyalists, stuffing it all in, to miss the gist and kill the punch line. So where is the proof it was ever funny, once so happy, really love? It was the *way* it happened, the excuse goes lamely like a cracked record, you should have been there. Should have been there.

Not at the scene of accident. Shock fails to illuminate life's darkest moments, no matter whose summer day is ending too soon. As in fact hers began, a more prosaic notion. But so much of what happened was prosaic routine, done before to be done again, which should have made it easier to reconstruct the picture. If you were in it and knew the difference, had actually entered the frame, live on camera, one of the missing pieces. And been there. Been there. Been there. With her.

But nobody was always. Or ever altogether, timespace being among the boring limits defining the human condition. So really there was no photo finish. But only us folks remembering different poses—for the eyewitness accounts to be circulated, the composite sketches drawn from mind's eye hearsay. Until finally it was all on the record, real and imagined equally legible, unerasable as the human psyche—less for society's justice than history's choice. A slower mill, but still the best hope that the written word may somehow outlast the darkroom print in the brave new world of magnetic tape. Where the medium's the message. I hear.

Also I've been there.

I am not a camera. Or even an auteur, though I wrote to order for a few she served, coming into the arena as I left, a moment in passing of no importance, until it became a lie.

I met her once. I saw an ingenue. *Le mot juste* then. Now, all that's left of a lasting impression to distinguish her from a host of starlets. Just a word, like all the others. (*Labels*, she said, never who you were.)

But she was different. And something about the illusion persists, more stubborn than my shadow, fading from the wall. My sister's shadow refuses to fade, though no more to me than I to her that she should cling to this shred of a memory, coming back like a breathless echo, endlessly sorry to disturb.

"Listen, I know it's late in the game but I'm just starting. And I wonder if you'd have time to help me . . ."

I wonder, facing a blank wall, reminder of some cave where the stories all began with any stick or stone or cutting edge at hand—the first medium message and still the only test. Until an act takes place, and the empty space is filled, or remains, is all.

Which day? Not now. The day is done, researched to a standstill. But the girl, sister, shadow, scandal . . . Which woman was she?

Take One

She woke up flirting. Not in so many words but with a reflex softening of tone when she heard the man telling her to rise and shine. "Why?" she asked him, whoever he was. And reached out a reflex soothing hand to the far place where her lover rolled when threatened by her telephone at night. Only it was 6:45 A.M. according to this voice and her lover's place was empty. No one to soothe but the puppy, jumping the short distance from the floor, all wide-awake licks and wriggles at the touch of her hand. "S'too early." She cuddled the puppy and the phone, snuggling deeper toward the center of her bed as she remembered her lover was still away so she had it all—double luxury, privacy and space. But not it seemed for long. There was a hair appointment to get to soonest, the voice reminded her. That's why the call was left for an early wake-up, honey. Maude Lee stopped cuddling and snuggling and sat up, unsteady on the water mattress, confused as always by the total blackout she had carefully imposed on the whole damn apartment. Her head throbbed.

"Whosis anyway?" she asked. Certainly not her hairdresser. "It's Hilda," the man said, "from the service."

Hilda—

"Hold, please, honey."

Maude Lee switched on the area spot, a minus in the morning, but there wasn't anything else to do until she could free herself from the welter of pink sheets and puppy love and get to those expensive vertical blinds. Rising in the pool of soft light which missed her eyes and the color of her hair, she was confronted with another morning minus—her own shadow image at once voluptuous and insubstantial, reflected into infinity between the glass-covered walls at both ends of her apartment. But she was into mirrors not narcissism as she sometimes had to explain, and anyhow concentrated now on Hilda's vocal sex change, quite an item in a relationship which was wholly vocal. So she ignored herself, picking up the base of her see-through Lucite telephone—she was also into Lucite —to carry it toward the windows, out of the spotlight. Nude leaving an impressionist painting. Dragging a fat puppy from a dog food commercial.

"Do you want to get us both electrocuted—or what?" She felt his weight before she turned to shake him off, knowing he would only shake back growling, until she bent down, her head splitting, to pry his bite loose from the twenty-five-foot telephone cord. Theoretically the extra length allowed convenient use of the Lucite telephone in the farthest reaches of her dressing room-bath around the corner, a handy substitute for private extensions she had discovered in the housekeeping hotel suites of Southern California. And imported before the puppy came into her life to mistake West Coast economy for a snake in the grass. A born New Yorker.

"Mutts kill me," she told him softly. It was their shared secret, the honeymoon foundation of a successful adoption: he had been chosen for himself over all the other bastards. In a final abandon of puppy love, he flipped onto his short hind legs, mounted her arm, and, humping like crazy, tried for passion. Hilda's voice came back on cue, basso profundo.

"Sorry, honey."

"Hilda for Chrissake—what happened—?" Maude Lee straightened, removing her arm, backing out of the puppy's range toward the windows, as Hilda explained not for the first time about the other board going with only the one girl to handle both on this shift, never mind her relief walking in late every other morning, anytime they felt like these kids, not like the uptown branch, but of course action was Hilda's middle name, and the clients midtown were a livelier bunch she had to admit, more like friends, honey.

"No, I mean to your voice—"

"Oh. Laryngitis."

"You sounded OK last night—"

"You weren't feeling much pain yourself!"

Hilda's roguish male laugh disintegrated into a racking cough which explained itself. Or could have. But having been asked a silly question, Hilda was off and running about summer colds, the way this one would now hang on, could have been fought off, as always before, with forty restorative winks on the job, if last night hadn't been such a pistol, honey.

Today looked sort of like a pistol too. Gray light filled the room when Maude Lee adjusted the cord of the wall-to-wall blinds, slowly, carefully, in the expectation of sun. But of course Hilda did not mean the weather. No local full moon could account for nuts all over America in different time zones suddenly choosing the same lonely hours to look for each other long distance.

Maude Lee got the message. But didn't quite remember it. "Including my nut," she offered, wishing her head would go away or get itself together.

"Well, Mr. Nedders only made the one call direct. The last time—12:59. You just missed it."

The memory of missing him came back dimly. Along with some of the pain she hadn't been feeling last night, the reason for the whole dumb dirty stay-out.

"The last time . . ."

"12:10 and 12:31 it was the operator. But like I told you, honey, we don't accept charges—"

"Well, neither do I!" Maude Lee said defensively. "When Ned hears my voice, he calls back direct. It's just a signal."

And a ruse. To save him wasting money on her service. Wasting money was a tricky subject between them. Until now, the trickiest.

"Well, he couldn't wait on account of catching the plane." (Which plane?) "Just wanted you to know he'd be coming in earlier than expected—so he'd be sure to get you for lunch."

"Lucky if he gets me for dinner—" Maude Lee sighed. "I mean it's really hell week at the office . . ."

"Yeah, sure," Hilda said. "Well, like I told him you could've been working late."

At one in the morning.

"I like to inject a note of humor," Hilda chuckled recklessly, risking another fit. Maude Lee decided to think about something else, like what to do next, or what to do it *in*, more to the point for the moment. She adjusted the vertical slats a little wider in the hope of a fast glimpse of rain or no rain against pane. But of course what she got, framed, was a typical scene from the hotel directly opposite her second picture window. (The shadowy crone on the top floor reaching out for the can of condensed milk on the sill; the yawning man below who wore an undershirt to bed—wore an undershirt anywhere— reaching down to scratch.)

"Listen," she interrupted the dwindling cough, "Hilda? What's it doing out—really raining?"

"I wouldn't know if it was snowing down here. We look out on the court."

"Better than somebody else's windows." Maude Lee snapped the slats almost shut again.

"If a girl wants her privacy!" Hilda's chuckling tone remained irritatingly true to her concept of lively clients.

"It's what I see that bugs me, thanks. The Suicide Arms Motel."

"The what—?"

"That fleabag behind here—the Morely."

"Welfare," the gravelly voice sounded shocked, almost offended. "There was a nice class of tenant at the Morely Arms before Welfare. Permanent crowd."

"Well, now it's transient—the crowd that checks in to jump out." Maude Lee giggled.

"You got some imagination!"

"I like to inject a note of humor."

"Some humor!" Hilda did not laugh with her.

Maude Lee had a sudden flash of a sick old woman staring at a stone wall, waiting for relief which did not come, with only the one girl alone all night, only the one room at home alone all day, the one man in the undershirt gone long ago. There was the distant sound of buzzing.

"Here we go again—"

"Ciao, Hilda."

"Bye now, honey. Kill the people."

Fifty. Had to be, talking like that. Maybe worse than fifty. Old and alone and disconnected. Like the dead line on the see-through telephone. Maude Lee replaced the receiver.

It was a low moment. The lowest. She didn't have that many. Everything sagged like the leaky end of her sofa, even the puppy collapsed in front of it, one leg still slightly raised as a memento to his vanishing erection, the rest of him sagging from there in a dappled semicircle on the shaggy white

throw rug. "You're too young is all," she said. Better than
being too old, God knew, but the puppy didn't, giving her the
perfect opportunity to take action—Hilda's middle name and
Maude Lee's only answer to life's gray days. She tiptoed past
him, trailing her telephone cord unheeded across his shaggy
castaway's raft, to kneel on the far side at the edge of the
black and white sea. Putting the phone down, she lay full
length, the upper half of her body cool against the tiles, as she
reached around the side of the sofa to unscrew the valve,
keeping her eye on the puppy through the chrome legs of the
glass coffee table so that she was almost sure he could not gal-
vanize himself in time to leap through the air and land smack
in the middle of the seat just as she took a deep breath and
put her lips to the valve. Ever hear a sofa break wind? It
didn't. She exhaled a whole lungful of air, possibly her last the
way her head swam, and slowly through stars she saw the
white vinyl mountain above her fill and right itself. Screwing
the valve shut again, she patted the fat white arm almost
affectionately as she rose, grateful for a little less sag in the
world. Reflected freshly into infinity, her daylight image
seemed suddenly leggy, almost angular from certain angles,
merely dappled like her puppy with softly white voluptuous
areas, where bikinis had kept breasts and buttocks sun free—
almost—always on the roof.

"Now, c'mon," she scooped up the see-through phone,
"we're going to watch for the lady who feeds the puppy
Alpo." Her walk was also not voluptuous. She held her free
arm straight down, a little away from her body, fingers stiffly
extended like a child's, toy-like phone clutched close in the
other hand, long hair bouncing, as she marched to the ar-
rangement of chrome-bracketed glass shelves, and Lucite cabinets on the opposite wall to turn on her see-through TV set.
But the puppy would not be diverted from the terrible defeat
of innocence. Nothing moved but his eyes, tragic and dark,

rolling back in his head so far they almost disappeared, following the action. "Oh, couldn't you just turn out to be a fag and forget it?" she wondered, only half kidding like many another mother before her. "And not have it be my fault," she added quickly. And not a fag—just as insatiable—neuter. God, male animals. They were all alike. Coming of age overnight, and looking at everything upside down ever after. Tragedians all, from the first faint hint of failure. She sighed. If you fixed them up with a mate, they were supposed to get worse. If you had them fixed, you were a castrator. And if you didn't, they did you. Terrific. "Well, everyone warned me," she told him as if he cared. As if she needed warning about male/female trauma in this particular week of the battle of the sexes. She turned away to bounce, straight-armed and phone-clutching, bare feet slapping bare tiles, into the foyer. Where the super had gotten last week off to a swinging start by calling her a whore.

Actually she had been the first to use the word. So now, it was her voice wafting hoarsely through paper walls which lingered to poison the foyer air. Not the guttural aura of him as always before, for all the other times he had tried unsuccessfully to find her anger.

"Vy I can't come—you are not alone?" He would shout from the hall outside the door, at any attempt to stall his visits, deliberately ill-timed to surprise male consorts on the premises. Even before there was one—really. While he himself would stall equally audibly the most urgent requests for service in the Foremans' apartment next door, unless and until "the Mister" were home to make it official. ("Take the sex appeal away from Stanley Kowalski and what have you got—B. O. Plenty," said Amy Foreman, who was older, pregnant on purpose, and philosophical.) He was a bad Polish joke on women of all ages throughout the building from sun roof to laundry, Superpig to whore and housewife alike.

Maude Lee, being neither, fell into a special category. As the super made perfectly clear, from the day he showed her the apartment, over two years ago, telling her pointedly about the *Nice* girls living three and four deep in only slightly larger quarters. The nicest of whom, a Swissair hostess in the bedroom apartment on the other end of the hall, had eyes for 14B to share.

"Not with me," Maude Lee said firmly.

"You already haf roommate?"

The roommates she already had were part of her motive for moving up from loft country. She wasn't looking for more.

"But is too much rent here for one girl," the super objected.

"Or one boy," Maude Lee agreed. "Let 'em room together."

Sex and the single boy, however, were only of peripheral concern, not being natural prey anymore even when swinging too far in the wrong direction, no real threat to the super anyway. Unlike the aloneness of Maude Lee Evans. And the money which paid for it. When in addition to doing him out of the Swissair matchmaking fee, Maude Lee's renovations did him out of a rake-off by involving her friends as suppliers and builders rather than his, suspicion turned to harassment. The *permanent* alterations he usually helped with and winked at were virtually forbidden by the terms of her lease, read aloud finally like her rights, by the shy building agent at a shoot-out in the rental office off the lobby. While Superpig muttered loudly—always, through everything—"See, see in the end you pay! You pay to take it all out!"

But in the end it seemed more likely she would be paid to leave it all in. Since clearly her improvements at last provided the Studio 3 unit with an illusion of space—as advertised. And conceded by the agent himself, shyly drunk at her housewarming party, volunteering to show Miss Evans' unit personally when the time came, promising gallantly the super would not be a problem. *Good luck*—old-fashioned men killed her—

but throwbacks like Superpig were here to stay, always too close for comfort, to be got around by the young and heedless like thoughts of death, any old way. Especially once the big renovation was over and the big romance had become serious and the super could only renew his raids by going over the management's head to bluff her sporadically with obscure safety codes and empty threats of building inspectors. Futilely —until last Wednesday.

If only she had not been so damn eager to advertise her aloneness at 7:45 A.M., pausing only long enough to pull on the terry towel robe she clutched around her, before she let him in. Unwisely. His eyes never left the toweling, checking for fallout, while she struggled to retrieve the cord from the puppy and tie it. The pretext for entry was identified as a fire law, violated, the super alleged, by new frail French shutter doors which, in fact, finally provided sufficient privacy to use the john hall beyond the foyer for a dressing area. Also as advertised. But this logic, triggering his true objections, only made him crazier.

"Vy you need privacy so much—you got men lined up out here?" he fumed, enraged to have picked the wrong morning for finding even one. "At this bar you've got here—while you undress for them?"

"I said dress—for a date—" She left the cord half knotted to grab the lower edges of her robe together. "Finish dressing—"

"So you make your house into a bar for your dates to wait? That is what it's for?" His eyes, roving up and down after her clutching hands, missed or ignored the mug of coffee already set out on the white Formica. So that he did not or would not see that the counter she had substituted for a partition really made the useless little foyer into a dining area. As advertised.

"I eat there—" She nodded toward the high chairs. "It's a *place* to eat."

"And there is a place to sleep?" He nodded the other way

toward the mirrored room, opening out of the foyer. "Where you give shows with your crazy lights going on and off, and your crazy music, even a piano—"

"That's a living area—for everything."

"With this great bed taking so much room—two tons of water in it—just for you?"

"That's my business, Mr. Walenski—"

"It's pretty good your business—"

"*What does that mean?* And what's a water bed got to do with a fire law anyway?"

Her voice, which had suddenly become low, remained deadly clear. So did his mutter.

"Maybe you break another law. To pay for all this, a little office girl like you." And there it was, the bottom line.

There had to be a man. If not a John who paid, a pimp to please. But a man to make her a woman like all the others, needing protection from feelings so strong they could overpower her terry cloth towel defenses, and force the truth out of her. Feeling her back against the Formica-edged counter, she almost wished so too, regretting the absence not of her lover but a proper rent-paying mister who could compel respect for her position, as Bob Foreman did for Amy. And thus having inwardly denied the strength of her own aloneness, Maude Lee lashed out at last to defend it, prove it against the super.

"If I were selling myself, I'd be paying you too much to say so."

His fists bulged, and so did his eyes, which met hers for the first time. "You think I take dirty payoffs—"

"I know you do—"

"From cheap little office hustlers with five-dollar tips at Christmas—"

"From every whore in the building. A hundred dollars a month."

It was the magic number, the going rate for services he was alleged to extract from one at least—the one with the heart of brass and a mouth to match, who lived and loved directly overhead, betrayed again when the super looked involuntarily toward the ceiling—exactly as Maude Lee had spoken—too soon, before he could stop himself.

So it was a standoff. Charges which could neither be pressed nor disproved were left hanging. The super took it out on the doors, gouging out the latches to satisfy his fire law. Maude Lee took it out on herself whenever she was confronted with the jagged holes, splintery and ragged-edged, like her nerves when she pushed the doors open. Last week she had put the whole hassle down to overreacting because her period was due. Now that another Wednesday had come and her period still hadn't, her hangover mood was even easier to explain, if not to resist, as she passed through the violated entrance. Well, better her shutters than her towel robe. She remembered his eyes. It could have gone either way.

She fumbled in the dark for the switch that turned on the fluorescent light she hated but somehow hadn't gotten around to changing yet. As, in fact, she still hadn't gotten around to installing a fun toilet seat or even do-it-yourself carpeting to cover the ugly floor, left bare when she ground to a halt right here on the threshold of yuk green tile, not knowing it would all stay yuk and doorless for more than a year after her housewarming party. Being almost equally distracted ever since by a new job and a new man, she had only recently felt ready for a last roundup of the fey friends who knew about wiring, even plumbing. And even now wasn't quite sure she could work up enough adrenaline to sustain another total war with the super —wouldn't he be thrilled to know it? Running out of steam, she discovered, was just as crucial as running out of money. Having done both, she thought she knew. But her lover, who had lived on steam alone, said nothing was more crucial than being poor. She was just occasionally broke. They taught each other the difference.

She dialed Weather 6-1212 while sitting on the john, and leaned sideways to turn on the taps for her bath while listening to the ninety degree possible high and ninety per cent precipitation possibilities. She brushed her teeth electrically while the tub was filling and then hoped against hope while getting on the scales, twice, to discover, twice, she had gained three pounds. She swore at the unreliable pill for fouling up everything, while following it with a diuretic—somewhat futilely in view of the extra glass of water it took to swallow down additionally: one Compoz, two aspirin, and a diet upper.

She swore at Bruce McVitty while easing into the hot water, swore she would never again go out with anybody who was into booze instead of grass while trying to forget how much she herself had wanted a drink after work last night. She gazed down disapprovingly at her firm and glistening skin while remembering, despite herself, that it was sharing the special grass hidden in top of her little white cocktail piano that finally sent them reeling to the refrigerator to consume one *entire* Sara Lee cheesecake stored for her lover's return. She counted the calories and carbohydrates already multiplying into fat cells under her behind or somewhere awful while she soaped her errant limbs. She soaped her breasts, which should have felt swollen preperiod but weren't, while seeing clearly her tummy was. Her hands came to rest there while her thoughts went back to square one.

It just *couldn't* show that way this soon, or she'd be going to the gynecologist instead of the hairdresser, bearing a specimen bottle to some lab somewhere, if it weren't at least one full week too early for urine to mean shit. Holding that thought—really attractive—she rose from the tub, splashing the puppy, paddling back among the living to ride her exten-

sion cord into the dressing area. Sliding open the doors of the
too shallow closet space, selecting flowered panties from the
overstuffed, too few, built-in drawers, moving on to reject
slacks which would drag in the rain for a pink shirt which had
to be dragged from the too tightly packed hanging area, she
wondered for the hundred thousandth time what in hell the
Swissair hostess would have done with her clothes.

"Maybe she flies them to Switzerland," her lover had murmured once, trying to find a hanger or an inch of space for his
pants. But his eyes never joked, tragically dark as the puppy's,
mourning Maude Lee's aloneness, longing to be the mister,
smoldering with frustration because he couldn't cut it. Finan-
cially, he thought.

"It's nothing to do with money!" She had told him a hundred times.

"Fuck it isn't."

"Fuck it is, Ned! My problem is making the commitment—"

"Jesus, you're getting to sound like a goddamn TV panel—"

"Sorry about that—we can't all be speech professors with
PHD's—"

"EDD! And I haven't got it yet." He had told her a hundred
times.

"So go get it!"

"Fucking right I'll go." Etc., etc. Door slam. One of *those*
conversations. Fuck misters.

Her thoughts slipped perversely away into secret grooves of
pleasure as she slipped the crisp pink shift off its hanger, over
her head, feeling perversely naked as soon as her reflection
was covered, secretly naked, with nothing on underneath,
even the flowered panties yet. Like the first time with Ned,
sweet Ned, soon to be Dr. Nedders, EDD, but even sooner her
lover. She felt again the dizzying sense of power it gave her to
kneel on the white vinyl sofa beside him as he lolled back un-
suspecting, laughing at her crazy new furniture. Until one of

them said or did whatever it was that shattered the kidding stage of shyness so that he had to penetrate the silence or let it fall forever, his hands moving so slowly up her legs under the little girl skirt she almost went crazy watching his face change—she would never forget that look—perversely stopping him, dizzy with power, saying that was all until he could swear he loved her, knowing he was too silly and too serious, swear on his mother and father, knowing he was an orphan, perversely unbuttoning her own middy shirt front and leaning over unbuttoned, to unbutton his, unfasten unzip, until she felt his skin as sweet as hers, his body surprising in the same way, no longer lost and ungainly in clothes, but achingly beautiful to the touch, begging for mirrors. So that for the first time ever, as much tempted as tempting, she could no more stop herself or him, whatever he did, than he could keep from swearing whatever she asked him to.

It was a pure high, and between fights they rang various changes on the theme to reach it again, make it last with a better class of grass, special sounds and lights reflected in the glass. But really, swinging from the same strap on a crowded bus could be enough; swinging with the swinging crowd at the Foremans' once wild parties could have been, almost was, too much. If one of them had not pulled back, if either had been willing to settle for less than the erotic purity of the sometime reflection they found in each other. ("Deprived boy meets greedy girl," said Amy Foreman.) Which made Maude Lee understand why all the thieves and grabbers who knew where treasure was buried came up empty when they found it. And made it worth her lover's while to risk wanting someone more than something. He had turned her on with the spontaneity of innocence, and she fought him for it.

And in fact, if they had made a baby together, it had happened super spontaneously, not in her water bower of methodical madness, but in his cold water pad off-campus, on his dumb, uncomfortable, pullout, three-quarter bed with the ridge in the middle of the mattress, sans pill or precaution, after the worst fight of all. *Typical.*

She sighed, sliding open the last of the closet doors to fill her arms with the sexiest flowered sheets saved for their bed tonight, if only they didn't fight in-between about where she had been the night before or where they would both be a year from now, all those questions which became unanswerable as soon as they had to be asked. She hugged the sheets with arms that ached for her baby, baby—meaning her lover not his seed—what *was* she going to do with her baby? Blindly she brushed through forgotten shutters, forgetting the super, and even the phone. Until it suddenly rang behind her.

She almost dropped the sheets. Her heart stopped, then raced like her mind, as she stuffed the whole armload back in the closet, figuring even if he were still at the airport waiting out the bus, even from Kennedy, he could make it before eight. Figuring no university or foundation would claim him for a meeting before nine. And certainly no hairdresser—indeed no job—could claim *her* if she could have him here the way she felt right now. She got to the phone in time to break the rule of a lifetime and pick up before the end of the second ring. So that she'd sound as if she were coming out of a dream —not just coming on with him, knowing it couldn't be anyone else at this hour. Unless someone had died or something.

"Yes," she began softly, with his favorite word.

"*Leesy*—?"

Someone had died.

"Leesy—it's Grace."

Not Grace. Which would have been logical since she was the oldest of Maude Lee's stepsisters by a long horsefaced length, though they all sounded alike, speaking in the same high-pitched, weirdly accented tones, intelligible like bats mainly to each other.

"God, I'm sorry to wake you—God!"

Maude Lee sat slowly on the stool in front of the mirrored vanity. But, it was her father's face she saw before she found her voice, his voice really, too breathlessly hoarse like his for a girl, contrasted with bat-shriek.

"S'OK, Grace—I'm awake. Something wrong?"

"Well, sort of—but not with the *family* or anything, I mean not at home, God!"

There was no home. There was no family. Only Maude Lee's father traveling dutifully back and forth between too many houses owned by the woman with too many names and too many children from the too many times she had married men with money, before Leland Evans married hers. (*I want a real home for my Maudie Lee.* "But Leland, why is Leesy crying?" *Don't, Mud, not at the wedding. Not at the airport, please for Daddy. Not long distance, Maudie Lee.*)

It got ridiculous like the rest of adolescence. Preferring by nature to laugh things off, Maude Lee found it all mostly funny now. And once she knew he was safe, today was not an exception.

Though Grace was indeed on a mission of mourning, staying at the Plaza overnight, en route to 11 A.M. services at the Lattingtown Church on the island. "God, if it's not a wedding it's a funeral," she groaned. Certainly nothing less could have brought her down from Murray Bay in this heat, but poor sweet Buzzy Cecil meeting with ultimate disaster, on top of all *that* family had been through, wasn't it awful? Could Leesy imagine anything harder on Buzzy's barely surviving spouse, poor CeeCee?

"Untimely," Maude Lee murmured. Unless they were both ninety.

But it seemed the cause of death was a crack in the eye with a polo ball—hit smartly into the stands by CeeCee himself, so rumor had it—which eliminated age as a factor. Except for the age of Big Buzz, who *was* ninety, in the shade, if you asked Grace, and going strong. But *not* to the Lattingtown Church. So that was the thing—flowers. Somehow to be delivered through the Plaza florist, rather than God forbid in person, chez Buzzy's Ma at the remodeled gardener's cottage. Only you couldn't just say *that* anymore, now that the rest of the place was sold off into those ghastly *Estates,* with hideous street names, and *numbers.* "God, Oyster Bay might as well be Great Neck." Grace sighed, "Isn't it *something?*"

"Everything's changing," Maude Lee suggested without risk, though really all Grace's questions were rhetorical till the last. The final straw. The end thing: in the midst of revolution, Grace had forgotten her Blue Book. So could Leesy be an absolute darling and look up Big Buzz's nouveau address?

"Right *there* under Mrs. Henry Lanahan—*Senior,*" Grace stressed. "Junior's in Payne Whitney for the duration."

"The thing is Grace I sort of can't." Maude Lee felt herself drawn over the old line into Leesy as she tried to break the news: she did not, in fact, possess the Blue Book. But Grace misunderstood.

"Does *anyone* when you need it, God! But the thing is Leesy, the Estates aren't *that* nouveau. Last year's book would be OK, if it's lying around—"

"Yes, but it isn't—"

"*Any* year's?"

"Grace, I'm not *in* the Social Register."

There was a beat.

"God," Grace said.

Maude Lee winked at herself in the mirror while it finally occurred to her oldest stepsister they had not been brought up together on the island or Murray Bay. Had not in fact even vacationed together on any of the jet-set yachts or villa beaches which came and went with increasingly exotic successors to Grace's pa, until Grace's ma finally found a man who

seemed as staid and Old World as her first husband. Leland,
the last. Dear old Leland, player of cocktail pianos, who
played the gentleman so perfectly even Grace forgot that he
wasn't.

"God—that's right."

"Your mother told Daddy we could have three letters written or something. But I didn't." (Wouldn't, but that was another story, beyond their language barrier.)

"You're not missing much!" Grace rallied gamely, but
frankly, half meaning it, sort of. Honestly, what *was* the use of
keeping book on so many Dilatory Domiciles, preserving the
illusion of Family with so many steps and halves you couldn't
keep track of each other. Better by far to go your way like
Leesy working for the TV, or whatever. And Grace would be
the first to say so to any daughter of hers, if she had one.

It finally occurred to the youngest stepsister that the oldest
was the heirless heiress, and would probably now remain so.
Suddenly wishing she really could have been helpful, Maude
Lee made a belated suggestion.

"Listen—Grace, why don't you try getting that address from
Long Island information?"

"God!" Grace said. "*They* ask *you* the address." *After* you
called information here to get the number of the one there.
The hell with it. Grace would simply stop en route and see
what could be done by Ye Old family florist, right *there* at the
Bull's Head light—something still had to be somewhere. But
change or no change, no known possessor of the Social Register was going to be found on the hottest day of summer at any
New York city exchange, call it Butterfield 8 or Yukon.

"Bruce McVitty," Maude Lee said.

"You're joking!"

If so the joke was on Bruce. Serve him right to find out how
the other half lived with a hangover.

"He's going to work downtown." One of these days. "You know, at McVitty Brothers."

"Yes, but now? I mean, are you sure? Isn't he sort of a partner?"

One of these years. "I'm sure, Grace. I saw him last night for dinner."

"Oh." Grace sounded relieved. "Then I guess you didn't keep each other up too late."

Her guess was as good as Maude Lee's, who repeated Bruce's number with relish—several times before Grace got a firm grasp on the sequence—and said *God,* she couldn't thank Leesy enough. And both agreeing they'd *have* to get together *this* fall *after* Grace got back from Murray Bay, definite date, *before* she went to Hobe Sound, they hung up in mutual relief, vanishing from each other's mind without a trace.

Except one. Staring at the mirror image she never really saw, Maude Lee could not help but wonder, if only for a moment, why it gave her a feeling of accomplishment to say she wasn't in the Social Register, when saying she wasn't a whore had made her feel like one.

There wasn't time for heavy speculation. There wasn't even time to change the sheets, only to straighten the bed—she never left it really unmade. She retrieved the shaggy white throw, neatly thrown as always over the little upright piano, where the pot should be hidden as always, reminding herself to look before she left and, as always, make damn sure. Always there was method, method in all her madness. Only her lover ever noticed how much, been around long enough maybe to notice the spine of efficiency, running flexible but straight through her dizzy tangents. Had even noted—jokingly jealous—that only the puppy ever really threw her off course, made her forget something essential by doing something ridiculous. As now, almost getting himself made up in the bed by jumping on it, just as she threw the throw.

"No . . . stop . . . no, wait . . . no, I've got to remember something . . . *will you stop?*" But of course he wouldn't. She had blown it, laughing and scratching. Blew it again, singing and dancing. Oh, how he loved it when she sang to him. . . .

> *"Our bonds and shares may fall downstairs*
> *Who cares? Who cares?"*

Not the puppy. It was like being distracted by her own childhood, when she had teased and tugged and gotten in the way, saying look at me, listen, I can do it, jigging in perfect time to the tunes she could always keep but never make musical, selling the words in her odd little composer's voice, like father, like daughter, in the days when she thought he not only played but wrote every air Astaire ever tapped to, and forsaking all rock and roll, she kept her only unto Daddy's music. Reprised now for the puppy . . .

> *"We'll pay the piper,*
> *When times are riper . . ."*

Only to break herself up, because he really was dancing, so was she, dancing to the counter to leave the phone and get the tote bag, don't forget the script, no, already stuffed in, dancing to the umbrella stand, where the leash also dangled, oh final craziness, who could forget the leash, who could remember the other thing she had forgotten, still to be done when she brought the puppy back up . . .

> *"Because you see we're dancing*
> *And we can't be bothered no-a-owl"*

Only they were, of course.

"Well, you're keeping bankers' hours."

It was young Mr. Lonelyhearts—so his heartless neighbors called him—fairly leaping into view from the studio across the hall, before Maude Lee could pick up her morning *Times* from the maroon carpeting. Still feigning surprise, he did it for her.

Her acceptance was bleak. "This is a banker's hour?"

"Well, actually some of our branch officers have a sort of informal breakfast club at Schrafft's Fifty seventh," he said grandly. As if it were the Racquet and Tennis. As if he hadn't been lying in wait, Johnny at the peephole, already primed with the knowledge of Maude Lee's early wake-up, waiting to press last night's advantage. Helped by the puppy, pawing the air with indiscriminate enthusiasm, and sharp claws.

"Look out for your pants—"

"Doesn't matter—old suit."

Hardly new with ninety per cent precipitation possibilities. Hardly the imitation Italian import in weather fit for imitation Brooks. Still, Lonelyhearts tried to keep the thin gray material from being shredded by shielding his legs with the black and chrome briefcase, so carefully selected at the local cigar store, but already betrayed by the cracked plastic loop which secured his furled umbrella.

"Down, boy . . . easy, amigo." He feigned affection for the puppy while tossing off the nouveau jargon featured last night by Bruce McVitty, cruise director of elevators. ("Hi, amigo— we'd have you in for el drinko—but somebody's got to walk el doggo, etc.") As if poor Lonelyhearts needed that much encouragement to do Maude Lee's dog-walking. Ever since she had included the whole floor in her housewarming, Lonelyhearts had mistaken their every casual encounter for another potential glimpse of Eden. ("On the make for a guest list," Amy Foreman said. "Don't invite 'im.")

Sensing implacably he wasn't at *all* on the make for her body, Maude Lee did not know how to be merciful. She gave it a swing when she saw him, but nothing could warm her eyes.

"Whew!" He actually said Whew, as they moved toward the elevator. "What a night!"

"Oh, come on, it wasn't that late." One drink and it became a night. One joint and it would doubtless be an orgy. Good thing she and Bruce had gotten rid of him before breaking out the grass. And then she remembered what the puppy made her forget.

"No, I meant afterward, after the drink—" Lonelyhearts was saying when she stopped short. "What's the matter?"

"Something I didn't do."

"Well, aren't you coming up again with el doggo?"

She'd have to now. No use trying to con him into it if she'd left the pot among the strewn cassettes on her Lucite cabinet. And even less use stopping to go back in and check with him trailing after her. *Damn* Bruce McVitty and all his amigos. She let the puppy yank her ahead to the elevators, both of which were sitting firmly on the ground floor according to the indicators. So much for bankers' hours.

"*After* the drink, when the Foremans started," Lonelyhearts persisted, pushing the down button. "Whew! How about that scene?"

"What scene?" She was mildly surprised. The Foremans hadn't thrown a bash, or even had a good row, since disappearing into a four-month trance of mystical communion, accompanied by deep breathing and other prenatal rites.

"Having the baby, the way it sounded."

"You're kidding!"

He looked as if he thought she were.

"Didn't you hear her? About 4 A.M.?"

The "her" was chilling. It didn't make sense.

"Amy's not due till next month!"

"Due or not, she woke me out of a sound sleep and you're right through the wall!"

"They don't sleep in their study." Now that it was a nursery anyway.

"Listen, your friend screamed down the whole apartment, the whole floor before he got her to the elevator—"

"They went to the *hospital?*"

"God, yes. *Finally!* Like you never heard anyone *go* like that, *sound* that way—"

"Don't tell me about it!"

There was a surprised silence.

"Sorry."

He wasn't, just taken aback, and a little offended. But Maude Lee was too shaken to care. A memory broke loose.

"Oh, God," she said softly, "I *did* hear her."

"Well, I hardly thought you could've slept through it." He was huffily vindicated. "I hardly meant to be the bearer—"

"I thought it was a nightmare." She had thought it was herself.

"Nightmares," Lonelyhearts said, "don't last an hour."

Maude Lee faced front brightly. One of the elevator indicators was moving.

"Well, it's all over by now."

He shook his head. "I'd have heard Bob coming home. Couldn't get back to sleep."

"Oh, the father *stays* after natural childbirth. There's this whole technique—you know like the breathing. Even screaming, I guess—probably just part of it."

"Didn't sound like technique."

"Well, of course, you feel *something*. But the more you express, the less scary it is. That's the whole point. You're not supposed to *need* anesthetic."

He shrugged. "She wasn't supposed to have the baby for a month."

The elevator shot past them to the penthouse floor. Watching the indicator stop on 20, Maude Lee silently rejoiced, hoping the welcome relief from Lonelyhearts' company would be a woman, preferably young, with a vested interest in discussing the reassuring possibilities of painless childbirth.

Irritated, Lonelyhearts punched the down button again—quite unnecessarily—and then, as if he had just thought of it, seized what was left of the moment.

"Hey . . . by the way . . ." (Of what?) "When the Foremans *do* get back to normal . . ." (As if Bob and Amy had *ever* been that.) "There's this girl from the bank I've been seeing . . ." (Dog. Maude Lee had also seen her.) "And she really digs cooking—"

"At the bank?"

"No . . . here." (Ever literal.) "I'd like to return some hospitality."

Maude Lee had a bit picture of it—Chopped Beef en Bordure Bank Teller, in an earthenware casserole on his walnut coffee table between the narrow foam-rubber couch-beds where they'd all sit facing each other, three on a side, boy girl boy, and girl boy girl killing a gallon of Gallo's Hearty Burgundy. Vin du Lonelyhearts pays.

"Well, it's sort of frantic-time for making plans," she waffled, letting the puppy drag her into the elevator before the door was properly open. Contrary to her hopes, the occupant was a young man who seemed too unfamiliar and embarrassed to be a tenant, reminding Maude Lee so much of her own lover's uneasy morning exits, she smiled sweetly upon him. But Lonelyhearts pressed in between them still pushing hospitality: "Doesn't have to be a big-deal *plan*. Make it spur of the moment like last night. Anytime you and Bruce and the Foremans—"

"*Bruce!*" Maude Lee turned, alarmed. That really *was* all her jealous lover had to hear, some dumb slip like that. "Why Bruce?"

"Just seems like a nice guy . . ." he fumbled, embarrassed. As if McVitty partnerships had never entered his mind.

"My childhood sweetheart," she nailed it, "but we're not joined at the hip." So Lonelyhearts couldn't forget or pretend to, which was more like it.

"Well, listen . . . you and anybody."

"Anybody's sweating out his doctorate." She nailed it again; sweaty students were the B guest list. (So don't invite 'im— here's your hospitality.)

"More birth pains across the hall?" Lonelyhearts still smiled politely.

Maude Lee didn't. "With Ned and me it comes out work. I'm due to produce a small television season."

"More screams in the night." The smile had an edge.

"But no more parties," she said. "Miles to go before we party. Thanks, anyway."

In view of her bacchanalian mood in the wee hours, this had to be a lying snub. Lonelyhearts could only back off into silence. She left it that way when the puppy dragged her out of the elevator into the yuk beige lobby. Sensitivity never was the slightest use really, with insensitive people.

Beyond the yuk mocha banquettes and fake shrubs planted in gravel, Maude Lee saw that the shirt-sleeved night attendant had been replaced by a youngish doorman she liked. Benjie was one of the few who had been around long enough to get his uniform fitted, and actually remember some of the tenants whose deliveries and guests he was supposed to announce. He also remembered the title preferred by most working women, along with the names—or non names—of pets in residence.

"Morning, Ms. Evans. How are you there, puppy?" Benjie even remembered Lonelyhearts. "And Mr. Lorrilard—morning." He greeted everyone cheerily, but Maude Lee was a special favorite. His eyes shone when she lit up the lobby. It was her first true mirror of the morning; she moved toward him gratefully.

"Hi, Benjie!" And then she saw the rain. So did the puppy, who sat down instantly, before there was a chance of getting him through the glass door, out under the blue canopy, no more shelter today than Lonelyhearts' umbrella. Caught without even that, the embarrassed young man from the penthouse floor could only turn up his collar before diving through the wall of water toward the crosstown bus. Lonelyhearts got equally drenched, umbrella and all, when he dove off in the other direction toward the downtown subway. Hovering, Maude Lee realized that *no* form of public transport could get her to Fifty-seventh and Sixth in half an hour, even without the puppy to delay her. And both Benjie's sleeves were already soaked from futile hailings of occupied taxis. It was a vertical flood.

"Oh no," she said. "Oh, Benjie."

"Ought to let up, if you can wait, Ms. Evans." He hovered with her, comfortingly. "You're early this morning."

"I'm supposed to be earlier."

She could just *hear* Jean Paul's martyred sighs as he dragged his sandaled feet through drifts of hair, shrugging helplessly at the line of unisex bodies waiting a turn ahead of her in his chair. It really did not matter how early she got to Le Salon, there was always somebody earlier to wait for, somebody's hair already shorn to walk through.

She ventured a step forward under the canopy, but the puppy went into his whimpering number, hanging back like an anchor.

"Oh, knock off!" she said. "Nobody's going to drown you."

"Tell you what—I'll take the puppy out when it's over."

"That's sweet, Benjie, but he probably won't do anything even for me with these puddles." More like lakes. She surveyed them dismally.

"So worst comes to worst, I'll put him upstairs. Walk him on my lunch hour."

"Oh, could you?" He didn't offer to do *that* very often. "Would you really?" She half hugged his arm. "Oh, you're an angel!" His eyes were startled. But Maude Lee was already handing him the leash, fishing her key ring from the tote bag.

"I can get the passkey from the super—"

"Not to my new top lock!" It wasn't exactly new. Weeks had passed since Bob Foreman, self-appointed floor warden, talked her into the extra security measure, but she had deliberately avoided making a key for the super, as most of the hip staff knew.

"Oh yeah . . . that's right, you don't want these just laying around here," Benjie remembered tactfully, "when I go off and all."

"So maybe you could put them in an envelope for me—?"

"Like last time. Sure, I'll find one in your desk."

Along with the pot, maybe. But she'd have to risk it. She had already spotted the cab drawing up, some Ivy League type in the passenger's seat leaning forward, rapping on the window, opening the door, to offer her a lift in his Ivy League voice, going her way wherever it was.

"Fifty-seventh and Sixth?"

"Take you right to the door."

She never had to open her umbrella. Why not trust to luck? She was lucky. Even with a hangover. Even in the rain.

That was the good news; the bad news was when her luck ran out.

But, for a while it held, the rain stopping before she came out of the hairdresser's three hours later, the sun even breaking through to shine on her hazily as she started down Sixth Avenue for the office, a few blocks away.

She sped along, twirling her candy-striped umbrella, her

long hair flying deliciously behind her, exactly as blond as she wanted it to be when heads snapped around and Con Ed men whistled.

"It's turning the same color your mother's was," her father said on his last visit, his voice always carefully devoid of blame or praise whenever noting any resemblance to the woman his daughter could not remember. "The same unusual combination," he said, "dark eyes and fair hair." He had never told Maude Lee the combination before; she found it without knowing.

"*I* found it," Jean Paul claimed, "on a chart, dear, in a bottle. Not your subconscious. *I* said Honeysun. You picked Mellowash—right here, on this chart." He could be vile, as today, vilest, trying to nag her into a boy-girl cut, saying long hair was over, only for hippies and teens. He even tried to nag her out of the color, saying it had already taken its toll, showing her the split ends. He just *wasted* time, drooping around in his girl-boy shirt, open to the waist, medallions gleaming on his hairless chest, his boy-boy denim pants so tight she had to squeeze the tip into his pocket, barely squeezing a goodbye smile from his reflection—Jean Paul was into narcissism, not mirrors. "Stay loose, dear," he said, refusing to the end to be hurried, resisting Maude Lee's breathless pace. He always did. ("Got to have it all *now*—right? The Emmy, the boy-friend, the pad beautiful, Big Daddy, Mummy's looks? Well, stay loose, dear—*something's* gonna give.")

Like what? Stay loose how? Only her hairdresser knew. Maude Lee could never let go—wasn't about to—of anything.

Even a baby? The thought came from nowhere, bringing her up short with more dutiful pedestrians, waiting for the light to cross Sixth. Her euphoria sprung a slow leak like the vinyl sofa; she looked over toward the networks, towering three in a row in the haze where her own small window, among so many others, could be so easily lost. (More easily than a baby?)

Not if it meant losing herself. Whoever she was. She'd know the bottom line when she had to—trust to luck. She took off, getting the jump on the light, and the rest of the latecomers. The ones who worried their luck away, climbing the walls of skyscrapers, never getting there. She jaywalked through the steamy avenue traffic, cleared the great puddles at both curbs, skidded down the sidewalk and through the great doors, slid halfway across the stone lobby toward the last bank of elevators, to make the last car before the door closed. Just as she knew she would, feeling more like her mystery self again, ready to take on the whole twenty-first floor. Until she got there.

It was a bad day at Boring Rock.

She hadn't gone a dozen steps across the pepper and salt carpeting before she got the word. From her least favorite source of misinformation.

"You shoulda stood in bed, Evans—wherever it was." Charlie Collins leered from the door of his office off the charcoal gray reception area, looking for brains to pick, as usual, on the day of a creative meeting. She tried to get past him.

"Guess again, Charlie. But not now, OK? I'm running late."

"Tell me about it—you got Father Phelps guessing! He's back there chewing everybody out for not knowing where you are."

That stopped her. Though autocratic, Austin "Father" Phelps was no administrator, being a man of artistic temperament, frequently himself off schedule. Maude Lee reached for Charlie's imitation Cartier wristband to get a look at his Timex watch.

"It's ten-thirty—look what you're doing to my pulse." It didn't take much to race the Collins motor.

"We're not meeting with the writer till eleven," Maude Lee said, puzzled. She was cutting it close on a crowded morning but normally Phelps would consider that her problem.

Charlie's leer faded to gloom. "You ask me, there may not be any meeting. We're getting flak from upstairs on the whole damn project." The "we" was royal and hastily reconsidered. "Like I've been warning you, Evans, been trying to tell the writer and everybody, all of you guys, all along."

As the Network Supervisor newly assigned to dramatic specials, Charlie had indeed met his obligation by saying the same dumb things over again every time the only finished script was revised. But today the mimeoed third draft lay virtually forgotten under the *Times* on his slate table desk. Clearly he was into heavier worries, nostrils flaring at the familiar scent of power plays on winds from above. His face was flushed and anxious, what you could see of it under the Brillo bangs, auburn sideburns, and wild mustaches. Too bad really, Charlie had been quite sexy-looking before he disappeared into an unset permanent to pass for creative—the fast route to TV status for fringe flak flunky executives. Charlie should have stood in PR.

"Now listen, relax." Maude Lee laid the voice of authority on him, but gently, soothingly. "Mr. Weldon read the script *himself*. It's *in*. They love it upstairs. Phelps told me." Phelps had also told her never to worry a worrier until you got him in the studio where you could ride a camera over him.

"Oh, come on. If Old Man Weldon's so high on it, we'd have script approval—"

"We're getting it—"

"When?"

"That's just a formality now. It's been set since last week."

"*Last week?*" Charlie's voice rose in anguish. "Oh well, forget it—Jesus, last week! That was before your ex-boss got to town, with his boom-boom boys from L.A."

"Israel?" Of course, Israel. *Always* Israel.

"Flew in on the red-eye yesterday."

"What's that got to do with a New York special?"

"*Are you kidding?*"

She knew better, of course. Israel Gold had to do with everything. That's what made him a nemesis and the quintessence of network VP's.

"So, big deal—he's here on West Coast business—"

"Which is screwing the East Coast, baby."

"Screwing the fall opposition—"

"*Both!*"

You couldn't snow Charlie on his own prototype. Wind up a Charlie doll and he tried to screw you like Israel.

She shrugged. "Politics. We're not into that scene. Let Phelps handle it—"

"So, why doesn't he? Why's he down here hollering on us? Israel's up there in flak city having breakfast with the brass. Phelps isn't."

Maude Lee giggled. "Anyone who wants Israel for breakfast can have him in a big brass dining room."

Charlie's leer returned. "Where'd you have him for breakfast?"

"Where I had him for lunch." The possibility that she might be sleeping her way from boss to boss, coast to coast, always excited Charlie, distracting him from darker suspicions.

"You gave at the office."

She patted his warm hand, which had somehow managed to encircle her arm. "Hang in there—you'll get a shot at a guess you can handle." She removed his caressing fingers before her skin could reward him with a shudder and, longing for the day when she could ride a camera over Charlie Collins, she moved around him.

"Our Gal Friday," he murmured after her, "never makes anything but coffee."

"I'm nobody's girl, Charlie." She kept going—guiltily. Because what she was supposed to be making instead of coffee was revolution. Not this dumb blonde entrance—letting down her side in the week of the West Coast invasion. Not to mention her sex in the Year of the Woman. Now that it had finally come to national television.

It was an event more overdue than Maude Lee Evans, shaking up the chauvinist power structure at all three networks to force its unwelcome way into the pictures on the tube. There, for the first time, starting with the annual February replacement of fall clinkers, women had finally joined blacks as unlikely junior law partners, brain surgeons, and investigative gunslingers. Since they went right on behaving as if they were clerks, nurses, and Mannix's secretary, the giant step up to the hour series from half-hour sitcom segregation passed virtually unnoticed. Except to be panned as a PR phony by the Movement press. It was this ingratitude which at last sparked the first genuine demand for the woman's point of view behind the scenes of nighttime programming. Hence the presence of such as Maude Lee on the twenty-first floor.

Certainly it explained her windowed office, almost as big as Charlie's and a lot nearer the corner suite of power at the end of this block-long, carpeted hall. And, if the executive in the corner suite had his way, it was also going to explain the revival of at least one anthology series of quality drama in New York, where he had made his name, and where, despite all his unmaking Hollywood experiences, Austin Phelps was still respected as a pioneer from the Golden Age of television. His was a class act of survival in a medium which made overnight monster-gods of the young, while eating its middle-aged for breakfast.

So even as she panted along her truant path, Maude Lee was fully aware that her foolish youth was another asset Phelps needed to borrow, helping to make her his golden girl, natural heir to his lost golden boys, to be similarly nurtured, protected, and fought for.

"It is inconceivable that someone of Maude Lee Evans'

abilities should languish as my assistant or anyone else's. At any network," Phelps had warned the brass upstairs in the now historic confrontation which resulted in her promotion. And his.

But there were enough of her sisters still languishing in inside offices as Maude Lee whizzed by, to remind her that such a fate was not in the least inconceivable. Capable women had been languishing for years on the fast crawl at the end of shows. Including Phelps' own wife, one of TV's great no-nonsense dames, whose legend name even after he changed it had never once appeared up front, where the great producer-director and his golden writers shared the credit that really mattered, each in a separate frame. Even though Phelps' decline in the West was dated from his wife's retirement by certain diehards on the twenty-first floor.

Among them was another great no-nonsense legend, Dame Bella Sweet, waiting even now, door open, to clock in the latest starter in the field of new girls who called the office manager Bella the Beast. She frowned at Beauty from her lair.

"Oversleep, Evans?"

"Wish I had." Beauty yawned, leaving Bella to her doubts that Maude Lee Evans would ever make another Nannie Bernstein Phelps. Maude Lee, herself, didn't want to, rather suspecting it was the third reason Phelps had hired her. The fourth being her head. Such was liberation. Especially on mornings like this, when she rounded the corner of his suite, only to see him moving down the hall ahead of her. *Hours* ahead of her. Already armed with a mug of his specially brewed tea, Phelps had changed into his army sweater as protection from the air conditioning, one stiff shoulder held higher than the other, his leonine blond-white head ducked against it, like an old fighter, wary and mean. It didn't take a diehard to spot his livid, legendary temper as he slammed through her office door, rudely ignoring whatever her secretary, Sally, was trying to babble after him.

"Oh wow," Sally whispered, rising from her desk when she saw Maude Lee. "He found out you were at the hairdresser from your service, but nobody could remember the name . . ." She flipped her address wheel futilely—"I couldn't find the name I put it under."

"The name's Le Salon. But put it under hairdresser."

"Oh wow," Sally gasped. "Of course—that's what I should have done . . ."

"S'OK, I should have called in." Sally was a hopeless secretary, but in the Year of the Woman all God's chillun were staff persons, sisters under the skin. Plus which Sally's best friend was Phelps' secretary, an unimpeachable source of news. Maude Lee leaned closer over the desk.

"Any idea what the flap's about?"

Sally nodded toward the mimeoed third draft, sticking out of Maude Lee's tote bag.

"Looks like *My Father the Chauvinist* may really get shafted!" Sally couldn't have been more indignant if she'd written it herself. "Cinny heard Phelps sticking up for you on the phone."

"Who to?"

"Not sure—sounded like a couple of people."

Israel Gold usually did. "Thanks, Sal."

"Good luck."

Maude Lee braced herself and went in to face Phelps and the rest of the music. He was standing by her desk with her appointment calendar in his hands. Unlike Charlie he was clean shaven, his craggy, lined face neither flushed nor anxious—expressionless. But his pale blue eyes blazed like dry ice when he looked at Maude Lee's hair.

"So that's what you've been doing," he said. "And all this time I thought you were a natural blonde, Evans."

She smiled. "No, you didn't."

And then the fight was on.

"Do this office a favor—save your beauty secrets for your secretary! She's the one with a need to know."

"Sorry—it was a mix-up—"

"The hell with sorry—"

"Sally has the number—"

"Now she has it! I've been in here since nine looking for you—"

"Well, I was here till nine last night—"

"Tell it to your message service. What do you pay 'em for?"

"To get me out of bed when I'm beat!"

"So you can sleep it off at the hairburner's? Don't take that as a business expense—"

"Only half—"

"Buy a goddamn alarm clock."

"Please, Father, I'd rather do it myself. Most of the time I can just set my mind—"

"But not your hair." He threw the calendar down on the papers littering her slate gray table desk. "So now you can cancel the lunch date you had it done for."

Maude Lee glanced down at the large question mark she had drawn over the lunch hour, and beside it a tiny exclamation point. She plunked her tote bag on top of both.

"It was only penciled in," she said loftily.

"And bloody well not for business!"

"I think it's really super how everyone feels free to mouse through everyone else's desk!" She yanked the mimeoed third draft from her tote bag. "Making these wild speculations about everyone else's private appointments and affairs—"

"I do not give a hoot in hell about your affairs, or any crazy thing you do on your own time—"

"Oh, great," she said. "Then I guess it's OK to tell you I've got this really vile hangover—"

"*Unless it conflicts with your performance in office hours!*"

"It only conflicts when you shout." Maude Lee moved past Phelps to her battle station behind the desk for round two. (Why be difficult, as her only stepbrother used to say, when with a little more effort you could be impossible.)

"Goddammit, Evans!" Phelps was really shouting now, as he slammed the door in Sally's frightened face. "If you don't want to produce that thing I will!" And coming toward her, he looked mad enough to seize possession.

"*Want* to produce it?" Maude Lee hugged the mimeo. "What do you mean *want* to?"

"So far all you've done is talk about it—"

"So far what I've done is get it written—"

"Rewritten—from a stage play."

"Which nobody saw but me! And rewritten again for you. And rewritten again to show a director—"

"Which," he thundered, "is exactly what you ought to be doing now, instead of toting it around—"

"Which is exactly what I did—last night! Luckily *I* toted two to P.J.'s." Lucky she'd gone there, even with Bruce McVitty. Thank God she got around, luckiest of all. "Because I ran into this director I was going to send it to and he ended up taking my other copy—"

"That's the stuff. Some drunken adman who shoots commercials—"

"Hardly. Billy Bee Bernard doesn't drink, period. Plus the last thing he shot was runner-up at the Cannes Film Festival—"

"There's a certificate of crap."

"Only *Frisco Guru* is different." She was primed for Phelps' views on ever so vérité cinema. "It happens to be making money!"

"In three-dollar bills?"

"In *Variety*." She knew he never read it. "Really, the word on *Guru* is good. Billy Bee's hot—"

"Nothing good ever came from playing God in San Francisco." A native of the heath, Phelps was given to regional ironies, a possible signal of returning good humor. She tried her smile.

"Oh, I don't know, Father."

"I wasn't some boy genius *filmmaker*." Just Jesus jumping off the cross in the drama department at Berkeley. Irony was out of it today.

"Filmmakers impress them upstairs." Salt in his oldest wounds, but true; hastily she applied balm: "Anyhow Billy's crazy to get into tape—he's got this theory about taping on location, using trucks or something—but with one camera hand-held style—"

"Oh, my ass. Art off a barge in Sausalito."

"OK, so it'll wind up in a studio like everything else—"

"With three cameras and the wrong scenery—"

"And you can take over," she finished. "Which'll suit me. It's what I wanted in the first place."

"Hell of an expensive way to get what you want on tape!" Supposedly the cheap medium, of course, but his own, so he couldn't deny that using it again was what he wanted also. Or that the network view of his executive obligations would require an emergency to stage a comeback this early. If instead, her friend the filmmaker conquered tape, she'd be making Phelps the father of a new golden boy. A no-lose situation, concluded with the master's own maxim.

"Better waste company money than our time," his golden girl quoted, about as safe at this moment as teasing a lion. But it proved a protégée's progress, if he really meant her to take the giant step forward into the role of producer, leaving his hands free for the cameras when opportunity came. "Ready when you are, Father Phelps—this is the draft I want to go with." She placed it on the desk. "All I need is script approval." And luck. She crossed her fingers.

He glowered at the mimeo, but no longer seemed impelled toward seizure. "You may have to fight for it, baby. Are you ready for that?"

"Yes."

"Whining about your hangover? Won't get you far with the big boys—"

"I don't mind fighting anybody but you," she said. And the fight was over. At least this round, part of the endless contest no one won or lost or was meant to. What it took to defuse disaster with Phelps was the will to outlast a blast, or the wit to divert it. Maude Lee, having willful wit at her weakest moments, found it hard to fathom why strong men usually didn't. But it gave her more edge than the Woman's Revolution. Every year was woman's year for Phelps, the teacher, best with those who had the most to learn. The trick for the woman in any year was working *with* not just for him.

"Now my goddamn tea's cold," he said accusingly—to no one. It was always cold by the time he drank it. But something in Maude Lee moved to take the mug, as if running down the hall for a refill was instinct. What then—conditioning? Whichever, suppression was a constant effort, wearing for both freed slave and master. She put the mug on the desk. He turned abruptly toward the floor-to-ceiling window, glaring into the glare from a city full of glass houses. The haze had lifted.

"Since you've been passing scripts around town like peanuts—"

"One script."

"—did you happen to pass a copy to the Coast?"

"I'd have to be crazy!"

"Someone did."

"Not me—I only had a dozen run off, on purpose so I could

keep track." Fishing methodically in the madness on her desk, she came up with a list. "Here—"

He barely glanced at the names before he started.

"*Two* to Charlie Collins?"

Nit-picking time. She sighed.

"He wanted the extra one to make notes on—" She knew it was wrong as soon as she said it.

"*Charlie Collins'* notes?"

But she was already thinking of the slightly larger oyster white office off the charcoal gray reception area, remembering Charlie's slate gray table desk, recognizably a replica of hers because Charlie never had anything on it but newspapers, not quite covering the mimeoed third draft this morning. One mimeo. Only one left of the two copies she had given Charlie Collins.

"That *fink*."

"Paid to be." Phelps threw the list back.

Prick then. He wasn't paid to be that. "Vile, vilest . . ." But then she remembered something else, the face, flushed and anxious under the Brillo. "Yes, but it doesn't make sense. . . . If Charlie is in on it, why's he so upset?"

Phelps shrugged, impatient. "Probably got double-crossed himself."

"Not until they leave," she said, knowing more than her fatherly boss cared to hear about the out-of-towners who used double agents to procure more than scripts. Perfect casting for Charlie. And even Israel wouldn't dump perfection in midstream. "Getting their jollies is half the trip," she pressed, heedless of storm warnings that Phelps' temper still rumbled near enough to deliver a thunderclap.

"Evans, we've wasted enough damn time this morning, without office gossip! Now can you possibly confine yourself to the matter at hand?"

"OK, OK, Father . . ." Her own had taught her the futility

of arguing sexual motivations with Victorian madmen, though
how either Phelps or Leland Evans got through a whole war
in any man's army remained beyond her. "What is it, exactly—
the matter, I mean?"

"The dialogue of *My Father the Chauvinist.*"

"The *dialogue.*" She blinked at him. "But the dialogue's absolutely right . . . you said so yourself!" And it had to be right
if it got by Phelps. Only a good writer could face him with
the juicier facts of life and get away with it. In a script.
Where he found life relevant. Since they were operating in a
foul-mouthed vacuum where the home screen was guarded
from home truths as from the plague, the clash of double
standards was frequently confusing. She felt her own anger
rising for the first time. "Look, if they're getting around our
artistic control by doing some kind of obscenity number upstairs—"

"Who said anything about obscenity?"

"What else *could* they say about the dialogue?"

"That it's ethnically offensive. According to Israel Gold."

"How the *hell* would Israel know?" Maude Lee exploded
with indignation. "He can't read!"

"Maybe somebody read it to him, thereby offending his eth-
nics—"

"*No way!* Israel can't even sit through a synopsis unless you
make it a one-liner." Ask the girl who had the job. "Plus he
wouldn't be ethnically offended if you hit him in the face with
a knish."

Phelps didn't exactly smile, but the lines in his face soft-
ened, going the other way. "With a what?"

"Oh, some kind of potato thing." The air had gone out of
Maude Lee. She sat down, glumly facing the dead eye of a
TV set under a gray on gray painting of a ball in a square, her
back turned to the world's most breathtaking skyline—as per
the inscrutable whim of the management's design consultant.

"Israel can't even get through a *menu*," she said, remembering. *Damn* him. "That's why he always orders the same thing. Ever notice? He just pretends it's an ulcer." Also a built-in safeguard against overdrinking. Cautious creepy son of a bitch.

"He obviously never ordered a knish," Phelps said. "You pronounce the K." He started lowering himself into her visitor's chair, warily, because it swiveled. She swiveled hers to face him across the window. "How do you know, anyhow—for sure?"

"My wife's quite a cook—"

"No. About Israel japping *Chauvinist*."

"That's a nice sentence."

A legacy from her father's service in the South Pacific. "OK, shafting *Chauvinist*—but how did you find out?"

Phelps swiveled toward the window. "The old man called me at home."

"Mr. Weldon? *Himself?*"

He nodded. "Last night."

"But that's wild . . ." Maude Lee faltered as Phelps swiveled back, and their eyes met.

Old Man Weldon wasn't really old, just mildly doddering and prematurely white. But his daily slow fade into nightly oblivion was office gossip raised to the power of legend. She proceeded at her own risk—with care.

"I mean, isn't it kind of unusual for him to call at night . . . you know, now—what with commuting, and all . . . ?"

"And all" was right. If Mr. Weldon couldn't pour himself into his midnight blue Eldorado in time to beat the rush hour, it didn't much matter whether he headed east to the island, north to Gracie Square, or just nodded off at his desk. He wasn't really there anyway. But Phelps let it pass, with matching care.

"Not much of a phone man," was all he said, though both of

them knew Mr. Weldon could take to the phone with a vengeance in his miracle periods of coherence—he underwent three
a year—crashing back through some instant cure to focus on
ratings and time slots and pretests, guessing right just often
enough to be considered prescient. Mostly by other networks.
Guesswork being now in abeyance at his own, the Vice President in charge of Programming was between miracles for the
summer.

"He must be really anxious . . ." Maude Lee murmured.
Certainly everyone else was anxious about him this year.
Clear-eyed as Rip Van Winkle, Old Man Weldon wasn't much
of a guesser on the subject of women. Young Mrs. Weldon
was living proof.

"Israel can be really persuasive. I gather he spent most of
yesterday worrying aloud."

"And fast." But even Israel would need a running start from
the airport to get in ahead of Mr. Weldon's morning drink.

"Well, the old man's supersensitive about ethnic issues. Especially this one. Something to do with being the only Wasp
upstairs when he first made Vice President. Israel knows that
better than I do—he was the first to call Mr. Weldon the
Company Goy."

Talk about office gossip. Phelps knew the kind that became
history. Maude Lee was fascinated.

"What's that make you?"

"Creative . . ." Phelps waved a dismissing hand. "In on a
pass." And it was literally true, of course. Creative staff were
on talent contracts, free-lance outsiders like the talent they
hired.

"The pass with the morals clause." Maude Lee giggled,
though Phelps had warned her often enough it was character
napalm. No joke if used against them.

"Management's glorified shit list," was how he described
their creative status now, proudly, seeing himself at the top of

the list, where he used to be, more artist than brass. "But I seem to be some special kind of Wasp Soul Brother to the old man! The kind with a non-Wasp wife, in this case, I guess." The tone was dry. "Anyway, he was sure as hell hoping I'd sound Nannie out last night—"

"Did you?"

Phelps laughed. "*Did* I?" he teased, as always getting a kick out of Maude Lee's concern with his wife's opinions. "Would I second-guess you?"

"Yes. Ah, tell me what she said—please?"

"I have. She said she wouldn't read this or any script. But her reaction to the *call,* you'll be happy to hear, was that Israel's trying to upstage you. An issue for an issue. Old Testament style."

"Israel's issue is old enough—right out of the fifties."

"Who isn't—me and Marcus Welby?" The smile became wry. "Why should Israel be any different?"

She brushed past the question and the moment. "But it's a ploy—just like your wife said. All bull, he's faking—"

"Hard to prove, kid. He came on real sincere over Weldon's line this morning." She knew that come-on. "Terribly humble about interfering. Just thought he could make a contribution if I'd come up for breakfast—"

"Without me, of course." She was getting to sound like Charlie, the spy.

"Well, Israel seemed especially concerned about offending you. *Very* aware of his delicate position. As your former employer."

All the words that sprang to mind were no-nos coming from her lips to Phelps' ears.

"*Blip,*" she said.

Phelps clasped his hands behind his head, his musing pose when most watchful.

"Mr. Weldon, on the other hand, feels it might be valuable for you to invite Israel to our meeting with the writer—"

"*Today?*"

"Unless you object, of course."

"Well, don't you?" He didn't answer; she couldn't believe it. "Then big deal what I think! I mean who really cares all of a sudden?"

"Everybody."

"Oh, come on—so I'm producing. It's still my first show. You're still exec producer . . ."

He sighed. "*And* the Company Art Maven. Like Weldon's the Company Goy, and Charlie's the Company Fink, and Israel's the West Coast Company pain in everybody's East Coast Company ass. But you, baby . . ." He unclasped his hands, to level a finger at her. "You, as you know damn well, are the new pressure group that worries everybody. The burning issue we damn well *can't* upstage—"

"Stay cool. You're all still Tarzan—me low girl on totem pole."

"Woman," Phelps corrected. "Company Woman of the Year."

"That's all they have to hear in CR," Maude Lee said.

"Well, forget it. The only consciousness that matters right now is Israel Gold's—"

"Who doesn't have one."

"We have to raise it anyhow. The question is how—letting him in, or keeping him out. I'm damned if I know—so you tell me. It's your decision. But make it fast." He looked at his watch.

She stared at him. "You're *really* not kidding . . ."

"Make a decision and see."

"Wow." She sounded like Sally, which was one up from Charlie but not much help the moment the buck stopped, really stopped passing. Feeling silly, she got up from under

Phelps' gaze to take her turn at the window. Vertigo. But then she felt something else, foreign and wonderful, up from her toes, from nowhere.

"Power," Phelps mused, behind her. "How do you like it?"

She looked wide-eyed into the sun. Power over Israel Gold . . . *Like* it? After all his endless attempts to make her and every other girl who walked through his office, his petty vengeance when he couldn't, petty contempt if he could. How would she like the power to call his ethnic bluff? The power to exclude him on the grounds of *his* offensiveness. To women. To writers. Not to mention performers, considering some of the shows he'd demolished. If she had Israel's power to use against him the tables had really turned. She faced Phelps, warily swiveling.

"Show biz," she murmured, but he shook his head.

"Industry, baby."

Of course. She had forgotten—Lesson Number One in Phelps' Video History. Show business had become The Industry the day the first picture moved, before it could even talk. Since the first banking baron invested in celluloid against the future of electronics, and called it mass entertainment. Soon to be mass communication, but mass was the operative word. Not for little girls to play with. Or little boys, one might have hoped, but it was ever thus pending maturity—or revolution. Transition, Phelps called it.

They were all transition figures. Pioneers lost on their own frontier, already mourning their golden age, selling out a miracle for a gold rush. Christopher Columbus, in it for the money. Einstein, trying relativity to see if it would play in Peoria. With a made-to-order advance man: Israel Gold.

She could spit in his eye. Israel would say it was raining, mark her for a target also, to be shot down later, with the script, job, title, the whole woman's issue if it got in the way— only success was hard to replace. Nothing else mattered. Even

Israel's vengeance would be purely coincidental. As irrelevant as principal. A by-product like art.

"I suppose *anyone* who's been snaking around calling our script anti-semitic ought to confront the writer . . ." She thought of E. V. Adamic's terrible scorn, and almost smiled. "Israel might just get a surprise."

"Right." Phelps nodded as if grading a test, his eyes no longer seeking hers, reserved for his watch again, as he rose. No E's for excellent today. She had taken too long. P for passing. "C'mon in my office—I've got a surprise too. A real live movie star for Mr. Gold—"

"In your *office*." So he had been that sure of her decision. But what if she'd gone the other way . . . gone wrong? Would he have let it happen—to both of them? There were lines in that face that nobody read. He was already opening the door.

"The more of a package we've got pulled together, the faster we'll look like getting off the ground. Might even help to call your surprise director—if there's time before the meeting."

"Maybe that's him calling me . . ." The light on Maude Lee's phone was winking. But behind Phelps she saw Sally half rising from her desk, wigwagging violently. Turning, Phelps saw her also.

"Oh wow," Sally gulped, flustered. "I thought you were through." She spoke past Phelps to Maude Lee. "I'm sorry I forgot to tell you before, but it's Professor Nedders for the third time!"

"That's a surprise, question mark?" Phelps said. "That's a director?"

"Not even a doctor yet, exclamation point." Maude Lee smiled. (Sally always gave a lover an even break.) "I'll be right with you—OK?"

Phelps frowned at his watch by way of an answer.

"Make it fast," he said, less agreeably than before. But when

he went he pulled the door to behind him, gently. Funny old
lion. Maude Lee celebrated by punching the wrong button.

"Hello, my *angel*," she said to absolutely nobody. Oh God,
if she disconnected him now . . . But the next button brought
him in loud and clear.

"Jesus H. *Christ*."

Right voice, wrong tone.

"Listen," she began again, "Neddy? I can't talk—"

"Look," he was overlapping, "could we make sense for two
minutes—"

"Where are you?"

"The terminal. I've been trying you since the airport."

"Angel, I know—but it's murder here."

"Want to try it in a phone booth with a bag and a briefcase
and two tape recorders—"

"Can't you check something?"

"Not before I check you—which is quite a trick."

She giggled. "You should have checked me for breakfast. I
woke up hoping."

"Sorry about that." He sounded pleased. "But I had to fly all
night to make brunch. By way of Newark—are you ready?"

So ready it killed her. Especially since it was out of the
question.

"Baby, that's sort of screwed up . . ."

"About meeting in your pad?"

"Just no way."

"Hell. I was counting on getting shaved."

She laughed softly. "Sure you were."

"Yeah . . . well . . ." He laughed too.

"If it's just that, a barber could fix you up, baby."

"Not with a shower."

"Counting on a shower, too?"

"And maybe leaving my gear, frankly."

"That's all?"

He laughed again. "Well . . . all I was *counting* on . . ."

"Too bad about you."

It was easy to keep it light with the bad news only half broken. She tried to leave it that way.

"Look—where can I find you in an hour?"

"Your office, if I can dump some of this gear when I pick you up. And maybe use the phone—"

"Yes, but you can't—"

"I'll smile at Sally."

"No, I mean pick me up."

"For lunch at *all*?"

Quitting while ahead was not her best trick.

"Well, not the way it looks—things are *really* screwed up—"

"How, for Christ sake? Didn't you get my message?"

"I also got my boss's message—bright and early."

"After working half the night? Shit, what kind of job is that?"

"You know. Crazy. Hey, don't make a thing—"

"*Me* make a thing—"

"*Neddy*."

"No, come on, this was your idea—you've been putting me on for a week about coming home early—"

"I never put you on!"

"What do you call it? Come home and surprise you last night, for Christ sake. That would have been cute. Break my ass and come home this morning so we can play house for lunch—"

"Because I want you home, damn you!"

It was like an electric current running through the cord between them.

"You know," he said, "you're too much?"

"Better than too little."

"Not this much too much."

"Yes."

She pulled her calendar from under the tote bag to see if the day was ever going to end.

"Come home for dinner?"

A sigh escaped him, deeper than any she'd heard before. "Mud, I'm tired." Of everything, the way it sounded.

"*Early* dinner?" Though she knew from her calendar it wouldn't be.

"I don't know . . ."

"Yes, you do. Because I'm going to cook something *fabulous!*" She tried teasing: "Like whatever's on special at the supermarket. Just to please you." Normally it would. "OK? No Gristedes, I *swear*. On my whole future." Anything to make him say yes before he asked when, but Sally beat him to both by bursting in, goggle-eyed with the usual compliment of wows, to announce that E. V. Adamic had arrived for the meeting *early*. An all time First. Today. Wouldn't it be?

"So say I'll be out in a minute—"

"Reception said to go to Mr. Phelps' office."

"Oh, God." Maude Lee spoke into the receiver: "Neddy—"

"I heard."

"Look, I'll call you after lunch at the foundation—"

"In the middle of a meeting? I'm giving my report to the whole damn board—"

"Well, I've got a meeting now, Ned!"

"Then say when at your pad."

The bottom line. She couldn't. "The thing is I've got to do a PR number at the end of the day for Mr. Weldon." Even Ned knew time stopped for Mr. Weldon.

"So I'll let myself in for once. Big deal—"

"That's all the super needs to see—"

"He won't be patrolling the halls for God's sake."

"Yes, but the doorman . . . and with your bags . . ."

"Mud—what the hell's the point of my having keys?"

Her reluctance to let him use them was an old bone of contention but preferable to confronting him prematurely with the evidence of last night's turn-on. She *had* to get there first and clean up. Vague guilt blurred into annoyance with the whole heavy mess. Who *needed* hangovers and ill-timed phone calls and jealous demands from boss *or* lover.

"Look, why don't you take your stuff so you can stay loose—?"

"Terrific suggestion. Check into the boardroom while I hit 'em for a grant—"

"Oh, come on, people have offices there too. It's better than schlepping back to the East Side in the rush hour—"

"For nothing. When I could schlepp up to 116th—"

"Well, why not? I mean you might as well get unpacked in your own pad later, where I can at least call you—"

"*After* you get through doing your number. Like last night."

"Not *that* late—"

"Not if it's PR."

"OK, Ned. What's that mean?"

"Why ask me? I don't even know what this morning means."

"That I'm *busy*—"

"Out PRing when I called before nine? Or just still out? You sure as hell weren't in your office—"

"This is *so* boring—"

"So's phoning it in to your service and your secretary—"

"Then don't! And I won't interrupt your meeting. Good luck anyway—" But he had already hung up, beating her to it for a finish.

"Professor Goodworks!" Maude Lee slammed down her receiver as Sally moved in sympathetically from the door. "Do you *believe* him? Nobody else's problems matter! *He's* the only one who's ever under pressure! If I'm busy I'm playing around!"

"Like, you know, ego," Sally said.

"Tell me about it. The biggest little ego in town. Closet

chauvinist, secret square." Raving made her feel better. "It's to die when he's really so smart—"

"And so humpy," Sally sighed.

"Oh, so's Charlie Collins humpy."

"Yeah, but without the soul it's not to die."

Exactly. Out of the mouth of a dumbbell. Just when Maude Lee least needed a reminder why Ned killed her. It was time anyway to change the subject before the rest of the day's surprises started to backfire.

"Here, Sal—I want you to make this call for me." Maude Lee picked up the mimeo to tear off the title page with the number scribbled on it. "It's where Billy Bee Bernard is staying—"

"*Wow!* For *Chauvinist?* He's a real *name!*" Sally could be had for an initial. She fairly snatched the page from Maude Lee.

"Just say there's so much interest in his reaction—I'm hoping he'll call in with it by noon. But on *my* extension for God's sake. I don't need some iffy arty 'Maybe' from Billy Bee in the middle of this meeting—"

"How about if he wants to call in person? I bet that wouldn't be iffy—"

"*Sally*—this is important!" Maude Lee borrowed the tone of authority. "Don't let's get off into anything personal—"

But Sally was already off and dialing.

Sometimes it was all too easy for Maude Lee to put herself in Phelps' place. Easier in fact than understanding what kept her flying along in his footsteps, up and down halls clutching script and tote bag, breathlessly trying to remember one single television show she'd ever seen that was really worth it.

What followed was one of those impossible interviews. Or series of impossible interviews, really. Maude Lee got a preview of coming attractions in Phelps' outer office, where E. V.

Adamic was still waiting, all five feet arrayed in new denim, under a ten-gallon hat.

Cinny, typing serenely, looked up from behind the black hatbrim to wink at Maude Lee.

"Oh, *fine!*" She smiled. "Now you're both here. So you can go in together." Cinny spoke as if it were all a pleasant surprise, the most marvelous coincidence, overlooking unusual earliness, breathless lateness, and even the paranoid little writer's well-known reluctance to budge an inch without Maude Lee Evans, who winked back gratefully. There was only one like Cinny.

"Thanks, Cin. Hi, nutsy—sorry." She kissed the writer's cheek.

"He's got someone with him in there!" There was a hoarse crack in the tiny voice to match the flint in the baby face.

"To meet us."

"*Why?*" Always why.

"It's a surprise."

But surprises were the food of conspiracy. The eyes shone darkly, framed by an inverted V of long dark hair under the hatbrim. Maude Lee took a fast practiced look to make sure the pupils were undilated, about all she hoped for now.

"C'mon." She held out her hand; it was grabbed as if by a child going in to see the doctor. Maude Lee led the way around a small corner into what looked like a country house library, surprisingly informal, and only a little too large to be cozy. It was a mark of the occupant's status that the décor could reflect his taste. And like a true fifties liberal Phelps had found a democratic way to take advantage of the privilege, eliminating what he called the movie mogul approach to his presence by positioning his hunting table desk immediately inside the door with his back to the book-lined wall. Thus, his arriving visitors practically fell over him when, as now, he was sitting there, on the lookout.

"Well, here they come at last! Our producer, Ms. Evans, and her playwright—" His glance flicked to the great black hat. "Ms. Adamic, the cow person." It was all for the benefit of his other visitor, of course. Phelps turned toward the comfortable sitting area at the far windowed end of the room where a man reading a script untangled long legs to rise.

"We don't have to get up—they're liberated."

"I'm *not*," said a voice everyone knew from somewhere.

With a lurch of the heart reserved for childhood gods, Maude Lee recognized the only movie actor her father had ever described as a gentleman, a star since distinguished by the swiftness of his falling. He loomed up now from the sofa and the past like his own ghost, late of the "Late Show," where indeed his stardom had been preserved, intact. He had not blurred the image like so many others flickering on in made-for-TV movies, to be had for a laugh on "Laugh In," had for a faked song and dance with any cheap MC on a game show. Or worse, had for real in the shallows of in-depth interviews. Not for him the show of old hands at the Oscars, political telethons, or public recovery from private despair in National Smile Week. He hadn't pitched public woo for ten years. When he went, he went. Like George Brent.

Yet suddenly, here he was, presto changeo—script in hand, auditioning for a TV power play. Nothing else seemed to explain his ghostly advance across Phelps' office, murmuring congratulations in the vocabulary of Maude Lee's father— ("remarkable dialogue . . . extraordinary . . .")—looking wholly unsure which of the two unlikely girls he towered over could have written a word of it.

Maude Lee gulped some kind of awed thank you, deliberately fudging the famous name in the faint hope that E.V. wouldn't be able to place him until Phelps could spring the trap—on Israel, for whom, of course, it was ethnically intended. Happily Phelps didn't seem to feel the need of an introduction as he joined the group to put a fatherly arm around the writer's shoulders.

"You missed quite a discussion of your father, the chauvinist, E.V. My friend here even tried a couple of speeches for size."

"Why?" E.V. looked blankly from Phelps to the actor, staring up at the once "gorgeous mug" everyone still knew from somewhere; unlike the voice it had aged, of course, though not so obviously as Phelps—the weathered skin was stretched too tight—but something had gone wrong underneath. No lift could put it right. Looking down from the brink of wherever he'd been, he answered with a question.

"Why not?"

"You're Irish." So much for faint hope. Like the rest of her breed E.V. was long on movie stars if short on manners.

Smilin' Ed Kelly smiled but not with his black Irish eyes and it wasn't the same.

"Irishmen read," he said.

"Especially aloud," Phelps laughed.

"Not for Jewish parts."

Phelps removed his fatherly arm. "Mr. Kelly doesn't audition for *any* part," he said quietly. "But he happens to be the Irishman who once played Shylock for me—"

"On *television?*" Maude Lee, astonished, forgot San Francisco.

Phelps frowned. "On stage." A golden age ago.

Not that E.V. cared where or when, *"Shakespeare!"* The tiny voice pronounced sentence on the dodo bard of drama departments. "What's Shakespeare gotta do with my kind of characters?"

"Prick him, he bleeds," the actor suggested.

Phelps sighed. "We could really do it now . . ." Back from the dead, such talent could do anything.

"Anything for laughs," the talent said, "Polish jokes, all kinds accents, female impersonations . . ."

It had to be a random collection of gaffes—Kelly seemed as far beyond the intentional slur as he was any real effort to please. But they were all fighting words to E. V. Adamic about to take Polish feminist umbrage.

"He can even sing . . ." Maude Lee leapt in, forgetting that the only time Kelly did her father had written the song, a can of peas she usually avoided opening.

"Yeah." E.V. pounced on new proof of conspiracy. "Your old man's hit."

"Well, I'm damned if I ever heard *that!*" Phelps said, looking as bemused as Kelly, who muttered the hope that he'd been dubbed as he sat on the sofa beside some forgotten musician's daughter.

"Daddy didn't stay in the business long," Maude Lee said, smiling, having learned long ago to make light of yesterdays with actors. "It was really more of a theme anyway."

"I'm afraid I missed most of those," the star said. "You had to see the picture to catch the theme."

"Not this one!" E.V. headed unerringly for Phelps' special wing chair before he could. "It was the title song of *Boys on Shore Leave*." She sat, her boots not quite touching the floor. "You did it in singspeak."

Phelps laughed, kicking his footstool toward the wing chair. "The things kids know . . ."

Kelly shook his head, staring at E.V. as he finally recalled what no kid could know. "You should have heard the starlet it was written for," he said. Kelly had run to starlets. He closed his eyes wearily against the past. "She was cut out of the picture—to protect the lot's singing lady, I guess, or maybe it was me . . ." It all got blurred. The cuts and the reasons, as he wrapped the system up in a nutshell. But not for E. V. Adamic.

"Why?" she asked. "Why'd everybody go along? Even stars, nobody could *make* anybody sign—"

"In those days," Kelly answered, "the East Gate of the studio was the end of the world." It was a flat statement, without recourse like the flat world it described. "They kept you in or they locked you out."

"For good," Maude Lee murmured.

"Yeah," Kelly said, nodding. "Like the songwriter." And then it all came back, more glimmers from the past. "Lee Evans." He turned to look at the blond girl with the starlet's face. "You're their daughter . . . ?"

But before Maude Lee could answer the enemy was upon them—gliding into their midst like a school of fish. Israel first, flashing white teeth, shooting white cuffs, round and tanned and fully packed, everything he wore looking like sharkskin, minus only the fin that could have warned them. But in his wake the shadow fins were showing—Charlie Collins, fink-pimp-spy, and behind him, the inevitable assistant with the special field of competence, left on the threshold, all fins; waiting as Maude Lee had once waited, to be identified. ("My young friend, the drama major, from Stamford.") The shadow's alma mater was the name that mattered, and the only one Israel ever got right.

"*Beautiful people . . .*" The soft voice spread over the room like an oil slick, embraces to follow.

"Father Phelps, you old lion . . . take me to your leader, the lady producer." The sea green eyes kept one embrace ahead, always hungry. "That's no lady, that's my Maudley!"

She held her breath against the wild aroma of colognes and talcums and oils and gargles waiting to engulf her as she was drawn up to his silky shark-front, turning her cheek before his silky lips parted, while his sleek arms went around her, silky hands on her back found her girdle-free and braless. How he loved *that* fashion news, the silky shark bastard.

"Hey . . ." She let her head fall back. "Were we lovers?"

He laughed, an oil splash. "I saw her first." The lips were gone but not the hands. "You guys, you guys, never give me credit, but that you owe me. Tell 'em, Maudley."

"Israel saw me first."

The sea green eyes found fame over her shoulder. "Well, I'll be a hermit's neighbor!" Letting go, one sly silky hand snapped her bikini elastic; he moved on. "We gotta come all the way here from Mulholland Drive to meet like Stanley Livingston?"

Kelly rose but not to be kissed. "Neither, I presume, Mr. Gold." He straight-armed Israel with a handshake.

But any rebuff could be turned to embrace. The actor's madras coat sleeve was shark bait. "Israel, Israel—why so formal? Not that I should even be talking to you, lousy neighbor." Kelly was too tall to see over. Busy clutching madras, Israel missed the wing chair. "This star's such a star we can't even get him to come next door for Dotty's buffet." A must for the television aristocracy, Dotty's legendary groaning board was therefore by definition a legendary bore to Hollywood's true *haut monde,* where Kelly belonged if Kelly wanted to belong anywhere.

"I might, now I've taken to eating," he said lightly, "but not without an invitation."

"Open house, open house—anytime." But everyone knew it wasn't. Not belonging was reckless, like showing blood to a shark; Kelly seemed not to care. Israel turned to the multitudes with his exhibit.

"You kids, you kids are too young to remember when Hollywood really had a star system."

"Were you there?" Maude Lee smiled, remembering damn well he'd been a New York space salesman.

"In the business, in the business. Before you were born." It was all pure Gold. When in doubt say everything twice. But

Charlie, who disliked being put down even once, moved hastily away from Maude Lee, to include himself with the big kids.

"I'm one media executive who's not too young to be a fan, Mr. Kelly—"

Israel all but yanked the madras clear of Charlie. "Ah, whadda you know from fans? Fans had clubs. It was part of the system—am I right?" He hugged Kelly's arm. "The studio said who had fans, how many, where, when, stay, go . . ." Looking at the creased madras, Maude Lee wondered what in the absence of the system made Kelly go now. Anywhere. "The studio made stars," Israel was chanting. "This star, you know how he started?" Israel patted the madras. "He was the threat to Gable. *Clark* Gable. *This* star."

Kelly's lusterless brown eyes sparked with something akin to hope. He wasn't disappointed.

"Barry Sullivan was the threat to Gable," a tiny voice piped up behind them.

Israel turned and gaped, obviously not ready for *this* writer, *this* writer, introduced by Maude Lee as E. V. Adamic. Some spy Charlie was.

"I think it's time we all got introduced," Phelps said to the shadow in the fishtail position.

"Oh yeah, yeah." Israel waved vaguely. "Samson Jones. My young assistant from the Actor's Conservatory Theatre."

"Jonas Sams," the young assistant murmured, shaking Phelps' hand. It was perfect. In the year of the woman Israel's new shadow was a black man. A faster second-guesser than Charlie, he was also trying to earn his shadow salary by gliding to the shark's rescue at the wing chair, an upstream effort as it turned out.

"Mr. Gold and I have wanted to meet you ever since we read your script, Miss Adamic."

"Ms.," E.V. said. "Why?"

Charlie the superspy made his move. "Mr. Gold has some very positive suggestions. Somewhat along the lines of notes I've submitted—"

"*Aah, shaddup,*" Israel said.

There were moments when apolitical amorality made Israel so wholly guileless he killed Maude Lee more than anybody. It was the one thing about him she had forgotten could always disarm her.

So laughingly telling Charlie that what Israel needed was a nice cup of Phelps' special tea, she unwittingly let the shark off the hook. As a look from Phelps told her, even before he called Cinny, setting off a chain reaction, about coffee for Kelly, and other special orders, for milk, no milk, and sugar substitutes. During which the blood faded from the shark's sea green eyes, no longer red-rimmed with anger, by the time she maneuvered him onto the sofa between her and the wing chair where she wanted him. All he had to do was lean forward to present his back, cool beyond cornering.

"I'm having a little trouble with this chauvinist father of yours." He spoke directly across the coffee table to Phelps, as if no writer existed, a media variation of the old stage maxim that the best writers didn't. And the same applied to token producers, finally just a pushy broad.

Phelps also leaned forward touching the memo that lay on the table like bait.

"Our chauvinist fathers gave everyone trouble. But the father in this script is something else. He's our generation, Israel. He's us. Giving our kids trouble."

"*Our* kids, Father? *Us?*"

"I meant contemporary."

The shadow leaned in slightly. "The problem of relating between generations would seem to be timeless—"

"Now there speaks a proud father!" Israel beamed. "Would you believe?"

Phelps looked at the shadow. "I wouldn't believe the father of an adolescent—"

"Makes no difference. Two months, two years, twenty, boy, girl—the feeling's the same—am I right, Jones?"

The shadow inclined his proud head.

"The *parental* feeling, that is," Phelps said. "Speaking as fathers."

"Father, forgive me—nothing personal—but it's the only way to speak. Frankly, you'd have to have a kid to know."

Ergo: Phelps didn't. First blood to the shark.

"Or be one?" Maude Lee said.

Charlie Collins laughed. "Really, Evans, everybody's *been* one. I mean we were all born somebody's kid—"

"And would you believe those of us who were born girls got the feeling our sex mattered to Daddy?"

"Maudley darling," Israel spoke without looking at her, "you're a gorgeous goyisha Princess and your father, the King, should never be embarrassed. But if you got in a jam and he didn't go bail, you'd yell down the slammer."

Unbelievably E. V. Adamic joined in the laugh, cackling disloyally from one side of her mouth—all smiles being admissions of failure. The sound was old like the sad toughness of midgets, but Israel wasn't ready for her noise either. He cut her off with a passive verb.

"What's written here, what's written here . . ." his silky hands were grazing the mimeo this time ". . . is a very specific type situation. An *unnatural* situation."

"*Unnatural?*" Phelps raised an eyebrow, chewing his pacifier now, which usually made Maude Lee want to smoke, but not today watching Kelly light one cigarette from another, not even filtered—where *had* he been, anyway? Thank God she didn't inhale. "Unnatural to whom?" Phelps looked at Israel, as if expecting a sensible answer, as if it weren't all a farce, travesty, waste . . .

"Unnatural to both parties." Israel tapped the mimeo of a ten-character, twenty-scene play. So he really *hadn't* read it. Big surprise.

"Of course there's only one father-daughter confrontation," Jonas Sams said hastily before Maude Lee could, "but I'm sure we all agree it's more focal than the peer relationships."

"Yeah, yeah," Israel said. "The title gives it to you." It had certainly given him enough. "But what I did, what I did—I checked into this peer angle. Would you believe I got a kid the exact same age and sex as the central character here?" He was holding the mimeo now. "We even call her the same pet name. Maudley can tell you."

There was a lot more Maude Lee could have told them about the forlorn Princess staring balefully from the forgotten half of the silver frame on Israel's desk. His thumb was usually over her face when he showed off her brother, the Prince.

"Dolly," Maude Lee said, "nee Barbara."

"Yeah, yeah. The girl."

(My son Aaron, heart of my heart. My daughter the girl.) Maude Lee looked at E.V. to make sure she wasn't missing one chauvinist syllable, but the gaze bent on Israel from under the great black hat was softly out of focus. What seemed to be tears blurred the agate eyes. Then the hatbrim dipped leaving all uncertain. For the first time since the meeting began, Maude Lee also sat forward with a jolt of alarm.

"What I said to Dolly," Israel was saying, "I said 'Dolly, do Daddy a favor. Tell me if this is what it's like to be in trouble at your age!' All I said, right hand to God. You know what she said an hour later? Ninety minutes the outside. Jones was there—am I right?" Jonas Sams nodded . . . "OK, you tell 'em—"

"She said that's what it's like when kids get in a hassle. But you'd get her out—"

"'But Daddy would have gotten me out of it.' Quote un-quote!"

"That was the idea," Jonas said.

"So what's the matter here?" The script he'd been pawing like Kelly's madras slipped back on the coffee table with a slap. "Maybe the writer knows a character like this. But he's a new Jewish father on me. Just takes off, never supports his family, couldn't care about his kids except to play the big shot. So finally his girl comes after him, just a teen-ager, but she gets in the pokey on some pill rap, like my own kid tells me could happen. So she uses her one dime to call the old man, in his own town, his turf. And here he comes talking big deals, dropping big names she knows he doesn't know. And that's it. What's he do? Nothing. Zilch. Doesn't lift a pinkie."

"Couldn't," said the writer, the only word she got in.

"So what'd he come for—in the scene?" Clearly in life only management's relatives were relevant. "You're supposed to show us—not tell us."

"She did," Maude Lee protested. "The scene shows what the characters lost—the love they both feel—" Still unexpressed, as this too was interrupted.

"Not in the script Jones and I got." Israel turned to his shadow. "You see any love for this guy's kid?"

"Well, there's certainly very little in terms of anything structured or supportive—"

"There's shit is what there is," Israel summed up. For fatherhood.

"Maybe you'd have to lose a child to know." As soon as she said it Maude Lee wished she hadn't, having forgotten *that* hollow feeling almost all morning.

"Come next door on visiting day," Kelly chimed in languidly, "if you'd like to try something in an ex-Catholic loser."

"The problem would seem to be nondenominational."

Phelps smiled at Jonas Sams. "As you said, timeless—and universal."

Israel blew his cool. "If it's so goddamn universal, if it's so goddamn nondenominational—be my guest." He rose. "Make it that way. Don't cast an Irishman—write it Irish. Write it black, Hindu, Wasp, Mormon, but let my people go. We don't wanna see ourselves as bigots see us! And that's what you got now—a dirty little dropout who can't get the ante from her cheap kike papa—"

"Broke doesn't mean cheap!" Maude Lee was on her feet, furious. "Or a kike—"

"Whadda you know from kikes?—don't tell me!" Israel roared. "*I* know. *She* knows. Her father knows. And he'd tell her the same—cut the delicatessen!"

"Why?" said E. V. Adamic.

"To get an audience—like the big-timers! Gotta be crazy—selling yourself short. Did what's her name make *The Little Foxes* Jews? Did Arnold Miller make the Salesman a Jew?"

"Lillian Hellman," the shadow murmured, "*Arthur* Miller."

"Who?" said E. V. Adamic.

Israel didn't know either. "Be reasonable, if it isn't 'Gentleman's Agreement,' who needs the problem?" His literary references exhausted, Israel turned to Jonas Sams. "Am I right? You're the ethnic specialist."

"Thematically, nothing ethnic is at issue—it's a dialogue brush—"

"Balls," Maude Lee yelled. "Would you tell a black writer to whitewash dialogue?"

"Is this a sitcom—whadda ya want from Jones? Soul is for schwartzas on public television—"

"*Well, so's our writer—that's her audience too. This is a special!*"

"OK," Phelps said, "OK."

"Aah, you can't stop Maudley, it's got to be so special

nobody looks! Jesus, that's her whole trouble—if she were thinking film, pilot, series, you kids might wind up with more than a one-shot. Like maybe a series. The dislocated home. Where the other half lives. Life with Father the Chauvinist on visiting day. Life with Mother, the divorcee. Back and forth with the custody kids . . ."

"The split family Robinson."

"So laugh, Maudley. So it's never been done—"

"Except for thirteen weeks on public television." Maude Lee smiled savagely. "'Loud' and clear."

"And every talk show ever after," he agreed, unperturbed. "That's what started me looking for the right fictional property. The fictional Louds. Well, we got it." *We.* "There it is." He pointed.

And there indeed it was. On the table at last. Loud and clear. Israel wasn't trying to shaft the *Chauvinist,* he wanted to steal it. Dizzily Maude Lee looked at Phelps, who had so thoughtfully baited the trap they were all falling into. Daddy. Let him get her out of it.

His hands clasped behind his head, Father Phelps seemed to be musing.

"The fictional 'Louds' . . . Or 'The Urban Waltons' . . ."

"*Hey!*" Israel said. "Hey," said Charlie.

"Only instead of the young boy as writer/narrator—" Phelps mused on, "we'd have the girl—in keeping with the times . . ."

"Yeah, OK," Israel said, "so we'd keep the girl."

"OK, yeah," said Charlie.

Phelps laughed and unclasped his hands to scoop up the mimeo. "Israel, we're way ahead of you. That's exactly the way we're going. 'The Waltons' also started as a special, you'll remember."

But obviously even Israel's shadows had forgotten. "Fluke—" he began, glaring at them.

"Our director doesn't think so." The tide was turning as

Maude Lee came in on it with the name of the filmmaker that impressed everyone, even the film buff in the wing chair.

"If we can't get a woman," the writer said before Maude Lee could kick her.

"Who can't?" Israel moved in under the hatbrim to start naming the exceptions on Coast sitcoms and soaps. But luckily Phelps had spotted the phone winking on his hunting table, and moved away to get the call which ended the argument. It was Weldon's office announcing that the old man was on his way down to pick Israel up for their lunch date.

"Before noon?" Israel protested. "We made it for one!"

Phelps shrugged. "They said he'd sit in, if he was early."

Everyone had a big picture of that, so the meeting broke up, to go into a holding pattern for lunch, with nothing, as usual, supposedly decided.

"Just when we were going good, Maudley," Israel sighed, rising. "Like the old days."

Old days in the oval office maybe, last days in the bunker. Maude Lee had never been gladder to see Mr. Weldon dodder through the door, one full hour ahead of schedule but unable to wait another minute. Hands shaking, voice trembling, he slurred every word, and got every name letter perfect. Including "Mlle. Adamic," congratulated for her work. While "Mlle. Evans" was reminded of her teatime PR rendezvous upstairs. Stardom of course received appropriate salutes ("Dear Kelly, finally come to us . . ."). Even the shadows were politely assigned to each other for lunch, with the suggestion that Mr. Collins show Mr. Sams some spot that was really New York. But Mr. Weldon himself was in rapid transit to the nearest oasis in a desert, gasping on his exit, like a fish out of water. It was a class example of how to go down the drain by drops, what made the old man still competition, and kept Israel scrambling to follow, slowed down only by E. V.

Adamic tugging shyly at his sharkskin elbow, saying she would think it over, about the dialogue. And all.

"Yeah, yeah, you do that. Later, baby. Play it by ear."

And everyone saying yes, that was the way to play it, making no commitments, the whole school of fish went gliding out the way they came, but slower because of Old Man Weldon, doddering in the lead.

Phelps threw his bitten-through pacifier into the scrap basket.

"How about lunch, Ed? Want me to show you somewhere really New York, like a sewer?"

But Kelly was ready for the showers. Or anyway the Men's Room.

"Me too," said E. V. Adamic, heading for the door. "C'mon."

"Are we going together?" Kelly asked politely.

"Yours is first. We'll show you."

"I'll catch up, E.V.," Maude Lee said, keeping her eye on Phelps as she had from the moment she found out what Israel wanted. If there was one thing she had learned about television it was the danger of the chain reaction. A request for tea could change everything; today E. V. Adamic, tomorrow the world.

"*Writers!*" She closed the door and leaned against it. "How can anyone so talented be so dumb? I mean why not just throw her script out the window?"

"It's sealed." Phelps smiled, refusing to be ruffled. *That* mood.

"After all the vile stupidities he got off—"

"Who in particular?"

"*Israel.*"

"I wouldn't say that to the dumb and talented Ms. Adamic. It might stop her from opening up—"

"And ruining her dialogue? I want to stop her!"

He shook his head. "Don't be so sure. Kelly did those

speeches straight, not even trying for an accent—he's too good
an actor, reading cold. And the impact was fantastic—"

"Because they're great speeches—but done right they'd be
even greater. E.V. was working from a very specific model—"

"And when she looked at Gold she saw it again."

Those tears.

"Heard it, you mean." And even that was half faked for the
occasion. "Israel can talk straighter than Kelly—"

"*Exactly.*" Phelps leaned against the desk, hands clasped
behind his head. "Evans, what would Israel Gold do—*after*
he bailed his daughter out?"

She didn't have to think. "Nothing."

He nodded. "You've seen one dead father walking around,
you've seen them all. That's what the play's about. Not accents." She stared at him in wonder. It was stronger than her
suspicion of all the others. "Take your writer to lunch. Reassure her. But leave her alone with her instincts. Let her feel
whatever she feels for Israel. She wants to tell him something.
Let her trust him—"

"The way I do you?" It just came out, to be answered im-
personally. Though with tactful care.

"It's all a risk—developing your own talent, letting someone
else's grow. But that's what producing is. The rest just gets in
the way . . ." He gestured wearily toward the scene of the
meeting. "Wasting time, yessing and guessing." He turned and
started looking for another pacifier under the papers. "In this
case the risk is minimized—it's our project, not Israel's. We
can protect it. That's *also* what producing is."

And what she longed to hear. She found the pacifier, wanting to give him something. "Here. No wonder your writers
had a golden age."

"It didn't last long enough to be an age. And it wasn't gold,
just not pure dross." He clamped the pacifier between his
teeth and started to unbutton his army sweater. "Sometime

when there's time I'll get you up to the country and show you
some kinescopes to prove it."

"*When?* You always say that." But it never happened.

"I'm not in a hurry to disillusion you."

That wasn't the reason.

The only time she'd been to the Phelpses' place it had gone
wrong. Even in a group, with all the others, even Charlie
Collins, hiring a car to drive her and Bella, even Bella, somehow Maude Lee, the greenest and newest, freshly released
from Israel, and thrilled about it, too thrilled maybe, had let
herself be awed. All over Nannie's new career of a garden and
the Phelpses' old love of a house, all over their lovely rolling
hillside, trying to hit huge English croquet balls through narrow English wickets, trying to help in the kitchen, help Nannie, who needed no help anywhere, trying too hard, maybe
that's what did it. That and babbling about her own father's
early retirement and how it was tricky, a half-truth anyway,
and perhaps Nannie knew it, if Nannie cared. But Maude Lee
had a feeling even then, there wouldn't be any more Sunday
outings for the new people in Phelps' career. Maybe she'd
done it, maybe it was all of them. But it was over by the time
Maude Lee got in Charlie's lap to go home, Bella driving because Charlie was drunk now, like whoever fell asleep in the
back of the car. Whoever, whatever made little difference.
Nannie, smiling wryly with Phelps' arm around her, meant
goodbye when she said, "Take care . . ." Phelps never mentioned any of it of course, except casually like today, raising
hopes of a second chance by saying they'd have to do this or
that. But he always changed the subject.

This time the switch was oblique—*her* family. He didn't
remember her ever mentioning that *both* parents had been in
the business.

"I wasn't around at the time."

"Making up for it?"

"Working *here?*"

"Here and there."

"No, Doctor. I'm not E.V. But while we're into a Freudian number, that name you use is your idea. I don't see you as a father either. Especially in that . . ."

He had slipped on his jacket. It was new, dark blue, and trim when he buttoned it. He looked five years younger.

"Yeah? Like it?"

She really smiled.

"OK, Evans. Go turn your charm on your friend, the director. It's wasted on me."

"No, it's not."

But anyway Kelly came back.

Meanwhile back in the Ladies' Room, E. V. Adamic was turning on. Maude Lee got the message at the door. It wafted unmistakably from the next to last cubicle, where the boots were plainly visible. Worse in the first, Maude Lee saw the nearest things to sling-back pumps you could wear and still be in the same century. The Beast. Maude Lee passed through a blast of Bella's Shalimar on her way to the source of pot.

She scratched on the door. "It's me."

"It's open."

Wedging in, she found E.V. standing in the corner, smoke coming out from under her hat.

"Have you *flipped*—?"

"Who hasn't around here?—*hey*—"

The joint snatched from the tiny hand disappeared into a swirl of water as Maude Lee kicked the handle to flush the toilet.

"You could at least save me the roach—"

"Shut *up*," Maude Lee hissed, gesturing wildly toward the sound of the other toilet flushing. "Come on—" She held the door open, urging the smaller girl out ahead of her.

"I didn't even bring an upper—"

"Good girl—"

"*Woman!*"

"Good woman then. *Move.*"

"Bet you're holding . . ."

"Not here."

"Even a *diet* pill?"

Maude Lee was in fact in possession of a large and sinister capsule, a peace offering from the vile Jean Paul, stashed even now in her tote bag in case it came in handy as a bribe. But not until the last gasp, she decided. Fortunately. Or they'd have been caught in the middle of a pill pass by Bella the Beast, sashaying forth from the toilet, pulling down her girdle. Bella still wore one for all occasions, plus an uplift form-fit under her classic wraparound silk jersey, hemmed at the knee-cap this year. Neither flood nor blizzard could bring Bella to the office in slacks, and only the total disappearance of Hat Departments finally forced her to the scene bareheaded. She smiled frostily.

"Hi there, girls."

E.V. ground her teeth.

"Bella, you know E. V. Adamic—who's writing our first special—?"

"Surely. We met the night it opened Off-Broadway." A veiled hint that Bella knew the special was a rerun. And indeed no loft or happening was too obscure for her frosty notice, as the favored date of the agents and executives who fought to escort power. A powerhouse, in Bella's case—she was no fag hag. A cold lady maybe, married to her desk and zoftig, but nonetheless—sexy. In her draggy way. "How are you, Evelyn?"

"OK. It was Off-Off-Broadway."

"Well, it's Right On now!" Bella liked to use such expressions once she got the hang of it. "Going to clean it up for us,

Evelyn?" Bella sauntered toward the basins to wash her hands.

"Well, of course E.V. had to cut . . ." Maude Lee followed to emulate going through the motions. Anyhow her hair needed brushing. She saw E.V. glaring into the mirror from behind them. "But the cuts are mostly for length."

"Name of the game," said Bella, reaching for a paper towel to pat her hands dry delicately. "What's the shade of your new rinse, sweetie?"

"Honeysun."

"I like it. Lighter." Bella unzipped the flowered makeup kit she had extracted from her black bag—patent leather to match the sling-back pumps. She started to set out the ingredients for full slap: lipstick (red, of course)—base cum powder, teasing comb for the old bouffant, and last but not least her handy purse-sized Shalimar blaster. Wrinkling her nose, she gave herself a shot. "Something smell funny in here to you?"

"Yeah," said E.V., moving away toward the door.

Maude Lee plopped her brush in the tote bag. "Listen, Bella, before I forget—we took a vote about asking you to join us in Consciousness Raising—"

"*Where?*" Bella paused in mid-tease.

"My office after five. Monday. E.V.'s coming too—"

"I've got a screening Monday."

"Consciousness Raising is *every* Monday, Bella."

"Oh." Bella smiled into the mirror. "Well, I guess I'll take a rain check, sweetie."

"I'm not coming if she does," E.V. muttered to Maude Lee at the door, which opened as Sally rushed in practically colliding with them.

"Oh, wow—" she said when she saw Maude Lee. "I just put that cute director through to you in Mr. Phelps' office—"

"*Sally!* I told you *not* to—"

"Well, but I knew the meeting was over—Charlie Collins came by to ask me to lunch." Sally giggled. "With his new best friend, Sam Spade." Then she stopped, head turning, nose a quiver. "*Hey!*" Sally said. "Who's been turning *on,* in here?"

"That's a good question, sweetie." Bella snapped the patent bag shut, coming toward them. "I was just about to phone and ask Security."

Maude Lee shoved E.V. out the door, down the hall, and into the elevator.

"You think maybe it's because of Jewish, not Jewish? I mean you hanging in with the great white father, and me relating better to Mr. Gold?"

"Oh God. It's too hot to think." Think fast anyway. Sixth Avenue had steamed itself out and started frying as they trudged north toward Fifty-seventh, and E.V.'s favorite health bar.

"Well, it could be."

"What?"

"Jewish, not Jewish—"

"Oh, E.V., it could be a lot of things. Like I've got a better job going with Phelps than I did with Israel. Plus you hardly know either of them."

"Maybe it doesn't matter anyhow."

"No."

"I mean about the dialogue either. Whether it's Jewish, not Jewish. Like they were saying . . ."

Maude Lee did not answer.

"What do you think?"

"The point is what you think, E.V.—"

E.V. stomped to a stop.

"Oh *boy*—what's *with* you all of a sudden? You're coming

on like my ex-shrink." She mimicked the professional tones: "Why do I think I'm about to cut my throat?"

"Are you?"

"We'll get to *Acting Out* in our *next* session. With a Ouija board. Meantime don't rule out our penis envy."

Maude Lee sighed. "We're the only ones who can. Look at the men in that meeting."

"Ah, whadda they got to envy?"

"Each other. And the way their wives can fake in the sack. They sure can't."

"The hell with 'em. I've got my own worries. Anyhow you're the only one I really listen to, I mean there's gotta be *some-body!*"

Fortunately their arrival at the health bar created a mini-diversion. "It's too crowded," Maude Lee said. "And I have to go to the john."

"Why didn't you go to the john *before?*"

"To keep you from getting busted for a big fat change." In fact Maude Lee had been too busy since arriving at the office; and even E.V. couldn't argue with the call of a diuretic. Instead, turning north on Seventh, they started arguing desultorily about the dubious merits of public facilities in hotels cruised by hookers; day and night, according to E.V.

"As opposed to some of the wonderful pads you've crashed in. Do you have any idea of the VD statistics in communes?"

"Neither do you, I bet. So, don't bother making 'em up. Anyhow everything's different now. I've got my own place, I told you."

What E.V. meant, translated, was that she had someone else's place to herself—a photographer's studio, this summer. Whether dog- or cat-sitting, E.V. wasn't into paying rent, and so remained essentially homeless. With scars on both wrists to prove it.

Finally at Fifty-ninth they both agreed on the Coliseum,

which was one, clean; and two, cool enough so they could at least *think* about lunch, or maybe even have it free, if the Packaging Show, advertised on the marquee, involved any kicky food samples. They were avoiding death in a safety zone in the middle of Columbus Circle, when E.V. spotted a picket line and said she couldn't cross it.

"Well, I can. They're not picketing the john, for God's sake."

On closer inspection the alleged line turned out to be a boy/girl pair of health bar rejects, who paused, leaning on their signs, to identify themselves as environmentalists, protesting all packaging on principle. So E.V. tagged along on Maude Lee's PR pass. They got as far as the first exhibit, something called a shrink tunnel, where a panting demonstrator was jumping up and down on a package to show that polyethylene poured over cardboard compressed to size made it virtually indestructible, obviously advantageous when shipping.

"Why?" piped E.V. from behind three lunch hour onlookers. "What happens when you want to ship it into the garbage?"

Maude Lee went to the Ladies' Room. When she got back the shrink tunnel had closed. And E.V. was outside walking the picket line.

"Where'd you get that *sign!*"

"The girl who was here had to go to dance class. She said she painted it herself . . ."

In bold letters, which read: "TODAY'S PACKAGE IS TO-MORROW'S TRASH." It killed Maude Lee.

"I've got to take it back to the office!"

Even E.V. laughed. "It'll sure kill *them.*"

"That's why."

But the boy, passing with a terser message ("SAVE OUR EARTH"), said these signs were no joke, man. Falling in step, it took Maude Lee several turns up and down to convince him that TV packaging was also a serious threat to the environment, which might better be honored by letting the network spring for a picnic lunch break under a tree in the park. In the end, he melted under her smile; his slender body was already melting through his shirt from the sun. It all reminded her a little of meeting Ned at some protest rally for Ellsberg's defense—if Ned had been bearded and aimless.

"And boring." E.V. glowered after the boy, as they followed him through a shortcut in the park. Though, in truth E.V. didn't like Ned much better, preferring at all times to occupy center stage even in memory, such as when Maude Lee rescued *her* the first time in the middle of a bust at Madison Square Garden during Star Spangled Women for McGovern.

"So stoned out of your mind you don't remember it yourself," Maude Lee teased, as she saw the writer start to drag her feet, feeling displaced and disconsolate. But E.V. dug in her heels for real when the boy led them to a hot dog stand, doing her whole Nader number, on the verge of fouling up everything by splitting for home, which, translated, probably meant into a pill bottle. So Maude Lee came up with the vile Jean Paul's vile capsule, and the boy went for beer to wash it down, and E.V. herself, relaxing, retrieved a final joint from under her hatband, and after a few drags down to her boots even passed it around. And ate a hot dog.

Maude Lee got the sign.

By the time it went waving out of the park, the boy was all for helping them picket the network, even following for a few blocks until they lost him. Which led to another argument about coming on with people to get what you wanted.

"Oh, what's so terrible if it just happens—?"

"Happens to you, maybe. I'm not a sex object," E.V. said, somewhat unnecessarily.

"All objects are sexual if you ask me—"

"People aren't *objects*—"

"OK, then people. But I've seen you come on, little girl."

"When I mean it—"

"When you're high. I use my own body chemistry."

But the chemistry E.V. was using made her feel too dopey even to argue. Anyhow they had reached the network. "If you paid street price for that upper, you got stuck." She yawned as she spoke.

"Who said it was an upper?"

The yawn went awry. "You're kidding! You wouldn't be such a bitch . . ."

Maude Lee giggled.

E.V. looked up at the giant sun reflector of a building and panicked. "How'm I going to get through meeting a director on a *downer*—?"

"You're not—till I find out if he's worth meeting. Go home and sleep it off." *Home* again. E.V. hesitated.

"Yeah, but what about the rewrite—do you want me to try it, or what?"

They faced each other. Maude Lee reached out impulsively, catching the writer by a tiny wrist.

"Oh, Adam 'n' Eve, just be true to your talent. Swear by your father, the failure—"

"Why'd you say *that*?"

"It's all I want—"

"No, I mean—what you used to call me."

"Not a bad name for a writer—being both—"

"Copout—I wasn't a writer then!"

"You didn't know what you were, baby." With scars to prove it. Maude Lee dropped the wrist to straighten the brave hatbrim. Leaning down, she kissed the soft cheek. "Be a good person . . ."

A twist of a smile came and went. "You must want that new dialogue a lot!"

There was nothing to do but turn away, trusting to luck— and Phelps. *That's what producing was,* he said. But he hadn't touched that scar.

"And fast, I bet—like tomorrow?" The tiny voice piped after Maude Lee as she went inside.

Was this how it felt to let go of a child? It killed her. All the way across the lobby. All the way up in the elevator. It would be easier, surely, not to give birth in the first place. But that's what producing wasn't. For Adam *or* Eve. Or both in one. *SIGH*, to quote the great Charlie Brown, master of interior monologue. Just plain *SIGH*.

The charcoal gray reception area was deserted, except for the relief receptionist reading the latest *Rolling Stone*. Even Charlie Collins wasn't back, which meant that Sally wouldn't be either. But at the turn of the block-long pepper and salt carpeting, Maude Lee took a fast peek into the corner suite and found Cinny, at her desk, diet cottage cheese already consumed, but still sipping black coffee while she improved what was left of the shining lunch hour by tatting serenely on her shining husband's new petit-point vest. He was a schoolteacher, from another world, like Ned, and they all sometimes fled office parties together, like two pairs of soul mates. It made for a bond.

"Hey, come in—I've got some good news." Unlike Sally, Cinny wrote hers down. "Mr. Bernard got in contact about the project, and Mr. Phelps wanted to be sure you heard it was *affirmative*." She pointed to the word she had underlined. "*Also*," she dropped her voice to dishing level, like any true soul sister. "*Also*—I left it *right there* like that, when Mr. Gold came through just now. So he'd get the message." They both giggled.

"Did he?"

"Well, you know Mr. Gold . . . There was time."

"Yeah. I bet. While you were fighting him off . . ."

"Mostly I told him how worried I am that I'm having a baby—"

"*Cinny—!*"

"Don't worry—I'm always worried." Cinny smiled. "Who could afford a baby? Anyhow he's inside, Mr. Gold, I mean."

Maude Lee had a spasm of longing to confide in Cinny, except that it meant asking Cinny not to confide in Sally, with implications that were complex. So, suppressing the impulse, she went straight in to Phelps' office, which was probably just as well anyhow, because she caught Israel leafing through the mimeo while he murmured into Phelps' phone. She waved her sign, to gratifying effect. He practically cracked his shark caps against the receiver getting rid of whoever it was.

"*What the fuck is that—?*"

"Today's Package Is Tomorrow's Trash—"

"I can read for Chrissake—"

No trusting to luck on that. "A funny thing happened on the way to the Coliseum—I got on a picket line—"

"Are you crazy—bringing that back here? Weldon could have been with me. You want to give the old man a terminal attack?"

"Not much. But if you do I'll trade it for that script." She leaned the sign against the hunting table.

He weighed the mimeo, and then leered. "You got better things to trade."

"Not with you." She smiled.

"Depends what's happening in your pad tonight."

"Nothing you can watch."

"Might have a problem watching Phelps—"

"*Israel!* Tell those problems to Charlie? He must be doing something right."

He laughed. "C'mon—admit you miss me, Maudley."

"Only when you're here," she sighed.

It pleased him enough to try a small proposition. "Tell you what . . . supposing we work a side deal. I take what I want out of this shit and run like a thief. You make it your way. I make it mine. And nobody's wise your flop is my hit."

She groaned. "Why the hell didn't you?"

"What would you give me?"

"Nothing now, dummy! It's too late."

"Ah, who'd care? Enough to blow the whistle."

"Phelps—among other people."

"Fucking parson." Israel threw the mimeo on the hunting table. "And for what? So old Father Phelps gets it up one more time—he's still a wipeout." He shook his head. "You of all people, throwing in with a loser. And *losing* to him—like his wife."

"Israel, there's nothing to lose if you're on the same side—"

"Wait till he crosses you."

"How? By lining up the director I chose while I talk a rewrite Phelps agrees on?" A light flashed behind the sea green eyes. Israel had read a lot into Cinny's memo. "We're working together—not behind each other's back. Because we both happen to want to do something better than mucho macho crap. Someone's got to, Israel. Can't you ever understand that's what it's all about—?"

"Yeah, yeah, sure, sure. Today's Garbage Is Tomorrow's Smash." He picked up the sign to twirl idly so that Charlie, walking in, mistook it for Israel's joke and *fell down*, laughing so much it *put him away*, collapsing against Jonas Sams. Who smiled.

Cinny interrupted the hilarity to find out whether anyone planned to cover the next appointment, which Phelps had forgotten, or not bothered to cancel. Somewhat to Charlie's chagrin since he had set it up. The arrivals were a well-known writing team of his acquaintance, a terrific couple in His 'n' Hers outfits, their credits suitably swiched to Hers 'n' His this year. To go with their latest, up-to-the-minute idea about a team of switch-hitting Ms. and Mr. double agents, who could exchange roles in various exhilarating ways that might confuse the enemy for a sitcom half hour. Or stretch to ninety minutes for a dramatic series pilot, if played straight. It could go any way you wanted, like the terrific writers.

"I gotta go to the can," Israel said, surrendering Maude Lee's sign. "Here's your murder weapon." And in a way it was —the coup de grâce, on top of the news about Billy Bee Bernard. All that was needed to make Israel feel ridiculous. She could tell from the way he glided unseeingly past Charlie, signaling Jonas Sams to follow.

"Goodbye, Mr. Sams," she said.

"See you later, Ms. Evans."

But they wouldn't. The shark had done circling, the mimeo bait left behind on the hook. She had won, or gained time, but was anyway rid of Israel Gold for a while. And as soon as he left, she was glad.

She forced her attention back to Him 'n' Her. "Look," she said, "instead of updating the 'Avengers' how about a *really* odd couple . . . ?" All eyes were riveted on her; her own eyes glazed over with boredom, but she flogged grimly on. Because the idea of a couple per se wasn't half bad, she had to admit —half a loaf being better than none. God knew it would be easier to get on than an hour series about a woman alone. The kind of woman Maude Lee had in mind anyway. "Why not something *new?* Why not a husband and wife team who really exist—in life—like you two do . . . ?" Eyes remained blank all around. "Like doctors—?"

"*NEW!*" Charlie howled. "Another *medical* show—"

"Name one that's got a woman MD as a running lead!" Maude Lee snapped. But she was watching the writers look at each other.

"Wait a minute . . . *wait a minute* . . ."

"Marcus *and Mary* Welby . . ."

"Sharing the same office . . . she's a pediatrician—"

"No, he's a pediatrician—she's a surgeon . . ."

"On the same staff at the medical center!"

The writers were pros. It had never been done.

Getting back to her own office was a real down. Ned hadn't weakened and called, of course—what he lacked in cool he made up for in pride. But Sally broke the news as if it were an obituary, and then followed it up by gushing over her lunch-time discovery of Charlie Collins' hidden depths. Or shallows, more accurately, since Charlie had confessed to feeling inadequate about not having a college degree like Israel's other shadows. As if anyone in the whole dumb industry *needed* a degree, but women and blacks.

"Where was Jonas Sams, BA?"

"Mostly on the phone." Thickening Israel's plot, no doubt, but it gave Sally this beautiful chance to know the real Charlie—in the middle of the jam-packed bar at Joe Allen's.

"*There's* somewhere really New York to take Sams." Maude Lee remembered Mr. Weldon's suggestion. "Except they've got one in Beverly Hills."

"Yeah, Sams said." Sally's avalanche of compassionate attention was selective. "Poor Charlie—"

"Poor *Charlie!*"

"A person's so different when you're alone with him!" She breathed new mystery into an old story. "Wow . . ."

"Wait till poor Charlie really gets you alone."

"As soon as Mr. Gold leaves town . . . we've got a date." Sally smiled dreamily.

"Did you mention living home in Forest Hills?"

"A girl can stay over."

"Not with Mr. Inadequate. Nobody's even seen his pad!" It was said instead that Charlie possessed a giant key ring, with a memento from every score, to choose from nightly. An ugly rumor, Sally had decided.

"And guess who started it."

"I don't believe it!" Sally was already mentally buying ash-trays and cheese slicers for the pad perfect. Obviously there was no talking her out of it. The great experience was going to happen *somewhere*—probably in Bloomingdale's furniture department.

"OK—I'll bet you one entire lunch at Joe Allen's." Maude Lee's hot dog was wearing off.

"Nope." Sally shook her dizzy head emphatically. "Bet you a coloring job at that place you go!"

Maude Lee stared at the bouncing brown curls. "*Why?*"

"Oh, you know . . . everybody's always talking about your *hair* . . ."

Everybody.

Ned. Who loved it more the blonder she got without ever really questioning the change. Though he was probably at this moment casing all the volunteers at the foundation, as a prelude to marrying a brunette on the rebound. Good luck to him.

"He'll call," Sally said soothingly, "he always does."

"Not unless I call first. Or at least leave a message."

"Well . . . ?"

They decided that Sally should do it—*sounding* official being one of her best things. They looked up the foundation—neither of them had *that* number, and Maude Lee coached while Sally persevered, leaving the extension of the network *Specials Consultant* (not a girl's name) for *Mr.* Nedders (not Professor) at the switchboard and the boardroom office, before they both broke up laughing. And became aware of Phelps in the doorway, leaning on Maude Lee's sign. Sally almost knocked it out of his hands in her haste to get past but he didn't seem to notice.

"Greetings." He looked strange. There was no telling how long he'd been there. "Thanks for your message."

"It was to put Israel on. I just wanted you to see."

"I saw. I thought it was for me. It's the thought that

counts." He leaned the sign against the wall and promptly kicked it over. He didn't seem to notice that either. She saw why when he lurched into her visitor's chair, heedless of swivel.

"Who got you loaded without me?" She was almost indignant. This was something she had wanted to see.

"Our friend who doesn't drink, period, but I got *him* loaded, as it happens."

"*Kelly?*" Surely not Kelly. Phelps wouldn't.

"Kelly watched. He is *on* the *program.* That's AA for on the wagon. Which shall be Anonymous." A loaded lion was an indiscreet one, not that she hadn't half guessed about Kelly, knowing the signs. Phelps was about the only man in his age group who wasn't in *some* stage of a drinking problem that Maude Lee had ever heard of. Her mind flashed to her own generation.

"It wasn't Billy Bee Bernard—!" But of course, it had to be. She could just imagine Billy with his hair tied back, all his leather thongs going, maybe even using one for a tie to get into "21" with Phelps.

"At Mr. Weldon's favorite pub, right?"

"Where else?" Phelps relished her reaction almost as much as he had Israel's. "Gold sure hated going out past our table."

But where Weldon doddered, Israel must follow, his only solace that Maude Lee had been excluded also, until she put him straight. It was worth missing it all just to know that. She laughed aloud. "You really swallowed a canary!"

He looked as satisfied as one of the stone lions in front of the public library. Until the smile faded. It seemed the canary had done too much singing while celebrating what Phelps called his unholy alliance with minors. "That bird's more of a baby than you are!"

"Just smaller," she said, not about to bring back satisfaction by revealing the age she always made a joke of withholding. "Small enough for me to handle. Don't worry."

"He's hot to handle you."

It was like something Israel would say. But the tone was rougher coming from Phelps, making her wonder if he was jealous. It seemed a good time to keep a low profile. She shrugged. "Billy never looked twice when I was Israel's reader," she lied. He had always looked, even as a UCLA film student. But now apparently he was leaping. "After all it's a chance to get into a new field at the top." In superstar company. "You, Kelly, even an interesting new writer."

"Who won't have to rewrite incidentally. Mr. Bernard doesn't feel there's any dialogue problem actors can't solve by making up better lines."

"Not with this script! And I *told* Billy that." Double-crossing, leather-thonged midget. It confirmed her first resolve to double-cross *him*. "All we need is a bunch of Billy's mumblers saying what they'd do if they were the person . . ." The new film form. Brando's Tango minus Brando. And half the editing. "Try and do it on tape in eighteen days! That's where you come in, Father—to the rescue."

"Shoving aside the man of the future?" His voice was sardonic. "They're pretty high on your filmmaker upstairs."

"Then let's lose him right now—say it was my dumb mistake."

"Not if your dumb mistake gets us an August shooting date."

"*Really?*" Excited, she saw him rise to stand over her. "Yes, but the script . . ."

"It'll all get handled . . . just stay cool . . ." He hesitated, as if that weren't enough. "And dream on, kid. You're doing OK—between hair appointments." And then unbelievably, on top of getting the best and most confusing grade ever, she felt his hand on her hair. Not a pat on the head, fatherly or casual like an arm around the shoulders. Phelps did not touch her casually. Ever. But almost before it had happened, it was over.

"Gotta go upstairs and keep Weldon impressed." He was moving away around the desk. "Want me to take over your PR number?"

"You're kidding!" She was supposed to cover for Phelps, not vice versa. "You ought to celebrate at lunch more often!"

"Shouldn't we all, question mark?" He was looking down at her calendar, as he said it, the closest he had ever come to making up for anything done in a temper. She was really touched.

"You're sure you won't mind if it runs late?" Unlike Weldon, Phelps *did* have a commuting problem, not being a driver.

"Probably miss my train anyway, outlasting Israel."

"What happens if you miss them all?" She smiled flirtatiously. It was easier to imagine Nannie driving in to fetch him than Phelps staying over on the town, but he'd started it.

"Fortunately," he smiled back, "you've got something better to do than find out. Exclamation point." Turning, he almost tripped on her sign again. "And take that home before it gets us fired. I only want your good ideas."

He was almost out the door, but she couldn't resist. "Are you going to tell your wife how good I was today?"

It was going too far of course, but he didn't have to answer, didn't have to stand there, looking quizzical volumes, all unreadable.

"I never tell anybody how good or bad I think you are."

She was so up after that she cleaned off her entire desk, feeling too up when she left to harangue Sally for real about covering the phones until Ned's call, knowing Sally wouldn't stay otherwise, but knowing also Ned would call home now, and come home sooner or later. A thought of such upness Maude Lee didn't even flash her sign at Bella, as usual clocking exits on the diamond watch imbedded in her pudgy wrist, frosty eyes looking sharp over the mound of paperwork on her desk—stacked but neat, like the Beast herself.

"Well, you're keeping bankers' hours!" As the day began so it would end. "You and your boys . . ."

"The boys in my band."

"In The Bar, you mean. Joining them downstairs?" Equivalent to upstairs after four, and never Maude Lee's scene, but one where Bella took few rain checks.

"Aren't you?"

"Not if I have to crash a creative meeting."

"What's so creative about meeting for a drink?"

"Phelps is buying."

Again? Then Maude Lee remembered. "Oh, that . . ." Obviously Weldon had adjourned the PR number to The Bar exactly as she'd feared when she warned Ned. "It's just a TV Key interview I got out of—thank God. It'll go on forever."

"*Time* magazine, Charlie said."

"Charlie?"

"When he left with Jonas Sams. Something about a piece *Time*'s doing. On some new director?"

Maude Lee was blank. "Not the same. Must be a West Coast number."

"Better make sure—they've only been gone half an hour."

"Bella, what am I going to miss I can't read in the papers?"

"You might miss your own picture in a story, sweetie." Bella smiled. "Why lose a morning having your hair dyed for nothing?"

Maude Lee smiled back. "I didn't, sweetie. I never lose anything for nothing."

But the smile died as soon as she moved from the Beast's sight.

Trust Bella. Always ready with a needle to spring another slow leak in euphoria. Maude Lee felt her whole body rebel indignantly under the pink shift, nipples rising against the material, protesting neglect; long legs longing to stretch, fire flaring between them, sandaled feet arching to make tracks. To shake off the dry-as-dust lust for everything but life that filled this place. Physically at least, she had *had* it. Had the daylong game of shaft and flirt in the glass jungle. Had the paper chase of fictional climaxes, unsatisfying and unsensual, draining her gray at the vital center where anything could happen if she opened up, if she let her energy rip, hit the target, let it all hang loose like her Honeysun hair, flying her true colors for color's sake. And the hell with waiting for the camera! The hell with smiling on cue, programmed for programming like Weldon, making nice with receptionists, letting a secretary fix up your sex life, every instinct becoming so mechanical you had to dial-a-release like Israel, or shiver along like Phelps in an army sweater, hung up on dry dreams fit for Charlie Collins—becoming a frosted-malt, Barbie-Doll lay, bitter as Bella Sweet, the organization girl.

And as paranoid as E. V. Adamic, half a minute later. Maude Lee was ringing for the elevator when the warning bell finally rang in her head. About that reporter she had met in P.J.'s last night, doing an in-depth piece on Billy Bee Bernard. For the Sunday *Times* magazine, she had thought. *Time* magazine, Bella said. But either way it came out the same new director: Maude Lee's friend, the filmmaker, feted by both press and network. *Her* network, meeting in public to announce her show. Without her.

The whole mellow end of the day fragmented into a berserk jigsaw puzzle, all the ugly pieces scrambling for a place. No way it didn't make distorted sense—all that unlikely sweet concern turning predictably sour. Phelps covering for her upstairs—so he could head her off. Bella warning her—but that was the piece that didn't fit anywhere. Bella . . . Why in the name of unholy plots would the Beast tip off Maude Lee Evans, of all people?

A wry inner voice answered, as the elevator door opened: Why not?

What better way would there be to defuse the blond bombshell of the twenty-first floor than to send her on a fool's errand, crashing a stag party where she *really* wasn't wanted? Who would know better than Bella, keeper of her place, beloved among the boys who made Vice President and thought that loving meant saying they were sorry every time she was passed over? There was even a perverse, glass-jungle logic to make the beast throw a maverick of her kind to the wolves, thus preserving the unnatural imbalance.

Maude Lee fought the thought, suffocated by it in the airless cabin, stopping and starting, as more business suits crowded in, forcing her to hide her sign between her legs. She was afraid she'd melt before she got to the lobby, even afterward, leaning against the stone wall by the starter's station, trying not to gasp for air, afraid she'd make herself ridiculous. Though the blood rushing to her flaming face told her this had already happened.

It was a trap, go or stay.

"How many of them are in there?"

It was her father's voice in memory, once again asking that odd question. An echo from the time when he happened to call her out of a meeting just as Israel seemed about to fire her. She remembered the dead pause on the telephone when she blurted her unmentionable suspicion—you never admitted being fired in Hollywood, even *after* the fact—but there was no polite objection from her father about jumping the gun, only that pause. And then the familiar tone changed, became hard, long distance.

"How many of them are in there, Mud?"

One then, easily routed. But part of a lynch party now.

How many was no longer the mystery, but why. And the way to find out was as simple as taking her rightful place among them, if it still existed, *before* starting the third world war over a possible misunderstanding. The idea calmed her down. That and the hot air outside, which was somehow comforting, for not being machine filtered and artificially cooled.

The Bar Downstairs was on the ground floor of a whole other network, part of a restaurant that ran the width of the building, completely accessible from two directions through plate glass windows. Maude Lee's route home usually led her more directly to Fifth Avenue, but all she had to do was detour through the side street that passed The Bar and take a good look inside. As lots of people did when interested in network off-hour capers. So Phelps called it "The Dangerous Corner." That thought cheered her as she turned it. Of course, he wouldn't let himself be cornered and caught out here, unless unwittingly compromised in some way that could be explained. She approached discreetly, ready to play it their usual way, cool and by ear, until she got the picture.

It was right there—at two pushed-together window tables. The Last Supper. If you could have it in a saloon, sans savior. Judas was everywhere.

So were the paparazzi, clicking away alongside the note-takers—including Billy's from *Time* or the *Times,* plus her own interviewer from *TV Key* and an entertainment editor and a columnist, all gathered together by the new head of PR. It was a flak dress parade for a true media happening. And a super ripoff frozen and framed, in a series of jump cuts flashing on Maude Lee's brain.

Kelly staring down into his coffee . . . seeing the system's gates close again. Weldon drinking, what else? Charlie Collins and Jonas Sams eagerly fetching their own beers from the bar . . . While a waiter bowing over the table served Israel his special, almost-Virgin-Mary. And then a two shot—the

Cover Boy Director, focus of all lenses, his own eyes only for his new guru and true predecessor, TV's Master Pioneer in person, leaning back to leave room at the top, hands clasped behind his leonine head—good old boy, Austin Phelps, the Godfather of them all.

The frozen scenes had a brief commercial message: The Year of the Woman was being bumped by a news item for all seasons—the day of the Rising Son. As tape would no doubt give way to film, words to mumbles, special to packaged pilot to series, *Chauvinist* to Loud-Waltons. While the absent E. V. Adamic cried all the way to the bank and the cameras rolled. Right over Maude Lee Evans.

The girl who had everything and learned to smile for more, until she got so much she didn't know what she wanted, lost it all. Lost the breath right out of her, standing there frozen, like the pictures in her mind. Became Leesy again in the long winter of adolescence, exiled to school because her step-ma was rich and her pa just good-looking, and home never existed anywhere, and never would, though wired for sound, and mirrored for love.

And as if to reflect that point, Phelps' ice blue eyes looked up—straight into hers—and looked away.

But that was going too far. Because farther back than Leesy there was only a child, with Daddy in mourning and the other mirror empty, Mud shut out, nose pressed to the window, wild with pain.

One instinct prevailed again—she raised her hand to strike back, palm flat against the barrier, with all her force. Only to rediscover it was inadequate, and physically painful, now as then. But this time she was armed. She thought of her sign.

Wood shattered against glass which was shatterproof, averting tragedy. But no one could pretend not to see her now. It was quite terrific. She held up what was left of her splintered message with a big smile for the paparazzi. While Weldon

choked and Israel pounded, and Billy Bee laughing in-
nocently, bounded to his feet beckoning her eagerly inside—
the only one who did. Though Kelly raised his coffee cup in a
joyless toast, and Jonas Sams made a sneaky V from behind
old dumb-struck Charlie, and Phelps never moved, the only
one who didn't. Except at the end when he reached out to
stop the waiter from coming out to get her arrested doubtless.
So she blew a Judas kiss and thumbed her nose and held that
pose for a finish, yelling, "Tell 'em who I am" to the VP of PR
before she split. Though he didn't hear her—nobody could
hear anybody. Who cared?—one picture was worth a thousand words and God knows she had waited for the cameras.
Let the little brass gods fire at will—they'd never get her cut
from their story now.

Her least favorite doorman was standing out under the canopy when she came around the corner hugging three bags of
groceries. All from the supermarket as per her vow to Ned,
casually sworn on her brilliant future. About as ill-timed as
her arrival on the after-work check-out line. She'd hate to
make *that* scene every day—or any scene, when she came
right down to it, remembering the good old Book of Changes
(she'd have to throw a hexagram when she got home). In the
meantime she had plunked a *TV Guide* into her cart at the
last moment. Nothing like hanging in with the trade papers
while on unemployment—there were just as many jobs left in
the jungle as ever came out of it. No way *her* world was coming to an end! Not so long as that sesame smile could open
new gates. Wherever she landed—with a bounce.

"Lemme take something, Miss Evans," the doorman said,
finally managing to see her as she hit the lobby, masterfully
grabbing for the wrong bag, of course. An unhelpful gesture
anyhow—she'd only have to grab it all back if she made the

waiting elevator before two other tenants coming from mail-boxes beat her out of it.

"Never mind, Walter," she tried to keep going, "I'm not coping with mail till I walk the puppy—"

"But you need your keys now!" He fished the envelope out of his pocket, with a sly smile to show he was onto her stratagem with Benjie. Which meant the super was too, Walter being a fink. She didn't have time to worry about it.

"Just throw 'em in the top bag, OK? So I can make that . . ."

"Hold the car, please," Walter called importantly. So naturally whoever it was took off. The other car was in the basement. "Won't take a minute." Walter rang for it, obviously bursting with his usual juicy social notes. "You probably haven't heard—about your new neighbor who's going to be movin' in."

"On my floor?" It didn't seem likely. Even the airline stewardesses were full up.

"Right next door," he beamed. "Come next week . . . You'll have a lovely seven-pound neighbor, mother and daughter doing fine."

Amy. Maude Lee had forgotten. Almost. "When did she have it, Walter?"

"This afternoon—Mr. Foreman said. He just came in from the hospital."

Since last night. "That's a long time. Must have been rough." For Bob too.

Walter nodded gravely, opening the door. "They're all rough, Miss Evans. But it's worth it after." He held up three fingers. "Thrice blessed. All worth it."

"Did you have any of them yourself?" She managed to press 14 before he could stall with his finger on it.

He smirked again. "The wife told me. You'll see . . . you'll be the next one to the altar."

"That's a hell of a place to have a baby!" The door removed his smirk from view rather satisfyingly.

But it occurred to her that confusing altars and cradles was precisely what was screwing things up with Ned, making it impossible to decide on sharing so much as an apartment. Pregnant or not, Maude Lee faced it, she just wasn't ready to be a mother, or maybe even a wife. But if she could commit herself to a job without becoming a brass monster—maybe some other kind, but not brass—it did begin to seem possible that she could make a personal commitment without losing the rest of her identity. So she won more bread than Ned—tough macho shit. He could at least count on a shower and a shave and love while it lasted. Obviously *some* new mini-horizon was in order, or today was the scene that could be forever.

It felt like home again when she got off on the 13th floor. Particularly after she went three steps and heard her phone start, along with the puppy. She dumped the groceries right where she was, tearing the keys from the envelope as she ran, praying she'd make it before the third ring in case it was Ned. Praying it would be, just plain had to be, please, God—Ned—not some vile fink-pimp from the office phoning in a pink slip. Or worse, far worse, Phelps, saying he was sorry.

She left the keys in the door, stumbling in past the puppy, trusting to luck—one more time.

Reaction Shot

He hung up fast. Two and a half rings were his outside limit
from a phone booth. Wouldn't she have the only answering
service in town that always answered? On her crazy see-
through home phone where nobody needed it while the
world's lousiest secretary screwed up the works in her big deal
office. He'd already wasted one dime on some dumb damn
receptionist, unable to say *when* Ms. Evans left for the day—
So solly. Well, up their Ms., and the revolution Ms. Special-
consultant rode in on—with her fancy urgent messages plas-
tered all over his foundation. A big surprise reward for his
two-week-and-three-hour achievement. Like she had a *clue*
what he'd been trying to achieve for any part of the last two
years! Except that *his calling was gravely important,* because
she liked the way it sounded when she read it off the wall of
the speech department, a plaque to the memory of some
founding father Ned of course had long since forgotten, didn't
even see anymore, when he passed by every day. Well, forget
it again—up *everybody's* calling! All he wanted now was

somebody like maybe, just *maybe* his girl, to share in his first small, hedged triumph—a qualified Yes. (*"On a limited* basis, Mr. Nedders, for a *pilot* project."*) Bravo, bravo, bis! And here was your Hot Pilot Projector, Ned Nedders sweating out his last phone booth, splitting the arena as he came, solo. Shades of Dr. Kissinger; but unlike Henry, Ned had to pick up his own marbles—a couple of tons of dirty laundry, and a load of tapes that would fill a golf cart on the way to a D.C. shredder. But here in the private sector, it was back to the old files, the manual way, via the Nedders method, a miracle of Yankee knowhow—called Hot Storage in Clammy Hands. So here went your great Hot Storager stumbling down the subway steps with his rush-hour companions, bound for the colorful Upper West Side, where the Groves of Academe met Needle Park, a far-out province—(*somethin' funky always goin' down* —*sheeeeeeeeeeeeit, man,* interchangeable with *mon,* also *baby*)—as per indigenous speech patterns daily observed by your great Streetshit Observer, practically falling on his ass to make the express, the way his feet killed him in these god-damn one-size-too-narrow Gucci loafers, Ms. Hot Shot's super idea of a super present as a send-off to Middle America. For the academic who has everything. Meaning herself. Flash—Ms. Herself being unhappily delayed at the crucial welcome-home moment would be in touch soonest. Right now of course she was busy cooling her maddening ass on some banquet in the Crapartist Colony, doing her thing. Called running old pictures through the wind machine that used to be a radio station. Now converted to *show* daydreams, at their lowest common denominator, natch, eliminating the need for even a child's imagination. In fact, eliminating imagination as an entity. Except when needed by Crapartists to put themselves on about *their* calling. The "grave importance" of which was beyond the comprehension of your effete intellectual snob colony, your straphanger society riding the academic gravy train, looking down their noses for somebody else to put a light at the end of their graffiti tunnel—(*Cesar Chavez eats lettuce*)—ah, the primitive archetypal wit, the native color on the old cave wall. How about a little preservation funding there, fellows? (And fellowettes.) All ye of the foundation board, the cutback crowd, biting the bullet for inflation—here's to somebody else's bullet. Now that Ned Nedders has got *his*. *Always* looking for a handout, these bleeding-heart meddlers, always out to *prove* something at somebody else's expense. Splitting hairs nobody cares about, separating wheat from chaff (and there went your chaff insecticides, remember?). And now this Nedders (no not Nader), this Nedders clown, with another new theory about separating the deaf from the autistic from the emotionally disturbed—child, natch, not even Nam Vets—while incidentally separating experts in all three fields from perfectly good theories that haven't worked for years, also privately funded or government supported—now down the drain. Good money after bad, and back to the old drawing board! Where none of the hairsplitters ever made anything but trouble. Except of course for the industrial engineers, or the practical crowd that *split* the atoms, didn't just *talk* about it. But your Goddamn Ivory Tower Talkers never made a nickel! Couldn't make a living if they had to, the honest way, competing in your open market for the Crapartist Sweepstakes, greatest little rat-fuck, rat-race ever run in this world. (*W! I! N!*) But forget the old team spirit on your US of A campuses—God forbid—took some good old law 'n' order to force your Militant Rad element underground there! (Making the world safe for détente. Tremendous concept.) Too much for your lily-livered liberals—shut *that* think-tank right up. So there went your Milquetoast Profs. No loss, ergo no balls.

Or one Ned Nedders would even now have hijacked *this* mother, been long gone, roaring into oblivion with the whole

West Side express, trailing can after can of sizzling human tuna, *Soul Train, Yeah, Brother!* But with only Yankee ingenuity to fall back on—and tons of it falling back on him, he had to admit to Art and Science's oldest nightmare—creative block, impasse. They were stalled. Somewhere between Ninety-sixth and 110th.

It was too fucking hot to *think*. Even as a game. Professor Goodworks trips again, she always said, going along, even with the parts that were savagely unfair—to her, not their great society pressing in around him. She was with him there. And at his best he had to admit that in her way she tried to fight it—they had that in common, that and professional dedication, which was always rare.

So he defended her way-out notions of what those TV fuckers would let her produce. And stood off his disapproving friends among fellow doctoral candidates, most of whom sensed all along Ned would have to choose between a life of missing connections—or missing her. After two weeks of doing both, in the same room with Billings, a hard-eyed advocate of sharing *any* chick's board—and this one's bread—Ned did not need Billings' advice to write off the option; the price of her life style came too high. It was ultimate distraction. Though she tried gamely to understand his first thesis chapter, what he needed was the kind of girl who'd have re-typed it by now. Though Maude Lee stood off *her* friends with her great respect for Ned's calling, forever quoting the writing on the wall—(*Life without speech is empty,* she said; *life devoid of communication scarcely better than death*), proving what Ned's work had in common with hers: words, she said. They were both hung up on words. (*We seek out those who are halting in speech* . . . like stutterers, she said, and writers . . . *We offer our help to those whose ears have been confused* . . . well, she said, that's everyone!)

Everyone but Ms. Confusion, swamping him everywhere,

utterly—except in bed. When all he needed was a bedmate who would make *his* work her hangup, not match it with a career of her own. Chauvinist or not, his was more important to him if not to no one else in this boob tube world, where cartoonists took the prize money for shocking kids senseless. Well, the man underpaid to pick up those pieces didn't need to hear reviews for his calling. Just hard news about the supermarket special, and how to stretch it, how to save with him for the rainbow at the end of his education. And if Maude Lee once took the time to think of him separately from her she'd know—he couldn't get there from here through her mirrored fun house. And he hadn't come all this way to bog down on the wrong detour. Despite the once-in-a-lifetime scenery which was spoiling him for his chosen lot: (*The communion of man is our concern.*)

But oh man did he want out of purgatory. Not just this train, finally creeping to a halt, but up and out of this shithouse station where the natives were so restless they sometimes shot up on the stairs. He wanted to see the last of the student pushers dealing on Broadway, and the last of the spades who stalked now and mugged later right on his corner, where the Jewish delicatessen and the Spanish chili counter were barricaded, like alien outposts unwillingly arrayed together against the dark. He was tired of turning into this once quiet block, where garbage used to be collected, passing the old-fashioned apartment building where old rabbis and professors and merchants took turns as volunteer vigilantes, one standing guard with a cane now as Ned limped past. If anything ever pointed up the incongruity of the big romance it was the loafers crippling this lonely return. As duly noted by the kids' Hostility Committee on his door stoop. "Dig four eyes in the dude shoes!" They snickered, not moving as he picked his transient way among them, because *he* had something down, wasn't four eyes for his health, mother-fucker, already beyond them, into something better, sheeeeeeeeit, movin' on.

Into something like a real life in a real home, since he'd never had one, never been a kid any more than these were, never had a childhood but would like to see one, watch a child grow from baby not from patient, his own kid. Sorry about that, liberated ladies, gentlemen swingers! But here's your great home-coming orphan, digging the mail out of his box, taking off the killer loafers in the entry hall, to start up four flights of filthy linoleum in filthy stocking feet with a hole in them. He needed a wife.

The most expensive shoes, he noted, plunking them in his open bag on top of mail and laundry, smelled like the cheapest—the other most uncomfortable pair he'd ever worn, had to stuff newspaper in because they were also bought the wrong size, too large, at the foster home where the kids' clothes requisition was regularly mopped. Well, the last shall be first; probably his expensive shirt (another present) had outsmelled all the cheap stinkers around him on the subway, and doubtless the stuffed made-to-orders at the foundation, where his new best friends, the trustees, would never tell him. But Ned's nose had been rubbed in the smell so long it was always with him, clinging to walls like these, waiting, more a part of the scene than graffiti—(2R sucks? Splendid news. Into the old memory bank.). With all the store of secret smelling shame. (Ah—a cur turd to trip on! Step lively, Old Footsore Four-eyes, Agile Shitskipper, and Transient extraordinary.) *Where the hell is the super?* Maude Lee had said the first time Ned warned her off some decorative vomit. Ms. Smartstreet was not Streetsmart coming as she did from lofts to luxury along chartered ways, where supers might never get off their ass—or yours—but they came with the rent. Like her doormen now helping to reassure Daddy, when he came through town, dangling allowances to lure her home (where he wanted her), promising trust funds, promising anything once he got a load of the entrenched crapartists that she never failed to gather around Daddy's piano. One, so Daddy could play it. And two, so Maude Lee could make a smiling show of independent indifference to the accumulated alimony millions of Mrs. James, Stoner, Vonsickle, Richards, Demilio, Evans, an exalted connection confessed to Ned after repeated blood oaths, sworn on his future, to keep it secret from all other nouveau or notso riche members of the circle. Except for a few sterling characters she trusted. Like Bruce McVitty IV, who knew her when. Bruce was almost as reassuring to Daddy as a doorman, "Sir? Could you play 'Just Too Marvelous'—for the road?" Only Brucie gave it the poltroon reading "Mahvelous" as in "Chahming" as in "How about 'You're so Dawn Charming,' sir?" Someday somebody would have to pass the top hat to fund a study of *those* speech patterns. An echo from the past that confused Maude Lee's present though she wouldn't admit it, needing Bruce on tap for Daddy. (Ned didn't *understand* the way it was, thrown with so many strangers as an adolescent, she said. But Bruce was the one who'd befriended her, the one she'd really grown up with— was always closest to. So close, she confessed, they made it at fifteen. In the deep end of the swimming pool, which was better than diving in for a midnight skinny dip as planned because the pool wasn't filled.) Bruce returned Maude Lee's nostalgic regard saying they were two sides of the same coin. To which Ned replied, "Then she's heads," getting a laugh from seven-and-a-half-months-gone Amy Foreman, one of the few laughs Ned ever got from anybody at a crapartist party, where his elocutionary tones weren't all that reassuring, especially to Daddy, who seemed to have a tough time even hearing Ned's name when reintroduced. Because he sensed Ned's *hate*, Maude Lee said, setting off their last fight in the middle of "So Rare," whispering in her dressing area, which she hadn't yet gotten around to papering with human hair or something terrific. Hissing that people had animal instincts too, could smell hate like Ned's. Now overpowering sensitive old Dads, to hear her tell it—whatever didn't fit omitted from her scene as always. So here came your orphan reject to put her straight. "I smell poor." That's how it came out. In a great snort from his deep, unconscious, inner nostril, as dread a secret to him as smelling rich like old lady six-names was to Maude Lee. But it was said. Though she looked at him so strangely he thought for a minute she hadn't caught it, or sniffed it out long before like all her crapartist friends, as if she alone didn't know why her lover got a wide berth. She even said, *"What?"* as if she couldn't hear, or had wax in her ears, couldn't *possibly* tell what made her lover walk out, or why. On *her? And Daddy's party?*

Until 4 A.M., following to creep into his bed, lips against his ear, she woke him with another whisper: "Neddy, you smell dear . . ."

Which meant she had to unlock all his mighty locks first—alone and unaided, he reflected, unlocking them now himself —seven, count them, one for every ripoff. Ms. Superblonde had a lot of fucking nerve for a girl from Mars, including the nerve to use *his* keys when nobody asked her. Not that *her* surprising *him* was their biggest problem, her visits from outer space occurring a fat twice a year, usually to make up after a fight. Except that one Sunday she decided to uncover the natural brick on the wall behind his desk, and uncovered instead the beaverboard under his plaster, an interior decorating note he needed like he needed another rathole, or the Gucci shoes, or the sound of her voice.

He half expected to hear the goddamn *phone* ringing, coming up the stairs—like at the top, that was standard MO, after he'd made the whole damn ball breaker—"Neddy? I'm home —come *here!*" Only of course it was too soon, she wouldn't be.

Only when he dialed her, almost idly, Jesus H. Christ, she was! He'd never heard a better busy signal, standing there, dropping his clothes in his tracks, so he could dial again, his spirits lifting like magic. And that wasn't all that was lifting, he noted, laughing as he made his shower cold and thinking of the way she laughed and teased him afterward, calling it *his throbbing member,* in her pulp fiction voice. Lying across his knees, looking down at his body so possessively you'd think he was made from *her* rib, taking his cigarette to puff experimentally like a little girl making up a story in her rest period.

"His throbbing member lay limp after plunging again and again deep into her dark pubescence. But when she leaned forward, her lips parted, needing his manness. His malehood quickened—"

"Malehood—!"

"Never mind. It's quickening."

Yes, quickening as life itself did around her. No escaping— not tonight; tomorrow . . . ? Who knew? Here was your manness on the bell again . . . still busy. Her fucking office— had to be. She wasn't a phone disher even with Amy Foreman, even in their heyday, before the big pregnancy turnoff nobody discussed. Which was OK with Ned, the Foremans being too much the perennial swingers for his dough. "You're just jealous of *everybody*," Maude Lee laughed. But both of them knew she was possessive of everything so that's how it went. Ned's gut tightened every time she smiled at her boss coming out of an elevator. And her smile tightened when Ned went away—like to the corner. But near or far one fact remained: he had never known her to talk forty minutes on the phone with anybody—except her father. Or her lover. So . . . if not Ned?

A new one would explain a lot lately.

Yet his mind, which so often went black with doubt against

her, suddenly turned another way when he heard the final busy signal, *after* he'd dressed, was all ready to go. What the hell *was* this? He asked the operator who got the supervisor who said she didn't know.

"I'm sorry, sir—we no longer verify busy signals. Unless the phone is reported out of order." So he tried it that way, with another operator who got another supervisor who got the verifier who took thirteen minutes to thank him for reporting the line out of order because it was.

Off the hook?

No way. Not ever. Maybe four times in a two-year relationship she had let it *ring*. But that was it. And her first post-coital move would be to call her service. She might not want to talk on the goddamn thing but she sure as hell couldn't rest till she knew who wanted to talk to her. The phone and the puppy were extensions of herself.

Something in his streetsmart heart turned over. He tried to deny it, thinking no, maybe *here*, but not there, not with her doorman and her super. . . . And then, knowing better, he was out of his own door, locking it, ready to use her keys this time, if he had to, traveling the dark stairs and still light streets the way he'd learned—one foot other foot—alert to the corner he was turning.

He made himself look for the Chavez graffiti all the way back downtown in the subway. Going across on the bus, he made himself count the taxis passing him, thinking how fast she'd have jumped in one, and how he couldn't, not three blocks' worth at the new rates, unless he wanted to arrive collect and call up for cash. But her house phone did not answer. The doorman already knew it. Someone had called the apartment house to get her. And indeed Ned himself had thought of that, of trying once more when he got off the bus, but some bastard in the phone booth, pretending not to know Ned was outside, kept turning away, ducking his head into his shoulder, bracing his arm against the side of the booth so Ned couldn't see him either.

And finally feeling ridiculous, hovering like some supplicant, Ned went inside. Just as the doorman got a call from 12B, reporting a flood from 14B upstairs.

"Maybe she's overrun her tub," the doorman said to Ned. But even then, running for the elevator, the word flood somehow conjured up the other possibility. Even before Ned got off on her floor and heard the puppy—not barking in the usual way, but screaming. Where were the fucking neighbors? Ned ran, not realizing he was yelling for them—for the airline stewardesses, for Maude Lee's good and great friends, the Foremans. Couldn't they hear? Didn't they know? He did not yell for her. Not yet. Though he wasn't aware of that either.

He'd forgotten about the new second lock but so had Maude Lee so he didn't have to pause for unaccustomed fumbling. The water was coming through the door, sopping all over the maroon hall carpeting so he didn't waste much time ringing and pounding, or worrying about the big deal of using his key. And as soon as he got the door open, the puppy came screaming up out of the water, jumping against him, past him, but, reaching down, Ned touched the wet fur as it streaked past. His hand came away pink like the flood; he could see the color in the light from the hall as he splashed into the foyer. And then he saw her looking at him in the mirror. From their bed. He turned to face her. She was lying across the knees of the man who was with her. His head was down this end and Ned saw the little, round, obscene bald patch on the top. It was the only part of the man not submerged in water except for his knees, propping her up, so she'd lean naked over naked malehood, manness, drowned. Only her eyes resisted, looked for an exit, still beating on the place where the door was, eyes gone mad as Ned started toward her, shouting. And then he saw the rest, under the water. Probably he screamed, certainly he fell, turning away so violently, he went down twice at least, maybe more, down on the slashed sofa, on hunks of slashed chairs, terrified he would somehow go under, unable to regain his balance, to scramble out from between those mirrored walls reflecting him into eternity, reflecting her eyes watch him go, the part of the reflection he would flee forever. But not yet. He would not confront, but could not abandon her. Someone must come, her mad eyes said. Somehow he must get to the counter where the see-through Lucite phone should be, dial the operator to dial the supervisor, dial 911 and cry murder. But of course the phone wasn't there, was with her somewhere, unhooked, trailing its endless extension cord under the pink water. While the other extension of herself, gone madder than her eyes, ran in circles, screaming in the hall.

Directly ahead of him, Ned saw the house phone, but he knew he couldn't make it, clinging like a drowning man to the counter. Her specially installed bar-counter with the Formica top. He fixed his gaze on the clean, white gleaming surface. He thought of her in space, or wandering Mars, without any of her funny goods or worldly chattels. And he thought of her unlocking his dirty pad, his locked-up heart and deserted life, and how he should have had the balls to keep her, lock her in with his seven locks, and keep her safe beside him.

No way of knowing how long it took, with no sands running but the puppy's scream, no clocks ticking, until the footsteps sounded, until the super came, yelling about the water, barging through her door, to find a man at her bar and another in her bed. Just as he always wanted.

Interior: Night,
Exterior: Day

Deduction is another story, a horse of a different color, heading back wherever it came from. The amateur following its zigzag course tends to make an ass of a zebra. Intuition need not apply. Detection is a minor art and an inexact science, but it requires a discipline as strict as its budget; its oldest routine is a fast shuffle—too much footwork for too few gumshoes trying not to track dirt in from the street. Its official track record must be spotlessly accurate: statistics confided to a computer and mysteries filed in triplicate. Findings are reported in a dead language—appropriate to Armed and Suspicious Individuals approaching early retirement benefits In a Dangerous Manner. Thus professionals keep safe distance, civil service mostly a formality, relations with civilians highly selective. Experience does not leap in the dark at the whim of hysterics getting what they paid for. The tip, the hunch, the creative thrust must come from the departmental gut—or a snitch the detective can muscle. Freud himself might get in the way of psychology applied at the precinct level. And the greatest

Renaissance genius could not hastily draw conclusions on the Homicide Wall. ("What do you mean *unusual* smile, Leonardo? Mona didn't smile much? Or just not at you?") It's wiser not to know the joke when The Female Behaving in a Humorous Manner gets involved in murder—whether as victim or suspect. Approaching her premises is involvement enough, the innocence of bystanders being relative. All are presumed guilty of something. Detectives question only of what to deduce whether the guilt is relevant. Which does not always solve the crime. Or even the enigma of the lady's smile. Or who smiled last. But detection can't take forever. There are too many other zigs and zags to follow, other cases still open in the files. And since the files are closed, who's to guess that the law got everybody *but* its man in some of those unfinished mysteries. The closest of survivors may be loath to file such linen on the front page. Or in triplicate on the networks. Deduction is another story. And there's another one every week.

But there are exceptions—fish too big to get away without a backlash. Nothing so fires human nature's suspicion of itself as privilege falling prey to scandal. With the rich and mighty loss, there is always a little impatience. It takes a President to pardon a President, life being unfair as a President noted shortly before meeting his own unfair fate. When golden career boys and girls end in dust, the workaday public tends to believe they made their own appointments in Samara. The same goes double for sadder falling stars, caught trying to cheat fate by flirting with the forces they couldn't beat. Acceptable only when copping to the State, which is otherwise more apt to prove collusion than rape, a crime so perfect it can scarcely be said to exist unless resisted, to the point of death. Even then the offense may defy resolution until it is repeated, and/or confessed by the butler who did it, ever the last word on the maid it was done to, generally presumed to be looking for Goodbar even in her own bed. Once violated, the most logical of all last resting places can also be the hardest on the fair reputation. As on the fair corpus—robbed, kidnaped live on tape, or found in flagrante post-mortem.

Alas, the last interference made itself in the double homicide called THE WATER BED MURDERS from the moment the first tabloid hit the street. The story took over, running away with its tellers. Even those who had to make the case were hard pressed to take the heat, flaring out of control, while witnesses were burned and a few branded, but none remained safe from inclusion in some smoldering postscript. Until the last ash was raked.

The first to learn the relativity of innocence was a bystander so forgettable he failed to deduce his own name when colliding with the barrier of police mentality. He was Sam Lorrilard, tenant of 14H, all anyone had to know about him. But the so-called Mr. Lonelyhearts was tripping home on a happier alter ego when he was brought to his first stop on the corner, mildly surprised to find the block jammed. Traffic stalled and onlookers gathered despite a lot of bossy advice from patrolmen who had caused the whole mess by double parking. They weren't telling anyone why. And for once Sam Lorrilard did not care. Having overstretched the cocktail hour to develop a lucky encounter into the best contact ever, he was too spent with triumph to sense disaster. And far too hungry to be curious. So he pressed on, shouldering his way through somehow, ignoring the psychedelic lighting flashing unnecessarily from every size of official vehicle, until he was blinded by brighter lights, white and hot, set up in the desk beyond his canopy for cameras already focused on the entrance. To his relief a cop was keeping it clear.

"Clear for what?" A man wearing earphones kept thrusting a hand mike into the cop's face, as if the argument were an interview. "Taking somebody in? Medical Examiner coming?"

"It's for the tenants—I told you guys . . ." The reminder was weary. "People live here."

And died there, reminders jeered wearily back from the dusk. They had told him too—calls for help could be intercepted. But not by the tenant from 14H, trying to get in out of the spotlight. Stopped on the threshold by the night doorman, fumbling with a checklist.

"Sorry, sir—gotta identify you."

"Can't we do it inside?"

Unfortunately it was Walter, the girl watcher, who couldn't do it anywhere, as usual confusing Lorrilard with the other faceless young men too dull or discreet to provide gossip. Left unprotected by the cop who took over at the house phone, Lorrilard was more than ready to pass for some dentist or closet queen in the A or B penthouse, until another hitch developed. The entire twentieth floor had checked in.

"I'm not *on* 20, Walter, dammit—" A mike was thrust in Lorrilard's face before he could proclaim his true identity and floor number.

"And occupation . . ." Somewhere in the dusk a hand-held camera ground dutifully. "This way, sir, so we get your reaction."

Lorrilard's reaction was to turn his back and call the law, but he was upstaged by a better entrance. Across the lobby the elevator door opened to emit a knot of official-looking men, moving as óne, shoulder to shoulder, except for a shirt-sleeved figure, out of step at the center.

"They're bringing somebody out—" the mike thruster shouted. The rest of the press surged in from the desk, catapulting Lorrilard across the threshold, and straight into the cop who underwent a startling change in personality.

"Clear the hell outa that entrance!"

Another cop came running from a side door that led to the basement stairs. Together the uniformed men threw their

combined weight against the crowd. Lorrilard was caught in
the middle. A mike slashed his cheek; a camera ground into
his back; something that felt like a nightstick lodged in his
chest. He lost both breath and balance with nothing to keep
him up but the crushing weight of two opposing forces, suddenly unleashing mutual hatred.

"Move it. All the way—"

"Get your fuzz hands off the camera—"

"Get your fuckin' cameras outa here—"

"Clear your ass off this sidewalk."

And then the pressure behind Lorrilard gave way. He fell
sideways, grabbing for a canopy stanchion, as the press scattered, mike thrusters jumping the gutter, cameramen cursing,
reporters shouting:

"It's the second car—they're taking the civilian car!"

It was true. Hanging breathless on the stanchion, Lorrilard
saw that the flying wedge was heading diagonally past him
across the sidewalk toward the open doors of an unmarked
sedan, suddenly and miraculously unblocked, as the police car
ahead of it edged away from the curb. Two of the officials
broke from the wedge to run interference with mikes and
cameras closing in again.

"The witness has no comment!"

"Witness or suspect?"

"Better ask 'em, kid!"

"Tell us your name—we'll ask."

"Hey, man—how'd you get the blood on you?"

The shirt-sleeved figure turned. All the cameras in the
world seemed to flash. Lorrilard found himself staring straight
into the bespectacled eyes of Maude Lee Evans' lover.

"Amigo . . ." he said before he thought. Nedders shook his
head and that was all. The men holding his arms on each side,
swung left, ducking as one, and pulled Nedders into the back
seat between them. The car started moving through the press,

still running alongside. Lorrilard turned and headed for the lobby. There was nothing between him and the elevator now, but the doorman, picking up the pages of his checklist with shaking hands.

"What the hell *happened?*"

The doorman looked up but not at Lorrilard, beyond him through the empty doorway, at nothing.

"He found his girl with the man next door."

It wasn't up to Walter's standard. Tomorrow he would embellish with details and famous last words. But tonight the gossiping girl-watcher had seen and heard it all, and could do no better. It was enough for Lorrilard. He knew the names and numbers as he knew his neighbors. Too well. 14B was between the elevator and the A apartment, the largest on each floor, running the width of the building, adjoining 14 H across the hall. The man next door to Maude Lee Evans lived next door to Lorrilard too. Bob Foreman.

Lorrilard decided not to stick around the lobby and broadcast his reaction to that, along with his occupation. He had more than a bank teller's job at stake now. Vistas of lunches at exclusive clubs, weekends in the Hamptons danced in his head; his whole social future was opening up—in slow motion like the elevator door. But Establishment doors slammed shut a lot faster, in the face of scandal, Lorrilard knew. So he barely breathed as he pressed 14 and stood waiting where only this morning he had been snubbed by the bitch now threatening to bitch up everything. It wasn't until the car moved that he saw in the mirror his cheek was cut, and swore, snatching the handkerchief he kept in his breast pocket for looks. He wanted no connection with whatever bloody row had brought the whole police force down on his neighbors. Even Foreman, who never got involved—in anything, really— just went along, his voice a murmur, as veiled as his heavy-lidded eyes. It was Foreman's wife who called the tunes in the living room next door, called the parties, and called them off, called Lorrilard Mr. Lonelyhearts too, though he hardly had to hear he was lonely through a wall. Not from Amy, playing cat and mouse with husband and neighbors until she went screaming away to have her kitten, leaving the game to get too rough. Some amigos! Well, Lorrilard was lucky to be out of it. That was the main thing, he told himself, the party was over. And then he stepped out on the unlucky floor and found it was only beginning.

As it was for the haunted. Ned was still in the car, stopped at a light, when the anesthetic of shock wore off. Gazing out a window at nothing, he suddenly saw the girl, hair flying as she came around the corner walking her dog. He squeezed his eyes shut, turning his head the other way, toward the younger detective, who was sympathetic, though he misunderstood.

"Just a blonde, Ned."

Ned knew, had already gotten that message. So familiar, inconsistent, and silly, it could only have come from memory. Or Mars. "They think I'm just some *blonde*," his girl always said, indignantly, as if it were all a mistake of identity, a hapless accident, perhaps of birth. And only Ned understood her soul's dark secret, come home to roost, like a lost rib, unceremoniously shoving in with the others. Instinctively he clutched the painful place of entry, under his shirt, still wet to the touch, resoaked and stained for real by the first cops through her door, so busy searching and yelling they had pushed him back into her room, down again too near her bed where the water was red, blowing his mind right out of his skull. Until the detectives, crowding in next, had stopped the melee, establishing Ned as a witness they needed. "The way he is, for Chrissake," the older detective shouted, the tough one now appraising the blonde who was just some blonde, not Ned's.

"Plenty like her around, Professor."

"Not for him, Frankovitch. *Jesus.*" The younger detective moved uncomfortably.

"Not tonight anyway." The one called Frankovitch leered out the window as the light changed. "Later, baby . . ."

The younger detective seemed relieved when they moved away, heading west. "OK, Ned?"

They were playing Good Guy/Bad Guy of course. Ned named the game, knowing he shouldn't, sounding too street-boy smartass for a bereaved lover called The Professor. But it helped to center his attention here in the car where he was. Not where he was going. Or had been. (*"Swear on your future you'll always love me? No one but me—swear on my life?"*)

Good Guy's indignant reproof overruled all echoes of future and past. This was no time to play *games*, he told Ned.

Bad Guy's answer was better. "You've been watching too much TV, Professor."

Ned could almost hear her laugh. "Not without me!" she could have told them. Not even with her sometimes. Until she closed his book or took the pencil from his hand. Never just for the commercial stuff, the pilots and series she had to watch. Only for the shows that were special, she said, and worth it. Like the time she surprised him, her head on his shoulder so he couldn't see her crying. "I *never* cry," she always insisted. But the tears wet his shirt.

"Don't make a *thing*," she always said. So he took another chance on the window, to discover with surprise the car was entering the park. So after all, the detectives weren't taking their witness to the precinct. He tried to feel relief, to think of a better place to go. Surely he could find safer company to keep than Good Guy with his treacherous snow job. Even among friends who had thought all along she was just some blonde and told Ned so. Even Billings, who preferred bru-

nettes and was probably already in bed with one, after two
weeks of conference dorm life. But Billings' pad had two
rooms at least, which was better than Ned's, and being truly
alone with that suddenly silent phone. (*"I'm home, Neddy.
Come here."*)

"Listen," he said, "if you're dropping me off, I don't want to
go home."

But he wasn't quite home free yet.

Nor was Lorrilard, though home base was closer. He might
have made it if he hadn't found the hall so full of whispers.
Tenants whispered to each other from the studio doorways.
Even the professional greeters from the airlines were clustered
in a whispering circle outside C, their backs turned to the elevators. While at the other end of the hall, whispering officials
milled inside the open door of the Foremans' apartment, apparently being used as a sort of headquarters. Even by the
press, Lorrilard thought for a startled moment, when he saw
two men with cameras coming out. But they moved too
quietly past a cop who let them into 14B, the only door be-
sides Lorrilard's that remained closed. While behind it even
the puppy had fallen silent.

It was this, finally, that got to Lorrilard, rooting him where
he stood. Dread turned to fear, reflected in the fear all around
him, stilling his first crasher's impulse to slip unseen past the
whole hushed reception line. So once again he was caught
flat-footed when the fire door beside the elevator flew open,
and a crazy lady in a wrapper barreled out of the stair well
and to Lorrilard's horror mistook him for a detective. Tears
were cascading down her cheeks like the water from 14B apparently cascading down the walls of her apartment underneath, though she'd been calling on the house phone to report
it since she first came home and discovered the leak, fast
becoming a flood. Now she was yelling for the man in charge.

"What's he waiting for—my ceiling to fall in? What the fuck are you cops *doing* in that apartment?"

Lorrilard tried to back off with the first answer he could think of. "Taking pictures—"

"*PICTURES?*"

It was a shriek to pierce the eardrums, drawing the attention of a real detective who hurried red-faced toward them shouting at the cop for allowing access from the forbidden stair well to the floor now supposedly restricted to its tenants.

"But I live here—" Lorrilard began, drowned out by the lady, tearfully invoking her five-year residence in 12B, where she was instantly advised to return. Since nothing in 14B could be touched—including the water—until the Medical Examiner came.

"Your friend can help you remove your stuff to the hall—" The detective gestured toward Lorrilard.

"He can't remove my new wallpaper—" she sobbed, leaving Lorrilard to explain he had not come up the stairs with the lady, but alone from the lobby by the elevator, which the cop finally used to take her away. The detective himself preceded Lorrilard into his premises to corroborate the time of arrival on the house phone, only to discover that the tenant from 14H had never been checked in at all. It caused more flap than the flood, setting off a shouting match about security, apparently a touchy subject since the first cops on the scene had found the basement entrance unbolted. The automatic buzzer system signaling its use upstairs was admittedly often unheard by the doorman, now so shaken he couldn't remember press from tenants.

"So this guy coulda been in the building all along," the detective raged at the cop downstairs. "Anyone could!" Or worse, if a tenant had just sneaked in past the whole police force, the perpetrator might have sneaked out. In vain, Lorrilard protested about his open and aboveboard entrance

through a mob scene. Wearily the detective took out his notebook for the chore that should routinely have been covered in
the next day's canvassing.

"Got a witness where you've been we can contact by
phone?"

"*Contact . . .*" The word was enough to banish all fears but
the first. "What for—?"

"To corroborate when you left—so we don't have to chase
our ass around checking—"

"You can't. I mean I don't know the number."

The detective sighed. "Name and address?"

"But nobody's there—we left together . . ." Spluttering,
Lorrilard fought to protect the name he would have dropped
so proudly almost anywhere else. The more frantic his evasions, the more he was pressed; until finally the detective
turned suspicious—the last and most dangerous change in
police personality, spreading through the thin walls to the
highest echelons, where Lorrilard, unlike the lady in the
wrapper, attracted the attention of the man in charge, retrieved from next door.

The Lieutenant, the detective said, had some questions. But
the Lieutenant did not ask them—except of himself. Muttering about where the hell the ME was, the great gray emi-
nence passed Lorrilard to walk heavily across the bare floor
and peer through the slats of the cheap venetian blinds. It was
like being in a TV cop show gone wrong. Only instead of the
knowing and limpid gaze of Kojak, Lorrilard felt himself
watched by the back of the Lieutenant's head. While the detective called Red—to match his face—sat down again on the
foam-rubber couch-bed to review his own incredible notes.

"Let's get this straight, Sam . . . You walk home every day,
the same way, the same time—"

"If my cash proves out—"

"Only today you ran into this party you don't know—"

"Don't know the name—a chance acquaintance—"

"And go home with him you don't remember where—"

"I said Sutton Place—"

"South." The detective nodded. "Which leaves four blocks of high-rises we gotta cruise to find one trick—"

"Chance acquaintance!" the Lieutenant's voice interrupted from the window.

"Sure." The detective smiled, and the hair rose on Lorrilard's neck. "Chance acquaintance is fine. Nobody wants to embarrass anybody, Sam. We're all adults. Our problem is time, not how consenting adults spend it—"

"Jesus sweet Christ, this man's not a faggot!" Lorrilard was so horrified he forgot to say he wasn't either. "He's a broker with a partnership in one of the oldest firms, the oldest families—"

"Sure," said the red-faced detective, "and a wife and kids in Long Beach—"

"*Long Beach?*" Almost a worse heresy than faggotry. "I said they were leaving for the Hamptons!"

"Only his wife hadda get through shopping—right—?"

"It wasn't his wife—just some date. He's not married—"

"Nothing against him." The detective remained broadminded. "Sometimes wish I wasn't—"

"Listen—will you please for God's sake listen—it wasn't anything like that. This guy's a contact—business, social everything. Like I never had. Like everybody needs. Like if one of you guys had a drink with the Commissioner—and somebody said . . . *Jesus* . . ."

The Lieutenant turned. "How does a bank teller meet the Commissioner?" It was the heart of the matter. Lorrilard looked away from the great gray face toward the door, and the scene of all contacts across the hall, where everybody met everybody on this floor, and would say so, if they hadn't already. He made a helpless gesture.

"Over there. But they used to go together—so for God's sake don't start that faggot number—"

"With Miss Evans?" The Lieutenant's tone was sharp.

"With anybody." But somehow Lorrilard already knew no one would start anything there anymore. His palms were sweating. For the second time he groped for his handkerchief, forgetting the blood. Until the detectives saw it and looked at his cheek. His hand went to the cut. Still wet.

"It happened in that hassle downstairs," he burst out bitterly, before they could ask. "When you took that guy in." So why were they hassling innocent people?

"What guy, Mr. Lorrilard?"

The one who did it. TV talk gone wrong. *Did what?* He couldn't say it. "The one who made the trouble."

"We've got nobody in custody."

"You've got Nedders. I know him!" Too much of an admission. "I mean by name. I saw them take him in a car."

The Lieutenant shook his head. "A matter of co-operation," he said. "Mr. Nedders is the witness who discovered the bodies."

"*Bodies.*" Not just a girl struck down in a jealous quarrel. But Foreman too . . . even Foreman—"Both of them . . . ?"

The detective nodded. "We've got a case, serious homicide here." Sirens were approaching as if to confirm it. "Two victims. And for all we know two perpetrators." So clearly it would be to the advantage of Miss Evans' close neighbor to search his memory for the name of Miss Evans, former boyfriend, thereby confirming both men were together at Sutton Place. Far from the scene where the sirens screamed, stopping now, right under the window.

"Check him later, Red . . ." The Lieutenant was already moving toward the door. "Here's the ME."

"And the Assistant DA," someone shouted from the hall, suddenly filling with officials. Lorrilard saw another moving knot of them coming from the elevator—two with black bags, one in white—all disappearing into 14B. It wasn't until the intervening doors had closed and he was alone that it really sank in . . . two human beings he had known lay dead across the hall, being photographed, examined, prodded, turned over, in water that dripped down the walls below. . . . He turned dizzily from the kitchenette and stumbled into the yuk green john, realizing even as he retched that his word for the tiles, like his view of the Hamptons from Sutton Place, had come to him courtesy of the same vibrant life. Now vanished like all his vistas, swirling invisibly away in the water flushed down the toilet, with Bruce McVitty's vodka.

Good Guy didn't blame Ned for not wanting to go home, promising to give him another ride, wherever he chose to go —from Homicide, where the unmarked car finally drew up. The fuzz were forever collecting behind new façades, but this one looked almost as impressive as it sounded—very modern for the West Side—until Ned recognized the building for what it was. Just another precinct. With another press gantlet to run outside, into the usual precinct night music, the locking and unlocking, the hassle and waiting, the forms to fill out and fingerprints taken, including Ned's. Though only, of course, to be checked against more suspect smudges that might have survived the flood, as Good Guy kept on explaining, while taking Ned for a ride in an elevator, to Homicide's HQ—just another squad-room bullpen.

The detectives retrieved their messages from bare-surfaced desks, anonymous work space used by men in shifts, while Ned got a glimpse of a separate cell where even their head man left no trace. Whether the paint was new or flaking, the effect was always the same—prison gray and blank like this. On purpose. It was a familiar though alien home-coming to an orphan street boy turned professor, long an alumnus of public

institutions before he followed the fuzz through the last door
to settle at a "conference table"—just another station-house
back room. It was a little smaller than the inside offices from
which Maude Lee and her ilk had been liberated. (*"Vile,"* she
always said.) But larger than the cubicles where Ned worked
with the afflicted in front of mirrors, rigged as windows for
unsuspected observers. (*"Vilest,"* she said the time she tried
it.) Well, whatever she thought was fair. Here, the observers,
suspected everywhere, were deadliest right up front. Like Bad
Guy opening his notebook, as if to take dictation when he
meant to give it. Letting Good Guy do the honors, pouring
and passing coffee, lending and lighting a cigarette for Ned,
since the witness remained so clumsily left-handed, his right
hand still clutching his shirt. Like a man with a gut wound,
Bad Guy said, when they finally noticed. And started probing.

Only she was both gut and wound that night, not hurting so
much if Ned held fast. Nor healing, he knew vaguely. But he
was in limbo and doing well not to spill his insides at the first
question. Limbo was no hospital for the mending process, or
morgue for embalming, but a halfway house to stay half alive
in. It was not for the quick to let go of the dead, but to wait
release, the only way to get out whole. Which in this case
could take a while, instinct told Ned knowing his love as he
did. But the detectives didn't.

They just knew how it had ended. A far cry from the way it
began. (At a rally for *peace*?) When Boy and Girl Met Cute
—(sometimes called a pickup) and Fell in Love at First Sight
—(sometimes called fast work). But not by the boy sweating
it out, scoring for a year before he got those keys, awarded
one by one, an honor no one else had been accorded. (What,
never?) Though of course there must have been prior bed-
mates. No man or boy expected to be first in the Year of the
Woman. What could keep any girl like that virgin, after she'd
seen liberation? But just between Good Guy, Bad Guy, and

the witness—while rights and disbelief were suspended—what could keep any lover in her pad after he'd seen that bloody reflection?

What kind of love had glued Ned to the spot, hanging onto a counter, standing in water? Doing nothing. Not calling for help, with the house phone in reach. Not running for it with the super, crying murder to alert the living in mortal danger from sun roof to laundry, as Ned was himself, remaining there alone, not even checking the premises.

"Why not, Ned?"

"It was too late . . ."

"How did you know?"

"It was over."

"Not for you. Or the perpetrator."

"For her."

Over and over it was all he knew, standing his vigil still, as if he'd stumbled onto the scene of some no fault accident. With no perpetrator. And only one victim. Not two. Never once wondering why he hadn't found her alone, instead of naked in bed with someone else. Not even wanting to wonder.

"Maybe she was forced to . . ."

"By Foreman?"

"I didn't know it was Foreman at first—"

"You knew it was a man—did you think any man could do that to a girl and then start on himself?"

Once again Ned closed his eyes, shutting out that impossible feat under water. And the implications forced upon him as the detectives pushed his memory back further. To the first moment when he saw her in the mirror, and shouted, stumbling forward, murderous with rage—before he fully understood, finally believed, what the puppy's screams should have told him.

"Didn't the puppy always bark?"

"Not like that."

"Couldn't it have been at someone else—in there ahead of you . . . ?"

Someone else with the same motive and key, and lover's knowledge where to grab the kitchen knife, found bloodying the water under Ned. Surely if Ned hadn't used it himself, he should want to help them find out who did. Would dredge up some possible key holder from her past. Or some current threat Ned might have suspected, in a jealous moment.

Didn't he ever have one?

Again Ned could almost hear her laugh. Though it wasn't too damn funny this morning when his jealous suspicions collided with her sense of possession, setting off one last famous fight, as some secretary could doubtless tell the detectives tomorrow. But they weren't going to hear it from Ned tonight. He had promises to keep and miles to go before he broke them.

"There was nobody else . . ."

"That you knew."

"I'd have known."

"Yeah," Bad Guy said. "Like you knew about Foreman."

Ned shook his head. "Whatever that was . . . it must have just happened."

"While you just happened to be away . . . right?"

(*"Promise you miss me,"* the voice on the phone said. *"I miss myself when you're not here."*)

"Like Mrs. Foreman—just happened to be in the hospital."

"Amy?"

"She had a baby today, Ned."

So soon. "I didn't know . . ."

"Your girlfriend knew. The doorman told her."

(*"I'm home,"* the voice whispered to someone else. *"Come here."*)

It was all beginning to blur, the image Ned clung to with the one in the mirror, until the moment of discovery became the whole truth, all he knew, or could ever tell them, really. It was over and he had lost her. Even in memory.

Amy Foreman, by contrast, tried to look sharp. Better than looking dull, she had long ago discovered. So she brushed her mousy bangs from her mousy brown eyes as she was cranked up from drugged sleep to face the latest news along life's rialto. Ready or not, it was straight dope—considering the source. Or sources. There were two lawmen phumphering around like guilty criminals, not that she'd seen much difference since Attica. But she tried to separate message from messenger, straining to meet the averted gazes, shifting past her, as if still seeking some overlooked exit. Though obviously all loopholes had been exhausted—her sister was somewhere on a boat, her doctor somewhere in a car, her lawyer somewhere on a case—or it would not have fallen to total strangers to inform Robert Paul Foreman's next of kin that he was dead from multiple stab wounds in a double homicide. Fuzz talk, but a lot less fuzzy than hospital terms like "expire." Or some ass of a friend saying Bob had "passed on," fudging how, when, where—and above all with whom, a heavy load for any messenger hoping to escape delayed reaction. But the detectives were pros who went by the book and while they were at it had brought one along from the Foremans' apartment. They took their own advantage of delayed reaction to place her address book on the bed beside her. In case she wasn't ready to crack, might even be up to refreshing her memory, now when such help was truly needed, if she wasn't too overcome, since they had already intruded perforce, and, having done their worst, were here anyway.

"So it shouldn't be a total loss?" Amy murmured. It was the first sound she uttered in a voice shot from screaming. But the detectives seemed not to hear her.

She wondered if it was standard MO in their line of work,

all that averting and avoiding. It didn't bode too well for the
snappy solution of a double ax murder. But then neither did
playing dead or dumb or whatever she was doing, feeling no
pain, nor reason for living. Though she knew damn well hers
couldn't wait, was already waiting to be embraced, more
pressing than the detectives' duties. One last reality along her
rialto—breast feeding. So she tried to make a start, feeling the
familiar leather with her fingers, as she opened the loose-leaf
folder, hardly a snappy solution either, being as full of false
leads as the Foremans' social calendar was empty. No more
relevant to murder than the Foremans' accounts, on which
more time would doubtless be wasted tomorrow at Audio Vis-
ual Concepts. Just the fancy name Bob gave the studio where
he did his free-lance number—dreaming up new looks for
banks, sound and light for factory showrooms, ideal office
space that existed only in ads—institutional gigs, remote from
the rat race. Which suited him and earned their bread. With a
slight assist from Amy's puzzles and games and How To Gim-
micks. How to Succeed Without Competing, Survive Without
Sweat—Own Things Done for Own Sake—like all the Foreman designs for living. No one could get murdered for any of
it. But How To put it to detectives.

"We're missing a link," was how she put it to Bob, a silent
step ahead as they made for the wings, like cha-cha champs
well met at a spa—retreating from the new hard rock. Violence. Violence was simply beyond the Foremans. The sexual
twist that went too far. One political giant step too many for
passive resisters. And so, hip to themselves, they had turned
inward.

But she couldn't exactly prove it by a page of crossed out
Committees for the Berrigan Brothers, with two detectives
looking over her shoulder for the names of sore losers.

"Some of our causes weren't lost," she said. Nor were all
their experiments causes. But she wasn't quite up to those

party guest lists. "Some of our best friends don't vote," she said, knowing from her protest days how little authority believed women who protested too much. Even widows, if militant. Which was why sex crimes were political. But not in the way the detectives might suspect if she blew their routine, now requiring a search for fictional characters. Disgruntled Former Associates, they said. Like Poor Mr. Lonelyhearts, all she could come up with but the detective took it for a description, nodding. Yes lonely people—even Poor Relations sometimes. Or Beneficiaries with Something to Gain. "Me," she said projecting funeral expenses while she waited for her sister's ship to come in. (That was the in-law with loot!) "My husband didn't insure his life." She would die, she thought, before they stopped. So she summoned all her spent underground strength, giving it the old Berrigan one two, the clean for Gene New Hampshire try, to switch the detectives off her fruitless past and onto the clear and present danger: the world where they were all hostage, hijacked, bombed, buggered by broomstick. "At random," she seized on the safe term, the best face to put on revolution. "Couldn't this have happened at random?"

Didn't everything nowadays? Friends came and went, got busy, got bored, changed addresses, jobs, even names but seldom themselves, and never that much. While any anonymous phone breather could get your number; any street-freak chemist mail a plastic letter. And poof, there went the perspiration of a lifetime. For Ireland or Palestine or just by mistake. Like on Eleventh Street or Oakland. Or Kent State. All the best places. Frequented by disgruntled Former Members of Society, Beneficiaries with Nothing to Lose. Nothing personal, old buddy.

But local fuzz and feds had different frames of reference, she discovered. Though it was always routine to check on known offenders, when it came to the Unchecked Unknown, city detectives mumbled statistics, conceding some change, a slight rise in percentages, but maintaining finally the old odds, three to one. In most homicides victims and perpetrators knew each other. Especially likely in the absence of forced entry, when nothing of value seemed to be missing.

Nothing . . .

They enumerated the nothings of value to drug addicts—TV, typewriter, and other appliances left in plain view, not to mention pills and pot. They cited the cash of value to everyone undisturbed in a tote bag, the jewelry of value to professional thieves left in a drawer, even on the victims. Twisting the place where her wedding band should have been, but for hospital security, Amy thought of its twin, still in place on Bob's finger when his life was taken. Violence was beyond no one.

Not when sex was involved, as the detectives were busily making clear, gazes averted, stoic voices droning on to enumerate the suggestive circumstances, the vandal fury vented on victims and property, making it impossible to rule out the oldest of theories—self-consciously pronounced—a Crime of Passion.

"Try the address book next door!" Amy's hoarse voice broke. "That's where it happened!" And where passions ran highest, love being young.

It was the next item on the agenda, anyhow. Any neighbor's opinion was valuable, even allowing for a widow's sudden urge to kill the dead. Over again. But Amy fought for her habit of cool, falling back on her own routine as she struggled to recall what Maude Lee had been before becoming The Other Woman. Fun in the beginning, and hard to resist always. But trouble finally, like all people who were passing.

Passing?

"For original," Bob said, first, for once, to pass judgment on the big statement in 14B. It was a pro's wrap-up of amateur ado—sound and light, he said, signifying nothing. His wife, the How To expert, wrapped up the rest for the detectives. "How to shock Daddy without losing your allowance. A nothing rebellion." Amy enumerated the nothings of value to Maude Lee but not the Foremans. Status career. Celebrity boss. Establishment background. Rad Chic friends. Even a Pseudo-Meaningful Relationship with an alleged Anti-Establishment Anti-Hero, who came on as uptight as any boy next door. A square at heart, when you got to know him.

"*Square?*" It was the first separate sound. The sharp questioner detached from the larger parent body—moving closer to pursue this unlikely description of Ned Nedders, unless the widow meant some other long-haired type with a claim. Or a key?

But she didn't. Not since the hippie helpers, when the only extra key she knew about was left with her, a security measure suggested by Bob during the big renovation. Once over, the key had been retrieved, perhaps for Nedders, though she had never seen him use one on either lock. He came and went at Maude Lee's bidding like her more Establishment dates, some at odd hours. Bob had tripped over an occasional embarrassed type on the way to work. Not lately though. Or often.

"Different men? Or the same?"

Amy shrugged. All cats were gray in the light. "Men look the same when they're caught out."

"The average guy, you mean . . . who doesn't want to be seen."

"Just laid."

"But from your husband's description, it could have been someone from her office."

"Or yours."

Maybe that did it. Or maybe it was routine to come on strong with multiple stab wounds, asking a sharp question for every sharp answer. As for instance: Did Amy have reason to believe her husband and Miss Evans were having a secret relationship?

"I have reason to believe the opposite."

Then why today of all days, would Mr. Foreman be found on Miss Evans' premises?

"Why not? She borrowed everything else."

As casual as that . . . ?

Wasn't everything?

But would the security-conscious Mr. Foreman have been casual enough to let himself be discovered in flagrante delicto with the top lock open?

"Not unless he was already dead."

So only Mr. Nedders could have walked in on them.

She shook her head. Why risk Nedders with safety so close? "You've seen our apartment." The Foremans had rooms and couches to spare. It didn't have to happen in either woman's bed.

But it had. So perhaps Nedders was expected . . . ?

"To join them in bed?" She almost laughed.

"It's been done."

Tell her about it.

"Things might have gotten out of hand, Mrs. Foreman."

Things certainly might have. If they let Nedders in for a scene like that.

"Would your husband have been a party to it—with any third person?"

So there it was. Cover up or come clean. Her own little Watergate. The pause that refreshed. She looked down at her leather address book.

"Not without me," she said. "Some of our best friends were Third Persons."

She threw it toward them, open, the book of false leads— full of couples who were interested in meeting other couples, the singles who were interested in everything. But love's young dream. Or dreamers making trouble—to the tinkling piano in the next apartment. Who needed Nedders? Most perpetrators knew their victims. Too well for that. Let Homicide dope it out, running around in circles, losing a murderer to break the swingers' code. She wasn't about to break it for them. That was the Foremans' bottom line. They leveled. About themselves and to each other.

"What's your name?" She looked past the sharpy to the parent body, with the kind of face that got beefy not lined, the one who looked married.

"Detective Sergeant Corio."

She didn't bother to put a name to the sharpy. What did sharpies know about love? Or whatever it was that lasted more than ten minutes. Ten years to be exact, counting the two when Bob just moved in. Amy borrowed the only honest thought she'd ever heard from her own mother on the subject: You walked off into the sunset, and then you beat the rap any way you could. "We called our way an open marriage. But the idea was to keep our act together, not break up somebody else's, or cheat on each other." The idea was to stay friends, despite being lovers—so nobody ended up out in the cold, or got left in the dark, to wonder forever. Not Bob, gone silently ahead. Not Amy doing the talking for both, as always. "You know how it is," she said to Corio. Either he did or he didn't. "You hang loose and it gets too Masters and Johnson. Or you hang tight until it gets too lonely. And that's how babies are born." Not to the Corios if Catholic. But the best laid plans for parenthood went awry, whether you used the rhythm method or did what came naturally. Good luck with naturally, if the baby came out on its elbows, ass over teakettle, ripping the best-rehearsed mother apart, until the best-rehearsed father screamed the place down for dope. . . .

"Oh my God." Her hazel eyes went wide. "That's how it happened!"

Surprisingly Corio was nodding, moving in sympathetically to agree. Pregnancy was a tough rap to beat. "As far as leaving each other out—"

"But we didn't!" Not like that. It wasn't what she meant.

"Yeah, but the first time, especially toward the end. Any guy could get himself in this type bind—"

"Not Bob!" Until today. Not Amy, clinging to Corio's hand and the Foremans' routine. He *had* to see.

"It wouldn't have to mean much," Corio said.

It meant everything. Her hoarse voice enumerated the everythings of importance to the Foremans—breathing the same breath, repeating the same mantra, keeping the same fast, swearing off the same distractions, straining the same muscles from the moment of conception to the bitter end when Amy gave out. And Bob got left, in the cold and dark with no one and nothing to go home to—not a drop, lift, trip in the whole pad. So he tried next door. However it ended, that's how it began.

Though it was hot broad daylight with every bar, liquor store, and trip parlor swinging when he left his wife. But Corio didn't mess with logic. The Sergeant must have seen it coming, already sitting on the bed, his arms ready to go around her almost before she flipped, really freaking out, beating on his chest, yelling, "It was the shot—it was the stinking shot!" While the sharp detective yelled for the nurse who misunderstood, yelling back that Mother wasn't down for more medication until Baby got fed, while Corio yelled at them both to shut up. And then the baby started. And Amy stopped.

"Give me my baby."

"Doctor wants Baby on schedule—"

"Mother's got the *Daily News* for Doctor—"

"Give her what she wants!" Corio rose, signaling the sharpy

to wait for him, though the nurse thought it would be better if Corio left too.

"Not until he and Mother have a cigarette." Also sworn off by the Foremans. "The Sergeant's seen a baby nurse before."

"I've even delivered a couple."

"Deliver me, Corio."

So he tried. He said, "You're grief-stricken. Don't add guilt." And passed her a lit cigarette over the baby's head.

"Thought for this week." But she never forgot it.

"Maybe your husband felt like a drink, maybe he didn't . . ."

"He said it . . . upstairs." Or was it later over the phone? Or in some dream? "Ask the nurse . . ."

Corio nodded. "We'll check it out. It could be very helpful establishing times. But feeling like a drink or a smoke's got nothing to do with getting a needle for a breach birth. *Capisce?*" He put his pack of cigarettes beside her and took the address book. "Don't overconnect—things just happen."

"At random . . ." It was a whisper; he leaned down to hear her, "That's my line . . ."

"That's life." He seemed to want to pet one of them, heavy hands brushing close to the baby. He murmured something about growing up gutsy as Mother to little Amy. But he had that wrong. Mother put him straight. "*I'm* little Amy," Amy said.

She looked down at the tiny pointed head which should have come first. Which would never be christened Amy, never christened anything. For all the sudden longing to believe it all again, to pretend Daddy's soul, winging to heaven, would meet Big Amy's, in on a pass. So it went unto the third and fourth generation—ego and myth growing back like cancer. Turn East for Enlightenment or West for Progress, if you couldn't make the distance you took the same shortcuts. Dope or the Dream. Maybe both. Praise the Lord and pass the anesthetic. Hers had been Episcopalian.

"In Daddy's house are many mansions," she lied to the baby. It was her favorite lie. "He has gone to prepare a place for us."

Sure he had. Or a needle. Gone to prepare something. "There," said the nurse. And the fix was in.

If it were not so, I would have told you.

"Wouldn't I, Corio?"

But Corio had left. And Nurse took Baby. With Bob gone, silence was nothing. Amy felt cold, felt herself falling. She called out once through paper walls, as she felt it all go, felt them all fall apart, despite all precautions—alone in the dark.

"Dom Perignon, yet! He sure bought her the best—but they didn't get to drink much." The Lieutenant's sarcastic voice droned on to whoever was phoning from Amy's hospital. As Lorrilard pressed his ear to the wall listening for his name. In vain. The big question next door was time. And Bob's champagne, left almost untouched in Maude Lee's kitchen, indicated an earlier interruption than originally supposed. Supported in the hall by the Deputy ME, as Lorrilard rushed shoeless to his peephole, to observe the medical team emerging from an hour's examination of the bodies. Lifted one by one to the dry bar counter, the under portions of both victims showed signs of puckering, common to bathers who had soaked too long in tepid water.

"Longer than it took you to get here?"

The Deputy ME nodded. "Matter of hours."

"How many? Two hours? Three?" The back of the Lieutenant's head blocked Lorrilard's view.

"Or more . . ." Allowing for any and all delays, Forensic's best preliminary guess put the time of death well before the moment of discovery, reported officially at 7:57.

Within five minutes of Ned's entrance, according to the super, who happened to be adjusting the air-conditioning unit directly overhead when he was alerted to investigate the emergency one flight down, as already confirmed with 15B's tenant.

A lady who had doubtless been quick to hand the super his pants, it seemed safe to surmise behind the closed door of 14H. But it would take a far nervier tenant than Lorrilard to blow the whistle on the henna-haired hooker and her arrangements with fixers rumored to include the Vice Squad. So Homicide struggled on unaided, grappling with the time factor that threatened to eliminate their star witness as suspect. Unless of course Ned Nedders had made an earlier visit to his girl's pad, before limping home, up his own stoop, suitcase in hand—an entrance not yet verified by neighborhood kids. Or timed to the minute by anybody.

"The suitcase sure would have come in handy," the Deputy ME said. And indeed Nedders' suitcase was the strongest point in favor of phoning the wild theory to Ned's questioners, best able to guess whether the witness had the cool to revisit the scene of such a crime.

"It wouldn't take much cool to walk a trunk *out*," the Lieutenant said. "Anybody could get past the security here. . . . Like this guy . . ." The great gray head suddenly turned, gray gaze seeming to bore through the peephole at the tenant, abruptly recalled to existence. Lorrilard shrank back, heart pounding. But almost at once the voices receded, official attention again distracted to the larger problem of getting the medical team out, past the press still waiting below Lorrilard's window, to be watched through the slats of his blinds until another arrival took precedence at the elevators. The Detective Sergeant of the Manhattan Homicide Task Force was heard returning from the widow's bedside to share a new problem with the Lieutenant of the 4th Homicide Zone. They called it Little Amy's Little Black Book, but the leather folder looked tan to Lorrilard, once again ready at the peephole when the rival chieftains approached 14B.

"Ten gets you five Little Amy's right—we'll find the answer in the other girl's book," the beefy Sergeant said, sounding almost resentful of Little Amy's competition, when he agreed with the Lieutenant's suggestion that they start with the names listed by both women. The respect accorded such a widow wasn't exactly routine, considering the extra legwork her open marriage might cause Homicide canvassers. Yet the very openness of Amy's book somehow earned her a note of sympathy, withheld from the victims. Especially the Other Girl, whose entire life style, by contrast, seemed designed as a hiding place. Maybe the perfect one for a murderer, the Lieutenant surmised, leading the way inside, grumbling something about a stash, or maybe it was cash, and something else about books . . . as the door closed.

Then silence fell, leaving Lorrilard to wonder if he'd be discovered in both books. Or only one. Or none, not even as Mr. Lonelyhearts—his whole joke existence left in abeyance by every contact he ever claimed, pretending friendship, like a left-out child, inventing playmates. Left to face another long night lurking, waiting the return of new tormentors, while still hoping for a sign from the old ones—one whispered hint by hearsay or phone—that his name too would somehow be protected in the company he stalked, from peephole to wall, listening for voices. Like a left-out child inventing ghosts.

Bruce McVitty IV had no problem deducing what was in a name. The value of his own had been deduced for him in the Blue Book at birth. And rededuced every fiscal year ever since by McVittys who adorned law partnerships as well as brokerage houses. Knowing exactly which name to call, Bruce flicked off the FM radio before the girl driving his open

Mercedes could finish gasping how sorry she was, how ghastly . . .

"Let's get off this goddamn expressway."

"Now?"

She braked from ninety to seventy—barefoot for God's sake. A cop could stop them. Bruce slipped his flask into her carry-all. "I have to find a phone booth."

"Well, but can't you wait till we get there?"

"We may have to go back, amigo."

"Oh *no* . . ."

"Sorry."

They had abandoned dinner plans in town to get an early start on the weekend. Forty-eight hours early to be exact, a decision made on the spur of the moment, the way Bruce did everything, like now looking for an exit from the fast lane with two to cut across.

"Because of this? I mean what can you do?"

"That's what I want to find out." From his uncle, the lawyer. If a dime could be found in his hundred-dollar chinos.

"Just because you *saw* her last night?"

"Not exactly . . ."

"Then *what?*"

"I know something," Bruce McVitty said.

The girl pulled off the expressway.

Benjie, the day doorman, knew something too. It was a discovery he wouldn't have made if he'd minded his own business when he took the envelope from her desk. Instead of helping himself to pot, lifting the bag so he saw something else. Something that stopped his clock. Looking right up at him from another one of those transparent drawers. There it was. This wild picture crammed in on top of some checks and junk. Crammed back now with Benjie's prints all over it. More prints on the drawer. Also on the switch for the spotlight over her bed where Benjie had gotten a better look, leaving his imprint everywhere. The whole wild picture flashed back as the picture of his building flashed on the TV screen, and he heard the word murder and her name, before his friend, the bartender, switched channels.

"Wait a minute—"

"It's just an early spot—we'll catch the news at eleven." The bar regulars, there for a rained-out game, wanted the bowling.

"Geeze, will you leave it—that's where I work!"

So all heads turned to watch the rest on the set suspended over the bar. The regulars whistled when they heard how the girl in Benjie's building got hers in bed with a neighbor, discovered by an unnamed boyfriend, flashed on briefly while the regulars laughed, kidding Benjie did he ever get a piece? Some job *he* had! Some building!

But Benjie sat there silent, hands frozen around his beer glass, wishing he'd kept his hands to himself, hadn't said anything, hadn't known all day something like this would happen sooner or later, when her hippie boyfriend came around with that key of his. The super had been right all along. She was asking for it.

The lawyer with the unfamiliar name and accent accepted charges from Mr. Mac. Or was it Big Mac, he asked, sounding amused by the subterfuge Bruce used instead of his famous McVitty name and the credit cards that went with it.

"From what your uncle told me, you're both worrying too much, Mac. That is if you told your uncle the whole story."

"More or less."

"Better tell me more."

"Well, there's no problem about today—I mean I haven't been alone since I left the office—"

"Then there's no problem."

"Except for coming up with the price of her abortion!"

Bruce hadn't explained the loan quite so baldly to his uncle, but it met with no surprise from this lawyer.

"Nothing illegal about abortions—this week."

"Nothing too kosher about it either."

The unexpected term met with a chuckle. Though the news wasn't going to sound too amusing over the Mercedes radio. Not to the girl Bruce said he was practically engaged to, sitting a few feet away in his open sports car, androgynous head capped tight in dark hair, white face turned toward the transparent phone booth.

"She's sitting pretty compared to the Evans girl," the lawyer said, invoking a softer silhouette in Bruce's memory. He kicked the door open, which got rid of the damn light. But it didn't help him breathe any easier.

"That's the best we can do—live through a scandal?"

"There's a crowd ahead of you in the headlines, Mac."

"Amigo—our crowd wants out of the whole story!"

The lawyer sighed. "The girl's the story. Always. And this girl's your crowd—"

"Not anymore." Never, really. "They're calling her a career girl on the radio."

"And when they catch wise who her father's married to, they'll call her an heiress."

"*Heiress!*" This time Bruce almost laughed himself as he often had with her. Laughed till they cried last night. Her great expectations in the will drawn up by his uncle, the lawyer, were such a joke.

A sick joke now. "Some heiress . . ."

"The best of families have black sheep." The lawyer's voice sounded like a shrug. "So the line formed on her left, you weren't on line—"

"Now wait—"

"—except for old times' sake. Isn't that what you're saying?"

"Not about Leesy!"

"Who?"

"That's what we used to call her . . . Ms. Evans." But it came too late, that silly title preferred by the Leesy he used to call, only yesterday. He choked on it. "Oh Christ, why did I jump the gun? She wasn't even sure—and now it's going to help cover her in shit . . ."

"Stop that, Mac—just hold the phone! Take a deep breath, and *listen*, y' got me?" The accent had to be pure Bronx, or Brooklyn, one of those places, but there was U. S. Steel in the guttural advice, worthy of McVitty partnership. "The worst that could happen to that girl has happened. Finito. Over and out. There's no way you can help or hurt anybody now, but a killer. And maybe yourself, depending how you handle your situation. All you gotta decide is whether you want brownie points for leveling about something Homicide knows already. Unless she cashed that check today . . ."

"No," Bruce found his voice, "she wouldn't." In the unlikely event she knew she had it. Even Bruce wasn't sure where he'd tucked it. Vanity? See-through desk? Tote bag?

"Doesn't matter, you know you wrote it. And the price is right if they find out tomorrow she's pregnant. Automatic in this type autopsy—"

"OK, OK!" Bruce didn't want to hear about the autopsy. "So I better not let it go for the weekend."

"Depends, Mr. Mac. I don't think Homicide can let it go." The lawyer sounded tired. "See, every guy in town who knew her is gonna head for the hills, pretending he didn't. Wanna know who really gets covered in shit?—it's detectives. Now you save them yours, save 'em a trip or a toll call, hell save 'em five minutes, and you'll come on more like a friend of the family. And maybe the department. Any friend of the department could get a break in the papers . . ."

"Then let's get it over with. Tonight, OK? Just give me enough time to get back and grab a sandwich . . ."

"And find your way. It's on the West Side—amigo." There was a hint of a sting somewhere under the words, almost too subtle for a Wasp to feel, as the lawyer spelled out his Latinate name, pronounced for the first time correctly. "Say you're Mr. Mac, meeting me on a precinct matter if you run into any flak. I'll mosey on ahead and meet you there. So long as I know *everything* I ought to . . ."

There was a pause too slight for the smartest lawyer to be sure.

"See you in two hours," Bruce answered.

The bartender couldn't get a straight word out of Benjie, known as a dreamer since high school, but never this spooked.

"I'm not going in tomorrow, Art."

"C'mon . . . sure you are."

"Not going back at all if you really wanna know."

"Easy . . . I'll get you a refill."

But every time a full beer was placed on the bar, Benjie's grip just froze on the glass again.

"I'm not even callin' in my notice."

"That's great. That's really smart. Don't call them, they'll call you."

Benjie shook his head. He had given the super his mother's number in Hillside. "All the old lady knows, I got a room off the boulevard—"

"Benj, will you shut up and drink your beer?" The bartender leaned forward, voice low, one eye on the other regulars. "Think the cops can't find a goddamn doorman? Like you're the only one ever had something going for a tenant? So she teased you along—so now and then you got a feel—"

"I got her keys today—"

"You left 'em there, man! You've been sittin' on that bar stool since you got off work. All you did, you walked her dog."

The stubborn head shook again. "That wasn't all."

"OK, what—helped yourself to a shot?"

Worse. "A joint."

"How're they gonna prove it—if you flushed the roach?"

"From the bag, Art—she left it laying right out in the open."

"So maybe it's gone altogether now—you don't know where it is!"

But not for one wild moment could Benjie entertain such hope about the other places he'd left his mark.

"I laid on the bed . . ."

"So did half the town." Or so it sounded to the bartender, though admittedly only Benjie had done it in a doorman's uniform, leaving fibers the dreamer was convinced the police labs had ways of detecting.

"Jesus God! Two tons of water, and blood all over—and you got a fiber problem!" The bartender sounded disgusted as he noted a couple of the other things police labs would be testing for in the watery bed between the mirrors. But Benjie was worried about just that, having shot his dreamy wad, lying where she lay, turning on . . .

More ways than one, as the bartender guessed, finally shaking his own head. "Picked a swell day to take your gloves off."

The blood mottled in Benjie's face, as each complication that compromised him led to a more humiliating admission of dreams defeated, dismally concluded in the john, leaving more prints when he shut the door on her randy damn dog, trying to get into the act, turning Benjie off . . .

Ditto the bartender. "*Dog*, for Chrissake—what kind of kinky scene did that girl have going?"

It was exactly the question Benjie had been asking himself ever since he saw the photograph that lured him to her bedside spotlight.

"She was in it, Art."

"In the nudie shot—herself?" The bartender whistled. "You sure?"

Benjie nodded. "The other face was blurry. But I know hers." As he now knew her body, so long imagined, felt so seldom, but naked under her dress today, nipples hard against his arm, when she called him an angel. Well, now the angel had gotten the rest of the picture, seen how it would have been with the full breasts naked, falling forward, touching him. "She was on top."

"Of one of these guys . . . ?" The bartender gestured toward the TV, but Benjie's head was shaking again.

"Well, but Christ, Benj, if it was blurry—how could you tell?"

Benjie, the dreamer, looked down at his hands curled around the glass, cold hands that hung useless from the sleeves of his uniform, never reaching except for the door, or the leash, or the goddamn photograph of those bodies, wasted on each other.

"It wasn't that blurry."

The bartender didn't seem convinced. "Yeah, well your police labs got ways of blowing up pictures too. Better let them decide which guy it was."

For the last time Benjie shook his head.

"Why the hell not?"

He looked up. The friends' eyes met.

"Because it wasn't a guy," Benjie said.

The media crowd almost missed its own news. Having hyped the year of the woman for months, the VP of PR spent the early evening living down the whole issue, dead anyway at the network, even before the woman of the year made her farewell appearance as a window display. He did his best to help the press forget, leading them directly up Sixth to the Plaza Gold Room, where a more official high level blast had been laid on. Unfortunately neither the East Coast host nor the West Coast guest of honor put in reassuring appearances. Instead Israel phoned Weldon's apologies from Gracie Square, where the old man, borne home in a taxi, no longer felt up to leaving for the country in the blue Eldorado, piled high with his wife's packages, below the Plaza windows. When the message was relayed discreetly, to young Mrs. Weldon at the caterer's bar, she tossed her coarse mane of Mellow Ash hair and gave discretion the horselaugh. The second big one of the evening.

"So Israel gets to put Daddy to bed and Baby gets the chauffeur!" she brayed, PR not being her specialty either, though she tilted a mean pelvis for the paparazzi. So the press was all but surfeited with blonde bombshell body language by the time Charlie Collins showed up again, fresh from a shower, to face another long night with Israel, though Evans' hassle had apparently made him too late to retrieve a fresh suit from the cleaners. Not that it mattered. Even in rumpled seersucker, Charlie looked pretty good to his former boss, sweating scotch until he saw a way to kill two birds with one stone. Or two studs with one bird.

"Why don't you meet Israel up at the Weldons'? If she'll let you see her home." The VP of PR pointed to young Mrs. Weldon, starting on her second carafe of sangria, specially prepared, from scratch. It seemed her tastes ran to complicated mixes on the theory—now being expounded to the press—that the best things in life were a trick to make. But Charlie was the trick she hadn't met yet, a welcome addition to the ranks of dance captains among her husbands' weary troops. Also he spoke her language.

Pelvis tilted to pelvis on sight. "Why don't we just take the party to Israel? I hear he's fun at parties," Mrs. Weldon teased as if she hadn't also heard that the kind of parties Israel was fun at were not given in executive suites of gold. Nor could they be transported to Mrs. Weldon's town house like the carafe of sangria she thrust at Charlie. Not tonight anyway. Charlie teased back with his eyes, but kept his tone deferential as he reminded her of the gap between bumbling youth and the VP in residence at Gracie Square. "Isn't the old man there? I mean . . . Mr. Weldon . . ."

She only laughed, savoring youth's bumbles. "Might as well be old."

"Wouldn't a party disturb him?"

"It wouldn't matter to Daddy if we had it in his room!"

That was news. She took a sip of her drink as she took Charlie's arm, obviously meaning to take it all—glass, sangria, and stud—home to Daddy.

Charlie remained doubtful. "If you're sure he won't mind . . ."

"Ask him." He talked. He walked. Maybe he minded. "But he doesn't remember." She pressed her braless breast against Charlie's second-best seersucker sleeve rubbing harder with every rhythmic step, one of his own tricks in reverse. He almost wished Evans were here to catch the exit and get a laugh. Mrs. Weldon paused at the door as if sensing his message. It was like that sometimes with body language. She licked her lips as she looked at Charlie's.

"Someone you want to bring?"

"Not here."

"There's a phone in the car."

It was still light when they left, that much everyone agreed on afterward. Even the VP of PR watching from the window as the sharp-looking chauffeur ushered his charges smartly into that custom-built back seat. The VP wondered if Charlie would catch that sharp look under the visor, and try to warn her about the smart eyes reflected in the rear-vision mirror. Only to be laughed at, even Charlie, to be told he sounded just like Daddy, poor Daddy, who still hadn't figured out why

it only happened here, as she slipped to the floor, threshold of
so many blown promotions.

The VP of PR felt too lonely to go home, too tired to sleep
anywhere, too old to freeload with the free press, too spent to
spring for some Junior Ms. on the make to be Maude Lee
Evans. Or Mrs. Weldon. What difference? He moved away
through the Junior Mr.'s, the assistant associates—dregs that
took over at parties like this when the brass didn't show to be
polished. He wanted out of the thrown-together rooms that
were meant to be gold. He needed the dark of the Oak Room
Bar, where a man could buy his own goddamn drinks. Could
but didn't. Though he was far from calling for the company
tab when his friendly colleague, the Deputy Commissioner of
Police PR, finally caught up with him. To be hailed as ol'
buddy. As so often before when ol' buddies met to ponder
some bullshit cop show about Woman in Jeopardy, favorite
media victim, of this and every year, now come home to roost
with a vengeance.

The Deputy Commissioner needed a drink. Almost as badly
as the VP of PR needed coffee when they moved to a private
table where the veteran visitor of the city's most celebrated
bad scenes bore shaken witness to the worst one. Though the
Deputy Commissioner had been there before, seen other career girls wasted in their beds, knew all the extra shockers the
police kept out of the headlines. But not this time, with hysterical civilians phoning in the details, not just about her, but
the other body. You couldn't blame civilians. No man who'd
seen it would be likely to forget what had happened to the
man.

"What man?" The coffee cup rattled, as the shakes seemed
to pass from buddy to buddy.

"Some guy she had in the building . . ." The hand that put
the drink down had steadied. "After she got through in the
office . . ."

Neither buddy was in PR for nothing. But a cop was always a cop. And this cop had come from a vision of hell via the Plaza suite party, where The Upstairs gossip about what happened in The Bar Downstairs was easily traded for the sobering facts—hard news needed by the press boys, to run with their pictures of the woman scorned. Until the diggers got the real dirt—the private reason for the public putdown.

"What was it? An office romance?"

"Nothing like that . . ." The VP waved away the dirt with a shaking hand. True, boys might be boys upstairs and down. But the kinky sex implicit in the murder could not connect Maude Lee Evans' private life with Austin Phelps. Hastily identified as her boss and mentor, solely responsible for both her career and behavior. While certain lines could still be drawn, certain distinctions made artfully clear. To distinguish the real network power brokers (with their office doxies). From the free-lance temperaments (with their artistic differences) forever going too far as artists will. In the creative area where talent really lived.

"It sure as hell isn't where this girl died! And the way it times out, your boys kissed her off. That was her next to last stop."

At first the VP of PR didn't want to buy the bluff, knowing from their many confabs that only in bullshit cop shows did Medical Examiners make instant autopsies, calling it that fast or close. Nor did real life deputy commissioners, always cops, drop hints and theories like some viewer of bullshit medical shows, waiting to second-guess the late news about the city's first water bed murder case.

"Water helps. Now what happened there after she left?"

What always happened? The brass went up in smoke. But the smoke-screen cover for a fast mass exit wasn't going to be enough. The bluff had teeth, cutting off retreat behind lines and distinctions, all to be connected—by time, the first and strongest link. Reporters asked Who, but cops asked When, then Where. As for example: when and where had the network Who's Who gone? Homicide had some such questions. And the PR Commissioner recommended fast answers. Now, starting at the top—where the girl had ended. And where, all PR VP's knew, co-operation must always be pretended. "I don't know who we'll find tonight, old buddy. Most of the brass commutes."

"After a party?" The drink was finished. "Want to check it out?"

Once secure in the privacy of a phone booth, the VP wasn't planning to talk art when he tried to find Phelps at his house in the country. But it didn't answer. Nor were there any answers at Kelly's hotel—though the producer had fled the fracas with his star. Leaving only the outsider Billy Bee Bernard at The Bar Downstairs, where he was doubtless still telling all to his Boswell, another goddamn reporter. So there was nothing to do but dial Gracie Square, unbriefed, letting the private line ring in the master bedroom where the master programmer lay waiting to be programmed, probably in a blackout and half undressed by Israel. A mutual out, needed as an alibi even by Weldon, the first brutal fact to bring home. Until the legal department could really get their act together. And invoke every clause, revoke every contract, cancel every project that could possibly associate the men at the top with a lost lady's cause, revived from overkill, smelling mighty like a motive. . . . There was the sound of a phone being dropped and then the old man's voice came on, thick with phlegm.

"Israel . . . ?"

"No, sir—Scooper." It threw him. "Israel's not there?" Swept away with Charlie in Baby's blue Eldorado, but where?

A pause followed as if for a search, presumably through the old man's head.

"Dropped me off—said he'd check in . . ."

"Yes, sir, he did check in—"

"No, no, no . . ." The phlegm was cleared, and a couple of brain cells. "Check with me, not you. About that girl . . ."

"The *Evans* girl?"

"Can't have that, Scooper. Not this year. Israel agrees. Sent him after her."

Israel Gold. Sent after Evans. By Old Man Weldon.

Who would have thought a token had so much blood in her? Not the VP hoist by his own PR as a press agent's dream turned nightmare.

"Maudley . . . Maudley . . ."

Israel was murmuring the wrong name, near the highest moment of his craziest kick, the kind that only happened when he drank like this. Which was why he seldom did it in L.A. with Dotty, the downer, always waiting to be faced. And was careful even in New York off limits. But tonight limits were beyond controlling. One bombshell had set him off, set him up for the other in this private bar peepshow, where this substitute image was smiling for *him*, wildly writhing . . .

"Jeeezus!" it said. And became Mrs. Weldon.

"There you are . . ." Old Man Weldon's voice echoed down the shadowy stair well.

Israel jumped off the bar stool so fast he knocked it over. On the other side of the bar Charlie Collins leapt clear of Mrs. Weldon and grabbed for the blender, zooming the motor in his frantic pretense to mix drinks, one-handed. Mrs. Weldon, having no zippers to contend with, got her diaphanous silks together more efficiently. When her hands appeared above the bar, each held a glass.

"For Chrissake, Daddy, you wanna give us a coronary?" Her face was chalk. But then Israel remembered the powder she wore. Only the fantasy had been tanned and shining, sweet skin flushing, angrily clear. Israel stooped to right the bar stool, not anxious to face reality in either direction. Behind him, but coming closer, Mr. Weldon was clearing his phlegmy throat, starting to cough, murmur apologies.

"What the hell are you doing, wandering around like that—?" And then Mrs. Weldon laughed. "In *my* robe!"

Straightening, Israel turned to see the old man pause in the double doorway of the softly lit living room. Mr. Weldon gazed down at himself, bemused. He had indeed groped behind the wrong sliding door in the long hall of closets between the Weldons' bedrooms, where he dropped the pants Israel had loosened, kicking away the silk drawers, impatient to find her before the world closed in on them, as he heard the sexy cassette downstairs and pulled on the first thing that came to hand. His wife's winter best, moiré and marabou. It hung loose and open as it did on her, but to somewhat different effect. The marabou edging started below the sunburn line, traveling up to frame the flabby white section usually covered by flapping trunks, dramatizing the dark source of power between Mr. Weldon's skinny legs—la petite différence, which in this case was grande. Grander—in fact even than Charlie, who gasped in envy, before pretending to laugh with Mrs. Weldon, murmuring proudly, "*Get Daddy . . .*" Even Weldon smiled sheepishly at the inside joke, known so long it didn't have to be proved. She could do no better—all that and money too! Only Israel remained silently unsmiling, trapped by the terrible secret of smallness. Until Mr. Weldon looked up and the bemused smile faded. As he remembered what he *was* doing there. "Oh God . . ." He gestured toward the bar. "Think I better join you . . ."

"For *what*, Daddy?" The diaphanous silk gaped wide as she leaned invitingly across the bar.

"Whatever you're having . . ."

She laughed. But the moiré and marabou closed firmly as Mr. Weldon sank on the petit-point love seat he preferred.

"Another stinger, coming up," Charlie babbled, already pouring it, anxious to escape, not realizing she still had him trapped until she winked and reached again for the zipper, while Israel, laughing, took the glass, his white teeth flashing, the substitute weapon to guard a small secret, as he glided toward the love seat, all shark again.

"Thanks." Mr. Weldon took the deepest swallow possible before putting his question. "You came back?"

"We wouldn't let him go—caught Israel just in time, didn't we, Charlie?" Charlie's answering murmur was so full of alarm, Israel frowned toward the bar, not wanting anything to start without him.

"I only got as far as the hack stand—"

"That's too bad," Mr. Weldon said, wondering if perhaps it was better. As Israel was hastening to add. But better for whom?

"The phone was off the hook, anyway—it'll cool down by tomorrow."

"No."

But Israel didn't seem to want to know why not, anxious to resume his grandstand seat on the bar stool as Charlie's alarm grew more audible.

"You're *crazy* . . ." Charlie still didn't believe it could be happening. Almost had for a voyeur's benefit, he was not about to be had to spite the Boss, an aging cuckold coming down from a binge, sitting there abandoned to thoughts of death. Saved, all of them, only by the doorbell, staying even Mrs. Weldon's hand.

"I'll get it—" Charlie cried, this time really jumping clear of her, zipping up as he made an end run around the bar, past Israel's high stool, Weldon's love seat, thanking God as he fled that the damn staff was in the country, that she'd shown him how to throw switches for lights and alarms before shooting open bolts. Left unshot by Israel and Weldon himself, now abruptly raising his phlegmy voice, just enough to reach everyone, at the last moment, before the door could be opened.

"The Evans girl was knifed to death in her apartment. They found her at eight. With some man . . ."

It was all anyone had to know about the murder, and might be afraid to ask. But go prove conspiracy. Charlie had all he could do to register the announcement that sounded like a warning, before he found himself again facing his former boss. The VP of PR ushered in the others, trooping silent as mourners, into the living room to be introduced as the Deputy Commissioner of this, the Detective Sergeant of that. . . . While the VP of PR got a load of the cast from the double doorway, and hung back with Charlie for an instant's exchange of whispers in the hall.

"Where the hell was Israel when you got here?"

"Outside—"

"Going or coming?"

"Looking for a taxi—"

"To see the Evans girl?" Charlie just gaped. "Did he mention going there? Anything about her?"

Charlie shook his head. He had forgotten hearing the murmured name, mispronounced at the bar, until he heard Israel mispronounce it again. Mrs. Weldon, dazed, seemed not to notice, seeking the safety of Daddy's love seat, where diaphanous silk and marabou-trimmed-moiré were drawn together, clutched closed against this awful intrusion—tale of blood thinning to water, rumor of rape, hint of castration.

It was, as Israel said, a helluva way to find out about Maudley.

Hearing the echo of his own murmur, Israel darted a glance from Mrs. Weldon to Charlie, standing in the doorway staring back in fear at the sea green eyes, as Israel repeated himself, teeth flashing this time. Helluva way, wasn't it, Charlie? To find out about Maudley. (Maudley . . . Maudley . . .)

Charlie did not know which froze him more, Israel or Weldon. The sick shark or the blacked-out old jock, stuck with covering for each other on their awful trips into nowhere—when either of them could have done almost anything. While Charlie himself, waiting his own turn, wondered if his former boss, the VP of PR, would cover for a change in that cover story—about not changing to a fresh suit: Charlie's best seersucker left hanging in his closet, since he got it back from the cleaners—the last time he went home. Tuesday . . .

It was a helluva way to find out, all right. About a lot of things.

Good Guy and Bad Guy were playing Go Back You Didn't Say May I. All the way back to Ned's exit from the foundation, which seemed at first a welcome relief from rehashing his entrance to 14B. He found it comparatively easier to recall what he had done with himself and his gear, dragged in and out of phone booths and subways, before he finally climbed his stairs to start dialing busy signals. But as the rehash went around and around, he began to tire of the subject of his dirty laundry, left spilling over from his open suitcase or strewn in his wake, all of it to be collected for an overdue trip to the laundromat today, or so he had thought when he dropped it where it lay. Before the subject became of sufficient interest to charge admission, if Good and Bad Guys wanted to come along and see for themselves while he retrieved his tapes and books to go to Billings' place—still thinking automatically of pressing on somehow to work, pressing on somewhere, if day ever broke. The detectives themselves seemed tired enough to take him up on the excuse for an exit, when they were all suddenly interrupted. A detective with a face like a red brick wall looked in to say that the rest of the squad was back, and the Lieutenant had some questions in his office.

The Lieutenant also had another witness—this one with a

lawyer, a surprising combo seen from the door, if anything
could surprise Ned anymore. Homicide was a great leveler. It
had leveled the likes of Bruce McVitty IV to the kind of
mouthpiece who wore a shantung suit and sweated through it.
Ned did not have long to wonder what someone so mahvelous
was doing in a spot like this, surrounded by fuzz, out on their
feet, leaning against walls. Except for the Lieutenant seated in
shirt-sleeves behind his desk, both other available chairs occupied by visitors. Until McVitty rose to make an awkward
pass at shaking Ned's hand, still clutching the bloodstained
shirt.

"Sorry, amigo . . ."

A camera bulb flashed in the dark of Ned's mind. Somewhere in the endless friendless night the word for friend had
rung falsely before.

Bad Guy had heard it too, muttering that everyone was
amigos all of a sudden. Unfortunately, the witnesses' mutual
amigo at Chase Manhattan remained a faceless cipher, with
results that seemed about to fray the whole department's pa-
tience, since the cipher whose name no one ever quite caught
had returned the favor by forgetting Bruce McVitty's. An em-
barrassment to the lawyer in shantung, who knew that no
matter who you and your uncle were, you could not call your
alibi what's-his-face, or even the amigo who walked el doggo.
Though the bank teller would not otherwise have been recognized on the street today, or amiably allowed to fill an empty
space between the brokerage partner's squash game and dinner date. A crucial space as it turned out when a detective
dispatched to the scene phoned back that the unannounced
visitor trailing Bruce McVitty remained as invisible to the vast
staff on Sutton Place as at lesser home addresses. Where Ned
now was the last hope of a witness.

"I had a drink with this guy you saw outside Leesy's," Bruce prodded anxiously for a ray of memory. "You know, he's always around—lives across the hall."

"Oh yeah," Ned said. "Lonelyhearts."

"That's it—that's what Leesy always called him!" Bruce turned triumphantly to his lawyer, no longer amused by the insy names in Big Mac's crowd, which were now turning what should have been a piece of cake into a trap instead of an interview. Especially since Ned like everyone else had looked right through the tenant of 14H.

"Doesn't mean he wasn't there," Ned said, a wrap-up of Lorrilard, who ended as himself in the files, an alibi left hanging on a stanchion, even by the fuzz whose turn it served to postpone the whole question of Mr. Lonelyhearts until tomorrow's canvassing. Some aliases fit. Some didn't. What had been provided in the confusion was sufficient leverage to bull past a lawyer, and play off the Friend of the Family against the Lover. So that the check made out to the deceased by the former could be shown to the latter, along with the tag identifying the evidence as a loan for an abortion. While the Lieutenant asked, in reasonable tones, which if either of the gentlemen present had made the lady pregnant.

The lawyer in shantung reacted first. "My client has no knowledge that she was—"

"He has more knowledge than her boyfriend."

As if by way of illustration, the blood drained obligingly from the Lover's face, as it rose under the Family Friend's tan.

"You were out of town . . ." Bruce started to explain but he didn't get far with Good Guy and Bad Guy.

"He wasn't out of touch!" They hardly needed their notes to reel off the number of Ned's calls picked up by the service—while his girl was out getting McVitty drunk enough to hit up for bread.

"It wasn't like that—!" Bruce protested. "*I* called *her*—on the spur of the moment."

Bad Guy almost groaned. Another boy scout. How did these guys think the girl got herself murdered?

The Lieutenant frowned. "Let's stick to McVitty's version."

"We just stayed out later than we meant to, but she was damn upset to miss Ned's call—"

"Because she wanted to tell him this problem?"

"She didn't say—in so many words . . ."

"Did she say it was his?"

"Well, I knew they were going together . . ."

"What about six months ago—the last time it happened?"

"*Nothing* happened!" Bruce couldn't look at Ned. "I told you, it was a false alarm—"

"Did she give back that loan?"

"There wasn't any loan . . . she didn't need it."

"She didn't need it this time either."

The Lieutenant reached for a tagged manila envelope and emptied the contents on his desk.

Money. It poured out. Some bills fluttering down separately, others in wads, every item tagged with the name of the book where it had been hidden. Even the pennies from her I Ching were visible in a separate glassine envelope, the only stash Ned knew about except for pin money, shifted from book to book, petty cash, not the kind that added up to a giant petty issue between lovers, like those big bills Daddy left, one or two C notes blown after each visit. . . . Yet here were five, six, seven . . . fluttering down on wads of fifties, as Ned lost count of the amount she had hoarded, for all her endless talk of debt.

And perpetual carelessness about cashing in her assets, or depositing checks, often losing those sent as gifts, holding others meant as loans, reconsidered but seldom returned, just left outstanding in screwed-up checkbooks like Bruce McVitty's. To be canceled and explained away by accountants, frowned on by lawyers at auditing showdowns while officialdom guessed the worst.

"Looks like she cashed a few other Johns' checks . . ." the Lieutenant said.

"Why Johns?" Stung, the Friend of the Family ignored both his lawyer's signals and prior knowledge to bluster a defense of blotted escutcheons. "Why not her family?" *Everyone* knew the Evanses had a fortune. "Leesy didn't need Johns, if she wanted to be supported—"

"She supported herself!" Ned exploded, his first real release of rage, triggered at last, not by murder most foul, or fouler sex, but filthy lucre—contradicting himself to defend what he hated, the money she made. "She earned enough to cash her own checks. Forget her family—and the damn fortune!"

"Like you did, Mr. Nedders? Looking the other way?"

"She was making it, man! She had a great job. Ask the network!"

But Detective Sergeant Corio of the Homicide Task Force had already tried. He introduced himself, filling the Lieutenant's doorway, his deep voice filling the room with the news of her jeopardized job blown sky high at a press conference for the brass.

"Up the brass!" Ned said, having heard it from her often enough. "Ask her boss—he's the only brass she respected."

"Can't find him, Sonny," Corio said affably, "if you mean the one she called Father."

The one who looked down so paternally, leonine head held quizzically sideways against a raised shoulder, as she smiled up in adoration . . . while Ned watched, waiting in the lobby, waiting outside her office, at her parties. . . . A warning darker than jealousy tugged somewhere else in beleaguered memory. But Bad Guy jumped in, to suggest that she might not have leveled about trouble on her job, if she hadn't thought to worry her boyfriend about recurring fears of having a baby.

"She'd never have told me that—she knew I'd want it!"

"Even if it was his?" Bad Guy jerked a thumb at McVitty, but the lawyer in shantung was already on his feet. "My client doesn't have to submit to this—I advised him to co-operate voluntarily as a friend of the family—"

"*Then let him do it.*" The Lieutenant towered over his desk at the window, ballast for Sergeant Corio, towering at the door. The Lieutenant still had some questions about the Friend of the Family's lingering visit in the deceased's apartment. And he wanted the lover to hear the answers.

"Why didn't you just drop her home last night—when it got so late?"

"I told you—that's when we really talked."

"You couldn't talk, drinking at P.J.'s for three hours?"

"There were other people . . ." And then Lonelyhearts butting in, on top of Ned's messages. "She was still upset—"

"So upset she turned on?"

"My client has no recollection—"

"Now, goddammit Orisino, this is material evidence," the Lieutenant thundered at the lawyer. "We found grass laying out there with her cassettes. Did the witness see it, or didn't he?"

"Yes," Bruce said. "But she brought it out afterward."

"When the other guy left?"

Bruce nodded.

"Where from?"

"The top of the piano."

"That jibe with your knowledge of her habits, Nedders?"

"Yes." It was the first thing that did.

"All this time—no dinner?" And until today no groceries stocked.

"There was some cake—in her refrigerator."

"Cake? A girl with a medicine cabinet full of diet pills?"

"It was for Ned coming home." That too jibed with Ned's knowledge of her habits though no one asked him.

"So she had Ned's cake—and you ate it. And then you left, Mr. McVitty?"

"Well, a little later . . ."

"How much?"

"I didn't check the time."

"Late like this—" The Lieutenant turned toward the window where the rest of the black world was turning gray. "Light outside?"

"I didn't notice—"

"Because of her blinds? Or were you too high?"

"I don't remember . . ."

"How about when you got downstairs?"

"I guess . . . it could have been just getting light . . ."

The Lieutenant sighed. "Mr. McVitty, do you recall seeing the super mopping up in her lobby. Or the doorman from the morning shift in yours?"

There was a pause. Bruce could not even look at the lawyer, subsided again into the chair, every line of the body under the shantung silently protesting the indignity of being surprised by his own client's withheld story.

"All right," Bruce said. "I spent the night. But I just passed out—"

"Where did you wake up?"

"On the bed. But fully dressed—"

"What about her?"

"Under the covers—"

"Wearing what?"

"Zero," her lover said quietly. "If you're still jibing with her regular habits."

"Ned," the Friend of the Family began, "I swear nothing happened—"

"How the hell do you know?" the Lieutenant interrupted. "Want to try and pass a polygraph there was no sexual contact—"

"I must advise my client he's under no obligation—"

"How about you?" The Lieutenant turned to Ned. "You still sure enough of your girl to take a polygraph she wouldn't cheat?"

The time for polygraphs was long gone, unless more than her spirit could be revived to lie beside him demanding his solemn sacred word on past and future . . .

"I will if you will," Ned said to the Lieutenant.

"I didn't know the lady."

"You know your own, don't you? You want to take a polygraph you've always been sure your woman wouldn't cheat?"

There was a beat, then an almost physical reaction, a barely perceptible move toward Ned, a reminder of rumors about things that could happen when there was no lawyer in stationhouse back rooms.

Only the man behind the desk remained immovable, betraying nothing, the hand that might have shown a ring shoved in the pocket of the shapeless pants, while the Lieutenant gazed at Ned through one-way glass. No one saw through those eyes but the Lieutenant.

"The woman I'm sure of," he said, "was never afraid to have a baby. She gave birth to three. No one ever had to ask whose they were. Nobody cut her open trying to find out—"

"Shut up—" Ned yelled.

"Nobody got deballed because she was doing them—"

"Fuck off—"

"Suck off, you mean—"

Bruce grabbed Ned before he could go over the Lieutenant's desk. "God Almighty—isn't it enough he saw what he did?"

"You would think so, wouldn't you?" the Lieutenant said. "You'd really think so."

Then he turned his back and looked out the window.

"Let's wrap it up, Chief—" Detective Sergeant Corio suggested softly. "We know where to find these gentlemen."

No one said a word in the unmarked car, Bad Guy driving this time, and remaining downstairs, so that Good Guy, left alone with the witness as they climbed the four flights, had a chance to break the silence and put things straight.

"Listen, Ned, the Lieutenant's a widower."

"Sure he is."

"God's truth. Childbirth—the third time."

"You should have let me guess."

"Nothing to kid about."

"Takes one to kid one."

Good Guy reserved his reaction to that, waiting out the unlocking, to have a good look around at the laundry while Ned collected some books and tapes, though quite beyond pressing on anymore, anywhere, except to escape the detectives.

"Satisfied?"

"For now."

"For good," Ned said. "Or next time I'll bring a lawyer." Not the expensive kind in shantung, but Billings had a friend in law school who had a friend in legal aid. There had to be some help somewhere.

Good Guy hesitated by the door. "Let me give you a tip. You're buying trouble for nothing with the whole squad—taking this type of attitude."

"Thank your lieutenant."

Good Guy shrugged. "You shouldn't have put your girl in with his wife."

Of all the deep wounds inflicted that night, the glancing exit line festered most. Possibly it satisfied the department sense of chivalry. But the best of the good guys didn't leave much in Ned.

Rough Cut

Nobody stopped to wonder if Nannie Bernstein Phelps could make another Maude Lee Evans. Not at first. They needed all the help they could get at 11 A.M. on Black Thursday at Boring Rock, when yesterday's great no-nonsense dame sailed off the elevator and right through the press siege on the twenty-first floor. The network's own newshounds barely spotted her before she passed, walking tall on those marvelous long legs, calling "Hi fella" in the same old way, with a wave of white gloves. Who but Nannie carried those anymore? The VP of PR did not care, gratefully returning that signal from the past. While the receptionist, shaken and young, just figured Nannie for a wife with class. And the wit not to drop her VP name. Or a brick as some of the VP's had. Like Israel, hearing her vibrant voice from his hiding place behind Charlie's door, opened wide, as Israel opened his arms, for once seeking comfort not a feel—to Charlie's surprise. He had thought Phelps' wife cold in the country that time.

"Nannie—thank God!"

"Fella dear . . ."

Everyone was fella, Charlie too, warmed in turn by the grip of that firm hand, used to gardening now but quick to the helm when old hands belonged. As age did today, even here— where she loomed so much larger than at home, larger than life, which could prove so short. The wavy brown hair, still worn college length, showed gray at the top to the few who looked down or, like Charlie, stood close, drawn by the soft gaze level with his. But the brown eyes that mourned had no time to melt. No-nonsense dames who were towers of strength wore sensible heels and moved right along. No fashion could diminish those legs. Nor yet the high breasts, still firm as the arms in the taut cap sleeves of that basic blue dress, too taut where the high waist was thickening perhaps, but still all woman, the girl-watchers sighed. And all lady, to the toes of her classic pumps.

So it went down the hall as the word kept her pace, never hurried or breathless though she'd obviously come fast when she got the news. Read it, in fact, standing out in front of Shay's Depot Drugs after Phelps' train pulled out, but she didn't say that. She was here, she was back, which explained itself. And her name said the rest to the good ol' boys as she called and waved, ready to nanny the scared new girls, fellas all, the sole exception being dead, so who was left to guess? Perhaps not even Phelps. At first.

"We are not going to adopt that girl," was the only verdict Nannie ever passed, watching Bella drive that loaded carful away while Phelps waved, already planning returns. And Nannie saw it all about to happen again—the endless working weekends *en famille*, the spontaneous staying over for week-nights in town, to cope with an ersatz father's charge, new fa-vorite at court, subtly restretching the fabric of married life to include a third. But not this time. Nannie hadn't retired to mother "Nobody's Girl," still looking for Daddy, Lolita style, while nestled unsafely in Charlie's young lap. Second best, but forgetting what could come from that, Phelps worried only about accidents, father style, when nobody called, while they waited up, insomniac style, since nothing came anymore from nestling in bed, even before Phelps brought the "child" East. "Worry tomorrow. Take her to lunch," was Nannie's last word, nor had they discussed how often he did—right past the next office where the worst was guessed with every exit and entrance clocked, and even Nannie stopped, knowing the worst after three aching years, so what was there to guess? Until last night.

"*Sweetie!*"

"Hi, fella," Nannie said.

Even Bella was fella, sashaying forward on her patent spikes to drag her old rival in by the gloves—no gauntlets today—even Bella was glad, though less surprised than the good ol' boys she left outside in the time-honored manner of good ol' broads, more separate but equal behind closed doors.

"Sweetie—I hoped you'd come!"

"Faster than trying to get through on the phone." And it probably was, though Nannie hadn't tried.

Bella had. "But I was pretty sure yours wouldn't answer," she said.

Nannie shrugged. "Forgot to turn the damn thing back on." Though she'd remembered it driving home from Depot Drugs —but who could call but the network or press? Not Phelps, opening his paper on the train, no village druggist to warn him off before he saw the name, faced that face with the shattering smile, where the story broke over from the front page even in the *Times*. "You don't want to read the rest, Mrs. Phelps," Mr. Shay said, coming out from behind his prescription counter before Nannie could turn to the tabloid double spread, and that picture captioned *TV MEN IN HER LIFE,* with Phelps staring out from that scene in the bar. So

different from the "meeting" he left to Nannie's imagination
last night when he finally got off the bus, exhausted from
missing trains. To remain "in seclusion" or "without comment," the morning line on turned-off phones, no matter
which paper Nannie read. No use turning on the phone after
that, to second-guess Phelps for network or press. Or the
police. So Nannie had come to the source, driving in on one
wheel, armed with white gloves. "Just to pinch-hit, fella," she
said. And Bella, weighed down with guilts closer to home,
could only trade lesser guesses, as yet.

"Sweetie, it's a mess—never seen it worse." A No Win situation, Bella said, quite a stark admission between sometime
accomplices pulling together, for different shores. But Bella
wasn't about to mist up her contacts, watching things go from
sad to worse, while all factions lost their heads, artists and
management cowering alike, albeit behind separate doors,
waiting separate interviews with the police, while separate
regrets were leaked to the press. Or issued officially by PR,
like Weldon's for the home team, too dull to quote, perhaps
by design. Though better than the epitaph Israel blurted on
arrival, speaking for the West as the deceased's former boss,
calling "Maudley . . . liberated in the true sense." A really
choice squib for some mag like *Time* to run with a pic of the
deceased thumbing her nose. Just incidentally making things
worst for the boss who had brought the problem East, and
simply ducked it on arrival to hole up in his corner suite. The
only one who had gone to work, Bella conceded, Phelps being
closeted even now with legal's negotiators, but making deals
for God knew what, since the only project ready on his hunting table had to be deader than Evans, after yesterday's mess.
Alas, the clarifying statement both network and press really
did need about that had so far been cursorily left to Sally and
Cinny, now tearfully typing up some compromise eulogy PR
couldn't touch. Nor could anyone else in management, from

Charlie's level up. Until and unless the Creative Captain got out in front of his fallen teammate and wrote finis in person to Evans' obit. It was up to Phelps.

"No," Nannie said. "A woman should do it."

"Not secretaries!" Bella gasped.

Nannie shook her head. She hadn't meant girls.

Which left Bella herself. "Sweetie, I'm network, too."

"I'm not, fella," Nannie said.

Bella blinked blindly like a mascaraed bat confronted from nowhere with a flying rat. Size was the real difference that kept them from being friends, far more than the sides they chose—or men. But it was the perfect stopgap solution, of course—just the right ploy to get rid of the press: Phelps' wife, not only his wife, but former girl Friday or whatever Cinny and Sally decided Evans was. "Would you *read* this thing, sweetie?"

To herself for a start. It was why Nannie had come. "Let's see . . ." she said, rising to rally the girls, followed by Bella, rallying the boys, all of them following Nannie, like a pied piper, leading Phelps' children, fellas all, back into their walled town. To work. Everyone scurried to help her set up temporary shop in Phelps' tiny screening room, a hole in the wall across the hall, but any port in the storm. OK for now, as Phelps agreed, sounding relieved when the news was phoned in, though he didn't come out. Certainly it was not necessary to explain his strategy, understood in one glance over Cinny's shoulder, patted comfortingly, while Nannie read the statement still in the typewriter—announcing the presentation of *My Father the Chauvinist* as a memorial special to its producer, Maude Lee Evans.

"With her bio . . ." Sally's voice was small. So was the paragraph prepared at Phelps' direction by Sally. "He didn't want anything personal . . ."

"Better for now, fellas—just right." Nannie's embrace was

big enough for both girls badly in need of warmth. No changes were asked, only their help in making copies, to be passed out after Nannie read *Chauvinist*. All she needed was the lunch hour (and perhaps a word or two with Phelps) before leading his new team of three to sing Evans' praises (and face the music) in the reception area.

There, the press, gratefully alerted, was temporarily lifting its siege to go eat, when a straggler nobody expected made an entrance so ill-timed as to all but negate the effect of Nannie's. The only member of Phelps' team who could possibly have missed such news, stepped off the elevator with a grubby fistful of papers, and marched unseeingly past the newscasters toward the receptionist's desk, where a tiny but piping voice was heard to ask for Maude Lee Evans. For E. V. Adamic there was only one. And there would never be another.

"What the hell was *that*?" a dazed reporter muttered as the hot potato in the cowboy hat was whisked from view, and passed down the hall from receptionist to stenographer like a baton in a relay race. While the VP of PR got on the phone to the screening room, to make damn sure that the author in denim did not meet the press. Nannie rose to the occasion in her usual fashion, warm hand outstretched to the apparition dumped at her door. "Hi, fella," she said.

But it was not an opener to grab a feminist, peering suspiciously around at the inside office, not only a bad scene but a probable comedown, in terms learned from Maude Lee Evans.

"How come I'm supposed to wait in here?"

"Just temporary. Like me . . ." Smiling, Nannie gave her full name. But E.V.'s handshake remained limp. All she really heard was Phelps.

"I'm a writer," she mumbled. Wives bored her a lot.

"You certainly are!" The mimeoed third draft lay open on the coffee table. "I've been trying to catch up . . ."

"Why?" E.V. asked.

Nannie hesitated and then gestured toward the sectional sofas, placed at right angles. "Let's sit down . . ."

"I've got this stuff to leave for Maude Lee." E.V. tightened her clutch on the pages. "I mean it's sort of a mess—nobody else could read it. So I'll stick it on her desk, if she's all that busy—"

"Mind if we talk first?"

E.V. minded. "What's the matter—isn't she here?"

Behind E.V. the beefy detective covering Evans' phones had come down the hall to beckon from the door. Nannie shook her head.

"Oh, swell . . ." E.V. misunderstood, unable to suppress her disappointment that Maude Lee, who was never sick, had chosen this moment to goof off. "After I wrote all night . . ."

"I'll explain it in a minute, fella." Nannie patted E.V.'s arm and moved around her into the hall, braced for another argument about mishandling bad news with sensitive people, tricky enough on the phone, never mind with a paranoid here in person.

"Hey, wait . . ." E.V. pointed to the winking light on the phone but Nannie had already pulled the door half shut for some heavy whispering outside. So E.V. sighed, more than ever misused, and sank onto the nearest sectional sofa to pick up and take the message as she had so often for her more informal mentor. Thus the detective missed precisely the kind of call he was here to intercept, mistakenly transferred to the screening room by rattled operators when Evans' office failed to answer.

"Extension 2111," E.V. piped, as Maude Lee had taught her.

Somebody laughed.

E.V. bristled. "What's funny?"

"Cunts like you."

First fella then cunt. "What a wrong number you've got—"

"You and that cunt Maude Lee Evans—trashing the people's message—"

"Listen, phone freak—"

The laugh interrupted: *"Today's Package Is Tomorrow's Trash!"*

So then E.V. remembered the hippie picket she hadn't wanted to mess with even yesterday, before he came on with spooky phone calls, about as funny as a ward in Willowbrook, she told him instead of hanging up. Suggesting further that he go fuck himself, which really brought the People's wrath down on her head. In the form of a threat about a bomb already planted in that cunt's office ready to go off right where she sat, and blow the whole network, a threat which E.V. heard out to pass along, thereby springing the whole floor for lunch early. Until the next threat suddenly got to her. About a knife, or knives, waiting to be used on any cunt who survived, like it was used last night on Maude Lee Evans and her hump and the water bed they screwed themselves to death on, and a few more graphic details E.V. never remembered, freezing, hearing whatever she heard, that made her know suddenly, finally, why she was here alone in this cell and Maude Lee wasn't, never would be, despite all those precious grubby pages dropping, scattering, as E.V. rose, and began to scream in her piping voice, shrieking and shrill like a berserk trapped bird, even after Nannie and the detective ran in, grabbing her, grabbing the phone, still she kept on. So that Cinny and Sally, stapling copies of their statements, dropped those pages too, so frightened they could not say what both of them thought. Someone else was being murdered. . . . They both ran away from the sound, into Phelps' office, where the network negotiators called Security who called the police, ordering the floor cleared, so that finally even Phelps had to rise from the hunting table and come out and face it all—detectives, bomb scare, press, and wife.

Their eyes met over E.V.'s hat in the hall where Nannie held the writer fast, until screams turned to sobs.

His lips framed words seldom heard from Phelps. "Sorry . . . thank you . . ."

The smile Nannie gave her husband was sadder than her eyes. "All we needed." It could have meant the bomb scare.

"Need you . . ." It could have meant the difference. If he hadn't said the rest, if he'd been reaching out for her, instead of his last, least favored foster child. "Need you both . . ."

But E. V. Adamic did not need to be needed, too far gone and far out to be used as a buffer when her whole little writing life had depended on a blither spirit to serve *her* as buffer against grownups' ways and graces. So she split. The warmest grip could not keep her from twisting free, fleeing down the hall to sanctuary, not via the elevator as Security required, but through the swinging doors to the farthest cubicle where her hatband could be probed for the only security she still trusted.

"I better stay with her," Nannie said, raising her voice over the hubbub, as the press broke ranks, and started in from the reception area, against the tide trying to get out. Divided outside the Ladies' Room door, Phelps and Nannie lost each other.

So did Cinny and Sally, swept against their better judgment into the stair well by a panicky wave from the typing pool. Somehow Cinny got ahead; she was halfway down the first flight when the stairs grew clogged. She could see everyone trying to get out the same door below, until someone blocked it and sent them on. Panicky arguments began to break out about inching along a step at a time for twenty more floors.

"Jesus, what if there *is* a bomb . . . ?"

Ahead of Cinny a contingent of housewife part-timers said

they weren't coming back, boss or no boss, cops or no cops. But one of them had left her bag. She turned.

A black girl beside Cinny blocked the way. "So they'll search your bag. Go back on up there, and The Man'll search you."

"All they search is the premises," Cinny said, hoping it was true, but for all the times they'd been the same route, no one was sure what to expect today. Not with a murder case hanging heavy over them, and those detectives into everything, wanting to talk to everybody who ever knew the victim.

"So who knew her? Did you know her?" a voice asked. Cinny said nothing, hoping Sally wouldn't. "That's how I knew her," the voice answered itself.

"Keep moving," a security guard boomed suddenly from the next floor down.

On the landing above, Sally felt a man shoving into line behind her. She almost screamed when he grabbed her waist, until she recognized his watch. And the touch.

"Charlie . . ." She sagged against him; his arms tightened.

"*Keep moving!*" the voice of Security boomed again.

"You heard The Man," Charlie whispered, but no one else heard Charlie, his lips brushing her ear.

"I can't move . . ." Not down anyway, the way he had her grinding against him, both his hands straying, lips parting . . .

She didn't want to giggle; she couldn't help but gasp. "Charlie . . ."

"Take you out for a quickie."

She thought he meant a drink. "I've gotta go back up and help Cinny."

"Won't take a minute."

"Not Downstairs." She thought he meant The Bar but she just *couldn't* after yesterday.

"The Warwick."

She sighed. "There'll be reporters all over every bar around here."

"Not room service," Charlie whispered.

She couldn't believe it. "Today? Now?"

"Kidding . . ."

But when she jolted down a step and turned to look up she saw from his face he was frightened too. It shocked her more than the feelings he'd aroused, distracting her to distract himself, until a scared little trainee stumbled between them, offering a new distraction.

"Charlie?"

"Catch you later." He had caught the trainee.

"Where?" Sally called. She couldn't help but think of her crazy bet with Evans about Charlie's pad. But she didn't want to cry, pushed by the trainee, pushed by Charlie, who couldn't help trying to finish what had started with the first pushover that came to hand. Any port in a panic.

"Keep moving."

"You heard The Man . . ."

The cops in the squad car commandeered to take E.V. home, helped the Detective Sergeant calm her down enough to let them make a detour past the Coliseum. Predictably no handmade signs were being waved outside the Packaging Exhibit today, but one of the guards remembered the hippie type picket well enough to promise help with a composite picture. E.V. didn't, barely willing to point out where the boy had led them into the park. Nothing could persuade her to get out and retrace their steps, when the squad car pulled up on the grass inside.

"I want to go home," she insisted stubbornly to the detective, sitting in back beside her. "You said they'd take me home!"

"Just show us which path he took, E.V."

"It wasn't a path—I told you. He knew a shortcut . . ." She gestured toward the hill where other groups of kids sprawled in a circle, legs and laps used as pillows, getting sleepy or whatever they got from whatever they had to pass around.

"That's where you had your picnic?"

"Sort of . . . farther on . . . We were under a tree." Where E.V. had propped her weary head, wearier now, propped against her hand, palm supporting the hat's crown, fingers guarding her hatband. No way they could make her jeopardize that. But considering the APB they already had out on the boy, she picked her words with care, as she described the picnic menu.

The Detective Sergeant didn't seem quite satisfied. "That's how your girlfriend got what she wanted? For some hot dogs and a couple of beers?"

"Well, she had to kid him along for a while."

"About seeing him later? Meeting him someplace?"

E.V. shook her head. "He wanted to come too."

"Back to her office?"

"Anyplace we took the sign. I guess he thought it was going to be a party."

"For all three of you?"

"He didn't care."

"Did she?"

"I told you. She was putting him on."

"How, E.V.?"

How did they think, all of them, staring out the car windows at a couple of other kids who weren't sleepy, rolling in the grass, kissing openmouthed through matching matted manes, sexes indistinguishable as they grabbed and groped each other's jeans? Like the long-haired boy grabbing Maude Lee, when she reached across him for the sign, signaling E.V. to get it instead, while the boy groped, blinded by her hair covering his face, mixing with his, blond on blond. How did any kids turn each other on like that in a park patrolled by cars full of fuzz?

"Maybe she got him kind of high," E.V. said.

"Just on beer?"

She shrugged. "I dunno—beer brings me down. I was like out of it." Down and out, until she jumped up to split with the prize, leaving Maude Lee trapped by the booby in the grass.

"Was she high, E.V.? High enough to dig him? See him again?"

"Not for real." Not on a few drags from a joint too hastily passed to a surplus boy. "She already had one at home like him." It just slipped out, Maude Lee's poor excuse for an exit, which hadn't worked then, and didn't work now. Except to serve as a reminder of poor creepy Nedders, in enough trouble, before the detective pressed the resemblance. Did Nedders look like the pickup, sound like a freak, could it have been Nedders on the phone?

"No . . . I don't know . . . I'm not sure who it was," E.V. stammered, wishing she could take it all back as she watched the cops up front eying the kissers, pried suddenly apart, scattering with their friends, finally hip to danger, but laughing as they split, still high, maybe still holding, in enough trouble, like most kids.

They were all the same to cruising fuzz, toying with door handles, caressing clubs, muttering about busting grass-stained asses. . . .

But homicide took preference over vice. The Detective Sergeant directed the driver to take the exit on Seventh and head downtown to drop E.V. before the squad car started cruising the Village, circulating the boy's description, on the outside chance he'd been seen following more than one girl yesterday. Had perhaps chosen the one who didn't have a boy like him waiting, when she got off the empty subway. Did not, in fact, seem to have anyone in the once cozy carriage house, now turned photographer's studio, bleak and empty when she entered. Except for two boxers, barking and bounding, enough to deter any intruder from forcing entry into her premises. But not the detective, determined to wait until E.V. answered the phone they both heard ringing on the sleeping balcony.

"Where's the extension?"

"There isn't one on the private line—" she protested. "Nobody's even got the number. It couldn't be anybody! I mean—like him."

But the ringing persisted. So did the detective, climbing behind E.V. up the ladder to the ledge that was filled by a double mattress, where the boxers bounded, slavering at the sound of their mistress' voice screeching long distance, just as E.V. had feared. No way the detective could miss a falsetto note from his Kneeling Room Only section on the steps.

"E.V., what's going on—I've been trying to get you ever since I heard—"

"I was at the network—"

"*Today.* After what happened?"

"I didn't know. The cops just brought me back—"

"You're kidding—"

"For my own protection," E.V. added quickly. "It's because of some creep that followed me and Maude Lee yesterday—"

"Followed you where?" The voice froze. "To my studio?"

"They didn't know if he came after me, or waited at her office—" E.V.'s voice piped higher, in mounting strain. "All they know, I got this freaky phone call up there today, and it could have been him, only nobody's sure, Toni—"

"So what are the fuzz going to do—?"

"I dunno—the detective's still here—"

"Christ, E.V.! Not with my files—"

"*Right here,*" E.V. interrupted. "I'll ask him."

She covered the receiver. "Listen, the photographer that owns this place—Toni Porter—she gets very uptight about let-

ting people in, with all this equipment and stuff . . ." E.V.
waved vaguely below toward a couple of light stands, a desk,
and a chair, no other equipment being visible in the studio.
Except for the aforementioned file cabinets painted out white
against blank walls. All four walls. "I mean if you're going to
mess with anything . . . she'd sort of like to know what's going
down."

"A routine check, not a search." His face remained expressionless. "Want me to explain to Miss Porter?"

There were times when Ms. was no help at all. "It's Mrs.,"
E.V. said, and passed him the phone.

"Detective Sergeant Corio, Homicide Task Force." The
identification cooled the long-distance protest, chilling the
summer air. There never seemed quite enough for the boxers,
panting on either side of E.V., wedging her in like bookends,
waiting to bound after the detective when he got through
explaining the routine security measures being taken to protect E.V.'s person and/or the photographer's property, and
backed down the ladder. At last leaving E.V. alone on the unmade bed, with the private phone. And the voice of Mrs. Toni
Porter.

"I can talk now . . ."

"Where's he going first?"

"Kitchen."

"Oh God—the darkroom. Those drawers aren't locked . . ."

Neither was the door, opening off the dinette.

"Nothing in there but fashion stills." Like the detective,
E.V. had taken a few looks around, for her own protection.
"Just your contacts for Viva, is all."

"And a safe full of film!"

"How's he going to work the combination?" It had taken
E.V. the better part of a year, watching and waiting.

"He's fuzz, baby—"

"Not Vice." Or some cop cruising the porno scene to bust kids' asses for kicks. "You heard—he's only into homicide."

The word made another silence, shifting the mood and Mrs. Toni Porter's gears.

"Look, baby, this is heavy—staying there by yourself. Why don't you take Bonzer and Sweets over to Del and Jean's for a couple of nights?"

"They've got Pat and Elly's cat."

"Oh Lord . . ."

"Anyhow they're splitting for the weekend. Everybody is . . ."

"Then you split too. Board the dogs with the vet."

"Could I come up there?"

It created the same silence as homicide.

"I mean, even if you're busy, we'd have Sunday—"

"Baby, we shoot this mother every day."

"Why? You're the producer—" Also the director, making Mrs. Toni Porter doubly responsible to her always unnamed investors.

"It's not my bread that's running out. Anyway the sooner we wrap, the sooner I'll be back—"

"Said that before." E.V.'s voice was muffled.

"What?"

"Nothing . . . he's going outside."

Mrs. Porter's relief escaped in a sigh as the detective opened the glass doors on the garden, a cement oblong bounded by geraniums, just large enough to keep him out of earshot for another moment.

"Look, we can't have detectives following you here—so hang in till next week. OK?"

"Toni, I'm beat . . ." Too beat to hang in, even with pills. "I worked all night."

"For her?"

"Sort of . . ."

E.V. looked down at the typewriter on the desk, remembering the pages she had lost somewhere. Loss engulfed her.

"I just can't make it alone—"

"Then get one of your friends to stay over. Like what's his name that works at Our Corner."

"It's closed for the summer."

"Well, the other bars aren't—you can try around."

"Sure I can. Like at La Seour. Some of my best friends—"

"The *boys'* bars, E.V.! I said friends, not tricks. And I don't mean any more closet switch hitters!"

The pot calling the kettle gray. "That's your scene."

"Only to photograph."

"Tell me." E.V. had seen the models—on location. "I got that picture." Also the message. Mrs. Toni Porter's studio was full of echoes. (*Turn, baby, click, this way, children, yes, click YES, come to Mamma—come beauty, come youth, come back to me . . .*) How long till the man from Homicide got it, staring in at the glass house, across the empty floor that made the studio so great for parties? How long till the neighbors repeated their complaints about the music, which made it so easy to imagine the dancing, like E.V., remembering the dancers—the blonde with the model's body that the brunette could only recapture with a camera, ten years apart, from two different worlds, brought together for a moment, perversely by E.V. Once. Only once that she knew of, threatened ever since by a bomb, still planted somewhere, unfiled, unfound, ticking in the mind. How long before the law heard it, coming back into earshot, trying and testing the bolts on glass doors. . . .

"You get pictures that aren't there, E.V."

"So do detectives."

"What do you mean—what's he doing?"

"Looking."

"Where?"

"Where your body's buried." E.V. did her sad midget laugh. "He's looking at his watch."

"All right, dammit—I want that whole investigation out of there—"

"Now hear this—"

"Anyway you can swing it—convince your detective you need privacy—rest—"

"How about if I sleep at the vet's—with the dogs—?"

"Tell him the one about working all night! With your funky producer—"

"Not last night!" E.V.'s tiny voice sank into a whisper. "Thanks a *lot!*"

"Wait till he hears about the other overtimes."

"Never on Sunday. That's your story." Blues. For blue movies only.

"Stay paranoid, pillhead," Mrs. Toni Porter said.

"With the help of my friend . . ." Not a trick, but the tricky beloved.

"In your *hat!* Pop another biggie when he's gone."

One was already popped, another palmed. "Don't worry . . ."

Mrs. Toni Porter sighed. "Oh, baby, what the bloody hell's the use of worrying now?"

Indeed their worst worry should have been over. But the source of danger was only playing dead when E.V. went down to lock Homicide out of Mrs. Toni Porter's studio. As, from other households, struck dumb in the killing pause that followed.

Jonas Sams felt like a forgotten man, as he wandered the dove velvet carpeting upstairs, peering into the oystershell suites where high-level executives had stayed away in droves. Nor could he locate his fellow travelers, now stretching interminable breakfasts into lunches. Jonas seemed to be the only one whose afternoon plane reservations home had *not* been canceled on orders from above. The secretary's secretary who handled such matters in Weldon's outer-outer office obviously considered the omission quite natural. After all, she said, higher-up West Coasters like Israel Gold had actually *known* Miss Evans well enough to delay departure, pending the announcement of a memorial service. Mourning was the only reason quoted in the outer-outer office for delaying even the most knowing eyewitness. Let alone one so casually acquainted with the scene as Israel's shadow, so far overlooked even by the pushiest official investigator. Possibly, Jonas himself suggested, because Israel had supplied the wrong name for the only black face in the *Daily News* group shot.

"Maybe they're looking to question Samson Jones."

The secretary's secretary smiled politely, unable to see quite what either a Jones *or* Sams could possibly add to the high level of information available to police from Messrs. Gold *and* Weldon. A token, by any name, was a token.

And black was beautiful, but Jonas decided to sound the depth of beauty's skin elsewhere. After he let the secretary's secretary speed him on his way via the nearest elevator. "I'll tell Mr. Gold you couldn't wait," she caroled, waving. "Have a nice trip."

"Thanks," Jonas said, and got off on 21 to ask for the nearest detective.

"You just missed half the police force," said the security man sitting in for the receptionist. "But I sure want to know it if you don't find one of those Homicide guys covering her phone now!"

"Thanks."

Everyone knew where her phone was. Jonas stepped over the cables left by the camera crews in the deserted reception area and started down the silent hall between the empty offices, so full of connivers yesterday when she got her token ass in a sling. No more poor career chick, flown from her coop, which lay straight ahead as Jonas turned the last corner to find some red-headed, red-necked Irish shamus, swiveling in her chair, feet on her desk, using her phone—apparently discussing the contents of a small glassine envelope dangling from one massive freckled hand. Jonas saw the flash of metal as he got close enough to overhear a few words.

"Lucky I stayed on top of these boys when they emptied the washroom trash—what do they know from evidence unless it ticks?" The shamus chuckled. "All I can tell you, it looked familiar to me, when it hit the tile. So if the lab says yes, I figured Frank and Reilly would want to be the ones, try it at her pad . . . instead of Corio's task force—right, Lieutenant?" The glassine envelope clinked onto the desk. Jonas thought he saw a key before the shamus looked up and saw him.

"Samson Jones?" All eyewitnesses in group photos did not look alike to The Man.

"Jonas Sams." The witness explained his boss's problem with names.

"We all got problems . . ." The problem in the glassine envelope had disappeared completely under one massive freckled hand, as the shamus hung up, and got busy fumbling with a tape recorder, clearly trusted less than his notebook opened and ready, by the time Jonas took a practice swivel in her visitor's chair.

"OK, Jonas—you're on the air."

Instead of on a plane. The witness set his wrist alarm for the flight still to be made, or canceled. "Just thought I ought to check in . . ." Before checking out. "In case you had some questions."

"You were right. What can you tell us?"

"What do you want to know?"

"Who gave her the shiv?"

"The one she got here?"

"And in Macy's window."

So that was it. Ass-in-a-sling time. Jonas wasn't about to add his neck to the tokens risked for any job. Like The Man said everyone had problems. But this murder was Whitey's. So were the little white lies Jonas laid on the line from the first West Coast conspiracy to the East Coast grand finale.

"This project Evans developed got so hot they took it over. They'd have dumped her boss too if he hadn't crossed her." Phelps should live and be well and never do it again, as Jonas' boss kept saying before murder robbed all of them.

The shamus might have already heard the whole story—or guessed it—the way he sat there, scratching an occasional note, mumbling, "Yeah . . . uhhuhh," as if he couldn't care. But you never knew what you were telling The Man until The Man told you, usually in a question that wasn't quite asked. The shamus seemed in no hurry to tip his freckled hand.

"Now lessee . . . you and Mr. Collins went down there together around four-thirty—right?"

"Four-fifteen." Jonas knew exactly, because of the wrist alarm he set when he left, to remind himself an hour later that he should phone if he was going to be late for his five-thirty date at Joe Allen's. But when the five-fifteen alarm went off, he was already in the street, parting company from Charlie Collins, heading east for home, as Jonas headed west.

"But the others were still inside?"

Jonas shook his head. "We all sort of left together. My boss and Mr. Weldon were trying to find a taxi on the corner, the last I saw . . ." A perplexing memory since Jonas knew them to be early for a party, within walking distance at the Plaza.

"How about Miss Evans' boss?"

"Right behind me with Kelly—for about a block. They turned down Seventh, for the station, I guess. Phelps had to catch a train."

"Uhhuh . . ." The freckled hand started riffling back through pages of previous notes. "Lessee . . . seems like there was a waiter or maybe a reporter . . . placed your crowd at their table later than five-fifteen."

Jonas shrugged. "PR still had plenty of press around, interviewing the director. Bernard . . ."

Billy Bee Bernard. The only star left at the table. Or in the clear. Like Jonas himself, cleared for departure as the notebook closed on an easily checked story. Jonas rose, hovering until the tape recorder was turned off.

"I was wondering if you could keep this confidential."

"Just a routine interview . . ."

"Yeah, but I wouldn't want to be quoted . . ." Just in case some other witness higher up than a waiter placed Jonas' crowd in The Bar too long.

"Never quote anybody," the shamus said affably, "unless we have to."

Ready now to oblige by sneaking out of town, Jonas headed down the pepper and salt carpeting, hurrying by the girls streaming back from lunch. Until he saw the only one he really liked, and knew well enough to draw aside for a parting word of advice. About the girls sticking together, not working in the office late, or alone, until The Man checked out the evidence found in the washroom.

"But you didn't hear it from me—right? You know how the dudes are around this place."

The trouble was Sally didn't. All she could think of was some key thief, some outsider like the phone freak, or creep from the park, running loose on this very floor, planting clues. Or bombs . . .

"Unless it was someone who works in the building," Jonas said carefully, hesitant to draw too many conclusions as her eyes grew round. "Like maybe just a dude getting rid of Evans' key?"

"Oh my God . . ." Sally whispered, at last catching on. "Oh my *God!*"

"When I finally got a busy signal, I was in the station. So I knew she was home . . ." Phelps said, to explain why he'd passed up two trains for a bus. "Seemed worth it. Until I decided her phone was off the hook. Guess I gave up about the same time you did . . ."

"Yeah," Israel answered.

They stood silent for a moment looking south toward the networks from the windowed living room of the company's favored suite in the Warwick. There was no sun to bother Phelps with the reflected glare that had filled Evans' office yesterday, blinding him. And her.

"Christ, Israel—if only one of us had gotten through when she walked into the apartment . . ."

"Forget if. At least you got through to the service." Israel hadn't.

"What the hell's the use if she never knew?" And all the time Phelps thought she was ducking his messages.

Israel shrugged. "Maybe she was—the cops could tell you if she picked 'em up."

"Evans would have checked her service," Charlie chimed in from the sofa behind them, where he was taking another peek at his own picture in the *Daily News.*

Israel shot him a look. "How do you know?"

Charlie flushed. "Well . . . I mean . . . unless it happened right away."

"Isn't that the theory?" Phelps glanced with distaste at the tabloid, which had given the most space to the effects of immersion, now making a big splash in journalism's first waterbed thriller.

"Aaah—theories. Forget them too. We got enough on us without buying the crap that sells papers." The rest of Israel's

were stacked beside Charlie, with the *Times* on top, Evans'
picture smiling up from the break-over page, still folded back.
Proof that for once Israel had read to the end of the story he
was rejecting wholesale. "Goddamn reporters guess for a living—including ours. Want to research a crime, hire cops."

The networks had done it often enough, and ignored the result. But the police researchers now stalking the halls weren't
there to alter facts to order, however lucrative the sideline,
which had proved inimical to cynical talents of the fourth estate. The cream of which was seldom left guessing in the
street.

"Police reporters work pretty close," Phelps said. "Some of
them were up at the scene, Israel."

"Well, they're not at this autopsy today—the morgue's
where your time theories get blown." Or proved, as sometimes
suited Israel's convenience. "Real cops need to get a timing
that stands up in court. Otherwise it'll be the same old story.
Could have happened anytime, up to or after this boyfriend
walked in."

Phelps frowned. "Not after . . ."

"Who knows when? Nobody saw him."

"Somebody must have . . ." Phelps gazed down at the
street where there was nothing to be seen but the tops of passing heads. Except for a man looking up at the window from a
corner pay phone.

"Detectives . . ." Israel turned his back, already tired of
seeing them everywhere, jumping at shadows. . . . "Let them
figure it. I never even knew she had a heavy boyfriend!"

Charlie stared disbelievingly at Nedders' photograph. "Who
says he was heavy?"

"He does apparently." Phelps left the rest a question mark
on Evans' desk calendar, despite Israel's urging that their own
embarrassing questions might become heavier if Nedders got
off the hook.

"I don't know where Charlie went riding with Mrs. Weldon while I was putting the old man to bed. But sooner or later we may all have to say what was going on for two hours, between busy signals."

"*Two* hours—" Charlie blurted, only to be silenced by a red-rimmed, sea green look that could kill.

Seeing it, Phelps came in on cue, with a noncommittal murmur. "Seemed like longer . . . in a phone booth."

Knowing how impossibly much longer it was, Charlie shifted his disbelieving stare to the stony face gazing back with indifference. As if even Phelps had resigned himself to the practice of researching facts to order, all fiction disappearing under one cover. Leaving Charlie to wonder why, shivering damply in his fresh seersucker, knowing he was part of it, but still not one of them. Doubting suddenly he ever would be, for all his hustling and hurting to keep up, somehow always just missing whatever it took to get what he wanted. Still not understanding that swallowing this bitter pill gave every shark an iron stomach, and the insatiable appetite that drove Israel in circles, after the lion strength of talent. In Phelps, in Evans, in anyone . . . all equal prey to the predator who lacked it.

The buzzer sounded.

"Room service—I'll get it!" Charlie bounded to the door, thinking to escape again, needing only an antidote from last night to save him. Like one of the dishes he could be having here for lunch, if only Israel had flown West on schedule. If only Evans had not dallied too freely, done in by the sweet streak of youth. The very same that beleaguered Charlie, unable to forget ifs, while he aged resentfully from contagion with aging men, sandwiching him in over the damn sandwiches on the room service table. It was a day for simple fare, not counting calories, Israel had decreed when Charlie did the ordering. He wished now he'd ordered wine, or at least refreshed a diluted scotch to wash down his chicken on white bread, curling at the edges, dryer than the sound of Phelps' toasted cheese, chomped slowly and steadily. While Israel got to the meat of the lunch, talking through every mouthful of pastrami on rye, as he worried aloud about their now endangered project.

"What I don't see, what I don't see, is tying the property in with Maudley."

"No way not to now." Phelps lowered his cup. "Damn coffee's cold." Like the tea yesterday.

"Who's gonna make connections, once the case is closed?"

"*If* it's closed."

"So what's to lose if we wait six months?"

"The talent."

"Talent, schmallent . . ." Once consumed, it all tasted the same to the shark.

But not to the lion. "I've got the star and director I want—for half the terms I'm empowered to offer. Plus they're both available now for rehearsal. And I've got an early shooting date—"

"So you shoot the mother, who gets it in on air? Just because Weldon's suckered in this far—"

"No one was suckered, Israel, but Evans."

"Except maybe you, Father."

"If you want out," Phelps smiled, "fly out."

"*Now?*" Israel sounded genuinely shocked. "And look like I'm backing out on her memory?"

"Aren't you?"

The shark rose to the bait, teeth flashing. "Goddammit, Father—you should feel what I feel for Maudley. She was one sweet kick in the head—" Among other places brought to mind as the guttural voice became plaintive. "But can I help it, can I help it, if she died teasing some—?"

"I am more interested," Phelps interrupted icily, "in how she lived."

"Not for any cockamamie show, believe me—"

"I believe my own experience—she put her job first!" The exclamation point remained on the calendar of record, as Phelps threw his napkin down like a gauntlet. "Nobody repeat nobody is going to smear what could have been a brilliant career with a lot of irrelevant conjecture—"

"It's done already—with this mess hanging over us! Every goddamn thing she touched is controversial."

"And every person, Israel."

"*So*—you know what that does to us upstairs?"

"You bet I know." Phelps pushed his chair back. "Same way you do. I was here in the fifties. But I'm not sitting still for this blacklist—"

"Blacklist—for God's sake!" Politics was all they needed. "Who's talking *blacklist?*"

"You just did." Phelps rose. "And I'm going to—before it goes any further this time."

Israel shook his head. "You're crazy."

"So sit there. Let 'em gag you again. Like Weldon and Scooper. *But not me!*"

He walked out of the suite, before Israel could answer.

Things were running a little late on the twenty-first floor. Half the newshounds were still out chasing leads from the bomb scare, when Nannie, somewhat relieved to be upstaged, led her troops to the reception area to drop the second bomb of the day, read aloud for the remaining mikes and cameras, while Cinny and Sally passed out copies. And the VP of PR stood by helplessly, until Nannie removed her horn-rimmed glasses to add a few well-chosen words to the announcement of the Evans Memorial Special.

"On a more personal level . . . Those like my husband, who

worked most closely with Ms. Evans—and have the most to miss—are simply too shocked to express what they feel. And ask your forbearance regarding any questions that remain—"

The first forbearing question winged back from the network's own legman: "Nannie, when were you called in to replace Ms. Evans?"

"I wasn't called in—I volunteered. As a sign of respect from a predecessor in the same field. Where there aren't enough women anyway—and no talent can be replaced—"

"Weren't they all set to replace her yesterday?" The follow-up came from a legwoman on another network's national news.

"Not on work already done. Her credit stands, that's all I know—"

"A posthumous screen credit?" The legwoman's tone was incredulous. "Won't the network have some reservations?"

"Would yours?" Nannie shot back. "If it happened to you?"

"Under *these* circumstances—?"

This time the VP cut it off. "The circumstances are under police investigation which can only be hindered by idle comment or speculation here—"

"Aren't the men here who worked with her wide open to speculation?" It came from a newspaper reporter, of course.

"Every woman or man among us," the VP of PR said gravely, "*wants* to co-operate fully in supplying any information that can help solve this tragic crime against a fellow worker. Further, the network plans to offer a reward—"

A magazine man who had been in The Bar Downstairs laughed. "How much, Scoop?"

"—a reward for ten thousand dollars, to be announced officially on the evening news." The VP of PR put a sheltering arm around Nannie. "Now I think the creative representative has spoken to the professional matter—"

"How about letting her speak as a wife?"

"I could have done that at home," Nannie said.

"*Thank you, Mrs. Phelps!*" the VP of PR called out, getting her off like TV's first lady for the benefit of the home team's local news. He could only hope for short shrift elsewhere. Until, as he soon discovered, the competition stole the whole memorial show story with a livelier interview in the street. Where Phelps, bearded like a lion for office gossip about Maude Lee Evans, lost his Puritan temper. Not at the media but its enemy—the new pressure group of Kooks coming on at The Industry from the lunatic left as well as right this time, and not just with cards and letters but bombs, setting off an explosion of character assassination, to raise again the specter of witch-hunts.

"It's too late to save our colleague's life," he thundered, "but we can damn well fight to save her life's work!" Which placed the network squarely behind him. And on the spot. As it was in the picture, sure to get national coverage by the time Phelps stalked inside the building. It was only a question of waiting for the camera.

The super and the lady tenants had been scaring each other all day. He kept trying to win friends by leaping out of his apartment across from the laundry, to help with heavy loads, fix jammed machines, as the ladies backed away, trying not to scream, and his wife laughed in the open doorway. "Maybe that teach you, maybe you be nicer," she jeered in English, siding openly against him, knowing he could not take it out on her today, with the police in and out every ten minutes. Indeed the super had barely eaten his own lunch after relieving the doorman for the usual hour, when Benjie called down to be relieved again, so he could accompany more detectives to 14B, this time to try some new key they'd found.

"Vat key? Found vere?"

"How do I know?"

"Say I meet them up there . . ."

"I gotta do it."

"Vy?"

"To go over what happened on my lunch hour yesterday."

"Again?"

"They want me to show 'em this time." Benjie didn't sound very happy about it, giving the super the last laugh on his wife. "Maybe this boy get too nice. Maybe that teach *him*," he jeered, also in English, so that the ladies would hear it wasn't the scourge of the basement, but the smart young favorite at the door, who was being called to account for knowing too much about extra keys, handed out to favorites in 14B.

Certainly Benjie would have given a day's salary not to go up there, cursing himself for letting his bartender friend talk him into coming in today, as he followed detectives Reilly and Frankovitch into the elevator, praying all the way up that the key in their glassine envelope wouldn't work, that the super would insist on returning himself with the master key. But the damn door swung wide, with the top lock still left open. Just as allegedly found last night by Nedders. And yesterday by Benjie.

"Did she often leave it this way?"

"Only when she'd figured she was coming back up—like with the puppy. She knew I'd lock it for her." He had said it all before, if not to them, to others.

"OK—now show us . . . what did you do with the leash?"

His heart sank as they snapped on the overhead light and he saw the water line ringing the little foyer, staining the tiles around the umbrella stand where the leash was always hung. But he stopped in his tracks when he got his first flash of the room in the mirrored wall. "Omigod . . ."

"What's the matter?"

Were they kidding? He gestured across the wreckage toward the paper cutouts of two figures pinned to what was left of the water bed. And each other.

"Routine . . ." the younger detective said.

Maybe routine to them. Not to Benjie, asked to move ahead and show them where he'd gotten the envelope, as if they didn't know, with all her stationery still there, or already put back, in the first transparent drawer, with the cassettes still strewn around on top, and a circle drawn in chalk where the pot had been, over the second drawer, the one Benjie didn't want to look at.

"See anything different?"

"There was a bag of something there."

"Did you find out what?"

"Yeah . . ." As if they hadn't taken his prints along with everyone else's to find out for themselves who touched what.

"Relax, Benjie—we just want to know if you left it where you found it."

"Yeah—all I did, I picked it up . . ." To see underneath it, something he didn't want to admit he'd taken from the other drawer, where everything also seemed as before when he finally couldn't help but look. A long look.

It wasn't there. Gone with the pot, wherever their lab was.

He closed his eyes and waited.

"Touch anything else, Benjie?" It sounded like the young detective.

"The light switch," he said. When he opened his eyes, they were both turning, toward the bed, nodding, agreeing with the blinds like that you needed some kind of light in here.

"Go anywhere else in the apartment?"

"I used the john," Benjie said.

"Pot again?" the older detective guessed, grinning. It was OK with them, if it was OK with her. "Pretty free and easy, wasn't she?"

Benjie didn't know what to say to that. So he nodded.

"How about with tips . . ."

He shrugged. "I guess she did what she could . . ."

"You liked her for herself—that it?" The older detective kept grinning, dangling the key in its glassine envelope.

"She was OK to me . . ."

"And a few other guys!"

"I didn't see much of that—being on in the mornings."

"How about guys leaving?"

"Just one mostly."

"*Mostly?*"

"Well, you know—other women here have men stay over. I couldn't swear which apartment except if I know 'em. Like this Nedders. But as far as this other key . . ."

"You don't have any ideas . . . ?"

Benjie shook his head.

The younger detective patted his arm. "We may ask you to come by and look at some pictures. Thanks for now, Benjie."

They moved toward the bed, murmuring about the key, about whether or not the phone was back in service, leaving Benjie free to go. Free to leave that glassed-in mess. He couldn't believe it. He shot one more terrified glance at the drawer he hadn't even had to lie about. Though they must have lifted his prints there too. Must have known he touched it. As they knew about the other one, the light switches, the bathroom, knew about everything. Except the photograph. It wasn't a trap. It wasn't in some lab with the pot. They hadn't seen it. Or taken it anywhere.

But someone else had. Benjie got out of there.

Except for the mirrors, suddenly hung like the windows with horizontal blinds, it looked like all the rest of her parties. "I'll get to *you*," she laughed the way she did, but it wasn't clear if she meant Ned or one of the crapartists crowded around her, all celebrating her return, telling the same story she was telling. Wasn't it wonderful, all a mistake, she'd just been away, not in Mars at all, but a perfectly reasonable place . . . like Argentina. The one called Father sent her, on secret business, hence all the fuss, why she could not imagine, not wanting Ned to make a *thing*, though signaling with her eyes there would be *more later,* much more to tell when he finally reached her, longing to embrace her, hold her, touch her, looking so lovely turning toward him, until he saw that her hair, her long blond hair, had been shaved from one side of her head completely.

"It's no use, Neddy," she whispered.

So then he knew it wasn't Argentina.

Wherever it was, Bruce McVitty had been there.

"You're heads and he's tails," Amy Foreman said, in the next apartment, heard through the wall laughing with Bob as the Foremans always did at Nedders, lying silent in the dark on the farther side of her water bed, estranged as so often when the party was over, and some absence or exit with someone like McVitty was left unexplained between them, while she talked on the phone across long distances to Daddy, telling lies about Argentina and the boss called Father. "I'll get to you," she said, her soothing hand reaching out in the spotlight for Ned, until he saw it was mutilated like her other hand, deformed, unable to reach or touch anyone, though he wasn't to make a *thing*, she was saying, making him promise to hush, *promise,* so he too whispered:

"But they didn't do anything to your hands . . ."

And then she gave that little, giving-up groan she sometimes did and he held his breath knowing she was going to roll over, so light so sweet, one last time on his chest, as he put one arm around her, then the other, slowly, carefully, so that too much would not lose all, before she said once, just once, she had loved him.

Because of the graveness of his calling . . .

"And because you would never wound me, Neddy."

"You said that before . . ." He had really heard her, not in some dream, but the memory where he held her, praying she would say it again, would let them all hear her. No matter what happened in Argentina.

"I always thought we knew how we felt about each other. No matter what happened anywhere." She had said that too.

But it wasn't enough! "Tell *them*—" he was saying aloud, begging her to tell them he would never wound her, arms still holding where she'd been, circling the air, when a blind went up, or a light went on, or seeped through a door, opening or closing, as Billings murmured, "It's only us," and tiptoed past with some girl who looked frightened.

The next time it was a phone ringing. Ringing twice while Ned lay silent on her water bed, hoping she wouldn't answer, wouldn't say she was here, she was home, come over, to whoever was calling. But it turned out she was hoping the same thing, lying very still beside Ned in his three-quarter pullout, asking almost wistfully for one so possessive, "Haven't you seen enough of that Billings crowd lately?"

"Let it ring," Ned whispered, but it wouldn't stop until he opened his eyes and sat up on the sofa, realizing it was getting darker in that always dark pad where he'd been left alone with Billings' phone still ringing, waiting to be answered.

It was Bad Guy. Calling on the see-through phone by her bed, no longer under water, Bad Guy said:

"Sounds like you're still in bed yourself, Professor."

"What time is it?"

"Five o'clock. Early for us working stiffs." Thunder was rumbling to explain the darkness. "Been sacked out all day?"

"On and off."

"Do any talking in your sleep . . ." as if they had planted a bug in his head. "Like maybe on the phone?"

"No," said Ned.

"Didn't make any calls?"

"Or take any." Though there had been a few other times when someone tried to get through. But nobody kept on trying like Bad Guy.

"Reason I'm wondering . . . some jerk phoned in a bomb threat to the network. Hear about that?"

"Not this week." Not this jerk.

"Said he was a hippie your girl picked up in the park—you know, yesterday—when she broke your lunch date."

"No, I don't know."

"She said he reminded her of you. Isn't that cute? Funny thing, the girl who got the call today said the same—seems he sounded like you too. Unless you were doing your hippie imitation."

"I never even knew there was a hippie—"

"Your girl didn't tell you that either?"

"I never talked to her after lunch—"

"Just had your fight and hung up forever!"

"No—we missed each other—"

By a couple of miles in Bad Guy's opinion.

"But you can catch up with her on the news tonight, Professor."

"Thanks. I've had the news." Including the water immersion theories about time that Billings claimed let Ned out. Long before Homicide let him go last night. "You guys know how to miss things yourself—when you want to."

"We got this habit of waiting for autopsies. Not that any of it's gonna help you, without an alibi—"

"I told you the kids on my block saw me—"

"Why didn't you tell us about the old geezers who patrol the building on the corner?"

Ned swore softly. Why hadn't he? "I forgot . . ."

"Sure you did. Because one of 'em saw you limping home

when he took his watch. And five minutes later saw you running out—"

"He did like shit—"

"Would a rabbi lie?"

"Would a detective?"

"Check it with him."

"After you got through shaking him up?" Old men, old men, getting everything wrong. Locking out the young before the danger got closer. "Thanks for everything. There goes my neighborhood."

"Now all I gotta do is place you in hers a little earlier—"

"Except you can't. So find yourself a suspect—"

"Don't make any mistake—you could be it." It was the first real thing Bad Guy said. "Want to know why? You've got the motive. Not her pickups, or the Johns, but the poor professor. The only one dumb enough to love her. Never mind if we just walked into her pad with a key some bastard threw away—"

"There's no other key—!"

"We found it! I've got it in my hand! So who was keeping who? Did you know, Professor? Was it one of the guys at the network?"

"There wasn't any guy—"

"OK—which girl?" Bad Guy's snicker was getting uglier, like his inferences about the company she kept—even female. From the sound of her chosen lady confidante next door, from the looks of E. V. Adamic, chosen writer and cruising companion—anything, correction, everything was possible.

Except listening any longer. So Ned hung up, dragged back from his dream to another displaced memory suddenly stirring in a darker shadow somewhere. . . . Something about her first love in college, misunderstood or misrepresented when confided in the night, forgotten until the cold light of a later dawn's fight, when Ned accused her of taking him for some college kid, like that sucker of a boy she went with. "Boy, what boy?" she cried indignantly, sustaining the high level of all such dialogues.

"The one you told me about—in college."

"Was a girl," she laughed. "You are nothing like her."

It could have been a bitchy joke, or a crush that meant nothing, could have meant anything, everything being possible, from the sound of the ugly voice on the phone, ringing again, waiting to be answered. While Ned read the note left beside it, about Billings and the girl bringing food back. It didn't say when and Ned didn't much care, stripping off his shorts and the stained shirt, gathered up with his jeans, and the Gucci loafers, to be dumped, all of it, in Billings' garbage. Before Ned took the change of clothes he'd brought into Billings' bathroom, carefully latching the door, so no one would walk in. No matter how long he stood in the shower, turned on full, so he could finally get clean, couldn't hear the phone ringing, couldn't hear Billings' greetings, couldn't hear the black and white news on Billings' Sony. Nor even the slightly colored views from Argentina. Just plain couldn't hear anything.

The storm had passed, settling nothing. The air hung heavy and gray as before, neither cooling nor cleared by the last clap of thunder, with no relief promised after the deluge, turning to drizzle. Just more of the same.

Certainly it was not the kind of weather to delay a Learjet from landing on a remote La Guardia airstrip, where a squad car waited with two limousines, one private and empty of passengers, the other full of officials. The big men from Homicide were first off the jump seats, leaving the Deputy Commissioner alone in the back with his civilian PR friend from the network. Neither was in any hurry to face The Original Shit Detail, aptly named en route by a veteran of same. Detective Sergeant Corio, former precinct prince of tact, had apparently been on general loan as a Big Case Bad News breaker, before the newly formed Task Force stole him, somehow making a sergeant the Lieutenant's equal, homicidally speaking. But such mysteries of rank were almost beyond explaining to outsiders, forever querying who was in charge of what investigation, while trying to follow its Byzantine procedures.

The Deputy Commissioner kept it simple. "Morgue first. Then it's up to them." He gestured toward Homicide's giants outside. "We'll just go along—stick with it, while we all have the chance."

"Won't they get their questioning done on the way?"

The Deputy Commissioner sighed, easing forward, as a uniformed cop reopened the door on his side. "It never gets done."

The VP of PR opened his door for himself. "Just so there's enough time for me to firm up memorial logistics."

"Out of our hands. Once the body's claimed."

"It's going to be out of our hands too—if I don't get a commitment." Though there was less to memorialize with every passing hour, some sort of PR compromise with the family still seemed preferable to a Cinny and Sally type uprising, spontaneously gathered in the network's name, against a chorus of blacklisting protests from Phelps.

"Wait till later," the Lieutenant advised, when joined in the drizzle, "at the hotel . . . maybe . . ."

"The *club*," the chauffeur from the other limousine interjected haughtily. Though any VP knew the establishment named on the East River was not the haughtiest of its kind, including as it did a minority membership of ladies. But that made it a sufficiently exclusive haven for the arriving royal consort, who was to be chauffeured there directly as per cabled orders from bigger guns to follow. The biggest gun couldn't follow soon enough from where the VP of PR stood, watching the passenger make his slow, solo appearance on the steps wheeled up to the plane. A minor figure, as remembered, though grown portly. Made less so by perfectly tailored dark gabardine. Never tall, but made less short by a hat of Bermuda straw, half hiding gray hair—with the brim, pulled low, half shading a face perennially tanned, while smoked glasses shielded damp eyes in the rain. As if such stratagems could save his presence, when a private jet hadn't. Or a family-owned island. Or the whole world of membership bought by wealth. Where now only officialdom could guarantee safe entry, secret from the press, and the highest level of police escort was here to say so, shouldering aside a mere chauffeur, as public servants took precedence.

The Deputy Commissioner went first, voicing PR regrets for the sad occasion and expressing appreciation in advance for co-operation. Painful but necessary, as explained by Corio, moving in next, massively gentle, to make clear from experience that swift action was meant to be merciful.

"And save time," the Lieutenant said, putting a merciless end to all formalities now standing in the way of the real job ahead. Which was the cue for the only other civilian to put in his own reassuringly familiar appearance, utterly unrecognized from the outset.

"Leland . . ." the VP of PR began unheard, forcing himself to try again, mumbling who he was. "From the network, Leland." And the past, limply revived with a limp handshake, and few limp words about a limper acquaintance during the hated days in Hollywood. Or was it the hated nights in New York? Neither man knew or cared. It was enough just not being cops, as one limp hand dragged the other to the safety of a private huddle, beyond the overpowering circle.

"Sorry about this . . . hate to intrude . . ."

"No, no . . . relieved you're along. But the others . . . must we . . . ?"

"Unavoidable, Lee. Perhaps in your car?"

"Yes, God yes . . . perhaps not all of them?"

"Might be better . . . get it over. Commissioner's a friend."

"Couldn't he explain? Have the rest follow . . ."

Apparently, he couldn't. In fact, the Deputy Commissioner sat up front, while the jump-seat occupants simply switched vehicles. The Lieutenant moved in behind the haughty chauffeur, the better to overrule costly toll routes with his police-wise shortcut to the free Fifty-ninth Street upper level. While Corio slid his bulk in sideways the better to confront the royal consort, helplessly surrounded, albeit in his own rented corner of the wide back seat shared by the other civilian.

It was just as remembered—the man was a pudding. The VP of PR cleared his throat ready to accomplish his memorial mission and maybe get out short of the morgue. He waited impatiently for Corio to get through his number, already heard at the Weldons', about the majority of perpetrators who knew their victims in homicides unaccompanied by forced entry, etc., etc.—complete this time with props, held at the ready: address books, calendars, even photographs from news clippings—but there the royal line was drawn. And held this time, unexpectedly. The VP of PR had remembered wrong: some puddings had starch.

"*No*," Leland Evans said. "We don't see the papers." Or the news on television. Any of it. "We decided it was better simply not to look at these things . . ." The royal consort turned away from Corio's props with such disdain as to perish the thought that the better part of "we" had been left behind, like the Learjet, now refueling to fetch the lady at her later convenience. Leland Evans fixed his damp gaze on the route to the city, traveled so seldom with his wife, so often with his daughter.

"We'd meet him if Mrs. Evans didn't come," Bruce McVitty had told the detectives. "Or Leesy would get someone else with a car . . ." Gaily phoning Daddy to hold the limo, usually needed anyway if only for the luggage, considering the size of sporty models like the Mercedes, whose owner, despite every inconvenience, remained Daddy's first choice for an escort in waiting.

"Young McVitty seemed to be her steadiest beau." He waved away the rest of the address book. "Bruce lasted the longest."

"Yes, sir," Corio said. "But as far as boyfriends, wasn't McVitty more like a brother?"

"Well, they grew up together—from the age of fourteen. But it's hard to tell what might have happened . . . when Maudie Lee settled down . . . and Bruce took hold on The Street."

Corio blinked through the window at The Street where lesser youths took hold—mostly of each other's throats. While Leland Evans sighed for a lost alliance with another royal bloodline, not to be dragged into *this,* of course. "As it happens, we use their family law firm—we're all very close." He turned to the other civilian to confide a nuance beyond strangers. "Golf with Bruce Senior every winter in Pinehurst."

Pinehurst. Winter. One of the damn Carolinas. "Tough course . . ." the VP guessed.

It got tougher. Letting that ball bounce to a stop, Corio persevered with the names of other beaux, none of whom came in a close second. Nor did the few faces finally produced like flash cards, Corio's ham hand covering captions, while he apologized for the awful omission of an up-to-date file full of blowups of the men in Maude Lee Evans' life. As if there'd been time to keep track, with the heavy end of the home team batting order getting blank stares from her own father. Foreman, Lorrilard, Nedders . . .

"Lorrilard—" Leland Evans interrupted. "*Stu* Lorrilard's son—from Tuxedo?"

The VP of PR could only wonder.

It was Sam Lorrilard, Corio explained, from across the hall.

"Oh. Neighbors . . ." Her father conceded she used to include them sometimes at her parties. "But mostly just a couple. From next door."

Silence entombed the limousine interior.

"The Foremans," the Lieutenant said, without looking around.

Corio took the dirty end of the stick. "Mr. Foreman was the other victim, sir. There were two."

"So I was told . . ." But *this* Foreman? The damp eyes sought the wrong photograph for the man met with a wife at parties. "This one?"

"No, sir. That's Nedders."

"Who?"

"He discovered the bodies."

"Nedders," the Lieutenant interjected, "is the boyfriend she'd been seeing for about two years."

"She saw a great many people," said her father.

"Yes, sir," Corio murmured gently. "But she gave Nedders keys."

"Indeed." Leland Evans stared down at the bespectacled face he would not be likely to forget, or confuse. Ever again. "Then he's your suspect—this Nedder fellow?"

"The best we can ascertain he was elsewhere—as far as opportunity." But as far as motive . . . Corio shrugged.

"That damn apartment." Leland Evans' damp eyes sought the rain. As if two layers of misted glass could save her presence from that file of men. Or her absence from the waiting skyline. "This damn city . . ."

Right all along, Bruce McVitty had said about Daddy's negative reaction. Unchanged since that first visit, when she broke the news by directing Bruce's Mercedes straight from the airport to the apartment building where the three-year

lease was already signed. A *fait accompli*, like all her breathless moves since Stamford—from the first jump to shared
sublets in Hollywood to the final long hop East and this full
stop in a glorified one room, then without a stick of furniture,
except some dumb little cocktail piano bought from the previous tenant for Daddy to play when he came. Instead of
Daddy's own baby grand, and two uprights, kept in tune in
faraway places for her promised return from this damn city,
this unholy rat race, which finally got to everyone, Daddy
warned her. Right all along, right as rain, poor bastard.

"This damn job . . ."

"You objected to the job, sir?"

"The whole damn business . . ."

"The way she was living . . . ?"

"It wouldn't have lasted . . . we had an agreement. It was
all a trial, just temporary . . ."

The network would have been interested to hear it, the VP
of PR reflected. Very interested along about 5 P.M. yesterday.
But it was too late now with the credits already rolling, the
whole crawl getting the royal blank treatment, clear to the
top. Sams? Collins? Phelps? Gold? Scooper? Weldon?

"Scooper . . . ?" That sounded familiar to her father. Perhaps from her parties. Or some face from the old days, "Like
you . . ." He turned again to his seat companion.

"I am Scooper," the VP said.

There was, however, no placing any woman, but her secretary. Not Cinny, certainly not Bella. Nor most of the mixed
bag of talent: E. V. Adamic, Billy Bee Bernard . . . Then
came Kelly.

"Smilin' Ed Kelly," Corio illustrated with an eight-by-eleven
movie star glossy, sufficiently dated and retouched to force recall of *Boys on Shore Leave.*

"Yes," Leland Evans said, "I knew him."

The reaction to comebacks, as to careers, discouraged all

but the most necessary follow-up. Doggedly the Lieutenant reminded Corio about other work she might have mentioned.

"We're interested in free-lance connections," Corio amplified. "An outside source for extra income . . ."

It was the closest her father ever came to a smile.

"*Extra* income was *never* mentioned."

Except the extra tax-exempt three thousand a year he provided, usually gone, before he made his next visit, still hoping that someday her extravagant dream of living on her own would give way to his more substantial dream of setting up trusts, ensuring modest incomes for herself and her children. "She wasn't very practical."

"No, sir," Corio agreed. Nevertheless she had accumulated considerable cash on hand, not accounted for by bank withdrawals. Or even loans. "We were just wondering if you happened to extend any help on your last visit . . ."

"Yes . . ." For some problem about shutter doors for a new bath and dressing-room area, designed as usual by her friends. "All of these people wanted to be paid in cash. It's possible she just hadn't passed it along . . ." But Leland Evans had covered the bill, with some to spare. "Twenty here, ten there. Probably enough to account for what you found—if it's in the neighborhood of, say, two hundred."

Nobody answered. Until they got out from under an elevated train and the Lieutenant turned.

"Mr. Evans—did your daughter ever have a dope problem— or do *any* trafficking in drugs?"

"Never." There, parental warnings had taken hold—so far as hallucinogens and hard stuff were concerned. But gage, the dated term Leland Evans still applied to her hidden marijuana, hardly counted as a very dire problem to a former musician. Any more than her Dexedrine, taken by prescription. "She was always concerned about getting chubby."

"Chubby?" The detectives who had seen the body exchanged a look.

"Tended to be chubby . . . as an adolescent."

She had come a long way, the VP of PR decided, as the limousine picked up speed on the turn to the upper level bridge, vaulting from Queens toward Manhattan's skyline, and the chic East Fifties, where a landmark could be proudly pointed out from the exit ramp Maude Lee Evans preferred. Like the Lieutenant.

"Isn't that your old club, Mr. Evans?"

"Wasn't mine. Just somewhere I worked once."

The Piano Bar then, a disco now, a sewer always, like all the rest, to Leland Evans. Despite the current rage of nostalgia for the Good Old Days. And the pride taken in his by his daughter, a memory rejected once again as the former musician shook his head.

"She didn't know what it was like. Too young to remember."

"She remembered," Bruce McVitty had said. Silence fell in the limousine, heading down Second Avenue, empty now of traffic, allowing such good time through the staggered lights that the VP of PR did not even attempt to slip in a few words of his memorial address before they got where they were going.

"Here we are, sir," Corio said.

Oddly, the morgue's ground-floor façade was bright blue, a jaunty footnote to the Medical Center across from Bellevue. And the overworked Deputy Chief Medical Examiner, alerted to be on hand, seemed as young and bright as the building. He was a better greeter than the Mayor, rolling out the carpet for the mourning party he led up and down steps, through the smell of formaldehyde, past lesser mourners in the lobby, guards in the hall, not toward that vast, overpublicized tomb of locker-like slabs, but into the discreet Identification Room, with the oblong screen of glass, the single demure window. Where finally there was no getting around it.

She came up in a sack on a dumb-waiter. Nothing showed but her face, sewn up in place to meet the hairline, Honeysun hair carefully rearranged so no one could guess what had been done to her, before or after. Except perhaps the man who had also identified her mother. The long ago suicide, long denied, became what it was in the light of murder. No accident but crime begetting crime, separated only by a generation. It could have been the same sack left open.

He gasped and turned, fighting for control but unable to catch his breath, to do more than gasp again—yes he knew her, yes could make the identification, yes of his daughter, yes to the forms, yes to the signatures, to the network's offer to take over the mechanics of transfer, yes to the choice of funeral parlor, yes even to the memorial service. Perhaps he did not know quite what he was yessing as he gasped and yessed his way out—back through reeking halls and lobby, down the last steps to the street where the limousines were drawn up. His was first, waiting to bear him away, in privacy. Followed discreetly by theirs. Or so they thought, until he turned on them, gasping not from grief but fury.

"This is an outrage—a goddamn outrage. You birds dare come to me—with your goddamn newspapers. Your gossip—prying! About *her*—her friends, her things, in her apartment . . . her money, her medicine. You *dare!* What the hell do you think you're doing? Where is your suspect—why haven't you arrested him? This Nedder . . . why isn't he the one to be questioned? Not my daughter—on that thing in there! How dare you—how dare you commit this outrage?" He turned, with his last gasp, shouting, "Driver!"

"Yes, sir."

"The club." The door was slammed, the driver, no longer haughty, sprinted to his place to start the motor, trying to get clear before the passenger could be seen to collapse to one side, the side away from the observers, could be heard, even through rolled-up windows, to start sobbing. As the limousine pulled away, and the starch went out of the pudding.

In Queens, the news on the set suspended over the bar had been full of talk of mystery boyfriends—with Benjie coming in for some more ribbing, until the bartender called off the regulars. He had already reserved the farthest corner stool for his friend's retreat from celebrity, now more unwanted even than last night, though for different reasons.

"That picture turns up," Benjie prophesied darkly, "they'll be talking about mystery girlfriends."

"So. What do you need obstructing a justice—? Like you're some kind of President?"

"I open my mouth, they'll figure I took the damn thing."

"C'mon—they'll figure her boyfriend first." Not to mention the mystery person or persons who committed murder and might still be in possession of the evidence needed to make an arrest. For which information the network had now officially offered a reward of ten thousand dollars. As per the promise of some network executive at the memorial show press conference, featured locally on the home channel.

"You're scared of the cops, we could maybe get to this executive, Benj—"

"No way."

But there were ways, the bartender knew from the days when he served a drinker, who drank with a guy, who ran with Breslin. The emergency number announced with the reward was a monitored hot line, for cranks or rubes to call— though copied down over Benjie's objections, just in case.

"I'm not calling anybody, Art—"

"Not yet for Pete's sake—"

"Not anytime . . . And neither are you!"

"Will you just wait and see how the news breaks?"

"The hell with the news—"

"OK, OK, simmer down—make up your mind on the job tomorrow."

"Nothing's going to change my mind anyplace."

Except maybe one thing, the bartender prophesied. Like maybe the thought of some delivery boy knowing about the photograph. Or any dumb dude who got in there lately. "Somebody's gonna try for that ten grand, Benjie . . ."

Which held Benjie's water, long enough to pour another refill, which held him again for the ten-o'clock news, topped at eleven on the good old home channel where private memorial services, arranged with the Evans family for Sunday, were respectfully announced by the same smooth executive. Only this time the bartender got the name. And just in case, despite Benjie's objections, wrote down what it sounded like: S C O O P E R.

On Friday morning, the frustrated press was still a few official false leads behind the game. So it was anybody's turn in the barrel. Including Ned, overdue for follow-up, since the fill needed for weekend editions was not yet to be had at the final dead end in the club by the river where the family's respects remained unpaid. Unwisely. No one knew better than the media that such obligatory scenes were better confronted fast, out in the open, while the curious enemy was still a visible presence asking for directions, not yet dispersed to find separate ways through the most sacrosanct ivied halls. As per some very worldly PR advice, sleepily offered again by Billings, though it never really did get through to Ned, trying to exit silently in sneakers, moving like an automaton through underground passageways on his usual shortcut route across campus, back to work. It seemed the most natural impulse left until it was short-circuited on arrival at the speech department, where once before he had discovered a fair visitor copying the writing on the wall.

(*The speech of the children of man is our interest and the communion of man is our concern.*)

But this new visitor was not truly fair, just smiling sentimentally to prove friendship with strangers. The smile must have hurt. Her lips were cracked by a sun sore, skin tanned to leather. ("Blondes have to be careful over thirty," the blonde who was never blond or careful, or thirty, would have said.)

"They say your girlfriend carried this in her wallet."

"Who says?" Ned asked rudely.

She protected her sources, lip sore with smiling. "I know a lot that could help you, Ned."

(*We seek out those who are halting in speech; and we offer help to those whose ears have been confused . . .*)

"The only way you can help is to leave me alone."

Two embarrassed colleagues, hovering to offer sympathy, got the message and kept on going into the speech department. But the press pressed, needing a story. Ned shook his head.

"Yesterday's news. You've written my story."

"Not in your own words. Sooner or later we'll get your statement. Why not now?"

"I'm going to work."

"Then when can we talk?"

"We can't," he said.

(*Life without speech is empty; and life devoid of communication scarcely better than death.*)

"Everybody has to talk to someone, Ned. And we're the best friends you've got now." She was blind to Ned's faculty adviser, sometimes thought of as a friend, beckoning a mother with deaf child to safety in his office. Only the child waved at Ned as they went. Then a door was heard closing.

"You'll be my only friends, if you keep this up. We treat patients here!"

(*"Therefore the duty we owe is sacred, and our calling is gravely important."*)

But her calling called for an interview, preferably exclusive, business being business even with the free and friendly press, known to put money where the mouth was, enough to come in handy when a lawyer was needed.

"Lawyer for what? I'm out of it." The witness was not, had never been a suspect.

She laughed and the lip sore broke. "You'll do till they find someone else to hang it on! Give me some names—why should you protect her other men?"

Why indeed? He couldn't tell a stranger what he didn't know himself. "I only saw Foreman." Wasn't that enough? The Lieutenant would have thought so. The reporter didn't.

"Who's the rich boy who came to Homicide. What's your reaction to this pickup they're looking for?" Her lip dripped, she smudged it with her hand. "How do all these things make you *feel*, Ned?"

He focused on the freshest wound. No one, nothing could stop the bleeding.

"You make me feel like dying," he said.

Sooner or later, all voices broke, went off automatic, and gave with a quote. Good for a lead, or properly twisted, even a head. ("Wants to Die Too, Lover Says.") Ned left her at her copying, heading through the silent speech department for the observation booth where his first patient was already waiting, bouncing off the mirrored walls. Billy was a screamer, and almost a relief after the long hall of closed doors. But today the eleven-year-old would not settle down at all, could not concentrate on pictures or play with toys. Except for the little red phone used to shout bye-bye at his own reflection. So beatific only two weeks before when he finally learned the word for smile after an endless exchange of same with his teacher.

"Come on, Billy, we're saying hello." Ned grinned into the mirror. "OK? Hello."

"Bye!" Billy slammed down his phone.

"What do we do when we say hello? Like this." Ned's grin widened. "Hello, Billy."

"Bye, bye, bye!" Slam, slam, slam.

So Ned tried again to go back to the beginning, holding up the picture which had led to the mirror, fighting the regression, caused, he thought at first, by his absence. "What's this boy in the picture doing?"

"Eating peanuts."

"No." Ned chewed. "That's eating." Then he smiled at himself, in imitation of the smiling picture. "This is what we do when we smile. Where's your smile, Billy?"

Billy reached for his phone. On a sharper day, Ned might have trusted Billy's instinct instead of wasting the better part of an hour before a student turned on the light in the observation area to reveal a photographer clicking away through the window mirror. In the melee that followed, Billy escaped his waiting mother to run shrieking in circles like Maude Lee's puppy, while Ned raced around to help the student corner the cameraman, in a physical shouting match that finally brought Ned's faculty adviser from behind his closed door.

"Ned, you just can't have these press people here!"

"I'm trying to get him out—without these pictures!"

"This university doesn't own my equipment—" The photographer pulled his camera free. "You can't keep me—or my film!"

"I can damn well keep you from violating my therapist-patient relationship—"

It was settled finally, in the faculty adviser's office. A series of well-placed phone calls to venerable graduates from the school of journalism, sent the red-faced photographer on his way with a lot of unusable film. While Ned, equally red-faced, was advised to let things blow over before continuing therapy experiments for his thesis, despite the new pressure of a foundation grant, normally a credit to the department.

"We'll have to talk about all that, Ned."

"What do you mean have to—I want to—"

"Not now." And above all, not here. "We'll have lunch tomorrow . . ." Easily arranged off campus on a Saturday. "At least take the rest of the day off after all you've been through."

"Thanks, Doctor, but I'm due at the VA," Ned said acidly, "they'll never look for me there." Even Homicide didn't yet know about the so-called professor's hospital duties. But his department champion should have. Considering what was written on the wall.

Press attention had wandered entirely from network reception areas, where PR's steady line of official pap lagged well behind the word on the office grapevine, now catching up behind the scenes, with the only game in town that really mattered to Homicide. And no one sensed it faster than the player taking her frostiest tone with the Detective Sergeant, approaching her desk for a rematch.

"Why ask *me* about the office chaser?"

"You run the office, Mrs. Sweet."

"I'd like to!" In the welcome absence of the press, she seemed impatient to resume business as usual. And today that meant resuming her usual kaffeeklatsch with the VP of PR, signaling from the door he'd come back later.

"Not too much later, sweetie. This won't take long." Eager for the rest of the airport dish, Bella glanced pointedly at her diamond wristwatch. But Detective Sergeant Corio stood his ground, sticking with his stated intention to pay special heed to female opinions in this year of liberation. And this case, where most of the boys were paying heed to boys.

"We're looking for the type of individual who might have had access to Miss Evans' apartment."

"Not anyone who works here, surely."

"Checking it out. Just routine."

So was Bella's answer. "Personnel has files for that kind of information. I can't keep up with the psychological testing required for new executives. It changes too often."

"So does this case." So had his official tone of polite apology. And with it the level of Bella's hospitality. She offered her visitor neither a seat nor coffee from her thermos, as she bore her second steaming cupful back to her command post behind the desk. Such posts were not won by dishing with outsiders.

"We're interested in the records you keep in your head." The detective himself was armed with his notebook.

"I keep figures in my head." Mostly for contracts and labor negotiations, routinely noted yesterday.

"And schedules." He riffled through the pages to find Bella's interview, which spelled out Miss Evans' late arrival at 10:32, but omitted the time of her early departure. "Any reason, Mrs. Sweet?"

She shrugged. "All the creative people left early—before five. They were due at a meeting."

"Not Ms. Evans." Who could have been ducking because her boss was gone, a possibility worthy of Bella's interest.

"She gave me the impression she wasn't needed."

"Or wanted?"

"That's not what she said."

"Did anybody?"

Bella took a protracted sip from her cup, pinkie extended, and patted her glazed lips dry with a hanky before she answered. "The creative people do not take network staff into their confidence. Nor can I keep track of free-lance talents not knowing the terms of their obligations—"

"You keep track of who's in and who's out, don't you?"

"That would take a computer."

"And someone to feed it."

"Try her boss. Mr. Phelps is the one to evaluate Miss Evans' standing. I'm happy to defer to his opinion."

"He doesn't seem to have a private opinion—he's referred us to you on the subject of all interoffice relationships."

It was the first surprise of the interview. Bella put down her flowered cup. "Because I'm the only woman on this executive level—and therefore likeliest one to gossip?" It was as close as she could come to a feminist reaction.

"Not exactly." The detective seemed to be reading a quote: "He said you are a better man than five out of six who made Vice President."

Better or worse, she was harder to flatter. "Who was the sixth supposed to be—his wife?"

The detective laughed and closed the notebook. "I think it was meant as a figure of speech. Would Mrs. Phelps get your vote?"

But nobody won Bella's vote for best man today. Certainly not her own sex, nor any artist over management. Nor West Coast over East. Though Old Man Weldon was barely in the running against Israel Gold, running too hard. And not about to get any farther either. Since wanting too much also gave the wrong image, said the voice of experience, wanting too little. "At this rate, none of them will make it. Just chasing their own shadows."

"And that's all?"

"All that matters around here. Girls come and go." Bella gestured wearily toward the hall where the parade less one continued, getting by for a bit on brains, where once looks had helped. "Evans would have done better when we had it both ways." A losing game since liberation. Especially in a field where the competition came from starlets who didn't have to be chased around casting couches. A born flirt, miscast as a token was simply more trouble than Evans was worth.

"Some men like a challenge."

"Not here—not men at a dangerous age." The age at which most media men were arrested.

"What would you call her age—safe?"

"I never quite knew *what* it was. Do you?"

The ages mentioned in the papers reflected the disparity between East and West Coast personnel records. None had so far quoted the family. Neither did the detective. "The concensus puts it at twenty-five."

Bella's penciled eyebrows arched in neat and permanent disbelief. "Really."

One thing was for sure, the Detective Sergeant said. She was young enough to get chased around a desk. "Especially by a rising young executive."

"Until someone got caught."

"Someone did, Mrs. Sweet."

Not by any executive Bella knew. And she knew them all. "That's my opinion." She rose to make the point. "I'm sorry, but if you ask me, the office chaser is dead."

Meantime, as if by secret signal, the home team brass was about to go public—lunchwise. To a man they chose the scene of their crime as if to show the brass of other networks there was nothing to hide or fear from return, and certainly nothing the least bit shady about continued co-operation with the authorities—met now, right out in the open. Indeed, table reservations in the restaurant side of The Bar Downstairs promised to turn their network's usual section into a veritable Homicide Squad Room. Surprisingly, the Creative Co-ordinator was due first, though running late true to form, when Detective Frankovitch presented himself to the maître d' at the dining-room entry.

"Mr. Phelps phoned he's been delayed by an interview. Would you like to have a drink at the table, sir?"

"No, thanks, I'll see if my partner's here." Frankovitch headed for the bar side, only to find that Reilly was already rising from his stool to greet Mr. Weldon, walking in from the street, soberly early, and with his young wife. The partners barely managed to exchange a passing word—and wink.

"Better check back with Corio, Frank."

"You got all the luck, Reilly."

Mrs. Weldon was already turning executive heads en route to the restaurant from the bar, where Frankovitch was left to call the home network from the empty booth nearest the street. The receptionist on the twenty-first floor put his call through to Mrs. Sweet's office, where it was transferred to Personnel, who transferred it to Cinny, where Sally answered, sounding as if she'd been crying. So that's where Corio was.

"What's up, Sarge?"

"Couple of things. You in that restaurant?"

"Yeah—hold on." Hearing a tap on the glass, Frankovitch turned to fold the door open, but it wasn't Phelps.

"I understand you guys are looking for me," Charlie Collins said. And held out a bunch of keys.

"What's that?"

"A joke . . ." Flushed purple under his mustache, Charlie took another wild look around the bar, before he blurted the rest. About his mythical key collection, made into a joke gift— a giant key ring full of jokes, presented with love from the girls in PR, at their farewell celebration for Charlie's promotion, all of it now backfiring to threaten his whole career. Like the stupid cover story he told to his former PR boss at the Plaza party. Which today had Charlie sweating in vain through his seersucker jacket. Too late to prove that his access to changing stations did not include, had never included a key to Evans' apartment. Though at least there was a way to place him in somebody else's stall shower after he left this damn bar Wednesday. But Charlie's witness, also connected with the network, was someone he honored, still hoped to protect. Certainly wasn't about to name here. And, he didn't mean Mrs. Weldon!

"Better tell Reilly to double-check the lady," Corio advised on the phone. "The gentleman's already lied once. And I'm the one who's looking for him. Right now—in his office."

So in the end it was Corio's Task Force that had all the luck when it came to leads. Not Reilly, from the ranks of Homicide regulars. Or his partner hovering by the table, listening to Mrs. Weldon, full of outraged innocence about how she merely gave that Collins *boy* a lift home to meet Israel, never having *met* the lowly junior executive before Scooper of PR made the usual intros at the VP party! *Much* too late to involve Mrs. Weldon as an alibi. For *anything* this Collins did! Or did not do on Wednesday.

"That's what Collins said, ma'am," Frankovitch assured her. "Just checking—"

"There's Phelps," Mr. Weldon interrupted Reilly's partner coldly. "I'm sure he can tell you more than my wife."

"Well, I *hope* so!" Mrs. Weldon huffed. "I mean I'm sorry any of these kids got mixed up in a murder! But it's really up to Phelps to say what was going on between his own employees."

Frankovitch thanked her, hoping the same, though Phelps' reaction when joined at his table was not much more helpful.

"Nothing could have gone on." Not between a Star Protégée and a company fink.

"What about his keys?"

"He obviously doesn't have hers."

"Well, not *now* . . ."

The rumor about the washroom discovery had yet to be confirmed at the official level, but Phelps wasn't much on rumors anyway. "Evans had no use for the type in general. Or Charlie Collins in particular," he said with finality, and signaled the waiter.

Frankovitch shrugged. "Lots of people get laid without liking each other."

"I'd be the last to know." True to form, Phelps ordered a Virgin Mary. So Frankovitch had to.

"Sounds like you have a good marriage, Mr. Phelps."

"I hope so."

"Never give your wife any of these extra curricular type worries . . . ?"

"No reason for any. But feel free to check with her."

Frankovitch smiled. "The ladies are Sergeant Corio's department." In fact, unless rerouted by Charlie Collins, the tactful terror of the Task Force was even now due for a very personal kaffeeklatsch in Nannie's screening room, though it seemed to be the first her husband had heard of it, Corio always being one to keep things discreet. Better at it than the younger men, Frankovitch conceded. Especially the good guy type like Reilly, looking rather swamped between the Weldons as the indignant lady beckoned to the VP of PR, now entering to join a bigger brass table, Phelps noted. Which left only one network county to be heard from. Los Angeles county. A cue for a welcome change of subject, though Phelps waited until the waiter served the Virgin Marys before voicing an untrue-to-form recollection.

"There was one thing Evans said the other day . . ." The last day, in fact. He turned ice blue eyes on the detective. "I thought it was a silly guess then—because of a script that Collins sneaked to the Coast. So I just dismissed it. I dislike gossip."

"Can be helpful. To us."

Phelps nodded. "She thought if Collins was spying for our crowd out there, he might be pimping here."

"When the executives come East?"

"Yes. Primarily Evans meant the one she used to work for. Israel Gold."

Phelps watched Frankovitch make a note of the name.

Home team one hundred. Visitors zero.

The detectives should have caught up with Israel before his wife did. He left her unpacking in the larger bedroom he wanted everyone to know the Golds were sharing, pulling the door to, but not quite closed, before he admitted Detectives Reilly and Frankovitch, cautioned to make it short, sweet, and quiet, as Israel ushered them to the sitting area where the pile of newspapers had grown higher on the sofa, formerly occupied by Charlie Collins—alleged fink-pimp, stud, and spy.

"Some spy," Israel muttered. Maudley, he said, Maudley was the one who sent scripts out, the way he understood and remembered it. And Maudley, definitely Maudley, had personally kidded to Israel about the office girls' delight—Charlie Collins—passing himself off as some kind of stud, would you believe?

"What's that about your friend Charlie?" The bedroom door swung wide and there she was, upon them: Israel's lovely wife, Dotty—one hand clutching a can of Superhold Hairspray, the other full of Playtex Superholds, with the rest of the world's supply of both products, already cementing her jet black upsweep and ample person. "What'd I hear you saying, Iz?"

"Nothing to you! Look how you look—" She paused to consider her traveling pants suit of magenta Dacron—"I mean with the bras and the girdles." Exasperated, Israel pointed to the handful of Playtex that so chagrined him in front of the de-

tectives, already rising to say they were merely here on a routine matter. To be checked with Israel, rolling his sea green
eyes, not Dotty, braying nasally, devil take Israel's embar-
rassment. "I never liked that Charlie Collins—"

"For God's sake, Dotty, what's that got to do—"

"You bring these people to our *home!*" Where she hadn't
felt at home since Atlantic Beach anyway. And no wonder.
She turned to the detectives. "I want to know who's suspected
of what—we got a daughter—"

"Three thousand miles away—"

"Where he brings them all—these boys from the New York
office. To escort our Dolly, at the Emmies. This Charlie—"

"With us along. That was different."

"What's different?"

"A nice girl with her parents—"

"The other girl was nice once too! That first buffet, I met a
lovely person!"

Israel blinked, unable to visualize the buffet when the
shadow called Maudley had seemed nice to Dotty, now turning to explain to the detectives that once this girl, so smart
from college, had been like a second Dolly to Israel, this
Maudley of his, brought low by office studs.

There being no hope of clearing Charlie, the detectives let
Israel clear them from the suite, hissing his indignation before
they hit the hall. "You guys gotta be crazy, starting with my
wife!"

"Didn't know you'd left your bedroom door open, Mr.
Gold," Frankovitch said.

"Neither did I." This time, armed with the key, Israel made
sure he pulled the suite door shut before walking them to the
elevator, to get the rest of it over with. For good, he hoped.

"As far as pimps, as far as pimps . . ." Israel had to laugh,
recalling Charlie's big plan for last night, which consisted of
maybe getting lucky with some secretaries at the office party.

Which even if Israel did such things wouldn't have thrilled him much more than baby-sitting with the Weldons.

"Some baby she is." Reilly gave an exhausted sigh.

"Forget her," Israel advised. "The Weldons—they're like honeymooners, would you believe?"

The detectives didn't seem to.

"Ask your commissioner. He saw 'em, with the His 'n' Her kimonos. Go figure," Israel sighed, pushing the down button. "Someone for everybody, I guess. Look at the Phelps . . ." he shook his head, "such a gorgeous girl like Nannie."

"What's the matter there?" Frankovitch asked.

"He's sterile. After sterile comes impotent. Or how come there wasn't any make with Maudley?" It was a stunning sweep of false assumptions, somewhat dazing both detectives. The older of whom, as appraised by Israel, was thirty, tops. "So what do you know?"

"Mr. Gold, what do *you* know, personally, about Miss Evans' makes—on the job?"

"Not enough," Israel had to admit, though ruefully. "Face it —what'd she need from me?"

"How about before? When she worked for you . . . ?"

"Fresh out of Stamford? In my own home state? With my wife like that?" He looked over his shoulder. "You young guys, you really are crazy."

The elevator arrived. The last they saw he was already hurrying down the hall to the doors he left open or closed so selectively. To guard or to expose his marriage, as needed for appearances. Like Dotty, last of the Jewish mammas, homesick for Hillside in Beverly Hills, on hold for life at forty-five. Israel had said it himself—there was someone for everybody.

The point was made once more for Sergeant Corio, reluctantly brought to Charlie Collins' home away from home at the end of a miserable afternoon of questioning. Buzzed in to the old-fashioned building from upstairs, the two men got off the converted self-service elevator to find their hostess appropriately changed to a hostess gown, waiting in the only open doorway out of four. Rising frostily over the compromising circumstances of their final encounter, Bella Sweet led the detective down the long narrow hall between an archway and windowed double doors, straight to her roseate boudoir at the end. She sashayed coolly past her pink moiré double bed with matching upholstered headboard, across her floral carpet to the last of three neat closets, the one reserved for Charlie's use, though he hadn't left much of a trace. Opened as dispassionately as a file cabinet, the door discreetly lined with a mirror, flashed a brief reflection of some clean shirts and shorts folded on a high shelf, an extra pair of slacks on a hanger, a seersucker robe hanging limply from a hook over the shoes he had switched for loafers on Wednesday. When, it was now confirmed, he had indeed showered and shaved and changed his shirt before hustling across Fifty-eighth Street to the Plaza. Leaving Bella, reclining on her pink satin chaise, satin drapes drawn behind her, as always when watching her console TV, using her remote control unit to switch from channel to channel during the local news, until she zeroed in on the home team's anchor at seven. Bella was a creature of unbreakable habit, Charlie being only one of many, sweating and flushing briefly in the background of her reflection in the closet mirror, before the door was closed again.

"I was gone by seven . . . already at the party," he muttered unnecessarily, again at the rear of the parade led back down the hall to the dinette archway, where refreshments, politely offered, were politely refused. Except by Charlie, left to help himself, mumbling and fumbling at the bar cellaret opposite the windowed double doors now thrown open to reveal a smallish living room, Bella swept carefully ahead through a suite of furniture, apparently inherited from vaster spaces, and proudly identified in response to the smallest compliment, as her mother's "things." The maternal taste had run to pairs—tables edged in gold filigree and topped in marble, twin wing chairs, even love seats, lovingly reupholstered in moiré, with satin pillows accenting more drapes of the same. The daughter's limited taste in fabrics ranged from formally sexy to sexily formal, tied together by a thread picked from the pattern in Sloane's oriental rug. What didn't pair matched. When it wasn't a boudoir, Bella called it a salon and colored it gold. To be used for entertaining only.

"Please sit anywhere . . ." Bella moved to the farther side of the fake marble fireplace, to enthrone herself on the love seat under an oval-framed décolleté study of her mother, done, as often noted, by a twenties master of pastels. A stronger family resemblance might have persisted had the too, too solid flesh framed by the hostess' décolletage also been magically composed of chiffon.

Without batting a freshly mascaraed eyelash, or emitting so much as a sigh of regret for the morning's evasions, Bella began by pointing out the need for Corio's discretion re the occasional residence of bumbling youth. All business, she cited the obvious age gap as if it were a figure in a labor negotiation which might make her bargaining position ludicrous in the office she was supposed to manage. Especially among the girls, forever giggling after Charlie, an office joke that could still provide cover, since the gigglers had never included Evans.

"Any particular reason why not?" Corio asked, taking out his notebook.

"We," Charlie said, entering in more forcefully with a scotch in his hand, "just never saw Evans much socially . . ."

"We," Bella said, the only time she said it, "don't see each other much socially, sweetie."

"Well, except at office parties, I meant—"

But only the biggest or most special, Bella explained to the detective. "The demands are different for Charlie and I." Incorrect use of the first person singular obviously sounded better than any form of the plural, while discoursing on separate command performances. Having enough of her own to contend with, Bella would not have gone if asked, for example, to Evans' housewarming and thus had missed the unveiling of the now famous décor. She surveyed her own with satisfaction born of many a favorable comparison.

"You didn't miss much," Charlie came through loyally, "before *or* after."

The detective looked up from his notebook. "Ms. Evans gave a party *before* her apartment was decorated?"

"Well, no—I mean I just happened to see it . . ." Charlie fumbled, flushing again as he hastened to explain that, in a way, even his first visit had been business, coming as it did at the end of a long Sunday-night drive back from a longer day at the Phelpses' house in the country. He turned to Bella. "We were all together that time, remember?"

"Yes," she said, at last batting an eyelash. Perhaps in memory of the weekend traffic which made it so hard on the driver, surrounded as she was by sleeping passengers, in the gathering darkness full of brightening headlights, making it harder and harder to see what anyone's right hand was doing while the left clasped a girl, like the one next to Bella in Charlie's lap, Phelps' new find from California, still tanned enough to go bare-legged in her mini skirt, worn so conveniently that fall by all the gigglers. But somehow that style note went unmentioned as the moment passed with the batting of an eyelash.

"I think I'll have a drink after all . . ." Bella said. Charlie jumped up, draining his scotch so that he could switch to "our usual" offered to the detective, who looked tempted, if only by nostalgia. It had been a long time between sweet Manhattans.

"Maybe a soda," Corio decided, "Coke if you've got one."

"We've got everything." Knowing that Bella always did, Charlie crashed off through the dinette into the kitchen.

Thus the hostess was free to wrap up the memoir of that tiresome Sunday rather more swiftly than Charlie might have. Coming from the West Side Highway, she had naturally dropped herself off first, leaving Charlie to drop the others and return the hired car. Evans being last had inveigled him into coming upstairs to save her another night in a sleeping bag by connecting the hose to her water bed, left unfilled by some hippie helper, caught in the act of fleeing. All of which reminded Bella that Evans' feckless moonlighters had included a few minor workers from the network's own set departments, any one of whom might, as Bella put it, have mislaid a key.

"We're canvassing everyone who worked on the apartment," Corio said noncommittally, though he made a note before accepting his glass complete with coaster from a lacquered tray, served Bella-style by Charlie, making points so he could squeeze in next to her on the love seat this time, crushing the silk gown with his thigh, as he mused on about Evans' weakness for hippie types, not only as helpers, but friends.

"Like this grad student she went with . . ." And picked up, according to the papers, as casually as the picket in the park.

"Or Evelyn Adamic," Bella said, reminded only Wednesday of the prior relationship between writer and producer, caught issuing from the same toilet, reeking from pot and whispering about pills. A throwback from bygone days when E.V. made her reputation as a prize stray, champion sponger, finder and loser of other people's keys . . . without a word on paper to her credit when she landed on Evans' doorstep, the way Bella heard it on the Off-Off-Broadway grapevine.

It was a new one on Charlie, who looked bemused. "Yeah,

but even if E.V. got a hold of Evans' key, how could she dump it in the Men's Room?"

Bella shrugged, eyes on Corio, still writing. "The rumor I heard didn't say which washroom the key was found in." It was a fine distinction not previously noted by any of the panicked gigglers, spreading rumors, still neither confirmed nor denied as Corio closed his notebook to rise, with only one more question to be asked, almost as an afterthought. . . .

"Oh, by the way, Charlie—that night you filled Ms. Evans' water bed, did you come back here to Mrs. Sweet's?"

It caught Charlie unprepared. "Well . . . I'm sure . . . We usually stay together on weekends—when we can . . ." He turned to Bella, also given pause, perhaps in memory of a longer delay, a deadlier silence full of imaginings.

"Yes," she said. "You came back here."

But when he came back from showing the detective out to the elevator the salon was empty—doors wide, lights on, the almost full shaker left with the glasses on the table, a break in precedent that shook Charlie, loading the tray to hurry after her down the hall, wishing she'd just once forget the news, so he could set the drinks on his table by the bed, instead of hers by the chaise. But he made himself smile as he squeezed in again, facing her reclining form, mountainous under the silk gown, against her satin mountain of pillows.

"You're in the way."

"Can't you watch at eleven?"

"I may not be back."

"From where?"

"Seeing Mother . . ."

"*Tonight?*" All the way to the *Bronx?*

Bella shrugged and switched channels. "She never knows the difference . . ." Did not even know Bella, Saturday after Saturday. "We've got the memorial Sunday. I need one day free."

Free from Charlie? A new ploy, but still surely the same game plan, requiring a turnabout, change of pace for the Queen of Putdowns after a hard week's reign at the office.

"Move so I can watch too."

"There isn't room."

"Since when?" He laughed and slapped the thigh, ungirdled under the silk, a reminder that she never wore one around Charlie, the only time . . . "C'mon . . . make room . . ."

Her lips were set; she crossed her legs.

"I didn't mean that way . . ." He slipped his hand up between her knees.

"Leave me alone, Charlie."

"Are you kidding? Quit playing games!"

The trouble was they couldn't. Their game was called Wolf Wolf, and the way they played no never meant no. But always yes—Pavlov's bell to make a wolf salivate after a bitch no longer in heat, just burning up for a fight she couldn't win, had to lose on chaise or bed, forced for fun until she gave, giving so much they couldn't stop, kept coming back time after time, spoiling for the sport, now missing somehow. Nothing seemed to give but the seams of her dress, pulled over her head to imprison her, rolled on her back onto the floor, as he freed one hand for himself. Until she bit his other hand right through the silk, showing her face to get it slapped. Harder than usual, too hard, like everything else since Wednesday.

Charlie had all he could do to stay on top, unable to spare his strength for the rod, almost whimpering with frustration. Like a Mamma's boy, spoiled rotten, sticking out his tongue once too often, he feared now to freeze that way, freezing Mamma by contagion, suddenly congealed to ice underneath him, hard heart pounding next to his in the awful stillness. Before Charlie let it all rip, like the tearing silk, and something that tore inside Bella, not ready, not wanting, not won, when entered. He was pumping at a well that had gone dry, beyond control or satisfaction, gasping for the ruin of a shared fantasy, not fully understanding it had become real. Until he raped her. An antidote of sorts to being had himself, but it left him without an antidote to Bella.

"Get out," she said as she had on the chaise, final proof the game was up, like Charlie, spent short of the mark.

"Not yet . . ."

"Get out. Get off . . ."

"Wait . . ."

She had done waiting. "I can't."

Neither could he really, just wishing the floor would open up or his pants close, when their bodies rolled apart, shorn of roles. But he could only lie panting where she left him, using the chaise to hoist herself up from the remains of her dress, staggering naked to the nearest closet, mirror flashing the other view: Bella in the round, sag assed and balloon breasted —old, cold, frozen the way she really was, when her lover laughed.

"Wish you could see yourself from here."

She was the one to fumble this time. Shaking hands reached for the nearest cover, the seersucker robe she had given Charlie, taken back to wrap around her, unable to find the armholes before she made the john, minus the old sashay at last. Poor old Bella with the blind staggers.

"Beautiful," Charlie whistled. "You oughta mirror the ceiling."

"And get myself murdered too?" He really didn't take in what she'd said until he heard the door lock.

"What's that for?" He jumped up, awkwardly holding himself together as he rushed over. "Who do you think you're locking out—?"

The trouble was she didn't know either. And never would know now, no matter how long he rattled the doorknob, shouting in protest that it was her fault as much as his, that he

meant no harm, wouldn't do any. Never had, to anyone, anywhere, anytime, including Wednesday. Not before or after he
found Bella dozing on her chaise, hair up in curlers under her
dryer, hardly expecting Charlie to let himself in between
office bar scenes, not even hearing when he tiptoed past. Who
knew when or for how long? With her console TV still playing
to no purpose, when he tiptoed out, covering his almost invisible traces, taking care to slip across the street unseen by anyone. Except some smiling whore, setting up bar in the back of
her extra-long mobile dream wagon, parked ready and waiting for the Johns still fumbling hopelessly with address books,
at the mercy of busy signals in Plaza phone booths. So that
Charlie, who never had to pay, almost wished he had time to
steal a march while the whore's pimp nodded off behind the
wheel. Snoring softly—just like Bella, now so silent.

Because of a moment's flash in an imagined mirror, a moment wasted filling some bed, all the moments, all the beds,
with Bella's so near, so wide, so empty.

"Fuck it then—it's your loss, lady." He wished it were, wishing for the strength to kick the door down, barely having
enough to struggle into his extra slacks, and pick the pockets
of his fallen pants for the empty wallet, the once full address
book, to be fumbled through for any number that wasn't busy
this black Friday. When even that little puppy bitch in Forest
Hills wasn't answering Pavlov's bell, no longer salivating to
audition in the chintzy walk-up Charlie was ashamed of,
though good enough, no, too damn good for Evans' pissant
secretary!

"You think I have to line up for any of you?" Grabbing his
own keys from the last picked pocket, he detached Bella's to
fling at her door, locked against him out of all the doors he
once could have opened, leaving him no way to get at her, get
back at any of them. Until it came like a parting shot—the
idea he needed. He got it from her patent bag gaping open on

the bed, with the usual wad in her money clip—the price of a spin in that mobile game room, parked downstairs, where credit cards were not accepted from those hard up enough to pay for hangups. Like Bella now, and Charlie.

"Want to know what really happened with Evans that Sunday? How many times? Want to know *where* it happened, Bella?"

She didn't answer.

He left it unsaid. The perfect last laugh. On both women. Traces kicked over, Charlie took the money and slammed out down the long hallway.

On Saturday morning Sergeant Corio returned to the hospital, but alone this time as per the widow's request. Even so, her sister withdrew reluctantly on the day of departure for home. "Please, not for too long—we don't want her upset."

"Good luck," said Amy Foreman, seeming very much herself. "Still wasting your time?"

"Some of it," Corio sighed, pulling up a chair as the door swung closed. "But a couple of leads fell in our lap."

"From your friendly neighborhood stoolie—no doubt."

"Not exactly. Got some photographs to show you."

Two folders full, in fact. The first were all men, a few of them obviously known to Amy. Like Lorrilard, resident bore. And Bruce McVitty, boring throwback, underfoot when needed. But from the network, she only remembered Phelps, more for his work than rare party appearances. The rest blurred, none more than Charlie Collins, who sounded familiar and looked like everybody.

"Could he have been the type that used to hang around Miss Evans' apartment?"

"Maybe . . . without the mustache . . ." But never with a key in the door, Amy was sure about that.

"Were there ever any roommates—even for a while?"

"No way—check the airline hostel at the end of the hall. She fought them all off."

"How about girls from the office, maybe just to stay over some night . . . ?" Corio closed one folder and opened another. Cinny and Sally remained faces in a crowd. But not the writer in the cowboy hat.

"Oh my God!" Amy laughed. "Nobody rooms with E. V. Adamic. You get custody."

"And Miss Evans did?"

"I shared it—we adopted E.V. together." At a rally of Star Spangled Women for McGovern. "It was sort of a rescue—she was causing a disturbance."

"A political disturbance?"

"Well . . . she took a political position." McGovern's might have been easier to revive for the benefit of a detective.

"Like?"

Amy sighed. "It really started as a joke . . ." The waif who stole down from cheaper seats was hardly looking for trouble, until roused from sleep, to emit standing raspberries at the podium ten feet away, where filmdom's most famous dramatic actress had chosen a rather odd occasion to plug everywoman's need to get a man, prior to singing about it off key. The star's riposte cut the heckler down swiftly, famous voice punctuated with famous hip action. "I speak" (jerk) "only for myself" (sway). "Some of us are luckier than others" (jerk sway jerk). A laugh followed, giving Maude Lee a chance to grab a raised fist and yank the miscreant back into her seat, where constraint was happily mistaken for an overture of friendship. The fist uncurled. A sly smile appeared.

"What's your story—wanna hold hands?"

"Just be a good girl."

"Woman."

It got them through the song about the man. But when Greece's answer to Bette Davis bounded on stage in what

looked like a tuxedo to sing baritone, E.V.'s one-woman standing ovation was predictably beyond controlling. Further
excesses, easily anticipated from the program, gradually attracted a cheering section of well-heeled liberals recovered
from shock, to turn benevolent, as always toward a mascot.
Until Armageddon came inevitably with the grand finale.
The grand dame of all good Democrats advanced to the mike
amid wild huzzahs and spoke, as per her family's custom, for
the star spangled woman's primary role, as Wife and Mother.
Accent on Mother. This time E.V. climbed on her stolen seat,
both tiny hands raised to form V's, as she shrieked her opposition straight into the teeth of the Establishment's most promi-
nent jaws. Which went on working, royalty remaining serenely unaware of E.V.'s mouth, also still going, all the way up
the aisle. It took one guard and two of the finest to drag her
out.

"Just for heckling?" The excess force seemed to puzzle the
Sergeant. "Not throwing anything, posing any threat?"

"Depends on your definition of a threat," Amy said. "She
called herself a Lesbian in Madison Square Garden."

"Jesus." Even Corio looked awed.

"And proud of it."

"That's a political position?"

"Can be. To a militant radical feminist."

"But as far as literally—she meant it or she didn't?"

"Literally, she was too zonked to tell."

"What on?"

"She reeked of beer, but who knows?" Since possession of
drugs could have made search more fatally embarrassing even
than seizure, it seemed the better part of valor to claim the
homeless waif as a friend and take her back to sleep it off in
the Foremans' extra bedroom. Where E.V.'s primary passion
turned out to be continued oblivion, sought by any means at
hand in the medicine cabinet, until Bob put his foot down,

and rousted the dormouse. When E. V. Adamic split the scene, she swung with the rest of his Seconals, Amy's tranks, everybody's uppers, and all the pot in Maude Lee's piano.

"How about keys—any of them missing?"

"Not ours. And we still had the extra set to 14B."

"Could Miss Adamic have had a copy made?"

"When? She was never awake long enough. Anyhow what for? She'd cleaned us out. I don't quite see E.V. coming back to murder anybody."

"Maybe not alone, but if she got high with the wrong people . . ." Corio let it dangle. "Could be she nursed a grudge against your husband . . ."

"E.V. didn't even recognize Bob when she got straight."

The artist no longer in residence reappeared in a subsequent season, but only by day to pursue her career. Writing by then was her primary passion. And the only real one, Maude Lee always said, from the first wild words she read, found abandoned in her typewriter.

"What happened to the interest in politics?"

"Sublimated probably." Or like Amy's lost. "Lots of women turned off."

But others had also turned terrorist, going underground to join the kooks. Like this kook from the park maybe, Corio said. "He had a girl picketing with him. . . . The girl was the one that made that sign." Girls did worse than that lately. Some made bombs.

"Fall guys. I don't see E.V. falling for it. Or anything but herself. Especially any scene that's male dominated."

"Like a Homicide investigation . . ." Corio said thoughtfully.

"Depends on the approach."

"I approached her." It seemed like a good time to try again, on Amy's phone, as suggested.

Under the circumstances, anyone else might have shown

surprise when a man answered at Mrs. Porter's studio. But the detective, ready for anything, just took notes, about E. V. Adamic's early departure for the network. With some dude called Charlie.

"Charlie *Collins?*"

"Dunno the dude."

"And your name?"

"Like who needs it?"

"Homicide—"

The man hung up.

"Don't say I never dumped a hot lead in your lap," Amy Foreman said, watching the writer's photograph disappear into a separate folder—with Charlie's, and a police artist's sketch of the wanted picket from the park. "Look—E.V.'s harmless, if anyone is . . ." Corio hesitated before he rose. "If anyone is . . ." he finally agreed. If no one was harmless, no one was safe. And the family didn't want the widow upset. Neither did he. "Stay well at the beach . . . I'll be in touch."

"Bet you say that to all your friendly neighborhood stoolies."

"Don't worry—we're keeping an eye on you, Amy."

"Sure you are," Amy Foreman said. "Until your next case breaks . . ."

The summons back to work in the corner suite brought E.V. down with a bump, once she realized it came from Nannie Bernstein Phelps, caught in the country without telephone numbers and thus forced to pass the word through Charlie Collins, an unlikely but listed gopher, as usual trying to make himself indispensable by going for E.V. in person. The way Evans would have wanted, he said on the phone, parrying E.V.'s usual whys with the unctuous phrase Billy Bee Bernard had already used to justify calling a casting conference before Evans was even in the ground. Which precluded the attendance of such traditional mourners as Israel Gold, the next magic name Charlie dropped, though he waited until E.V. got in the cab to undermine her relatively clear-eyed recovery from Seconal, with the shark's latest thrashings about exploiting the dead. Charlie himself felt he had no choice but to lend his Liaison presence, as per network creative policy, he explained, rather inventively, the network having none. And anyway, he finally admitted on arrival, he wanted to meet Doreen Lunarhorn. But the Oscar runner-up for her supporting performance as a teen-age hooker in *Frisco Guru* was in town only for a day, and thus returning her guru a one-time-only favor by reading for the teen-age addict in *Chauvinist* at the glorious exchange of vibes the director clearly expected when he charged across the lobby toward E.V.—so surprised to see a man her size that she smiled and greeted him first.

"Here's our writer to meet us, Dor," he cried to the dirty blonde in a floor-length muumuu wafting ahead into an elevator with a languid hi to Charlie Collins, easily mistaken for one of the scripters—they scripted in squadrons where Oscar runner-ups came from. A minor gaffe, discernible only to E.V., since the actress' voice projected even less than her face, blank as a movie screen waiting for an image, until the vacant gaze finally focused on the figure in denim stamping through the elevator door that closed them all in.

"Hey—that's funky!" The boneless body propelled itself toward E.V. for closer inspection, not of the writer, but her hat, pronounced *really* funky, and appropriated right off her head to repose on Miss Lunarhorn's tangled tresses with Billy Bee's blessings.

"Let Dor wear it—like y'know for the essence," he exhorted, oblivious of E.V.'s alarm as he led the way down the hall to show Phelps, who turned out to be elsewhere delayed by an interview. *Temporarily*, everyone was assured. Not to be counted truly absent, like E.V.'s champions. Not yet anyway.

"You certainly look right for the part, fella," said Nannie, left in charge to greet Miss Lunarhorn, who yawned, not knowing where in the hat to look. Indeed even Smilin' Ed Kelly looked righter, once again untangling long legs to rise and be recognized with another blank stare from the Pepsi generation, succored on the star's old image by a mechanical baby-sitter, called the boob tube for every good reason. "Let's get you two together," Billy Bee urged, prophesying the hailstorm of Emmies sure to follow, while rearranging Phelps' furniture to appropriate the wing chair for his actress, placed center stage, opposite an ottoman carefully positioned off center for Kelly. Stepping away into a crouch, the director kept his back to the sofa where his new writer was left to sit with Nannie. Or stand alone. Or fall out the window.

A feeling of *déjà vu* gone wrong overwhelmed E.V. It was all so different yet the same, with Charlie hovering in the middle, still angling for a way to get in with the big kids. But today there was no one to nudge her when the Liaison on Specials tried to play director, knees cracking as he too squatted, for a really swell back view of Billy Bee, framing the empty air with his hands, first forming squares, then larger and larger rectangles. A hint that it might take a wide-angled lens indeed to bring the protagonists into focus, since nothing seemed to connect them but the common bond of growing, mutual distaste. It was a far cry from the longing to communicate shared by the estranged daughter and father of E.V.'s original vision, going up in smoke, to be replaced by a colder void of the director's choosing.

"We all know the situation . . . the jail visit and so forth . . ." Billy Bee waved vaguely toward the script still unopened in the actress' lap, as he fixed his rapt gaze on her frozen frame face. "Now let's use this one . . ." Another vague wave included Kelly. "So we can relate, like you know, to what's really happening . . ."

"Like with my real old man?" The actress rewarded him with a flash of real hatred, disguised as a laugh.

"Yeah, *yeah* . . ." Billy Bee's head turned toward the other player as if at a tennis match. "Get that, man? Like with your real daughter."

Kelly looked over his reading glasses. "I have two . . ."

"OK—which one do you see here?"

"Neither." What little Kelly had learned about his children while paying for their endless educations did not apply to the kin in the wing chair. Where all he saw, he said, was an actress. So far.

"Oh, man." Her head drooped against her wan white hand. "We're really into a phony bag."

"It could get phonier," the actor warned grimly.

"How—with cue cards?"

"They don't hardly make 'em big enough." Not to jog a drunk's sense memory, lost beyond reach of instant Stanislavski. "I seem to have mislaid my kids' formative years." Most especially their adolescence, sacrificed to continuing Kelly's as a failed Catholic turned failed neurotic, drinking himself off the couch in one long Freudian slip to nowhere, until he found his own level at the bottom of a drunk tank—four more marriages and a failed career later.

"Use it, Ed," Billy Bee entreated. "Use how it felt to face your kids when you woke up to that. Make us feel it . . ."

"I'm not a writer." Nor a bear to be baited. Kelly went back to his script. "It's all here—in the last speech."

"Oh wow," the other player moaned, "always with the words, and *speeches* . . ."

"Have you read it?" Kelly looked up politely.

"A whole page?" Her tone was incredulous. "Who *talks* like that?"

"Who listens?" Billy Bee snatched Kelly's script and threw it toward the coffee table. E.V. watched it hit the edge and fall on the floor. "Now let's forget the lines and the props—and fuckin' talk to each other, man—"

"Using what for words?" the star asked.

"Any old shit," E.V. burst out. "It's an improv."

"Right on, Evelyn," Billy Bee answered without turning. "We're using the actor's instrument to enlarge the writer's meaning. Part of The Work. Maybe even an improvement—"

"It's the wrong way to spell improve," E.V. said, shaking off Nannie's restraining hand, in memory of a stronger influence, as Kelly smiled and Billy Bee pretended to, remembering Evans' cute little joke. Though with all due respect, he said, it came from a very limited experience, in terms of calling shots, which Nannie agreed was up to the director. "We all have our methods." Billy Bee faced his actors. "And mine calls for one flash of what I'm gonna get—if you two let something happen between you."

He got half a flash. Suddenly covering her face, the actress hunched over, then straightened, tearing her hands away to confront herself with the man on the ottoman—her eyes blazing.

"Like, Dad—where *are* you?"

It seemed impossible the actor would not speak—staring back so long even E.V. listened in wonder, though not for the words she had written, the only answer that Kelly could make. So finally he rose to pick up the script.

"I am at an audition," he said. "You are reading for the party of Baby. I am playing her father. The scene is on II/8. My line is 'Long time no see.' That is your cue. Your line is 'I knew you'd say that.' From the top . . ." Instead of covering his face as she had, he adjusted his glasses, to find his place among the masks all actors need. Then leaning forward, he reached out, removing the hat that was hiding hers, to look for the daughter in the script. And smiled in the way that had made him famous.

"Long time no see," the father said. Drunk again. Any child would have smelled it.

E.V. held her breath, this time for the answer she knew too well, the only one the actress couldn't make, cheated like everyone else of climax as the mismatched partners spited each other. It could have gone either way, but not both.

"I told you he'd play it like I was auditioning!" Miss Lunarhorn turned to vent her frustration. "Like *I'm* the one's reading a one-scene cameo—for my own director!"

E.V. laughed. "Don't worry, Dor—we all know *that* situation—"

"OK, fellas," Nannie intervened. "We haven't got that much time to waste. So why not go through the scene once, the best way we can—"

"Not for me—thanks a lot!" Billy Bee started gathering up his leather folders and pouches. "Not with Evelyn doing her snarky number. I'm getting vibes that are wrong for me—"

"Getting names wrong too!" E.V. bounced from the sofa as he came out of his crouch; they went for each other like terriers.

"You've got the wrong director—"

"With the wrong girlfriend—"

"Who *needs* this?" The actress flew out of the wing chair, into the fray. "Like who's doing who a favor—?"

"You are, fella!" This time Nannie topped them, rising from the sofa. "I think it would help if we all remembered that Miss Lunarhorn is the *only* one here who is not committed to this project—"

"*Verbally* committed." The way the worst of the terriers snapped it out, even the word for words turned to ashes, though binding in television, as Nannie observed pleasantly, reminding them all this wasn't some mañana movie. "If we waited for the fine print, we'd never get a picture on the tube."

"And where would all the flower children go?" Kelly mused, toying with E.V.'s hat.

The top dog went for the corporate throat, slipping his leather leash to get control. "Artistic control—those were my terms!" Over script as well as casting, more than could be claimed for any writer. Least of all an Off-Off-Broadway novice looking wildly now to a surrogate producer, Phelps' wife Friday, who had spent her whole professional life looking to a man who wasn't there, his power lost to a boy genius filmmaker, laying down new laws: "At this stage of The Work, we're only into subtext, and I need time alone with my actors!"

"No problem—E.V. knows we're all here to serve her property." Smiling at the writer, Nannie waved E.V.'s grubby pages retrieved Thursday from the screening-room floor. "Come on—we have some revisions to discuss."

"Why?" E.V. said. They weren't even going to use the script they had. "I'm going home." Face flaming, the writer picked up her copy, the only one she could protect in the absence of the fighting spirit, so central to the project, only last Wednesday.

"Here's your hat. But what's your hurry?" Kelly held onto the brim just long enough to delay a total rout and put the director on red alert. A star in revolt was not unthinkable. "I was hoping you'd stick around, Sport—to help me on some interviews. About the meaning of it all." The star winked. "You wrote the subtext."

Seeing the director bristling jealously, Charlie drew on his PR background to get in the act. "Isn't it a little soon for that kind of promotion?"

"That's up to Kelly," Nannie cut in firmly, drawing on star system protocol, as she glanced nervously at the figure in denim, jamming on her cowboy hat. "We just thought it might be too painful for E.V.—the girls were so close. But of course

that's up to her." Having exercised authority by dividing it
like All Gaul, Caesar's wife ran out of parts and got very
busy emptying ashtrays. Woman's work was never done.

So the writer, saved a last shred of dignity for an exit,
agreed to talk it over at lunch with the star, picking him up
where she left him the last time, as he suggested, winking
again. They might have been making a tour of the talk shows
instead of a rendezvous outside the Men's Room. But, even if
it was all just an improv, it shortened the distance to the outer
office, as E.V. stumbled away to head down the hall toward
her familiar haven in the Ladies' Room, only to be foiled before she reached the door, by a strange brunette coming out.

"E. V. Adamic?" The brunette had a tough broad voice that
carried like Mrs. Porter's. "I've been looking for you . . ."

"Why?" Heart sinking, E.V. stopped in her tracks. This was
no improv, but a real live interviewer with a notebook ready.
E.V. wasn't. "Listen—nobody's supposed to be up here—"

"It's OK—I'm Detective Wilson." The brunette flashed a
badge to go with her metallic smile. "Sergeant Corio sent me."

"From *Homicide?*" Vice seemed more likely for a woman
detective.

"I'm with the precinct. But, we get borrowed sometimes
. . . to run the boys' errands." The brunette laughed cozily,
just between sisters. "*You* know . . ."

The opening was hip. So was E.V. "What's the errand?"

"Just routine . . ." All the same the brunette was hoping for
a more secluded place to talk than the reception area where
E.V. led her, all the offices being locked, like the building,
empty, as E.V. assured her, except for cruising security
guards. All the same, the brunette settled very close on the
gray velour sofa, bare knees touching E.V.'s through the denim,
as the tough broad's voice was lowered to inquire about E.V.'s
nameless boyfriend, no longer answering the phone or door at
Mrs. Porter's studio, when the cops followed up Corio's call,

to make double sure it wasn't that wanted hippie, sneaking in there somehow, bothering E.V.

E.V. shook her head. "It was Aldo," she explained. Just Aldo, staying over as a favor. Aldo with the funny last name E.V. never could remember, knowing him mostly from the corner bar, which he tended when it was open. But in summer, E.V. wasn't quite sure *where* Aldo worked. "He's just around—like he walks the dogs sometimes, does other stuff for us . . ."

"Us?" The brunette smiled.

"Mrs. Porter—the photographer that owns the studio." Where E.V. herself also worked part time, doing stuff like feeding the dogs in the photographer's absence, though now with her new-found bread from television, the writer would be saying goodbye to all that, preferring to rent her own place, of course.

"Of course . . ." The brunette nodded, segueing easily from there into the brief period of E.V.'s Evans/Foreman residence. And apartment access.

"Oh wow—I don't remember anything much about that! You better ask Amy Foreman." Like they hadn't. But it was another one of those hip, cozy moments, between sisters. "I was like really high a lot—before I started writing, you know?"

The brunette knew all right. Narco, not vice, E.V. decided, suddenly trying to change the improv by pleading this luncheon interview she had to do with Smilin' Ed Kelly, the famous movie star.

And famous drunk, the brunette remembered.

"Oh, he's straight now, too," E.V. said, very straight, as she got up to go.

"E.V., did you and Ms. Evans ever have words on this job—about using drugs?"

"Are you *kidding?*"

But the brunette wasn't even smiling. "No, E.V. Were you kidding Ms. Evans—or was she on stuff herself—and kidding you?"

"You guys must have searched her place—don't you know?"

"Yeah," the brunette said. "How about you?"

E.V.'s eyes flickered. "I don't know if she was hooked. . . . But she sure didn't care who else used what. Like she'd offer me uppers so I'd write all night—or push downers if I got upset. That's the closest we came to having words—"

"Hard to stay straight, with friends like that."

"She was my producer—she was getting my show on. We had to stay friends!"

"Here's your other friend," the brunette said, and flashed her metallic smile at Kelly, coming toward them, followed by Charlie Collins, who was Detective Wilson's next prospect as it happened. So they all rode down in the elevator together. It wasn't until they parted company in the street that E.V. really got the shakes.

"Rough on you, Sport," Kelly said. "All this stuff mixed up together—friend, show, memorial, investigation—"

"It's all a fake!" E.V. lashed out. "They don't want to hear anything but knocks. Everybody dumping on the one that's not here. Making you say things you don't even think!" It had to be somebody's fault but hers.

"*Sauve qui peut,*" the actor murmured, not bothering to translate. She didn't really care until he said the next thing. "Better get a new act together."

"What act?" Startled, she turned to face him.

"The fuzz may be onto that one. It's as old as the hat trick," Kelly said.

He knew. Not from pushing and prying in her hatband like some detective, or in her head like the shrinks. Not from her past, like Maude Lee Evans, who had never pried, or pushed anything. Shame welled up too bitter to bear as E.V. faced herself in Kelly's eyes. He knew because he'd been there.

"What's the matter, E.V.? Ever been able to level with anyone?"

What was so terrible she couldn't tell Papa, her own papa had said, that last time she saw him in some bar where she couldn't answer either, wondering which terrible thing Papa meant, if Papa had ever really meant anything, wondering still if Papa had cared. . . . She shook her head no, she'd never leveled with anyone. No lie ever stuck in the throat like that truth.

"One of the tough guys." Kelly sighed. "C'mon, let's find a place to eat."

But he must have known she couldn't even swallow, wasn't so tough, lacking even the breath to push for a health bar as he passed up the chic east-bound streets to head downtown for some plate glass window, ablaze with signs pushing the special. Like all the halibut fingers they could eat for $3.75. If they didn't mind standing in line with the tourists, not pushing anything but Kelly's smile, recognized at once by the middle-aged hostess. "Stick with the stars," Kelly murmured, and somehow E.V. did, passing up her longed-for side trip to the Ladies', to follow the formerly pied piper all the way to the plastic booth. Where he was recognized for real by the middle-aged hostess as by the brunette detective.

"Would you like to have a drink, Mr. Kelly?"

He answered with another smile, no answer at all if you watched his eyes or the way he reached for a cigarette. "Can't have everything," he said.

So they passed up all the halibut fingers they could eat for coffee, lots of coffee, before and after the hamburgers, pushed down to fill the void of wanting everything that could never be had. Passed up in time by everyone alive. Who stayed alive until the feeling passed, to be replaced by more possible dreams. Like the one in the script that lay on the table, an actor's dream that could have played itself, given any luck, Kelly said, unless luck ran out with Maude Lee Evans.

"She dreamed up the scene—I mean the father coming," E.V. told him. "It wasn't in my play."

Or anywhere else. A hard thing to admit in any interview.

"Might not have made as good a scene, if it really happened," Kelly said. "You lose one, you win one, Sport."

But the odds were really not that even, considering the ratio of hearts and minds, broken for every pimp on Broadway. Looking out at that street where no one else was safe, Kelly really knew better than to play God or even father, unless parlayed in winning combination. Looking out at the city for a fast way back, any player would have guessed. Godfather III was the part to shoot for.

Much farther uptown on the dirty white way, where the rooftop dining hall looked down on the neighboring state of Harlem, Ned's faculty Godfather contemplated the view, wishing he were still on top of it. Instead of just sitting here stranded, waiting for yet another of his brightest best students to come flailing back from yet another protest, right past a table full of history lecturers, busily pretending to split their lunch check. As if historians weren't part of history, hadn't felt the same shift of power, slipping and sliding away since the sixties when it all began with some uprising over open admissions to a gym, still unbuilt in Morningside Park below, where admissions were now open to a guerrilla army of muggers turning wartime protest into peacetime crime wave, sweeping over from the neighboring state of poverty, no longer contained in benign neglect. Not at any border outpost where the threatened and their threateners were united only in common helpless hatred of the few who were safe. Somewhere else. Like Switzerland, where they kept their money. Or some land of closed admissions where they kept their families, while they kept themselves on boards of directors and trustees, wining and dining each other at clubs where deductible tabs never had to be split. Except with the government, honored to support the only deluxe class on welfare—untaxed and untouched, the style which became Society's benefactors. The industrial, military, complex, rich.

"It's the Evans family all right . . ." Ned slouched violently back into his chair. "Her father wouldn't even come to the phone."

The adviser pretended to advise. "Be reasonable—the man's bereft."

But so was the brightest and best of the advised, bereft of future as of past, the ground opening at his feet to swallow him again in that cave of a park, where black knifing black made the police blotter. But one more nonminority academic falling from the ivory tower would never be missed or protested anywhere. Not in this man's bankrupt city, shocked to its excavated moral foundation by the folly of Liberated Woman. As yet another Slain Career Girl, Renegade Heiress joined the mountain slide of tokens burying Do Good Movements in living proof that survival should be restricted to the fit. Ergo: Those who could not take the heat belonged in the kitchen, ghetto, back of the bus, end of the line, where only junkies on methadone still dreamed there was anything better than the next fix. Or fixer. Everyone knew one. Even Ned.

"I said all I wanted was McVitty's number, not to bother anyone. I offered to hang on—wait for a message . . ."

Any message, hanging on until the dime ran out, dialing again to wait some more until the message came. Mr. Evans was sorry—the family had nothing to say to Mr. Nedders. *The family.*

"So now we know what happened to my grant."

His adviser sighed. "By that reasoning, Ned, you got it through pull—"

"The hell I did!" Ned showed a flash of his old indignant pride. Who knew Wednesday that McVitty Brothers was the foundation's law firm? Or that Mrs. Evans' trust was behind the funding?

But that was the point—no one knew. "It's only one of many trusts, Ned. People like that don't keep track either."

"Until we all make the same headlines—"

"There may not be any connection . . ."

"Come on . . ." Ned tried to laugh. "At the meeting it was yes. Now it's no."

"Now there's a delay. That's all I've been told. And not just on your study. They've been helping with the whole developmental program. And all our grants are renewable—"

"So why fight for my lousy fifteen-G project—just peanuts in Grant City—?"

"Ned, we both know better." No one could fight refusal of private endowments—all autonomous and beyond appeal. "It would be different if you'd been promised federal assistance. We could make a stand against the slightest hint of discriminatory reaction. That's why if you were in any emotional condition, I'd advise looking into a government subsidy, applying for a loan—"

"Whose government—the Shah of Iran? Ours is broke!" Also in the news, yet another yes from yesterday, turning into no by wild coincidence. "Man, I could be teaching for bread by next winter—I'm three months from the finish line—"

"With plenty of loose ends to clear up on your own. Take this time for extra reading, color coding your data analysis—"

"*Color coding!* While some dude from that New Mexico workshop proves *my* theory in *his* thesis—?"

"Let's keep it down . . ." The adviser reached nervously for their check as the historians rose from their table.

"That's what it's all about, isn't it?" Ned watched them file past to pay the cashier. "Not my emotional condition."

"Sort of hard to separate these things, Ned."

It was easier to separate one tuna sandwich and Coke from the vegetable plate with dessert and beverage. Having eaten the lion's share, Ned's adviser tried to tip for both, as if to somehow personally augment the available official support, exhausted in one public appearance.

"Thanks a lot!" Ned dropped his own quarter. "So now what do I do—take my MA and run? Transfer and teach elocution somewhere?" Somewhere the admissions were so open the cretins couldn't even read headlines. And bye bye to Billy, the screamer, halted in speech. The dime had run out on his toy phone. As on his hot pilot experimenter, lining up to pay the cashier.

"I hope that won't be your decision, Ned."

"What's my choice?"

There was nowhere to go from the roof but down. Ned's adviser got off, halfway, where he lived, hanging on at mid-management level, free to advise but not consent.

"You're overreacting, Ned. Jumping to conclusions."

"So's your buddy at the foundation."

"He doesn't run it."

"He sure gave a good imitation at that meeting."

But only an imitation. Like the girls at Ma Bell, and the boys at Con Ed who only worked there, authority's voice grew weary from explaining nobody really ran *anything* bigger than a self-service elevator.

"Ned, I want you to remember—all you got or could expect Wednesday was a conditional OK on a fair hearing—a verbal agreement, nothing binding."

Except in television, the medium that moved too fast for print. But slowly, when it wanted to. A pioneer in the use of the unspoken no, cruelest of all delaying tactics, hanging up the brightest and the best, twisting slowly since the fifties.

"Like blacklisting all over again," Maude Lee Evans' boss had said in some interview on the channel that got the clearest reception on Billings' black and white portable. Where every fuzzy newscast on her channel offered a reward for information, run again and again as if to emphasize that no one where she worked had any answers to the ten-thousand-dollar question: Whodunnit?

Suddenly aimless as he wandered across campus, Ned began to wonder, really wonder about that. For the first time.

In the street outside the club by the river, the media cameras had departed. The thinning press lines were no longer rewarded by even the thinnest trickle of members, long gone for the weekend. Inside all was austerity downstairs, the dining room long since closed for summer. Upstairs in the only occupied bedroom there was no TV set to tempt disruption of the total news blackout. No newspapers were delivered with the trays bearing breakfast from the kitchen, lunch and dinner from a favored restaurant, most of it untouched when the trays were borne away, sometimes still littered with unreturned messages. No calls were made and none taken. Until the one so long awaited.

When it came, the charges were reversed unbelievably. And like Bruce McVitty's, from a false name. Clearly the woman who had too many for small scenes, none big enough for this one, did not trust the phones in friendly villas, wherever it was that yachts tied up and jets touched down this season.

Leland Evans accepted the charges, hearing his name called with a question mark, her voice breathless from the long-distance effort, crying she couldn't hear him even before he answered, only to be interrupted with how awful it was. God so awful for him, was it too awful? Well, he said, yes, pretty awful. But the police claimed to be sorting things out, narrowing down suspects not yet in the news the Evans family tried to ignore, blaring everywhere, everyone having TV's, she said, even over there. So she knew the way her own friends were acting what it must be like, what was being said, or whispered, as she whispered now: Lee? Lee? Wouldn't it just be worse if she came, the way the press always treated her, thank God they hadn't found her yet. Well, he said that was up to her, but she would have to hurry to make the funeral. *Funeral.* Well, sort of memorial, tomorrow. *Tomorrow?* Oh God, she wished they could really talk. Usually it was so clear as if they were in the next room. Well, he said, they weren't and asked her for a number to call. But then the switchboard would know where she was, probably bribed to listen in for the press even at clubs, which might be the reason for the stinko connection, from this awful anonymous upright coffin off some hotel manager's office. Lee? Lee? She sounded frightened, wouldn't it be better to try again when the circuits were clearer, and they could understand each other? Which did not seem to be in the cards even before static overcame them, and the connection was broken.

He sat on the side of the bed, without moving, waiting for the phone to ring again. But it was only the overseas operator asking if he'd accept the overtime. So then he understood the conversation was really over. Like so many other phone conversations with first wife and daughter, calling Lee? Lee? Calling Daddy? Daddy? Calling collect, would he accept charges? The question marks were getting mixed, like sound tracks accidentally rerecorded, never again to be heard separately. No matter how hard he tried to remember that the youngest voice, husky like his, was the strongest. That despite all accidents of birth—child bride smile, dark eyes and fair hair—the last loving spirit had been true. Not a coward. Not a liar. Not a crier or a copout. Despite all accidents of fate, Maudie Lee was the one who was different.

But none of his women ever had been. And like the rest of the charges he couldn't pay, he finally accepted it. Sitting there on the side of the bed, in the club by the river, deserted for the summer, by the seasonal membership he had chosen.

In the East Eighties pub where overachievers gathered to exchange reviews, there was always someone in town. Two-fisted drinkers stood at the bar, in all kinds of weather, though the hungrier egos who dined on pasta hadn't yet appeared, when Phelps walked in to grant one more audience—his last and most dangerous. Not granting it, however, might have been more so. This invitation came from The Cork.

It was Phelps who had once given that name to the buoyant little jester he discovered, popping up like a true original in a court of solemn writers. Where The Cork returned the compliment by dubbing the master Father Phelps. The sly, cracked voice, since lost to fame, reached the former ruler at home by night. Last night, before Nannie turned off the phone.

"Father, dear Father—what's *hap*pening?"

"Murder. It's already happened, Cork."

"Oh no, *no*, Father!" Only someone else's murder had happened. But greater killings were to be made. And curiosity was killing The Cork, with more than a cat's nine lives to bob back from—quality TV, Little Magazines, slim volumes of memoirs, bobbing up larger and larger, into Big Movies, Big Magazines, Best-Selling Exposés . . . as youth's buoyancy slowly ebbed, and The Cork learned to float to the top on the flotsam and jetsam left by disaster.

Any disaster. Even his own—fantasy triumphs in a cork-lined closet, trotted out to join the latest minority, marching into vogue. For further profit, real headlines were mined, or better, the secrets of those who made them. As The Beautiful

People aged stark naked in the less than candid company of a little miked Minox, numbering their infanta birthdays for a wider public than Proust. So The Cork kept bobbing up, up, up . . .

Met head on suddenly by Father Phelps, calling in old debts to request silence. Or worse, discretion.

"But you must be *jesting* . . ." The jester smiled, secure on his new Special Table turf, where only Special Brands would serve to toast the once, not future protector of talent. "You know, Father, you were always *over*protective!" And over the hill in New Journalism's jungle where the tieless and braless set talked tough. Preferably on talk shows, personal appearances being so much more *Now* than appearing in print. Though sooner or later, Entree depended on signing *something*. About *someone*. Preferably someone everyone knew. Like the girl in the story Father Phelps could tell. Not that PR release about a memorial show, but the real inside story.

"All right," Phelps said as he'd known he would have to. "But let's see some of the old work." Real work. Not gossiped from drunken memory. But documented with long hours of research from a movable feast of material about another minority march—inspiration to tempt a talent, gone to seed. Which Phelps of all past masters to be toppled really remembered. He had seen it first. His only ace. And still The Cork's. "So if you're serious, I'll open the files . . ."

"But Father—it's her *life* I'm after!"

"Her career was a big part of her life."

"And part of her *death*, mayhap?"

Death was the final disastrous surface on which to bob, triumphant. But more than any other it had to start with a plunge to the depths. Quite a feat now. All kinds of Special Brands had made a balloon of The Cork.

"You can look for a connection to the death, if you want to." But Phelps added a condition. "Just don't make one up."

"Like everyone else will—in my absence!" Still The Cork sucked air like a blowfish, clinging to the surface where minnows fed. "Advance me one sample goody from your files?"

"You have my offer." Phelps' only offer; he pushed his chair back to stand pat. "Consider it this weekend—if you need time to think."

"Oh Father, you know I think faster than that!"

Father knew too well. "Think deeper," he said.

"And *while* I'm thinking deep . . ." The pouched eyes glinted, as if gauging the muscle of the once, perhaps future, champion of talent. "Are you by any chance fighting for your own life, Father? Or just playing for time?"

Father smiled before he answered.

"Not half as hard as you do, Cork."

"God," Grace said. "Henry Halpers has gone!"

"Who?"

"Oh, just this sort of drugstore where we used to lunch when we had summer jobs. Buzzy and I on *Junior Bazaar*." Not the best of subjects, all but Grace now being gone. With the wind and Henry Halpers.

"Looks like the whole building's going," Leland said. And indeed the windows had that new deserted look, like blinded eyes, as weirdly empty as Madison Avenue itself on Sunday. Except the part where their limousine was headed when the light changed, and Leland's gaze wandered emptily forward. Grace fixed hers on the chauffeur's cap and tried to think of something that had stayed the same or at least survived.

"*Harper's Bazaar*'s still with us." *The* Bazaar, outliving its Junior, to arrive every month from wherever, with *Vogue* and all the rest Grace still subscribed to in Murray Bay, but leafed through less and less, confused by the fashions as by the people in the magazine of the same name, the one that used to be *Life,* if *that* was any excuse for showing bare behinds on beaches, *where* Grace could not think. Even in the Hamptons, bathers of both sexes and colors did not lounge about in strings. Or less, in that rag she drew the line at, where the fannies fell *out*. Hard rock porno, if you asked Grace.

"Hard core," Leland offered, knowing that rock was alleged to be music, in the blatant new world of nude photographs. "But they're soft core porno if you mean *Playboy*."

She turned toward him, teasing, "Why Leland Evans, how would *you* know?"

"Your mother gets it."

"God," Grace said.

Though really, it was no more nor less than could be expected from a woman near sixty who still spent a month fasting at The Golden Door for every year she lived it up. Until the last time dissipation was sculpted from her face, when she finally had her whole body lifted. Only to split the seams, or some such tragedy now upstaged by a more final passing of youth's ephemeral beauty. Stealing scenes had been a habit of Leesy's since she turned overnight star at sixteen, beginning an exile that was now permanent. Leaving poor Leland alone, as usual in the middle, trying to rise above this last unforgivable breach of absence. And while he was at it, giving a rather better imitation of a gentleman than Grace's own huffy hubby in Murray Bay, blue blood rushing to his head long distance, as he shouted out all his pent-up disapproval of the family whose fortune had merged with his at that rather too flashy ceremony, with three half- and two stepsisters in bridal attendance. The last and least of whom the groom never saw before, or *since*, as he kept roaring to bully his wife back home where she belonged—out of that mess! Until Grace erupted herself, declaring the whole thing shitty, just too shitty on Leland, her exact words, *tellement* chic, but *tant pis*, dearie. There she *was*, right on the island, with everyone knowing she'd already flown down for one funeral. No gentlemanly pretense could

cover flight from that with some last minute airport phone call
to Leland's club, her voice going up an octave, a reflex habit
with her ilk since boarding school, when dealing with other
people's parents. Though really Leland was nearer her husband's age than her father's, near enough in fact to have
courted the ugly duckling, free as air when the swan was chosen. Obviously, as Grace's husband meanly put it, Leland didn't
want an heiress on a white charger. Which made Grace feel
her horsefaced worse as she rode to the rescue, barging in unannounced, to take her chances that she wouldn't blurt the
wrong thing. Until she saw Leland's face, as he rose cornered
behind his breakfast tray, trapped in pain. And understanding
dumb animals better anyway, she just went over and put her
arms around him.

"Thought no one was coming . . ."

"Ah, Leland . . ."

"Shouldn't have . . . didn't expect it . . . too much."

"Not for me. I just talked to Leesy . . . only that day . . ."

And only to get a telephone number, for more important
calls to follow, the first to Bruce McVitty, safe by then in his
own trundle bed, though Grace blurted no mention of that
conversation, already quietly confirmed with the police
through McVitty Brothers, quick to cope as family lawyers for
their own, but not about to play family friend for Leland,
quick in turn to get the message, the many messages, some
saved to display in tactful proof. Everyone was sorry. No one
was coming. Not even Bruce.

Just good old Grace, quick to blurt out the mourners' only
acceptable truth—they could both use a fast Bloody in the
bar, sure to be dead empty, an unfortunate phrase but what
living soul would be there now?

"Members," Leland prophesied correctly.

"The hell with them." She waved brusquely to the only em-

barrassed couple in view, as she stomped past to the farthest
window table. "Let's have doubles."

But the Bloodies were wearing off, and there seemed to be
less and less to blurt, the nearer they got to this TV spectac-
ular at an undertaking parlor, where surely even TV people
would have the taste to omit the coffin, having already run
one of those things about omitting flowers in favor of some
fund for the Families of Victims of Violent Crimes. Hardly
the Heart Association. But better by a long shot than Buzzy's
bier Wednesday, heaped high with garlands in the Lattingtown Church, awful reminder of the accidents that happened
in the best of families, for which no charitable exemption
existed.

Few survivors knew it better than Grace, graceless member
of so many weddings before the one that gave Leland's name
top billing. An extra added attraction to be dragged in the
mud of today's festivities, far from the hush of the Lattingtown churchyard. In fact they were still two blocks from
Campbell's, when traffic slowed the limousine in view of the
sidewalk where the same old strangers who waited to see
strangers stretched their necks from a crowd that stretched
out of sight around the corner. It had waited forever for a funeral like this one.

"Don't get out, driver!" Grace warned sharply, linking arms
with Leland. "Wait for the police!" There were plenty for
once, to open the car door, more than usual, to run interference, but never enough for the real enemy.

"Press, dear."

"Yes, Leland." No need to warn the swan's ugly duckling,
face that haunted a thousand clips, ruining the shots she
couldn't escape. Crowds melted, negatives never. Only stars
could break the cameras that loved them but hated Grace. So
she fought back the best she could, charging head down, head
averted, past flashbulbs, past lenses, past the crowd straining

at the barriers for a glimpse of her mother, but settling this time for Leland, as the next of kin clung together, knowing better than the cops, or the man from Campbell's or media PR that none of them could make it five feet across the sidewalk, before the barriers gave, ropes trampled, wood splintering . . .

"God," Grace said, once breathlessly inside. "Why put barriers *up* nowadays?"

From the PR point of view, the turnout was a bust. Not that Leland Evans didn't cut a convincing father figure with his silver hair and leisure man's unworked-for tan. But he had looked like a banker before he had a bank to save in, and so did several character actors present. Unaccompanied by the lady with the names that backed him, the gentleman songster came on like a Lamb, a player of pianos in a club of Players, First Family Tin Pan Alley, show biz old boy, nothing more. Nor could Grace's presence save him. The Princess Royal spoke only for herself, not that portion of family stock tied up in voteless trusts for the matriarchy's lesser females. The great estate of Mrs. James, Stoner, Vonsickle, Richards, Demilio, Evans were more directly represented by white camellias cabled to the altar, along with an unspecified, charitable contribution, pledged in the name of a victimized stepchild. The rest of the message telegraphed itself. One hundred and fifty million bucks was waving ta-ta from a safe distance. Halfway around the world.

As money went to money, so billions followed millions. White orchids and a well-advertised reward, left as a tip for some stoolie, represented the patriarchy on the other side of the aisle. Not Old Man Weldon the only higher-up to take a pew. Right up front, in regal splendor, as seen from the back seats where Cinny and Sally were crowded. But not from the sidelines where the VP of PR stood, the better to stay on the fence, while power felt by its absence sent up smoke signals from the house of mergers, where the real old men voted their collective holdings for their good ol' boy: The Chairman of The Board, alleged to be in Europe, but quietly flown home to express the corporate will. He was swimming even now in his Westchester pool, rings eddying out from the first dropped hints of top level reaction, not to be telegraphed but filtered down, pieced together like two and two, until the net result was puzzled out from its hiding place in the corporate "we." ("By the way . . . we were wondering up on 33 . . . who *hired* that girl?")

They sat, both of them, in the aisle seats directly behind Weldon: the first and last captains of her fate—shark and lion caught in the same memorial net, fin and claw hidden in black sheep's mourning. Not yet, however, to be confused with lambs, like the gentleman songster lost across the way. Her bosses at least were still in business. And men enough in their own households to prove themselves by bringing their women.

But these were not first ladies. Not even Nannie Bernstein Phelps, publicity notwithstanding, though she'd done damn well for a scholarship girl from Barnard. Far better, even in retirement, than Bella Sweet, who had neither made Vice President nor married one, and was therefore seated several rows back. Doubtless envying everybody—even poor Dotty Gold, summoned only for looks, and never looking quite right, as this time, for God's sake, in a hat! While a bleached blond shicksa sat bewilderingly bareheaded in the first pew, perhaps the sharpest reminder of the wives who should have been there, ahead of Mrs. Weldon.

Shifting his weight, the VP tried to shift his attention to the stage or whatever you called it at a nondenominational show biz memorial. As per Israel's self-serving suggestion, the West Coast's first female sitcom creator was here to do the speaking honors, symbolizing the rise of today's woman, as she rose above her sister's fall. Sisterly reminiscence, necessarily brief, was kept for the finish, hearsay culled on the plane East from Dotty, who had at least met the deceased. More often if less recently than Smilin' Ed Kelly waiting stage left to recite a psalm no one believed from a memory no one in the business trusted. As per Phelps' self-serving suggestion, on the grounds that the star was a friend of the family. Though Leland Evans had shown no glimmer of recognition for friend or foe among the mourners, there being no resemblance to his daughter, living or dead, for him to recognize in the eulogy, now winding up with a description of her smile, from an eight-by-eleven glossy. Next came the actor, rising, eyes by habit unfocused, to face the house. Or whatever you called the place in which the Almighty's absence was interpreted as Divine Presence somewhere else. Heaven. Buddha's belly. Westchester. Or the mind of the believer, where God's existence remained the one indisputable Creation.

"The Lord is my shepherd, I shall not want . . ."

Head bowed, the VP's mind wandered from still waters to legal phrases, looked up in a dozen different clauses.

"Contractor has conducted and will conduct him/herself with due regard to public conventions and morals . . . has not done and will not do any act or thing or make any statement to degrade the artist in society, or subject him/her to public hatred, contempt, scorn, ridicule or scandal, that will shock or offend the community, or any group of class thereof, or reflect unfavorably upon the Company or any of its affiliated companies, or the entertainment industry in general, or tend to do any of the foregoing."

Tend to . . .

A tall order. And once committed to fine print, a tall story. Also signed by Phelps, now spreading guilt by association, sometimes known as the domino theory, and ambition's best hope for ridding the network of the whole memorial crew. Yea though they walked in the valley of the shadow of death fearing no evil, all it needed was another little twist, devoutly to be wished: Or prayed, as psalm gave way to hymn, calling them to Jesus o'er the tumult.

> *. . . day by day His Sweet Voice soundeth*
> *Saying "Christian, follow me."*

Having no hymnal to follow, the VP's eyes wandered to his watch, as he counted verses.

"Saying Christian love me more . . ."

Cinny's suggestion. She said she thought Evans would have liked it.

". . . Saying love me more than these."

Saying Amen, for God's sake—and out the side entrance ahead of the crowd.

Strangely Ned still didn't feel the heat even after an hour in the sun, beating down on the museum steps where he'd been sitting facing Fifth, watching for the crowd now surging toward him. So he knew it was over, though not why he'd come or what he was waiting for, no longer being needed to keep a vigil. He would have kept it at the service, had the voice he loved ever once spoken for him, where more powerful voices spoke for her now. He wondered how long they would keep it up, once safe in their limousines, inching forward, through hysterical pedestrians shrieking recognition of celebrated mourners. Here her father, there a movie star, media mogul, top cop, snoop—all mourning the passing until they passed. Some looked frightened, some just looked, sometimes for others lost on foot.

Like the one Ned recognized backing away from the crowd

to step off the curb by an occupied phone booth. Even at a distance and from the rear, the stance was familiar, leonine head tucked against a raised shoulder, as the figure waited, beckoning to a woman Ned had never seen. He watched them turn uncertainly, moving away from the phone booth toward the posh hotel on the next corner. Whatever had made him come, made him get up, and cross the street to follow still not knowing why as they walked through the hotel's sidewalk cafe into the lobby, lost among other funeral refugees, by the time Ned entered. He wandered toward the bar, still not understanding why he bothered, what he was looking for, or trying to remember, until he saw the sign that said TELEPHONE and it happened again. The man in the booth spotted him too and turned away, leonine head tucked against his raised shoulder. And then Ned knew where it had happened before.

He took the few steps that separated them, and reached for the doorknob.

"My husband will be out in a minute."

Somehow she was right in there, ahead of him, Super Wife in white kid gloves, moving fast for a big mother—the deliberate kind that never took foster kids, just adopted. Too late anyway by twenty-three years.

"I want him—not the phone."

"What for?" No getting past her, over or around her, dark-eyed lioness at the mouth of the cave.

"He knows."

She knew Ned. The dark eyes said so, "Look, fella—everyone's upset from that service—"

"You look, lady—I couldn't get near your service without starting a riot. I'm the boy the fuzz yanked around in front of every camera in town!" The rage Billings had said Ned should feel welled up so suddenly it choked him with words that wouldn't stop. "Hassling me everywhere I go, hassling me at

work, hassling patients—Jesus, hassling me out of my goddamn grant! Like I'm some fat cat executive with fucking
stock options—"

"I'm sorry—" She was frightened, mentally backing off with
no way to go, her back to the door.

"Your old man's not sorry!"

"But they're hassling him too, the whole office—"

"I don't care if they trash your whole network! All this time,
every frigging minute, he could've squared my ass—"

"How, for God's sake? He hardly knows you—"

"Well enough to tell 'em he saw me that night!"

"But that's crazy—"

"So it's crazy—we were standing this close—"

"Then why haven't you told somebody yourself—all this
time, with all these detectives—"

"I didn't make the connection." His hand jerked convul-
sively toward the booth. "He was phoning from her corner
when I got off the bus."

Right between the eyes. Good and Bad Guys would have
taken notes. But they did it for a living. A dime clinked
behind her, a faint sound, but more audible than their choked
conversation seemed to be in the booth. Phelps was busily
dialing another number. She exhaled as if from holding her
breath.

"You thought you saw the man she worked for—any man—
there that night—*and you didn't make a connection?*"

"Until he just tried to duck me the same way again—"

"Austin Phelps was trying to make a train Wednesday—on
the other side of town! He walked from that bar to the station
with a friend. And from the station to the Port Authority. And
called me from both places—"

"What'd you expect him to tell you—?"

"The truth! That he was calling her, to try and fix things up before he caught the bus. As we've both told the police who have checked every word, every step—"

Ned's anger made him laugh, surprising them both.

"Their ass they checked. They're up to here in snow jobs just like you are. Or how come they're still bugging me about him having her key, keeping her, like every other bastard she worked for—?"

"Probably to get a rise like this! Some sick cruel afterthought—"

"Lady, it's the truth. I swear . . ." But there was nothing left to swear on. The hand he raised was as wet as his face when he tried to wipe away the sweat. Hers folded together tightly in the white kid gloves, washed of the whole mess, as her dark eyes turned away, trying to turn him off.

"If you believe that yourself, I'm sorry. But nobody else will."

"Unless he says so."

"Fella, you're mistaken. Can't you even see that you might be?"

"Ask him."

The white gloves came apart. "I'm not about to wound him that way now—neither are you—"

"*Now.*" Ned repeated the operative word, triumphantly, almost smiling, calm inside for the first time. What did she know from the wounds he'd seen, standing vigil in his bloody shirt, over that real jungle cave? "Let me tell you something, lady—the longer you wait, the harder it gets." He was the one to turn away, content to leave them to each other.

Ned walked out into the sunlight he didn't feel, knowing no beast could hide forever, guarded by his mate everywhere but the cave that brought them together. Good and Bad Guys had taught their professor the art of letting doubts fester. But it had taken that moment in the phone booth to make Ned one of them. Turning north toward another bus stop, he turned a corner in his mind, limping a little like any convalescent up too soon, still unaware, or unwilling to face that the damage he did might be permanent. Because the hunters were pros out to get a girl's killer. He was an amateur. After her.

Despite the air conditioning, the VP of PR was sweating before he hung up the phone in the limousine and turned to his friend, the Deputy Commissioner.

"Would you believe that jackass Phelps won't stop hyping his memorial show for twenty-four hours? Christ—all I'm trying to do is save him *some* face! Gonna look like he's fronting for a panel of suspects."

"Maybe he is, ol' buddy," said the Deputy Commissioner.

"Oh, come on," the VP wasn't buying, "just because some of the boys play with fire . . ." Just enough to get fired, but not, God forbid, to be accused of murder, just because one of the girls played for profit.

"We haven't established that's what she was doing." A policeman's phrase, carefully worded before it was carelessly brushed aside.

"With that setup of hers?" And that body of hers, mirrors all over, and bills in the books. "Only one thing it could be for."

"Two things."

"What's the other one?"

"To look at." Rating at least one camera eye, in addition to the naked human variety, though the Deputy Commissioner sounded faintly surprised to have to point it out to a VP from the media, armed now with a grand of the media's cash, as down payment against a ten-grand reward, for information about a pornographic photograph, not only the first hard evidence yet reported to be missing from the scene, but further alleged to involve the victim's own person, also a media phenomenon. Like the rest of Phelps' panel of suspects. Not to mention such traditional mourners as Israel Gold. "Face it, Scooper—there's all kinds of money in the voyeur business."

The traffic on the transverse looked just as bad as the funeral cortege, so they decided to ditch the limousine altogether and walk across the park. It was a pleasant summer afternoon, not that hot. And they had plenty of time.

"What happens when we get there?"

"Makeup I guess . . ."

"On a *news* show." E.V. sounded dismayed. Also disgusted. "Why?"

"Lights . . ." It had been a long time since Kelly faced them. He wondered what was used to cover that now.

E.V. scowled. "I'll look like a clown." In whiteface, perhaps with a cherry nose, easier to imagine than mascara and rouge on a thousand-year-old child, though today she seemed to have made, for her, a special effort, changing from denim to dark tie dyes. And the funeral hat had at last found its niche.

"You look very nice," he said. "You'll be fine."

"No way in that junk." She pulled her hatbrim lower as if to hide. "I'm not wearing lipstick is all."

Kelly laughed. "Neither am I."

He did not tell her how often before the same bottom line had been drawn by the tough guys. Today there were broader Rubicons to cross. Acres of picnickers surrounded the ponds, and sprawled on the grass, mostly in family groups. On Sundays the kids looked bored—and safe. Though tomorrow it would be as before, when they all changed back into pickets and pickups and passers of joints, cruised by society's watchdogs in squad cars and newsteams, all armed with that composite sketch of a face E.V. had tried to forget.

"Having second thoughts?" Kelly was watching for the signs.

"Just so we stick to the script," she said, "and nobody starts all that other stuff." Kid stuff to be left behind on the grass.

"Waste of time and tape—they know we can pass." Kelly had said as much in their breakfast briefing with the researcher, quick to agree the artists had been invited to talk art, not murder. Or suicide. A panel of experts was on hand for that. The artist's segment was only one of many on a syndicated hour, called "Wrap Up" because it wrapped up one or two stories a week, mostly with studio interviews taped cheap. What made the difference—and the growing ratings—were distinguished guest interviewers like Harvey Grant, dean of the flaming fifties' liberals, and still a friend to his fellow old-timers.

"I can get Harvey to let you off the hook—if you have any doubts," Kelly said, remembering Nannie's.

"They'd probably just call in that sitcom writer who doesn't know anything." Preferred as a eulogist to a no-name writer who knew too much. But entrusted to be true to her talent, E.V. saw her one and only chance to get in her own licks ahead of Billy Bee Bernard already jealously warming up for bigger and better bookings. She sighed. "Guess it won't kill me just to *sit* there . . ." And clam. If that was the worst that could happen.

It seemed so to the star. As long as she was sure.

Sure enough to keep on going. So they left the park and the kid stuff behind them.

Phelps did not speak until they were alone in the station wagon, although they'd been alone in the crowd since he emerged stony-faced from the phone booth to stalk beside Nannie to the garage. He slammed the car door as he slid in beside her.

"All right," she said. "What?"

"Our own PR department tried to warn Harvey Grant off

Kelly's guest shot today. On an independent station! Ready for that?" He glared out the station-wagon window as she steered them east into the crosstown traffic. "Scooper even confirmed the key story, told Harvey more crap about the money, and something new coming up he keeps hinting about —*Jesus*, this mess—" He broke off. It was the farthest he'd gone. He veered away as if to an afterthought. "What the hell did her boyfriend want?"

"The same thing you do, probably."

"What's that supposed to mean?"

"I gather he'd like his life back too—you know—name, reputation, work—?"

"He ought to try his luck with network PR."

"Maybe he will, fella."

And then it burst out. "God knows Evans would! Star member of the PR generation. Almost every damn thing she did was a puton!"

"The worst thing to do at twenty-four," Nannie said, "is not get to be twenty-five."

"Unless you'd rather die than grow up." Even youth's wasted promise had been less than it seemed. "Nobody knows how old Evans was. Her own father's brainwashed, she gave so many ages—all probably fake, like the rest of it."

"Except," Nannie said, "for that sign." Phelps glanced sideways, surprised. His wife's dark eyes were downcast. She seemed to be looking at a crook in her arm where the crepy skin could have been covered by sleeves—everywhere but bed. She still slept naked, but now only because of hot flashes. She was having one. She wiped at her forehead with a white kid glove covering the hand that never lied. "Today's Package Is Tomorrow's Trash," she quoted softly. "Evans told the truth that time." Which made her just old enough perhaps to know it.

Phelps' head turned to the window again. "So much for liberation. In the year of the woman."

"And the age of the man," Nannie added.

"This man's age must be starting to show." That was no child Father Phelps had adopted. "Should have listened to my wife—kept my eye on the sign." All the signs.

"Instead of the smile." Nannie kept her eyes on traffic, finally picking up speed as she turned north on Park.

"It wasn't the smile."

"What was it, fella?"

"The way she looked at me for the answers, I guess. All the answers . . ." He laughed or tried to. "Probably did it to everybody. Even Charlie Collins—Christ, Israel too, for all I know. . . . But even in that bar—with all of them there—she made me feel I was It, the only one—solely responsible."

"Let's just say she made you feel," Nannie said. "How responsible you are is anybody's guess."

He gave her another sideways glance. "Is that what the boy was doing—guessing—while I was on the phone?"

"In which phone booth?"

He didn't answer, except to start searching his pockets for a pacifier. The silence stretched for blocks. Until he gave up and reached into Nannie's bag for the cigarettes she had stopped carrying for a year because of him.

"No, dammit, Austin!" She snatched it away. "You're not putting that on me too!"

"What's the difference—?"

"You tell me—you're the man with answers."

"Sure I am. For the girl who had everything." His voice was shaking with anger. "I certainly got Evans' number, didn't I? Knew right where she really lived, was at, as the young would say. But unfortunately being vague, I misplaced her address—and I wanted to call her apartment building." To see if they could rouse her on the house phone, an old, impatient habit of his, hardly worth mentioning under ordinary circumstances. "So I went over there . . . OK?"

"Not OK." Nannie braked at the light and faced him. "You'd have used the house phone yourself, not a phone booth—if you went for business. And you'd never have lied to me about it."

"Not intentional—simply no time."

"You had time. And opportunity. And what's that other thing—?"

"For God's sake . . ." The lines in the stony face were like cracks. "It had nothing to do with the murder!"

"Until you lied to the police—"

"Stalled—"

"And let me do it—"

"Only to salvage what was left—"

"Your career. Your name."

"It's yours too."

"*Thanks.*"

The dark eyes closed, mortally wounded.

"Hey, come on . . ." He reached for her hand. "You're still my Bernstein . . . remember?" She shook her head, denying it all from the day it began. When both of them had used her maiden name at work, partly to promote the fiction that her first marriage was already coming unglued, though until she met Phelps, only his was. Yet it had been his escape that took forever, took precedence while Nannie waited, alone at home, isolated in the office. The way it began was the way it would end. Even the words were the same. "Come on," he said, "keep the faith. You know I'll square it. Just let me handle it my own way—quietly—"

"*Quietly?*" Her eyes were wide open now. And dangerous. That was the difference. "Using Kelly and Harvey to front for your little memorial? Quietly, hell!" Quietly was the way he used Nannie.

"What do you want me to do? Go on the air to comfort that boy? Throw what's left away for a weak moment—"

"You already have."

"Because I made one mistake in judgment? That's all it was —a lousy ten-minute walk in the wrong direction!"

"Who knows what it was now?"

"Our shrink knows!" Resentment rose against her. "At those goddamn rates, I'm obviously not the man with the money! And despite your infinite belief in miracles, I still wouldn't have much use for a key."

"Unless you found a cheaper miracle worker—in one of your weak moments!"

"Hardly cheaper—" A horn blared behind them. The light had changed. He faced forward. "We're due at the Weldons'."

She shook her head. "I'm going home."

"Without me?" There was only a morning train to miss on Sunday. And an afternoon bus that ran too early. "I can't just drive off with this show airing—"

"Then don't!" She hit the wheel with her gloved hand. "Stay over in town tonight! The way you wanted to Wednesday."

The bitterness of life's mistimed opportunities was beyond denying. Phelps didn't even try.

"You don't have to drop me," he said. "I'll walk."

She let him, watching him go, shaggy head tucked against a raised shoulder. Then she turned the wheel in the opposite direction, heading west for her rolling green hills, her growing garden, her warm barn siding, her lovingly refinished furniture, wondering as she drove what would be worse to part from—hearth or husband. She knew from experience she'd have to do the leaving. There was no Other Woman to make it happen this time. Except in the mind.

Coming from the East Side, Ned didn't have to pass the rabbi's watch on the Broadway corner. He hardly needed that on his first trip back, ill-timed at best. But he had no choice. On Sunday he took a private patient. If indeed even this source of income hadn't been scared off by the TV news, assigned ironically as a comprehension aid for the confused in speech. It hadn't done much for the comprehension of old neighbors letting Ned pass in silence. As always, the kids' hostility committee had adjourned for weekend fun and games, leaving the sunning space on the stoop to their parents. And victims. Picking his way up the stone steps between them, Ned Nedders, alias Four Eyes, at least was not yet suspected of stomping senior citizens. Or ripping off the tenant known as Lame Lady in the basement apartment where Ned tried to remember to deliver his rent so she wouldn't have to gimp four flights to collect it. Perhaps it was this that made her relent when he paused between the open doors to get his unwanted mail, so the stuffed box couldn't signal his absence. He needn't have bothered. Somebody, Lame Lady said, had just gone up right past it.

"Didn't say what for . . ." She shrugged her bony shoulders letting the world go by anew. "Nobody knowed where you was anyhow."

And cared less, the other bony backs said.

"Thanks . . ." Ned hesitated. "My regular visitor?"

Someone cackled a laugh. "Wasn't no detective!"

In a way Ned should have known. No accident of nature or subway had ever deterred the aphasic gentleman, pushing sixty, who was trying to escape the effects of a stroke before impatient relatives dumped him, cheap, on the sunless steps of a nursing home. A dapper dan with his walking cane, Mr. Kincaid always arrived at Ned's door on the dot, allowing for a brief rest on each landing. Climbing to the first, Ned wondered wearily if today the stroke victim had also allowed for fear, surmounting even the risk of a racing heart to continue past the waste of words on the wall. The power to waste, or use, words might even be worth braving a murder suspect. Leaning over the banister, to call a reassuring greeting up the stair well, Ned knew he could not expect an answer, when the familiar bald head peered down in silence. Until Mr. Kincaid thought to wave his cane, a gesture gallantly repeated each time Ned looked up from successive landings. So he needn't have worried about that either. The nearer he got the clearer it became. The aphasic, who had trouble telling hot from cold, was still in touch with deeper feelings, struggling for expression, as the dapper dan hung his cane on his arm to grasp Ned's hand with both of his. Usually Ned waited, but today, struggling himself, he was the one to start their conversation backward.

"Thank you . . ." he said, anticipating kindness. "Thank you for coming . . ." Among other things, too hard to express. But the best and brightest never stopped trying.

"Lost Fred . . ." Mr. Kincaid began, "not Fred . . ."

"No. But thank you."

"His friend, no yours. . . . Oh why can't I say it?" Sometimes words came so easily, a whole phrase escaping on wings, but seldom the one that was wanted.

"You're saying it . . ." (Lost Fred, not Fred, his friend, no yours.) The teacher waited.

"Goddamn!" They could almost always swear. *"Your* friend . . ."

"Yes," Ned said. "I lost my friend."

One Sunday when Mr. Kincaid came, the girl with three names had been there. Though the names were a life sentence to an aphasic, his perception of the meeting had not altered. She had made them tea. She had made them laugh. She had been Ned's friend.

"Wrecked the law . . ." Mr. Kincaid began again, as Ned got busy with his seven locks.

"The law?"

"Not the law." Mr. Kincaid had been a lawyer. He would not have smiled at wreckage of the law, as he did when the door was finally opened to reveal what he meant—the patch of beaverboard covering a futile search for brick which Mr. Kincaid's visit had interrupted.

"The wall . . ." He pointed.

"Yes," Ned said, "she wrecked the wall."

And that wasn't all. But the least and lightest of offenses was clearer than the darkest, to Mr. Kincaid, if not Ned anymore. Or he might have enjoyed the first decent conversation he'd had about her. Instead he changed the subject, explaining he'd been staying with another friend, as he kicked away his open suitcase, so they could take their accustomed places side by side on the pullout sofa opposite the slatted coffee table. Ned dusted it off before laying out the usual pictures. No need to explain there would be no follow-up quiz on current events, illustrated with photographs cut from the papers, as might have happened had these not created holes in the memory, wreckage beyond the patching on the wall. So they started instead where they had left off three Sundays before. With the nep, nib—no pen. The licnep, lamp—no pencil. The leap, peal—no apple. The reap, no rape, no God no, rip . . .

"Not rip, repair . . ." Mr. Kincaid was sweating. "Can't get it."

"You're getting it." (Reap, rape, rip, repair.) The teacher waited.

"Pear."

"Yes," Ned said. "The pear. Let's try again."

"No," Mr. Kincaid said, nodding yes. Somehow they got by pear, and kept going to another set of pictures. Or tried to. Until they heard the heavy footsteps on the stairs, and the voices coming nearer, finally interrupting with a rap on the door, not the wall, but the law, announcing itself for sure. Mr.

Kincaid stayed surprisingly calm—just shaking his head, reaching out as if to detain Ned, though the voices were calling they knew Ned was here, and Ned knew the voices.

"It's OK," he reassured his patient. "I'll tell them to come back." He was ready with information to trade, more than ready to handle Good and Bad Guys this time. Back again, they said, for another look at the premises, now that Ned had again taken up residence.

"But you were supposed to tell us when, Professor."

"I'm only here for a therapy session—"

"Sorry. It'll have to wait."

"You wait. I've had enough patients upset."

"Not by us, Ned."

"Only because you can't get on campus!" City police, unlike the press, had to mind university manners.

"Well, we can get in here—want to see a warrant?" Bad Guy made as if to reach into his side pocket, until he spotted the individual behind Ned, doing the same in a suspicious manner, used as an excuse to shove past and apprehend the dapper dan, babbling everything backward and dropping his cane, but stubbornly coming up with the card that proved he was once an attorney of record.

"What's that—give it over."

"Dark, no card. For Fred—"

"Who's Fred?" Bad Guy couldn't find any Fred on the card.

"He means friend—*me*." Ned appealed to Good Guy blocking the doorway. "The man's had a stroke . . ."

Bad Guy did not bother with niceties. "A busted mouthpiece. Just what you need!"

"Will you give the card back and let me get him out of here."

"You're not going anywhere, Professor."

"He'll make it fast, Frankovitch." Good Guy moved in from

the doorway, toward the suitcase he had already looked at. For other reasons.

"Come on . . ." Ned reunited Mr. Kincaid with his cane, guiding him toward the landing. "I'm sorry—we'll make up the lesson . . . I promise . . ."

But Mr. Kincaid kept shaking his head, obsessed with the card, now pressed on Ned. "Go write . . . no, not write, dammit—try . . . say Fred."

"I'll try." Ned nodded. "I'll call your office."

"Yes. No. Not then . . ."

"Now—the home number." There were two. "I'll tell your partners I'm your friend. Please don't worry . . ."

There was a sharp sound of grinding metal, a file wrenched open too violently.

"Oh God," Ned said. "My data . . ."

He rushed back in before Bad Guy could upend an entire metal drawer, and scramble six months of work, yet to be color-coded, one of those loose ends Ned's adviser had advised clearing up.

"Jesus—don't get that stuff out of order!" Six more months hung in the balance as Ned grabbed the other side of the drawer. "I'd have to start over—"

"Shoulda thought of that before you messed with evidence—"

"What evidence—there's no evidence here—"

"It was missing from the scene. We got a sworn affidavit—"

"Show me! It's got to say on the warrant—I've got a right to see—"

"You got nothing!" Bad Guy wrenched the drawer away. "Hutzpah's what you got—sitting at Homicide all night with that photograph on you!"

"*Photograph*—where?"

"You tell us. What did you do—eat it? Shove it—"

"I never even saw it—"

"Somebody did, Ned." Good Guy moved in. "The one we're looking for was in her place that day. And there may have been others. Maybe even film, sound tracks . . . tapes." He picked one up from the pile on the desk. "Like this. Now, if we have to, we'll go through all of yours . . ."

"Make us do that," Bad Guy said, "and you may just get some back erased."

Even one erased made all worthless. "But they're lab recordings . . . vowel sounds . . ." Miles of vowel sounds, choking Ned, months of lab. "It says on all the labels . . ."

"Labels." Bad Guy laughed, resting the drawer on the edge of the desk. "It says on the label you're smart for Chrissake! Our smart eyewitness—the absent-minded professor. Falls over the bodies, walking in on his girl!—And all you can tell us—you missed the big scene. Like maybe at a snuff flick, if she got it on camera . . ."

Ned stared from one to the other. "No, come on . . ."

Good Guy shook his head, but not in denial. "Could have happened like that. You saw what went down . . ."

"And you know what she was into, Professor. You got freebie peeks—"

"No," Ned said softly, but the ground had opened. This time they would never reach bottom.

"Sure you know—you helped her spend the loot. Dirty money from dirty pictures. She was in the business."

"You had to know if she was, Ned."

But beauty that proved untrue led only to the eye of a blind beholder, blinking at the truth in the sworn affidavit, now repeated verbatim.

"I didn't know."

"Well, now you do . . ."

"Sure you never had a clue, Ned?" If not, why not, Good

Guy wondered like Bad Guy—but their street-smart professor stared blankly past them at the patch on the wall, no more able to explain than Mr. Kincaid how he had lost his way as he lost Fred.

"You sure as hell suspected her of something, Professor. The way you acted. Always checking on her, hanging up phones, walking out . . ."

Jealous, the label said. Of everything.

But never this.

"It was all kind of too much . . . the way she lived . . . where I live . . ."

But other couples worked out such things. Good Guy, for example, name of Reilly, was himself about to marry Bad Guy's sister, name of Frankovitch, reconciling differences of religion, plaguing both their houses. True lovers always found a way.

"Not us . . ." No way.

"So you knew something was really wrong somewhere . . ." Not just her money, but where it came from. Never just for profit, always partly for kicks. Sorrowfully Good Guy sighed and shook his head. "Man, level with yourself, will you? Do us all a favor. There are other girls to protect in this town. Real live girls, into very crazy numbers. Our job is cooling the freaks—not making judgments. All we know—this picture is a link. Nothing else was missing. So if you ever saw it, or anything like it, maybe a hint you didn't even want to see—try to think, and tell us now, OK? There had to be once when it came up. Maybe some extra job, extra dough that took extra time—and maybe caused one of your fights. Like some lie she couldn't explain, some date she broke. Or maybe just a conversation you didn't understand—like on the phone, at a party, some name, some place. But something, Ned. You were in there. You were closest. Now help us."

First the body blow. Then the soft pitch. Then the silent wait for the new wound to fester, as the file drawer teetered on the desk's edge. And behind it, half the cabinet gaped empty—dented, tinny, gray-green and rusted. Not painted out steely white against white walls, file after file, almost invisible in memory. Like love, when Ned gave up the ghost.

"There was a party once . . . in a photographer's studio. Some fashion hotshot. Used to be a model. I forget her name." And the address. And whether it was spring or fall, though warm enough to use a terrace. "This photographer was kidding around about shooting a porno—"

"Just kidding?"

"I wasn't sure." Even then. "They were all like laughing back and forth about posing."

"Your girl too?"

His girl especially. Right in front of him—or across him. "You asked me about times we fought—that was one of the beauts. I wanted to go home. She wouldn't. So I left her."

Laughing, the label said. And dancing, the last Ned saw, all he saw before he split.

"Just dancing, Professor? Ever discuss what happened after that?"

"Like for about a week." If yelling was discussion. "She said nothing happened."

"Any mutual friends we could check with?"

Ned shook his head. "It was a pop crowd . . . models, artists, a couple of rock types, transvestites. I don't know who they were. Except for that writer—you know E.V., and she left with me—"

Bad Guy almost dropped the drawer. "*Adamic—?*"

"Only as far as the bar on the corner—she was staying at the studio."

"Wait a minute—" Good Guy moved in again. "This was *Adamic*'s place?"

"Well, her roommate's. But E.V. didn't dig the scene either. Not that night."

Motive, the label said.

"Jesus, Professor. *Now* you tell us!"

Good Guy turned on his partner. "Now we ask him!"

"The jerk held out—I checked him on Adamic—the whole angle!"

"Not about pornos," Ned protested. "I forgot E.V.'s connection." As he'd forgotten the rabbi connection that destroyed his alibi, and the Phelps connection that restored it, no more to be forgiven when finally blurted than more doubtful lapses, deliberately suppressed. Bad Guy wanted to yank him in again to make a fuller statement, one that better check out this time!

"*Later*, Frankovitch!" Good Guy glared at the other half of the team who had caught the big case for the regulars. "Corio's following up the right lead, for God's sake." For the Task Force. "C'mon, this can wait." Like the tape Good Guy threw on the desk. And the file left teetering on the edge, as Bad Guy reluctantly let go of his theory, better late than never, but too soon for Ned, as usual too slow on the uptake when he made his move, grabbing at the drawer, contents already slipping, starting to spill from folders, almost in slow motion, before the whole thing went over, scattering everywhere . . ."

"Nice eye," Good Guy said.

They had to wade in paper to get to the door, trampling graphs, charts, tables, as Ned had let them trample on his rights, against the advice of a busted mouthpiece.

"Bastards . . . pig mother sons of bitches." There was no warrant to cover this.

"You did it yourself, Professor."

Who needed a warrant? If they'd ever had one. They left

him to wonder, owing him nothing as they hurried away to make up for the time his delusions had cost them.

Suckers all, the label said.

The Sergeant from the Task Force seemed better equipped. He was hardly bluffing, when he gave up ringing and announcing himself to wave down the cruising squad car so he could use their radio and finally their wheels to locate the party required to be on the premises when he served his warrant. He could not serve it on the boxers, locked out to bark distantly from the cement court, where they could not drive the lookout crazy. Not crazy enough to answer, a mistake made yesterday. Today the boy remained silent, ear pressed to the door, waiting for the squad car to drive away, before creeping back up the ladder and across the mattress to dial a warning.

E.V. watched her face disappear under what had been described as a *light* makeup before Kelly went upstairs to the set.

"We *always* do a light makeup for public affairs shows, Mr. Kelly," said the man, now laying a really vicious blue on E.V.'s eyelids. Even the researcher dashing in from the hall took a beat to locate the guest in the mirror.

"Oh, there you are—you got an outside call."

"She isn't finished," the makeup man began, but E.V. was already out of the chair, and into her hat. "You don't need your hat to answer the phone."

Little did he know. "Where's the call?"

"Across the hall on the PA's line. But we gotta move, OK? They want you on the set." The PA's office wasn't big enough for two. So the researcher dashed back upstairs to explain the new hangup. As soon as she was gone, E.V. shut the door. Just in case it was one of those calls.

"E.V.?" It was. "That fucker just came back to search the joint—"

"You didn't open up—"

"Are you kidding? Now they think I'm that creep from the park!"

"Why? I told them who you were—sort of."

"Well, they didn't believe you. They think you were hiding the creep."

In Mrs. Porter's studio! "But *why*—?"

"E.V., don't start with the whys. I've had it—I'm going over the wall—"

"With that fuzz car cruising—?"

"They're on the way up for you—all of 'em—with a friggin' search warrant. E.V., you were right about pictures of Evans."

"Oh no . . ." She sat down slowly on somebody's typing chair.

"Baby, just don't ever tell the fuzz you knew . . ."

"I didn't."

"Well, that's what they're looking for—I couldn't hear why . . ."

"Three guesses." The chair was broken, forcing her to sit very straight. And still. "Aldo, call location—ask about the pictures. Ask what else to take—"

"Outa the safe? You gotta be *crazy*—"

"You're crazy if you don't. You know who's backing Toni's movie—they're backing your bar!" All in the family.

"Oh Jesus. What am I into?" He was crying. So was E.V. Smudging the makeup. How vicious was that blue?

"Ask Toni what we're into." A mad gay whirl? Or Murder Incorporated.

High risk questions. "You know her better—can't you call, E.V.?"

She stared at the phone. "Not anymore." Somewhere beyond the world of Mrs. Porter, the guest was wanted on the set. "Tell her I'll be on camera when they get here. Tell her I can stall . . ." E.V. was already groping in her hatband for the stash of pills, half to pop now, half to palm for later. After that it really wouldn't matter. They'd have to pump her stomach first anyway.

"Bye, Aldo . . ."

"Listen—"

But she couldn't. Footsteps were approaching. She threw the keys of Mrs. Porter's world into a wastebasket full of papers, before she opened the door.

Young Mrs. Weldon, white-faced and reckless, was back at her old stand, refusing the assistance of her staff to page a friendlier bartender over the low-voiced babble in her living room. "Where's Charlie?" she called, ready for another carafe of sangrias. Or should it be stingers? Wasn't Charlie here?

Almost all the mourners were. Even the real ones had been included. Cinny and Sally stood talking tearfully to a subdued Billy Bee Bernard, nervously facing a long ordeal to be capped by a solemn viewing of Kelly and E.V.'s TV debut, when they too arrived for the Weldons' buffet. Which Bella Sweet planned to beg off, once she saw the VP of PR was missing. Like Nannie Bernstein Phelps, a more mysterious defection, stonily explained away as exhaustion by her husband before he started drinking for two. Weldon, himself, remained mysteriously sober, listening to his wife call Charlie, hiding with Israel behind Dotty. But there was no hiding place from women scorned. Bella joined the Golds.

"Here's Charlie, sweetie," she caroled out to her hostess. Caught between the devil and the deep, Charlie headed for a bar stool, determined to keep the bar between himself and his boss's lady, already leaning across it toward him with that look he dreaded. Crazy . . .

"Ready for a stinger?"

"A little early . . ."

"Bet Israel's ready."

Charlie didn't think so. "Not with Mrs. Gold here." The traditional mourners were drinking seltzer. This was just not playtime, as Charlie tried to indicate tactfully. "You see, it's been kind of a personal loss."

Young Mrs. Weldon saw all right. Not being blind. Or deaf. Or dumb. "I'll bet," she said, "I'll bet it's personal. You two think I don't remember what Israel called me the night she was killed—sitting right there?" She pointed to the bar stool, as Charlie tried to slip off.

"I don't know what you mean," he stammered idiotically.

"Maudley . . ." she whispered, "Maudley . . ."

Charlie was too paralyzed to move in any direction, feeling Bella's and Dotty's presence behind him, Weldon behind them, and Israel everywhere. "For God's sake—he'll hear you—"

"Why should I care?" she said. "He's the sicky—"

"You want what Evans got?" It was a last resort, all he could think of.

Mrs. Weldon stopped smiling. It was the first time he had ever seen her eyes look halfway normal. As if she didn't know him.

"What did you say?"

"Just don't kid—"

"Don't you kid—not like that! Not with me, Collins! Don't you ever dare—!"

"Who's kidding?" It was Israel's voice coming softly from behind Charlie, a sound more frightening than any whispered imitation. She went a sick pink under the white makeup, shrinking back as she had from the police that night, looking wildly past everybody for her backup. For Daddy, sobered and withdrawn, withdrawing further to the hall, though the staff was ready to answer the door, could have answered the phone ringing on the bar, where no bell could save anyone. The voice everyone knew from somewhere asked for Phelps, ready and waiting for a call from home. Not this one.

"Speaking, Kelly."

"I'm at the taping," Kelly said. "E. V. Adamic just flipped out."

Phelps took his time answering. He didn't want Israel gliding in, scenting danger. Like Nannie, right from the first. "On camera?"

"You got it."

"How far in?"

"Early enough to edit," Kelly said, "but what the hell's the difference?" They couldn't blip memories. Not on a news panel jolted silent by the tiny figure in the cowboy hat, jumping from her seat, fists raised in defiance, at the first challenge to her friendship with Maude Lee Evans.

Phelps leaned casually on the bar away from the others. "Harvey said he'd stay off that."

"It wasn't just Harvey." The VP of PR, now entering the Weldons' hallway, had gone higher. To the show's producer, bringing on a change of cast. "There was another interviewer," Kelly said. "They threw us a curve."

And the curve was The Cork.

Phelps swore under his breath, not that it mattered any longer who heard him. There would be no end now to the wild speculation, spewing out even as E.V. fled the lights, leaving Kelly to sweat with Harvey, trying to interrupt, get a word in, change the subject. To the awfulness of violence, awfulness of gossip, of TV, to the awfulness of anything but The Cork. Until the control room wrapped the segment.

"Wrapped hell." Phelps' tone was grim. The least they could do was kill it.

But unfortunately for a better story. Or worse, as Kelly saw it. "There's some kind of a warrant out on E.V. Cops just brought it."

Another cop had just brought the news to Gracie Square. Beyond the suddenly hushed living room, Phelps saw the Deputy Commissioner following the VP of PR into the old man's study, saw Weldon close the study door. Saw Nannie close her eyes in the station wagon. He turned his back, and lowered his voice.

"Kelly, get out. Get clear . . ."

"Of the kid? I can't find her—"

"Clear of the whole thing—all of us." He covered the receiver with his cupped hand. "Clear of me, Kelly."

Phelps disconnected.

Kelly got clear of the sound stage itself by simply walking away with his makeup on, past all the police and show assistants trying to get clear of each other. In fact he might have gotten clear of the building if he hadn't spotted young Reilly, so different now from the day he routinely questioned Kelly, no longer a landsman but a hard-nosed detective, sweating the lone studio guard in the booth at the street entrance, so different from network security.

"Now you're telling me the girl's still in the building?"

"I'm saying I check everyone in and out!" The ledger was pushed forward. "And that street door don't open until I release it." Aggrieved, the guard illustrated by pressing the button.

"Anyone could do that while you were in the basement."

"It was only once—to take a fast leak. And you gotta know how to jam the buzzer."

"If she wanted to go, she could have gone," Reilly said.

"Anywhere . . ." Kelly was looking toward the open stairs, winding into darkness in both directions, while backstage, everyone rushed around, checking the locks on access doors.

"Nobody gets in my basement but me," the guard said defensively. "And the offices are locked up there."

"But not the johns . . ." Still unlocked, backstage, the actor reminded them.

Reilly frowned. "My partner and I will check everything, Mr. Kelly." His tone was a brush-off as he moved away, but Kelly moved with him.

"Look, I know it's police business. But I got E.V. into this."

"Not the mess she's in." Reilly glanced nervously toward the sound stage. "But we sure as hell don't want it on the air . . ."

"Don't worry—they're making up worse."

Reilly doubted it. "There's been a suspicious individual apprehended on her premises. Could add up to harboring a fugitive, maybe even suppressing evidence. Believe me, Mr. Kelly—you don't know from the questions we got for Miss Adamic—"

"Well, you may have to move to get the answers," Kelly said. "She's holding enough speed to fly a horse. And it has to be an hour since she took off."

Reilly moved. He yelled for his partner to take the basement, and ran ahead of Kelly up the stairs. The first floor was dingy, full of cutting rooms, some kind of work space, with a single washroom, found empty as Reilly's partner joined them, taking the lead up the next flight. Kelly fell back, slowed by his trick knee, cartilage waiting to be replaced. It would wait for Medicare at this rate. He was limping when he reached the neater hall of the executive floor and saw the light at the end, heard the detectives shout, running toward it, knowing it had to be a washroom. There were two for executives. True to form, the light was on in the one marked MEN. Kelly saw a flash of urinals as the detectives flung the door open. It closed again before he caught up, pushing it wide to limp past the urinals toward the booths. There were only two. They found her in the last one.

Her boots showed under the locked door. When she failed to respond they looked over the top. She was slumped to the side, cheek resting against the metal dispenser, hat in her lap. Except for her color, she looked quite peaceful, until they got the door open and dragged her out on the floor. And really saw the color in that overhead light. There wasn't much peace after that.

The boat had sailed for Adam and Eve who put to sea with Pinch Me. Adam and Eve went over the side. So who was left? the old joke went. They knew the joke, they pinched her to see, and slapped and called and then saved their breath for mouth-to-mouth until the ambulance came and saved the rest.

They knew what was saved.

Let her go, Kelly thought, though he had not and no one could without going overboard from the same boat. So long as there were signs of life, even signs the color of death, there had to be hope, the adage went, as old as the hat trick or the joke. *Sauve qui peut,* Kelly had said, the name of the game, or who would be left?

They knew who was left.

Kelly knew best: Long time no see. Long time no hear. Long time no speak.

Pinch Me.

Pinch Me was left.

Every line but the first had been changed in the dialogue, lovingly laundered for Israel, and delivered so promptly the next day. It took Phelps quite a while to read all the smudged, rewritten pages he found clipped together on his hunting table with a memo from Nannie recommending that they stick with the original. Evans would probably have agreed, but directly, without the memo, a difference more of style than substance. Both were right, but so was Israel. Had Phelps been running the show he would simply have kept the writer on the set to reword speeches as needed for Kelly. The ethnic flavor was implicit, not a matter of accent. But E.V. had worked too hard to replace it. So hard Phelps could not help wonder how she'd gotten involved in suspicion of murder on the same night. With or without the boy caught in her studio, or a picket still uncaught in the park. Confusion on this point remained unresolved at press time Monday morning, but some guilty connection seemed indicated by her suicide attempt, as reported on all three channels. Two of the newscasts were shot outside Homicide, a pretty good hint where the hints came from.

So Phelps folded her pages into his jacket pocket to show to the detectives when he kept the appointment he had requested, to nobody's great surprise. The Lieutenant, it seemed, was ready with some questions despite the big break in the case now being so widely advertised. A hint perhaps that bigger breaks were needed, to be pursued as usual, in private, for as long as possible. But with sources like Nedders on call in the background, the phone booth story would finally come out, like all the others. At Homicide today, on the news tomorrow. So each rumor flickered and faded. Everyone had a turn in the barrel. Phelps rose from the hunting table to turn off "A.M. America," sparing himself an exclusive, eyewitness interview with The Cork. The viewing was better from the corner office windows where he had watched night turn into day. Though, somehow he had missed the crumpled pack of cigarettes now spotted on the ottoman. Phelps needed sleep, breakfast, and a shave. But the cigarette he found, battered and forgotten, was what he wanted. Five years of resolution would go up in smoke with the rest of the visions if he reached for the book of Sherry-Netherland matches. But he did. Better his five years than Kelly's six months, he told himself, falling off the wagon for both of them. Inhaling, he waited for the dizziness to pass, prepared to wait a little longer, for more serious dizziness to return, with no Nannie to save him this time. And no work to be saved for.

This then was the beginning of the end, the slow-motion death throes he'd seen so often. The sublime to ridiculous slip into soaps, Canadian exile, Spaghetti Westerns, corner saloons, crack-up country for lost big-timers who couldn't get arrested, media executives without portfolio, running out of talent, out of the money, looking for jobs that no longer existed. As always the pioneer would be too good for the company he kept. But merit, in itself, was never enough. And somehow Phelps had fallen short as a bastard, had chosen the wrong bitch in Evans, or so they would all say when he finally blew it—going the way of all slow-motion failures. An inch at a time. The change in status would be gradual, coming at first in the form of a stall. Related to budget, availabilities, and of course to his having gone a bit overboard, bringing a conservative crackdown from upstairs. No big deal, they'd say. Just a few delays and postponements on his decisions, while lesser projects got preference all around him, were done wrong, done on shoestrings, done by dunces, by anyone but Austin Phelps, finished like his career by inches not only here but in the business, if it took them the two-year length of his contract.

But about that he was mistaken. Or he might at least have had a word for Cinny. He owed her so many when he passed her in silence, went down the long hall past Bella's door, closed for the first time in kaffeeklatsch history, he noted, wondering why. He found out in the reception area where he met Weldon doddering off the elevator from a three-martini breakfast. On the wrong floor or so it seemed to Phelps, the old man looked so confused. But today all floors were wrong.

"We're fired," Weldon said, in a voice so utterly mystified he obviously couldn't believe it either. Talent—yes, always hanging by a clause. But not VP's like Weldon and Israel, on executive contracts, insured by stock options and pension plans, seniority's severance, to be paid in perpetuity . . .

"They want us out today," Weldon said. And that was it. They were cutting their losses.

Sometimes the finish came very quickly.

She decided it was a new art form. Sand graffiti. She executed several examples before the tide came in. Contemporary stuff, in keeping with the environment. "Therese and Isabelle '69." "I'm a ferry—fly me to Fire Island." Her brother-in-law forced a laugh when he found her. "Don't you know any straight jokes?" he asked. And she said yes, but not with happy endings.

She had found her feet over the weekend, spending most of her time on the beach. By herself whenever possible. If she saw a familiar face she'd retreat over the dunes to the house, and if guests dropped by, to her bedroom. Or the baby's where she wasn't really needed except for feeding. There were three in help, smiling South American look-alikes she preferred to old friends from childhood. Her sister and brother-in-law kept telling each other, she'd get in the swing if she just relaxed, stayed on, spent the summer. So on Tuesday she walked from the ocean to the bayside, as if to test the possibility of escape by watching the people get on and off the ferries. She didn't mind people if they were strangers. Certainly she had no way of expecting that the last human being she wanted to see would be standing there as the crowd dispersed. There wasn't much chance to turn away. Or much point. He must have sneaked her sister's name and address from some Homicide folder to have gotten this far. Obviously he wasn't here for the sun. So she waited where she was and let him spot her. He came across the dock slowly.

"Got a moment?"

"That's all?"

"Yes."

She had always found him slow on her kind of uptake but this time she sensed a hard-edged difference, as if he'd added a protective layer. Along with some cool new shades clipped to his glasses.

"What's the disguise for—fuzz still after you?"

He smiled faintly, also new. He used to smile only when he felt like it. Seldom. "They found a couple of other types with longer hair." And worse, if ultimately provable, alibis. Even the hippie from the park had finally surrendered in a camper where he claimed to have been all along with his entire commune.

"What's with the big snuff movie theory?"

"No evidence." Lot of blue film, but no negatives of the still they were looking for. "They turned the studio upside down," he said, "they like to do that." And once done, no place or career or person thus upended could easily be put back together.

"E.V. . . ."

"Looks like she'll make it," he said.

"Just make it?"

"Nobody's saying for sure."

"She's made it before . . ." But scarred was different from turning vegetable. "For *nothing*." It was the bitterest sound Amy had made on that island.

Nedders nodded. "It's beginning to look that way, isn't it?"

They started wandering in toward the sea on one of the boardwalks that linked the houses.

"I turned her in," Amy said. "In my own cute way. To this one very special sergeant I trusted."

"I turned her girlfriend in by mistake," he said. Who knew they were *really* into porno? "I thought it was a private joke." At most.

"And you were never much for laughs, were you, Nedders?"

"You had enough laughs for both of us."

She stopped and faced him. "Joke's over," she said, though his moment wasn't. "I've got to see a baby about some milk."

"I could wait . . ."

"Anyone else, I'd say tag along." But he looked hard up, and he was one man she would not want to turn on, at the best of moments.

"Don't worry," he said. He was the one man she couldn't.

An idle boast, considering the nature of the beast stalking ghostly prey across dune and sea. To wind up beached with the shipwreck's other sole survivor, both suddenly more aware of sheer physical aliveness than they'd been since they were struck by the same bolt of lightning. Perhaps it was partly the romantic setting—a Victorian castle in the sand, veranda set about with white wicker, cool interior invitingly empty, everyone else gone to the beach, barbecues, Bay Shore dentists, except for one South American having a siesta. High time at high noon, heat getting to Amy, perhaps trying to get to Nedders, despite herself, when she brought her baby outside, to unbutton her blouse where he sprawled on a settee, waiting for his moment. He looked pale in the sun that tanned so quickly, made her drowsy, until aroused by tiny jaws, arousing the watcher, trying to look at the baby, not the mother, both breasts showing, nipples rising, alerted to the danger of his almost forgotten remnant of malehood, manness, a sign of life, watched in turn by sharp hazel eyes, still looking down, when he looked up, confounded.

He couldn't move from the settee, but he shifted his position. "She wasn't pregnant," he said finally.

Amy shifted the baby. "Was she supposed to be?"

"That's what she told McVitty." Never Ned. Nor had the fuzz told Amy apparently. They didn't tell *anybody* everything. Pro *or* con. But Billings' brunette knew a nurse going through college on a grant to study alcohol- or drug-related deaths, requiring attendance at the Evans/Foreman autopsies, neither of which revealed significant relation to drugs or alcohol. Nor any sign whatever of a fetus.

"So maybe it was just a story to get bread." Told to McVitty a couple of times. And perhaps to a couple of other guys, the way things looked to Ned. "Could have been an abortion shakedown, I guess."

"Is that what you guess?"

"You don't have to guess, do you, Amy?" Finally. The moment he had come for.

Her lips curled down as smoke curled up, getting in mother's eyes instead of baby's, but still too close for comfort. "Here . . . take this . . ." They had to look sharp to transfer the cigarette without touching. "I never heard that one," Amy said.

"But you'd know if it was true." Like all the rest.

"Would I?"

"The same way we knew about you." The new hard edge changed the voice Amy used to hear, raised in objection to the neighbors, until it was breathlessly put down for squareness.

"We might as well have been in there with you sometimes," he said.

Amy laughed. "Maybe it would have saved a little trouble."

"Look," he sat forward, "it doesn't matter anymore to me either. Not the way it did. All I want is to get straight—"

"How straight," she wondered, "can you get?"

"In my head. So I'll know what happened from what didn't and get the fuck over it."

"Don't let me stop you."

"You could stop this whole craziness. I wouldn't have come if there was anybody else. But somebody's just got to level—"

"Nobody's got to, Sonny boy. Believe me." Hadn't he learned? Mothers died forever.

"I'd tell you—I swear—"

"Tell me *what?*"

"The truth—if I could. You know it—"

"*You mean what I heard through a wall?*"

Even at Homicide he had not faced such contempt. Except the contempt he felt for himself when he woke seduced by empty promises, still breathlessly waiting to recur in his sleep, and he couldn't go without sleeping much longer. No one could exorcise belief like this witch, fresh out of the milk of human kindness as she burped her baby. But, alas Mother had her own nightmares to face, out in the cold, alone in the dark, on the sunniest beach. Hadn't he heard? Fathers went first.

"That's the whole damn trouble with summer," she said. "You wake up screaming and the shrinks are on vacation."

"That's all you can say . . ." The humiliation of special pleading had been anticipated, but not this awful writhing against refusal. "*Shrinks,* for God's sake!"

God for God's sake.

"Sorry about God." Even shrinks had better answering services. Only the fuzz came when needed, but with questions, not answers. So it didn't do to importune blank walls—in the end all you heard was the sound of heavy breathing. Nedders was making it now.

"Thanks a lot!" His mutinous gaze fixed on her breast, rage rising against the tiny rival jaws, at it again.

"Jesus—doesn't he ever let up?"

"She."

Self-pity like contempt was total. He hadn't thought to ask. Still didn't care, made desperate for succor by adult needs. "Another girl, born to liberation!" His jaws had teeth. He let her see them in that pretense of a smile. "Great timing. Maybe she'll grow up to assassinate a President."

Amy smiled back. "We can't all be victims."

Victimizing everyone, chain reaction wiping out the whole human family. Brothers too. Like fathers, like sons, next to go. "When did you get so thick with the sisters?" His hard edge sharpened—like a knife. "After you dumped on dike city? What are you bleeding for?" His eyes burned behind the cool shades. "One of your swell sisters helped your husband dump on you! Why cover with me? What do we owe either of them? Both of us got screwed . . ."

"Not lately . . ." Not from where Amy stood, eying her hard-up, hard-edged assailant, as she shifted the baby to her shoulder and buttoned her blouse. "There are times when everybody needs a mercy hump." Needing wasn't getting. Hadn't he noticed?

"That's what you call it—what they did?"

"Never call it. Unless I'm there."

"Well, weren't you? Ever?" It caught her in the doorway and turned her around. "Not even to test the water? Just for laughs . . ."

"Lay your own ghost, Nedders."

"Goddamn bitch!" He was on his feet, heedless with rage. "What the fuck kind of human being are you? What was she?"

Amy pressed her cheek to the baby's hard little head, soft somewhere, like hers, or she wouldn't have let them in for this. "Funny . . . we were just asking ourselves that very question. About Dada . . ."

"Oh for Chrissake—he was a man." A knee jerk reaction, kneed from a jerk, betrayed by his own sex as he stood there, proving the hopeless difference between them. Up down up. He couldn't help it. She couldn't help him, couldn't even relieve him of her forgotten cigarette, burning his fingers, before he dropped it to grab her wrist with a grip that could break the bone, both still blindly unable to gauge the strength of their effects on each other.

"*Hands off!*"

"Not till you level about her! *Now.*"

"*Shmuck,*" she said. Poor dangerous shmuck. "What the hell can I tell you? She was this girl . . ."

On Wednesday it was drizzling again.

"No press to bother us today, sir," the club doorman said, opening an umbrella for the departing guest.

"Yes, I know, thank you." Leland Evans thought it was because of the elaborate precautions he had taken, sending the limousine on ahead with his luggage, to be checked through on the commercial flight, discreetly booked by McVitty's law firm. He himself took a taxi, carrying nothing but the small urn, his raincoat folded over it as he placed it carefully in the cab beside him so that nothing could show in the rear-vision mirror. But unfortunately the springs were broken so the urn kept tipping over. Finally he held the whole business in his lap, directing the driver to take the fastest route—via her bridge, never to be taken again, he thanked God, as his burden grew heavier—only, of course, because of the urn. Though discreetly unmarked it seemed too unmistakably what it was to entrust to any plane attendant. He would wedge it, he decided, under his seat. Deliberately arriving at the airport early, he could first check it in a locker before risking recognition at the airlines counter, to be conducted from there to the V.I.P. lounge. Where privacy was assured, he knew, from all but V.I.P. friends or enemies who might guess why he was flying West to familiar home ground, with the ashes wanted nowhere else.

But this did not bear thought at all, so he kept his mind on the missions to be accomplished, anticipating nothing after that but a drink in the lounge's farthest red-carpeted corner. Alas, it was occupied long before he got there by another compulsively early traveler, already hidden behind his paper, lowered almost carelessly to order more coffee, since the place had proved empty except for some hustler working out of a briefcase. Until suddenly Leland Evans entered. So then there were three, in the V.I.P. lounge, and two knew each other. Naturally Kelly had to rise. And naturally the hostess left them together when she hurried off for more coffee and a double Bourbon.

"Appreciated your message . . ."

"Not at all . . ." Kelly flicked his butane lighter waiting for a cigarette to be extracted from the gold case monogrammed L.E. Their props had changed hands, with the changing times, but it was a relief to discover they both still smoked, good for a few nervous lines as Leland Evans shot a few nervous glances at the briefcase hustler to make sure they weren't attracting attention. Yet. With a star in the picture, attention had to be waiting somewhere.

"Your PR people running interference with the press?"

Kelly shook his head. "Yesterday's news," he said. "They've got another story." And so did Homicide. Leland Evans was probably the only man alive in the media-crazed world who didn't know it. Hadn't seen the headlines in Kelly's paper, now featuring the city's latest caper: a bank heist, complete with fallen guard and taped communiqués, claiming credit for new daughters of the revolution. Local Girls Making Good were knocking each other off the front page. Where none of them should ever have appeared in the first place. Leland pushed the paper back across the table.

"Don't any of them ever settle down and get married?"

"Mine are in no hurry," Kelly said of the daughters who described themselves as singles, somewhat incomprehensibly. He thought of the eldest living off campus with her bearded guru, of the youngest, playing second banana to a feminist starfish in a pond too small for Kelly's shadow. He thought of E.V. "Marriage doesn't seem to be a career for some women." He thought of Evans' second wife with her six spouses. He thought of his five. "Or some men," he added.

"And show business is?" Leland Evans asked quietly, eying the coffee that came with his double.

Kelly shrugged. "It's always been the same for performers, Lee." Tell two old performers about it. "But the others need something else on the ball." Their eyes met. Kelly took a deep breath full of smoke. "Your kid had it." He exhaled slowly. "A real pro. You could tell . . . even at this age. It happens early now."

"Too early."

Though not so early as noted in the papers. Even an actor, practiced at vagueness in such matters, knew that a child born before his had also been born before her own mother died. "How old was she, Lee?"

"Thirty." Would have been. "In August."

It was a relief to say so, without disloyalty, to another father who could have guessed anyway, must also have heard from his own young that thirty was the cutoff date for youth. Curtains. Thought a little premature for a heroine's exit, since Act One death scenes were for minor characters. Just one more lousy modern perversion of sound dramatic convention in a slob's age. So just between two old performers, as his next double came and the last was ordered, Leland Evans brought himself to ask his one and only question about the career so dear to his daughter.

"This show you're all involved in . . . will it be going on without her?" Didn't all shows have to go on? Without someone . . . ?

"Not for the time being . . ." The actor chose his words carefully, without recourse to the TV page. "Frankly, it wouldn't have been the same anyway. Once these things change hands . . ."

Or voices. "Yes," the songwriter said, "I remember." More

than he wished to. He drained the second double. The third came just as their flight was announced, causing some confusion. Once upon a time the old performers had smuggled many a roadie past many a stewardess, and even a few conductors, overtipped, coming and going, by the star's entourage, forever in waiting. But now Kelly stood silently beside an empty coffee cup watching Lee's Bourbon go down in one gulp before they made their unheralded way to the gate, down the ramp, onto the plane, hesitating only when they were faced again with sitting together in the half-empty first class.

"We can spread out later," the drinker suggested, "if we feel crowded . . ."

"Yes," Kelly said, already feeling crowded by fumes of alcohol, more ordered before the takeoff, to waft past his nose the moment they were airborne, as their solicitous flight attendant, the lovely Ms. O'Riordan, announced herself anxious to be of service, overanxious, knowing who they were. The whole section knew before she had done with her hushed good intentions.

Just making a bad thing worse, as Leland Evans observed, louder than he thought, growing expansive. The next drink made it easier to see a friend in Kelly. Not only a friend, but an alternative to facing the end of the road alone. "Nothing formal, of course, under the circumstances," he murmured. His pride had forbidden even a suggestion of interment among closer allies on grander family grave sites. Leaving only the one in Hollywood, also unmarked by headstone or ceremony. "Perhaps more appropriate . . ." Being forgotten.

Like mother, like daughter. "Oh my God—!" Suddenly Leland Evans went the color of ashes. He started searching through his pockets. "Oh my God, Kelly . . ."

"What's the matter?"

Even the key was not to be found. "I must have left it in the locker." With the rest of it.

"What locker?"

"I don't remember . . . I did it before I checked in." Before the drinks.

"Then it must be right near the entrance."

"No . . . I walked." But how far, before he found one far enough, going to what lengths not to be seen? "There's no way to find it."

"We can get them to radio from the plane—"

"Christ, no—not on top of everything else. I can't have this said!" Couldn't say it himself.

But Kelly could. "The urn will be found, Lee." And labeled lost. But nothing else.

"There's no name on it."

Unnamed remains, not to be claimed to Ms. O'Riordan, sister under the skin to the V.I.P. hostess, all too quick to find out what was the matter, supply what was wanted. Another drink.

"Lee, we can't just leave it like this."

"I can't claim it."

"Somebody has to."

"Not you for God's sake—that's worse!" A bigger name to lend fuel to the pyre.

Kelly watched the drinks come and go and thought of the drinkers who'd done the same. And then of his AA sponsor, Meegan, an anonymous name with an Irish lilt that should do the trick with Ms. O'Riordan, sure to know Ms. O'Redhead in the V.I.P. lounge. Kelly got up, ready to take responsibility for leaving Meegan's mother in a locker. That, as the girls were sure to agree, was what came of cremation.

"Where are you going?"

"To handle it." He shook off the trembling hand to move forward. "Quietly. Don't worry."

It had been a long time since absolute right presented itself so clearly, free of any shadow of a doubt left by atheist night or Freudian hour. Here above the clouds where the sun was alone, soul believed in soul, however pagan the disposal of parts willed to science or entrusted to memory. One dusty answer served all godfathers. That much of the role the actor could improv. Life honored the death of what it loved. You scattered the ashes before you lost them.

Kelly did not put it quite that way to the girls in their summer uniforms when he opened negotiations over coffee. But it no longer mattered to the Boy on Shore Leave, alone in his seat, eyes closed as he slumped against the window, not even waiting to hear the outcome. Lee Evans was listening to a different tune, played for a child jigging in a dream, crying Daddy look at me, Daddy jig with me. . . . They would pay the piper when times were riper. But they were dancing. And they couldn't be bothered now.

Rerun

She woke up finally. Not so much to answer her Princess phone as to make it stop. She reached out blindly, fumbling until it fell, cradle and all from her littered bedside table. But nothing stopped. So then she knew it was the intercom from the street, buzzing on and on in her kitchenette, like some heavy John was really leaning on it. Let him. No way she would answer, would even have heard it through the whole floor-through, if the last man out had closed her bedroom door. Fuckups. No way this one would let her get back to sleep. She shoved her sleepmask up and waited, lying there looking up at her used reflection in the round mirror clamped to the ceiling over the round bed, like a lid. Now about to slam on her broken music box head, buzz buzz buzzing. *Jesus!* She couldn't believe it. The digital radio clock half hidden by a bra seemed to say eight. The winter white light filtering through sleazy curtains said it was morning, dawn her time, waking the dead after two hours sleep in a lidded coffin, lined in black satin. Her used body ached in the used sheets. Her eyes were watering, her mouth parched dry. Her feet froze as she swung them to the floor, kicking around for her fun fur mules. Some fun. What she'd give for the real thing wall to wall. And forget the scatter rugs, scattered across the bare floor, like her see-through clothes. Last night's fun. Her teeth were chattering before she got herself wrapped in her old flannel faithful, always kept out of sight in her closet. She braced herself for the drafty living room, even colder. God-damn landlord ran ice through the radiator, only one between the windows, two tall windows here, neither blocked by the fleabag that faced her bedroom, so the winter white light got even brighter, blasting through more sleazy curtains as she stumbled over the warped wood threshold, misjudging every distance because of the hangover, clipping her hip against the varnished arm of the stinking Danish sofa, with the tied-on cushions. What she'd give for some wall-to-wall upholstered comfort, with no one on top of her, or trying to get there, like all she had to give was body heat anyway. No wonder she'd used up her life in bed. But she wasn't open for business at any 8 A.M. The day she got ready to punch that time clock, she'd be back behind some frigging counter. Not hanging onto the oilcloth-covered board in her kitchenette, watching cockroaches climb the walls. Nothing poisoned roaches, fattening on lead peels, and so inured to buzzing, one of them scurried behind the intercom box, while the rest vanished into the filthy, food-filled darkness of her wooden cupboards. She decided to impersonate the slob ex-whore she paid to clean up after her.

"Who dat?"

"Karen?"

"Dis de maid." Like any ex-whore would call herself that. But, what did Johns know? "Nobody home."

At 8 A.M.! Madame must still be dining. If Madame made house calls.

"*What?*" Like he couldn't hear.

Like she couldn't either. "Call her back after . . ."

"Can't—" After what? "Hey wait—" he was yelling, ready to hold it two minutes, if she'd roust the other bastard. Let someone else wait. "Hey, it's Red!"

Like any name mattered. Only his did. To maid or whore. Sleep or no sleep. She groaned.

"Oh, come on, Red—s'too early . . ."

Like he didn't know it. "Late for me. Just got off duty."

Who hadn't? Who cared? "So you hadda wake up the world?"

"C'mon, just for breakfast—brought coffee and Danish."

Sweets for the sweet, also freebies, but all the profit she'd see for a long hour's work, requiring new sheets, white for Red, and a whole creep thing in the bath, paid off with a promise of Official Protection, myth enough when it came from Vice instead of Homicide, no longer even in the damn precinct. But The Man with the badge was The Man with the edge, collecting at his pleasure, on the pad. No way Karen could keep Red out of hers.

The street door slammed while she was still pressing the button. She heard him whistle, running up the two flights of uncarpeted stairs, shaking the whole brownstone. God, the man was an elephant. Then suddenly there was silence, probably a pause for him to pant in, before he started again, buzzing and calling, barely giving her time to get down the hall from her kitchenette, where luckily the police lock he once helped her install had already been opened by the last man out.

"Karen?" He sounded as if he hadn't caught his greedy breath yet. "You home?" Like he didn't know.

"Will you lemme open the door?" But when she did, he had the nerve to stand there looking surprised, like she really could have kept her police lock on its hinges once the son of a bitch got in the building. And then without warning, he burst in, pinning her to the wall with his goddamn containers, hot coffee coming through the brown paper bag on both of them.

"Take it *easy!*"

The door slammed behind him. And words were screamed, also behind him.

"GET IN THE BEDROOM."

Red's lips hadn't moved. His pig eyes were round.

She froze. If it had been anybody but a cop she would not have scared that easily, would have figured there had to be some way to handle the scene, given all the scenes she had handled. But the egg all over Red's freckled face told her instantly there was something in his back, knife or gun. And whichever it was, whoever was holding it, screaming with that voice, was crazy.

"TURN AROUND!"

Red nodded. She turned and started down the hall, past the kitchenette.

"WAIT!"

She stopped so short, Red piled into her.

"Easy," he whispered.

"SHUT UP." Behind Red there was the sound of a drawer opening, then the sound of metal.

"*GO!*" The crazy man had what he wanted. A knife. So the thing in Red's back was a gun. Why both?

"MOVE." Feeling Red pushed against her, she got the answer, as if by osmosis. The gun was to hold. The knife was to use.

Holy Mary, she thought, Mother of God pray for us—

"THERE'S NO BED! WHERE'S THE MIRROR?"

The crazy man had seen it. He had been here.

"This isn't the bedroom—" she began.

"WHERE IS IT?"

"Show him," Red whispered.

But if he had been there, why didn't he know? She stumbled again over her threshold. Containers shifted, Red reached out to help.

"DON'T TOUCH HER!"

Then what were they here for?

"What'll I do with the coffee—it's leaking—"

"POUR IT ON THE WHORE'S BED. RUB HER FACE IN IT."

Red moved abreast of her throwing the whole mess on the bed so that the bag burst and the containers opened, spilling out a pool of coffee, brown stain spreading in the black sheets. It was steaming.

"HER FACE! HER FACE!"

Red had already grabbed her, was shoving her halfheartedly across the bed in front of him, but covering her, so she could try to fake it, with the maniac screaming again ahead of them, onto the next kick.

"TELL THE WHORE TO KNEEL AT YOUR FEET."

She was already down. So Red pulled her around.

"TELL HER!"

"Kneel there," Red said. He pointed a little beyond him, so he could keep his back turned, protecting his service revolver somewhere under overcoat and jacket, all she could think of, as the maniac screamed objections.

"NO—WHERE I CAN SEE! NOW GIVE HER YOUR OVERCOAT—DROP YOUR PANTS—"

"Which first?"

"UNDO HIS BELT—TAKE HIS BELT. OPEN HIS PANTS."

"All right—" Red was saying. "OK, wait a minute."

But the man could not wait. He was dancing from foot to foot now, screaming at her to drag down the pants, the shorts. She could see him from the corner of her eye. It was a shadow she had caught before, watching her from shadows, doing that dance.

"Hotel," she tried to tell Red, as they struggled and fumbled with belt and zippers. "Watches me." There was no freak too far out to fit a pattern somewhere; the gamut ran from the ones who made it en masse in spotlit mirrors to the ones who waited in darkened windows making it alone, but when either broke the pattern to go after the other, the lid was off the whole freaking box.

"TIE HIM UP WITH HIS BELT."

She looked up at Red, the belt in her hands.

"HANDS BEHIND HIM! BEHIND HIM."

"How about my jacket?" Red's left hand was already going for the button.

"PUT BOTH HANDS BEHIND YOU!"

"Don't you want the rest off?"

"I'LL CUT EVERYTHING OFF WHEN THE WHORE HAS YOU READY!"

She was nothing this time. Not even an object, but a means to an end. If she got her throat cut it would be incidental. Even Red's throat wouldn't be the climax of the orgasmic frenzy. It was not death the crazy shadow had come for, but another man's sex. And watching Red struggle to get his jacket open, she saw that he knew. It means more to him than life, she thought, more to the crazy man, all of them. How could it still surprise her?

"YOU WANT ME TO START CUTTING?"

"Like this?" Red knew better. "What's she down there for?" Down anywhere for, not kneeling to pray, but to breathe life into genitalia, limp as the shirttails hanging pathetically below his jacket. But looking up past those gartered freckled legs all she saw was the shoulder holster for his substitute weapon, at last coming toward her.

"LET HER TIE YOU FIRST—TURN THE OTHER WAY."

"Which way?" Red was halfway around, his freckled right hand obediently behind him, but of course not the left, already groping, now or never, though she was kneeling in the line of fire, would be eye level with the maniac's target when the detective came full circle, with his gun in the wrong hand. Save me too, what was left of her whispered, though in the end she knew she would have to save herself, fall to left or right, when she heard the safety go off, one split second before they opened up, blasting right through her, Red and the freak both, if she was still in their way.

"HOLD IT! LEMME SEE THOSE HANDS TIED! BOTH HANDS! *NO! WAIT!*"

No way she would ever hear the safety, falling anyway, face down in the shaggy throw, whole body pressed against the bed's box springs, flush with the floor, allowing no cover, heart crying Hail Mary, Mother or Magdalene, blessed among women, pray for us sinners now and at the hour of our death. . . . As the lid blew off over head.

The snow-clogged street was jammed with traffic, two ambulances, blocking each other, blocked by police cars. The Lieutenant had to get out of his and walk. Smack into Detective Sergeant Corio of the Homicide Task Force always ahead of the game. And the regulars.

"I heard Red's asking for you."

"I heard too." Why the hell else would the head man drag ass to an open and shut shoot-out, disgracing his squad in a Yorktown cathouse, serviced by a different Homicide Division. "Which ambulance?"

"First." The noisy one. Nobody was dead yet in either, but the crazy with his face half shot off in the second wouldn't be giving out dying confessions or famous last words. He didn't have any left to go. Just a few breaths. In the wagon up front, things were different, saints forgotten by the whore being shoved inside, face down on her stretcher, because of the bullet that just missed her spine to lodge painfully in her upper left buttock. "In the ass, you asshole," she kept screaming over the attendant's explanation, trying to divert some attention from Red, already there ahead of her, lying on his back, across the aisle, fighting to stay conscious despite the greater agony of a gut wound, taken, she said, to save his precious balls.

"Saved you, didn't he?" Trying to keep his overcoat clear of the bleeding forms on either side, the Lieutenant crouched between them. There wasn't room for Corio, left outside to try and overhear whatever it was Red wanted to tell his Lieutenant.

"Here I am, Red . . ."

Red groaned. So did the woman, louder. "You know how long he's been waiting for you?" Fighting a needle upstairs and down, while she screamed for a shot of her own booze, now left hopelessly behind, no help to her or any man with a gut wound. "You mothers . . . Only poke your nose in when nobody wants it." Noses, hell. "Cop hotshots . . ."

"Tell me what it's about, Red." Ignoring her, the Lieutenant watched the waxy eyelids flutter, then close.

"I'll tell you," she said, "if you'll get me a drink."

The Lieutenant turned, gray eyes close to hers as he leaned a little over her, ready to lean on her.

"Watch out—!"

"You tell me now."

"Water bed," she gasped. All she'd heard. "Something about a water bed . . . maybe that killing . . ."

The Lieutenant bent low to speak low to Red.

"Evans Foreman—?" The eyelids twitched open. "What about Evans Foreman, Red?" A bulb flickered behind the waxen freckled face.

"Same . . ."

"Same what?"

"Setup . . ." The bulb went out in Red's head. And went on in the Lieutenant's. He stood up.

"I'll see about your booze," he told the groaning woman.

"The spic said he'd get it . . ."

But the other attendant said the spic's ass belonged on the other wagon. Theirs was moving out. The Lieutenant stepped clear with Corio and jerked a thumb toward the second ambulance.

"Anyone know who he is?"

"Was. Just died."

"Identification?"

Corio shook his head. "But that's where he lived . . ." He pointed to the eight-story building with the sign that said, ROOMS, looking down on the whore's next door brownstone, and all the other crummy buildings on the block. It seemed a long way from the mid-Manhattan neighborhood canvassed so exhaustively last July, full of mod lux bldgs except for one—a fourteen-story eyesore called the Morely Arms, backed up to all those picture windows, including two in a glorified one-room, misadvertised as a Studio 3. On a Hi Fl! Tactfully misnumbered 14B. Same setup. Except for her blinds.

"Let's look at his room here first," the Lieutenant said.

It was like old times with Good Guy and Bad Guy together again—though no longer partners apparently. It was Good Guy, now reassigned to Corio's Task Force, who climbed the five flights to knock on the door after Ned came home from the VA to finish packing. There was nothing much left but his clothes. He had moved his books and tapes the weekend before. With the data analysis, long since crated—graphs, charts, tables—still not color coded, when thrown in piecemeal, growing every day more dated, as they waited to be unpacked, on

Ned's new Long Island campus where such weighty matters weren't really in it with extracurricular activities. Like coaching dramatics, the most lucrative but time-consuming sideline awaiting teachers of speech, no longer halted.

"That's show biz," Ned said, when apprised of Homicide's sudden concern for the graveness of his interrupted calling. Even the Lieutenant had nothing but good wishes for the department's smart eyewitness, first to get the good news from the team who had caught the case, now reunited to tell him how it was broken. Or show him, one picture being worth a thousand words. And indeed the Lieutenant had one last little question about the outstanding matter of that famous lost photograph, found this morning in a Yorktown rooming house, among a deceased killer's weirdo effects, and now tagged as evidence for lab examination at Homicide. Where it was hoped Ned would help with the identification.

"You mean the big man wants me in there again?"

Just like old times. But Good Guy was shaking his head. "Frankovitch is bringing a copy over." In an unmarked car already parked by a dirty snowdrift where good old Bad Guy waited, all smiles, glad to see the professor doing so well, from the looks of Ned's Christmas present to himself—a new fleece-lined three-quarter-length jacket. Some kind of suede— more pseudo than ultra. But not quite like old times.

"Let's get this photograph thing over with," Ned said.

The thing was in one of the familiar manila envelopes on the front seat. Ned got in beside Bad Guy, Good Guy craning to look from the back, the interior lights still on, as the Bad Guy pulled ahead to a street lamp so that Ned could really see in the fading light. Winter days ended so quickly. But not that endless summer night, flooding back in one flashbulb instant, when he pulled out the alleged reasonable facsimile of a porno nudie. He stared at it, braced to identify the girl he had loved and hated. But not prepared for the other stranger.

"Oh for the love of God," he said softly. Because indeed, both were familiar. "It's one of those double exposures . . ."

Two bodies. But only one person. Maude Lee Evans, clear as crystal, was superimposed on a fainter pose of her own see-through outline. A worthless piece of defective film, Ned had thought she returned for a free replacement at the store where he bought her the ten-dollar Polaroid: called, oddly enough, The Swinger. A birthday toy, put away on a shelf the summer after he met her. Like the Christmas puppy put away by her family a year later. According to a previous detective story. Though the camera, they thought, might at least possibly still exist to be sent for as evidence.

"If that's where this thing came from, Ned. You've seen the picture?"

"I think I took it . . ." But like so many innocent happenings in 14B, it was no longer a memory he could swear to. So it would only be poetic justice if he of all people blurred the image, recognized now less from life than from his own descriptions, too often supplied. Too easily confused with all the others that concentrated on the image's violation. He put the picture back in the envelope. But it was the same with her neighborhood, when they headed out of the park for the block of mid-Manhattan luxury, once so familiar, such a source of mixed feelings, memorable now only for the times they'd been denied.

There was, however, no reason at all to remember the Morely Arms, since he had always heard it called The Suicide Arms Motel. Had never even seen the front where the car stopped. And only glimpsed the back through vertical blinds, hung so impenetrably across the view, while walls were mirrored to compensate, an equally silly extravagance. Since she was only after all into space—not exploiting or hiding her own

reflection. An explanation Ned had stopped trying to sell the
detectives. Or himself, last summer.

But now it was winter and they knew. It was because of the
blocked windows, that a peeping Tom just hadn't figured,
they told him, leading him through the scruffy lobby, past the
shellacked wood desk where the killer's signature had been
identified, though he used a different name when registering
here, a month before the Water Bed Murders, to jump a
week's bill the day after, as duly recorded in some canvasser's
notebook, and filed in a Homicide folder. But nothing really
fell into place until they came back today to visit his room—in
itself a dead end and facing a blind alley. The real clue was in
the elevator. The highest numbered button. A big 13. Pressed
again now, as the story was again reconstructed, to show that
the creep, freak, frequenter of fleabags might not have known,
could not have guessed how often mod lux floors were tactfully misnumbered. Since everybody in the fleabags got out on
13 and walked down to the end of the dingy, brown-carpeted
hall to the door marked ROOF. Crowded every day in summer. While in winter it was deserted completely, though the
door at the top of the gray cement stairs was still open.
Pushed wide by the detectives, advancing through the slush
on the tar paper to the waist-high parapet—where the answer
waited at eye level. Not below, on the thirteenth floor behind
those expensive blinds bought cheap by the next unsupersti-
tious occupant of 14B. But directly above, in 15B where the
super's favored henna-haired tenant could be seen at her
work, though only in silhouette against the sleazy matchstick
curtains, now framing the figure of her departing guest. The
real target, watched from lengthening shadows by a killer
dancing from foot to foot, until he couldn't stand it any
longer. Not even needing to count the floors before he rushed
over, slipping through the unlocked basement door, past the
super's apartment and the laundry to the elevator, where he

punched 14, to get off on the wrong floor. And wait in the stair well for her next caller, as he'd waited all night in the Yorktown brownstone. And so, mistaking Foreman for a John like Red, had followed the wrong man into the wrong apartment to surprise the wrong girl.

While right overhead the whore let the super in to get her air conditioning fixed. Shivering out in the cold where they watched her remake her warm bed, the detectives moved from foot to foot in unconscious imitation of the killer they took turns cursing, as they cast shorter shadows in the gathering winter darkness.

"Cockless psycho, freaking out on whores . . ."

"Doing his scumbag number on innocent people . . ."

"Frigging pervert—probably never knew the difference . . ."

The third man laughed, a startling sound, and detectives didn't startle easily.

"Why should he know the difference?" Ned Nedders said. "None of us did."

She stopped at the newsstand on the way to the park to get the latest editions of the papers, both morning and evening. For once they all ran photographs of Bob. Not the snapshot sunbathing with Maude Lee, but alone. Or with his wife, a fitting illustration to the updated story of a respectable married man, celebrating the birth of his first baby by visiting a respectable neighbor, both fully clothed when forced to strip at gunpoint to commit unnatural acts, resisted until fatally climaxed with a knife. "It makes you think," a heretofore silent thinker among former neighbors was quoted as saying of their tragically violent times. "A thing like that . . . it could happen to anybody!"

Like another star survivor, the constant reader was moved to laugh, reading that one aloud to her constant companion, the baby in the carriage who waved a triumphant fist. More

Power To The People. When fully clothed and respectable, of course, her mother agreed, fist raised in reply. Which really cracked the baby up, gurgling uncontrollably, bubbles bursting from her lips. So the hell with tears, finally welling, now of all times, to pour salt in the wound. Leaning over the carriage, Amy saved her handkerchief for the baby's happy spit. "Let's hear it for Dada," she said softly. "That's telling 'em, eh fat lady?"

Fast Crawl

In the weeks following the breaking of the case, all traces of the Evans Foreman homicide faded from the headlines. But in the spring related items began cropping up elsewhere in the papers, inspiring feature recaps. For instance on the television page, where Weldon's replacement, the former VP of PR, kicked off his first season of summer replacements with a sitcom called "Our Dad, The Dealer," developed, as one columnist noted, from an unproduced Evans special about "urban Waltons." Closer to the mark, another network announced the fall premiere of a four-part maxi-doc entitled "The Voyeur," an in-depth examination of Society's latest reject—a peeping Tom turned murderer. As semifictionalized, his opposite number was a composite cop, known as The Lieutenant, designed to become the central running character if the pilot spawned a series. As per the master plan of Voyeur Productions, the independent packaging company formed by Israel Gold and Charles Collins, who quickly set Billy Bee Bernard to direct the opener, with Doreen Lunarhorn to get cameo billing as

The Voyeur's career girl victim. Despite the smallness of the part.

While in even smaller typeset, literary circles hailed the lower-case name of e. v. adamic, returned to the living from Central Islip with a magazine novella, "blackout," about a bumbling father's hospital visit, alleged to have sparked his institutionalized daughter's partial recovery from drug-induced amnesia. This fiction was soon to be followed by fact: a more commercial article about another rescue, a real one. Entitled "star spangled woman," it celebrated the writer's only surviving memory of maude lee evans—their meeting. Since this event revealed rather more about e.v., it finished the job of establishing her as one of the tough guys—or girls—in the brave new wave who Told All. But only in print. Not for family viewing. Or any camera, manned by auteurs.

On the grave pages reserved for serious business, more inevitable progress was also recorded. Such as the full senior partnership in a family brokerage house, now awaiting Bruce McVitty IV, come home at last from a prolonged foreign honeymoon, already given flightier space in Social Notes from all over.

It required a big appetite to digest so many little-known facts of little interest. But Sam Lorrilard no longer of 14H had not changed his habits with his address. Thus he caught each and every item over many breakfasts at Schrafft's Fifty-seventh Street. The last was the one he didn't want to miss. Surprisingly, however, it did not affect his pace along the familiar route home from his old bank to his new East Side efficiency apartment. Nor did he look to right or left, or lurk on corners as he continued day after day past Sutton Place. This time McVitty could call *him* amigo.

But in fact McVitty called him "cher ami." At first Lorrilard only heard the familiar voice, still calling when he turned to see the familiar figure, waving from the opposite corner until the light changed, and McVitty, this time the one to cross over, came closer and called him something else.

"My funny alibi . . ."

With a smile. The very rich were not only different from Lorrilard, but from each other. This was a slicker article than his senior partners. Or lawyer uncles. Under any sky Bruce McVitty would find cover. And discard it when the sun came out.

Lorrilard managed not to smile back. "Sorry about the alibi. But I didn't know what to say without hearing from you, Bruce."

A cloud passed between sun god and sun. Not to be mistaken for eclipse.

"Nothing to say . . . cher ami," said yesterday's amigo. "You and I had a drink . . ."

"Like we had a drink with her the night before."

McVitty laughed. "Long time between drinks." The smile was back to dazzle. "Want to try for three?"

So the ami, amigo, friend of the family remembered where he had passed out that night. In 14H, not 14B. Was even ready to laugh off the part that was true. About nothing happening. At least until aroused at dawn by the ill-timed labor pains next door. "Maybe I should say—try for two and a half . . . ?"

The labor pains had gone on too long with discouraging effect. More than made up for, the following afternoon, at their next lucky, chance encounter.

"Wasn't it right on this corner . . . ?" The blond head turned, beautifully vague.

"I don't remember," Lorrilard lied.

A challenge. Something was different. A hand reached to find out why.

"Somebody's been keeping you in shape." The hand that encircled Lorrilard's arm squeezed gently.

"I worked out this winter."

"On the slopes?"

"At the Y."

"We can do better than that." Like they did last summer? Twist again. The hand strayed to a button, "Good-looking jacket." Somebody, the tone said, was keeping somebody in style.

"I got a promotion."

"We both did."

"And you got married."

"Time to celebrate—open new horizons." And the jacket. "If you like me, you'll love my wife."

"Other half of the same coin?"

The hand stopped, surprised. "How did you know?"

"You said it before. About someone else."

The hand hesitated. "Look, if you mean Leesy, stop worrying. She'd have understood what we had to say—"

"You mean you had to say. They didn't ask me where you slept."

"Well, I couldn't tell them—and the worse that could happen to her was already over." So his lawyer had said. "What are we supposed to do—commit hari-kari on television?" The hand was warm inside the jacket. "C'mon, chéri, have a drink with me. Forget it."

"I've got a date," Lorrilard lied again.

"Have her join us."

"It's a he."

The hand left. Lorrilard buttoned his jacket. It was no big deal resisting Bruce, with so many other scenes to cruise, where some nicer boy or girl might really someday make a difference. The tough part was passing up the best contact ever, left behind in the shadows under the canopy, like the new horizons opening up beyond the privacy of Bruce's penthouse. But Sam Lorrilard worked in a bank. He'd been promoted from the counter to a desk on the floor for adding things up until they came out right. And this never would. So he walked away, not one of your big freeze frames. But it defined him.

And that was the way it was as one of the anchor persons said nightly, winding up the news before the last commercial, credit crawl, logo, station break. . . .

And Fade.